EVA GARCÍA SÁENZ

THE LORDS OF TIME

Eva García Sáenz de Urturi was born in Vitoria and has been living in Alicante since she was fifteen years old. She published her first novel, *La saga de los longevos* (*The Immortal Collection*), in 2012, and it became a sales phenomenon in Spain, Latin America, the United States, and the United Kingdom. She is also the author of *Los hijos de Adán* (*The Sons of Adam*) and the historical novel *Pasaje a Tahití* (*Passage to Tahiti*). In 2016 she published the first installment of the White City Trilogy, titled *El silencio de la ciudad blanca* (*The Silence of the White City*), followed by *Los ritos del agua* (*The Water Rituals*) and *Los señores del tiempo* (*The Lords of Time*). She is married and has two children.

ALSO BY EVA GARCÍA SÁENZ

The White City Trilogy

The Silence of the White City

The Water Rituals

The Ancient Family Saga

The Immortal Collection

The Sons of Adam

Other Novels

Passage to Tahiti

THE LORDS OF TIME

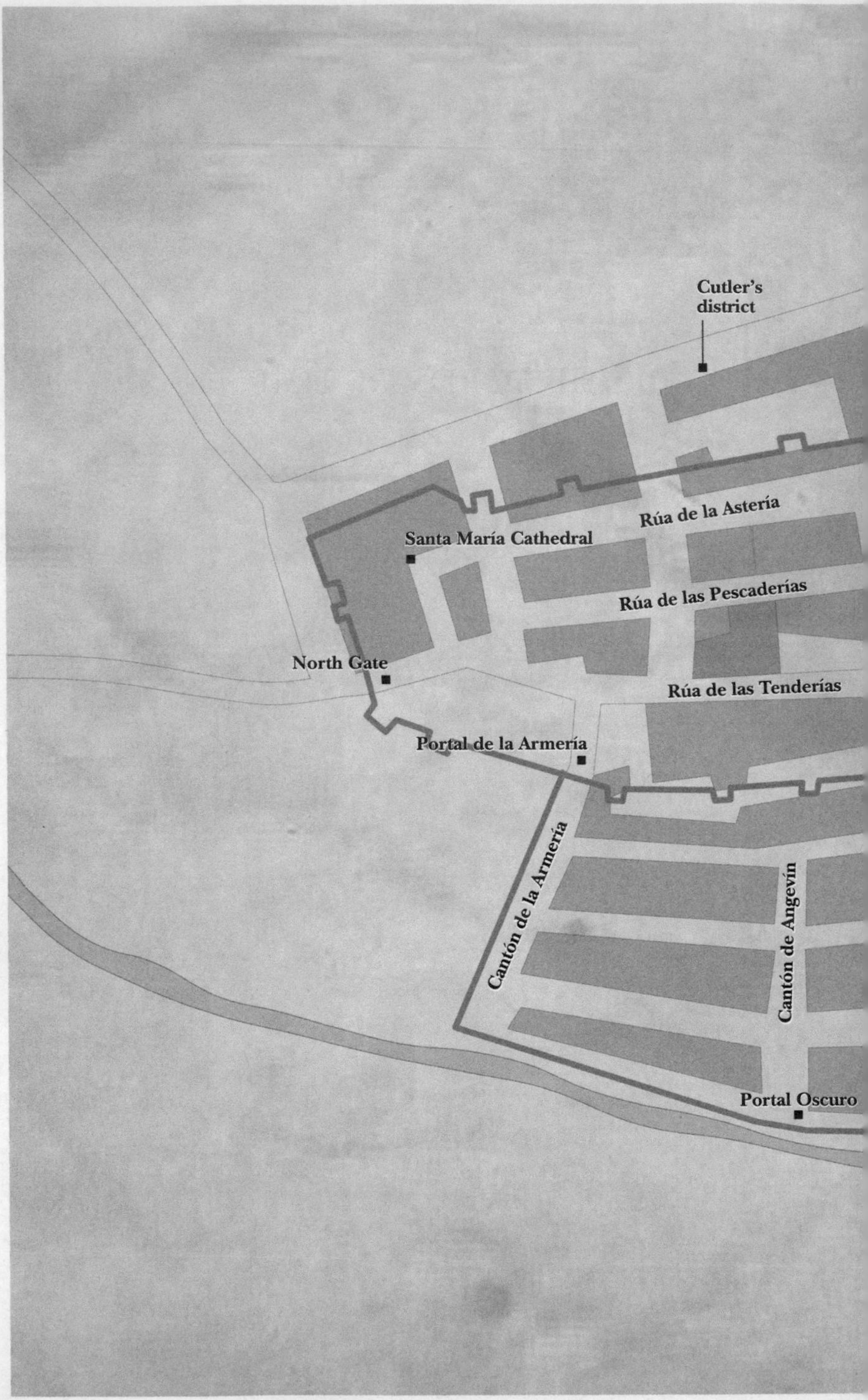
Cutler's district
Santa María Cathedral
Rúa de la Astería
Rúa de las Pescaderías
North Gate
Rúa de las Tenderías
Portal de la Armería
Cantón de la Armería
Cantón de Angevín
Portal Oscuro

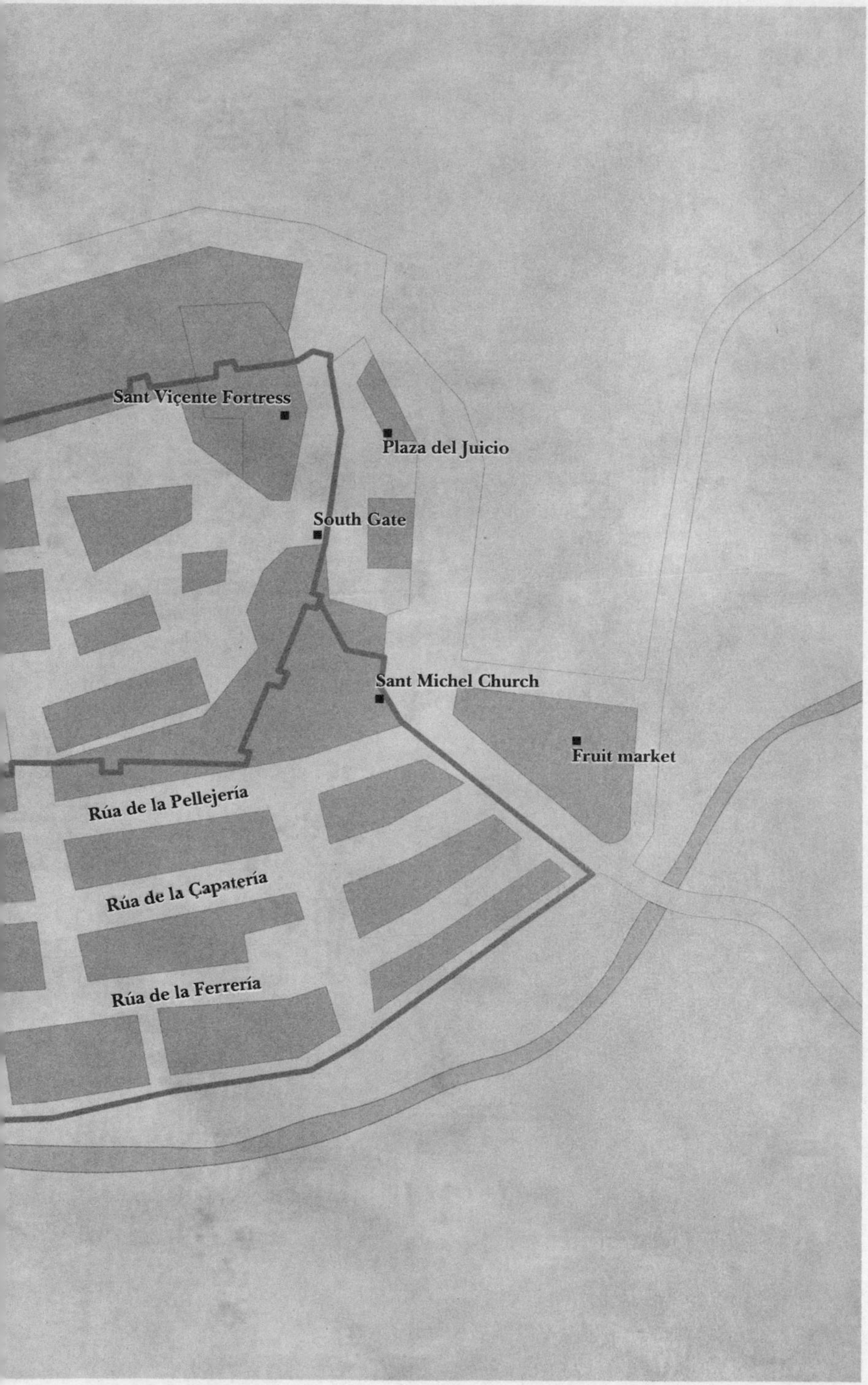
Sant Viçente Fortress
Plaza del Juicio
South Gate
Sant Michel Church
Fruit market
Rúa de la Pellejería
Rúa de la Çapatería
Rúa de la Ferrería

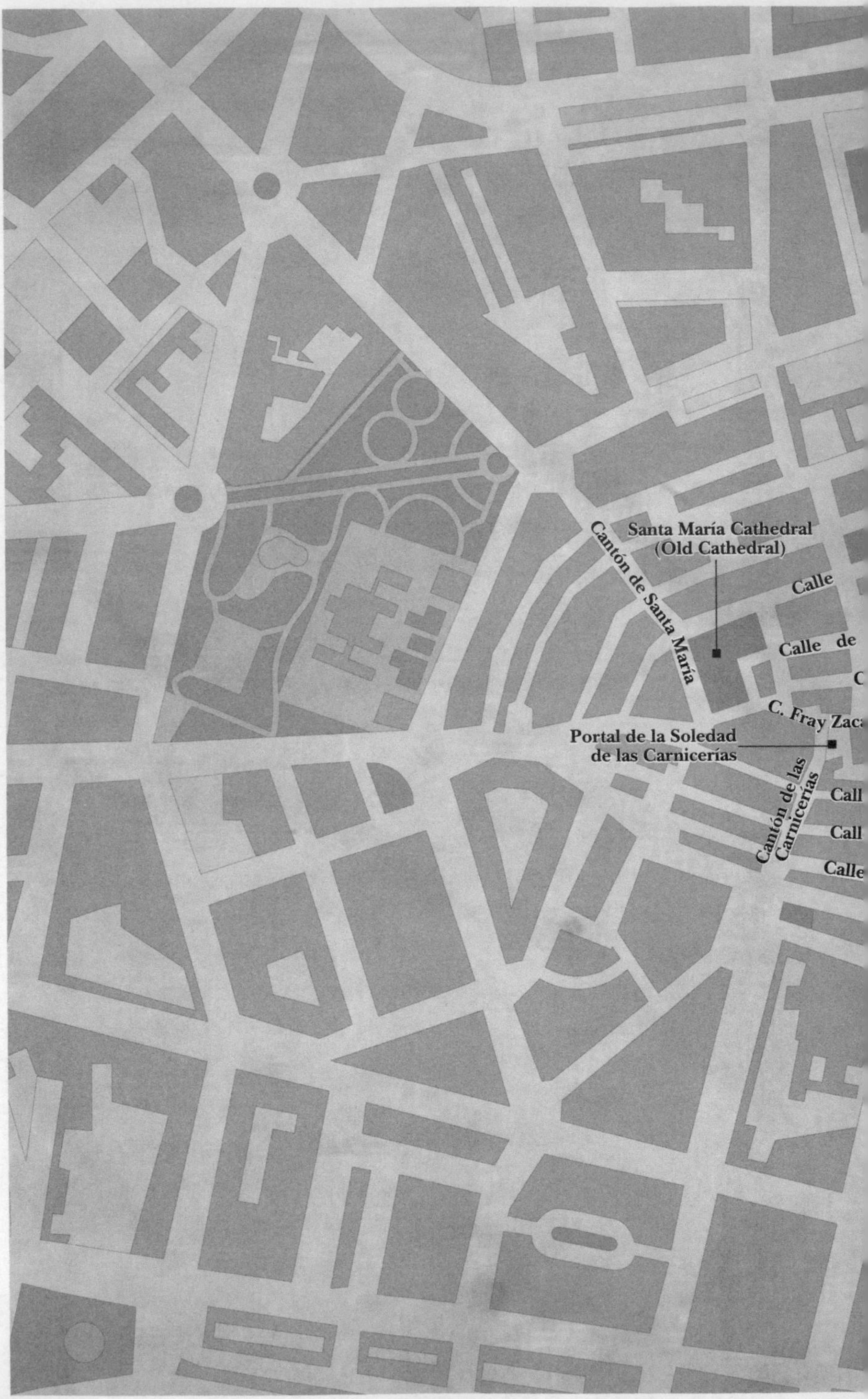
Santa María Cathedral
(Old Cathedral)
Cantón de Santa María
Calle
Calle de
C
C. Fray Zac
Portal de la Soledad
de las Carnicerías
Cantón de las
Carnicerías
Call
Call
Calle

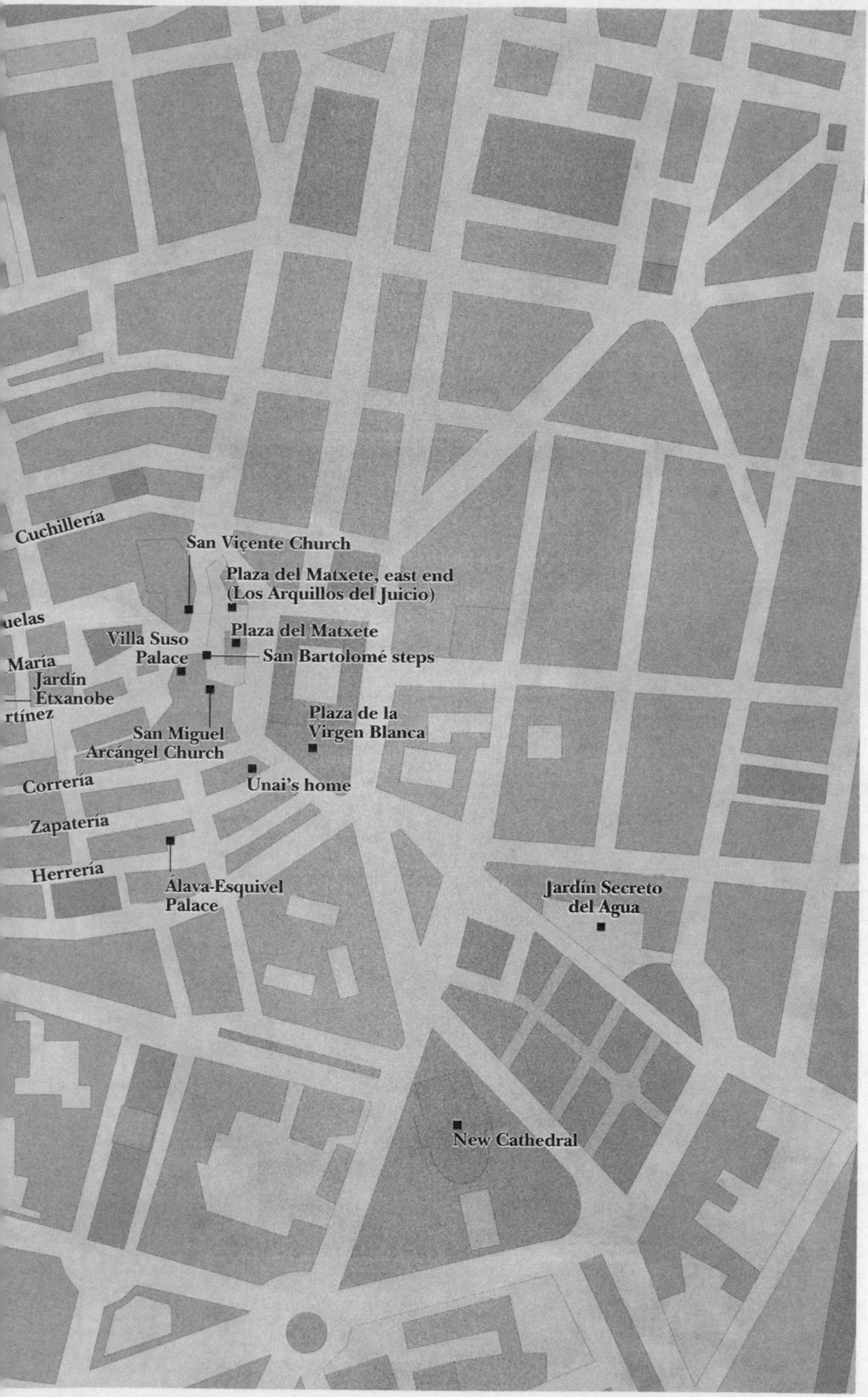

Cuchillería
San Viçente Church
Plaza del Matxete, east end
(Los Arquillos del Juicio)
uelas
Plaza del Matxete
Villa Suso
Palace
San Bartolomé steps
María
Jardín
Etxanobe
rtínez
Plaza de la
Virgen Blanca
San Miguel
Arcángel Church
Unai's home
Correría
Zapatería
Herrería
Álava-Esquivel
Palace
Jardín Secreto
del Agua
New Cathedral

THE LORDS OF TIME

EVA GARCÍA SÁENZ

Translated from the Spanish
by Nick Caistor

VINTAGE CRIME/BLACK LIZARD
VINTAGE BOOKS
A Division of Penguin Random House LLC
New York

A VINTAGE CRIME/BLACK LIZARD ORIGINAL, JULY 2021

Library of Congress Cataloging-in-Publication Data
Name: García Sáenz, Eva, author.
Title: The lords of time / Eva García Sáenz ;
translated from the Spanish by Nick Caistor.
Description: New York : Vintage Crime/Black Lizard, 2021.
Identifiers: LCCN 2020050162 (print)
Classification: LCC PQ6707.A7325 S4613 2021 (print) |
LCC PQ6707.A7325 (ebook) | DDC 863/.7—dc23
LC record available at https://lccn.loc.gov/2020050162

Vintage Crime/Black Lizard Trade Paperback ISBN: 978-1-9848-9863-0
eBook ISBN: 978-1-9848-9864-7

Map illustrations © Gradual Maps
Interior illustrations: first lines of the Vitoria population law granted by Sancho VI the Wise in September 1181, Jurisdiction of the Population of VITORIA, private collection © PHOTO HOZ
Book design by Elizabeth A. D. Eno

www.blacklizardcrime.com

Printed in the United States of America
10 9 8 7 6 5 4 3 2 1

THE LORDS OF TIME

1

VILLA SUSO PALACE

UNAI

September 2019

I could begin this story with the shocking discovery of a body in Villa Suso Palace: one of the richest men in the country, the owner of a ready-to-wear fashion empire, poisoned with *la mosca española*, or Spanish fly—the legendary medieval equivalent of Viagra. But I'm not going to do that.

Instead I'll write about what happened the evening we went to the book launch for *The Lords of Time*, the novel everyone in Vitoria was talking about.

We were all fascinated by this work of historical fiction, especially me. It was one of those books that completely transported you; from the opening paragraph, it was as though an invisible hand grabbed you by the scruff of the neck and drew you into this ferocious medieval world. It was magnetic. You couldn't resist, even if you wanted to.

It wasn't so much a book as a trap made of paper, an ambush of words . . . and there was no escape.

My brother, Germán; my alter ego, Estíbaliz; my entire *cuadrilla* . . . No one was talking about anything else. Many people had polished off the four hundred and seventy pages in only three nights. Some of us, however, preferred to enjoy it in small doses, as if it were a poison or a bewitching drug, prolonging the experience of being transported to the year of our Lord 1192. I was so immersed that sometimes when Alba and I were enjoying our early-morning rendezvous between the sheets, I called her "my lady."

But there was an added attraction to the experience—a mystery: Who was the elusive author?

A week and a half after the novel was released, it was flying off bookstore shelves, but there was not a single photograph of the author anywhere, not on the novel's cover, not in any of the newspapers. He hadn't given any interviews, and there was no sign of him on social media. He didn't even have a website. He was either a pariah or an anachronism.

Some people thought that Diego Veilaz, the author's name, was a pseudonym, a nod to the novel's protagonist, Count Diago Vela. It was impossible to know anything back then. The truth had not yet spread its capricious wings over the cobbled streets of Vitoria's Medieval Quarter.

The evening was sepia colored as I crossed the Plaza de Matxete carrying Deba on my shoulders. I was sure my two-year-old daughter (who already considered herself grown-up) would not be a nuisance at the book launch, but Grandfather had come along to help out just in case, even though it was the night before La Fiesta de San Andrés, and he would be celebrating the patronal holiday in Villaverde.

Alba and I were delighted when he'd appeared at our apartment. We were desperate for a chance to relax.

The previous two weeks we'd been working overtime on a case involving two young sisters, aged seventeen and twelve, who had disappeared in very strange circumstances—and we needed sleep.

We were hoping for a few hours' respite after fourteen fruitless days of investigation, time to collapse under the duvet and recharge our batteries. Saturday was already shaping up to be just as frustrating as the past couple of weeks had been.

All the routine work was done. We'd organized searches with volunteers and dogs, and we'd gotten the judge's authorization to seize family's and friends' cell phones. Our team had examined all the CCTV footage in the province, and the forensics team had painstakingly gone through the family's vehicles with a fine-tooth comb. We had interviewed anyone who had come into contact with the girls over the course of their brief lives. And we had found nothing.

They had vanished into thin air.

There were two of them, which meant the drama was twice as intense, as was the pressure Superintendent Medina was putting on Alba, his deputy.

People had lined up for a mile under the warm streetlights in the Plaza del Matxete, waiting for the book launch to begin.

The event coincided with the traditional September medieval market. The paved square was filled with the smell of corn on the cob and *chinchorta* cake. Furious violins played the theme from *Game of Thrones*. A performer dressed in green velvet juggled three red balls, while a bullnecked man stuffed the head of an albino boa into his mouth.

The square that had once been the city market was busier than ever. The line of readers disappeared under the Arquillos del Juicio, where vendors were selling pottery and lavender essential oil beneath the arcades.

I suddenly caught sight of Estíbaliz, my partner in the Criminal Investigation Unit. She was with Alba's mother, who had adopted her as one of her own after their first meeting and had included her in all our family traditions ever since.

My mother-in-law, Nieves Díaz de Salvatierra, was a retired actress who had been a child prodigy in 1950s Spanish cinema. She had now found the peace and quiet she so longed for as the manager of a hotel in Laguardia. The fortress-like space was set between vineyards and the mountains of Toloño. The range was named after Tulonio, the Celtic god I prayed to when the universe turned dark.

"Unai!" shouted Estíbaliz, waving an arm. "Over here!"

Alba, Grandfather, and I headed in their direction. Deba gave her aunt Estí a sloppy kiss on the cheek, and we were finally able to enter the Villa Suso, a stone Renaissance building that had stood proudly for five centuries on the hilltop where the city was first built.

"I think the family's all here," I said, extending my phone to a sky that was already turning a deep indigo. "Look here, everyone."

Four generations of the Díaz de Salvatierra and López de Ayala families smiled for our selfie.

"I think the launch is in the Martín de Salinas room on the second floor," said Alba, cheerfully leading the way. "Such an innocent mystery, isn't it?"

"What do you mean?" I asked.

"The author. This evening we're finally going to discover his identity," she replied, intertwining her fingers with mine. "If only the mysteries at work were so innocuous—"

"Speaking of mysteries," Estíbaliz broke in, pushing Alba as we entered the room. "Don't walk on the woman trapped in the walls, Alba. The security guards say she appears at night in the hallways near the restrooms, and her moans are terrifying."

Alba jumped to one side. Swept along by the crowd, she had accidentally stepped on the glass panel that covered the skeleton of a medieval woman, according to a plaque on the wall.

"Don't mention ghosts or skeletons in front of Deba," she said with a wink, lowering her voice. "I don't want her to have any trouble going to bed tonight. I need her to sleep like a hibernating bear. Her mother desperately needs rest."

Grandfather smiled, the half smile of a centenarian who had many more years of assessing people than we did.

"You're not going to scare the *chiguita* with a few piles of bones."

I could have sworn there was a touch of pride in his gruff voice. He seemed to really understand Deba. They shared a simple, effective telepathy that excluded the rest of us. Deba and her great-grandfather communicated through looks and shrugs, and, to our bewilderment, he understood better than anyone what made her cry, the reasons she refused to wear her rubber boots even when it was pouring, and what the scribbles meant that she drew on every surface she came across.

We finally managed to get into the room, although we had to settle for seats in the next-to-last row. Grandfather sat Deba on his lap and let her wear his beret, which accentuated how similar they looked, turning her into his tiny clone.

As he entertained my daughter, I tried to forget my worries from work for a moment. I looked around the narrow, stone-walled chamber with its thick wooden beams across the ceiling. Behind the long table with the three empty chairs and three unopened bottles of water, a faded tapestry of the Trojan Horse dominated the back wall.

I glanced at my cell phone. The book launch was almost forty-five minutes behind schedule. The gentleman to my right, who had a copy of the novel on his lap, was fidgeting, and he wasn't the only one. None of the speakers had appeared yet. Alba shot me a look that said, *If they take much longer, we're going to have to take Deba home.*

I nodded, stroking the back of her hand and silently promising that we would enjoy our night together no matter what.

How good it felt not to have to hide in public. How good it felt to be a family of three. How good life could be. For two years now, from the day Deba was born, my life had been marked by the pleasant accumulation of family routines.

And I really enjoyed those innocent days with my ladies.

Just then a stout, sweaty man walked past me. I recognized him immediately: the owner of the publishing house Malatrama.

We had met a few years earlier during the Water Rituals case. He published the graphic novels of the killer's first victim, Annabel Lee, who was, among other things, the first love of my entire *cuadrilla*. I was pleased to see him again. He was followed by a man with a thick goatee. Could he be the elusive author? An expectant murmur grew around the room, a murmur that seemed to forgive what was now almost an hour's delay.

"Finally," whispered Estíbaliz, who was sitting on my other side, "another five minutes and we would've had to call the riot police."

"Don't joke about that, we've had enough to handle over the last two weeks with those girls disappearing."

Her flame-red hair brushed my face as she leaned over and whispered in my ear. "I've told you a thousand times, they'll be home with their mom and dad soon."

"May the good fairies hear you so we can get some sleep for once," I replied, stifling a yawn.

I had almost completely recovered my ability to speak after the Broca's aphasia I had suffered in 2016 as the result of a gunshot wound. Three years of intensive speech therapy had made me a loquacious investigator once again. Other than temporary lapses due to exhaustion or stress, my oratorical skills were triumphant.

"One, two, one, two . . ." the publisher squawked into the microphone. "Can you all hear me?"

Everybody in the audience nodded.

"I'm sorry for the delay, but I'm afraid the author cannot be with us tonight." He nervously stroked his bushy, curly beard.

The reaction was immediate. Quite a few people left the room. The publisher watched them go disconsolately.

"Believe me, I understand your disappointment. This certainly was not the plan. I don't want to waste everyone's evening, so let me introduce Andrés Madariaga. He is a history professor and was part of the team of archaeologists from the Santa María Cathedral Foundation who excavated an area only a few yards away, on the Villa de Suso hill and in the Old Cathedral's catacombs. He was hoping to speak with our author tonight and explain the incredible parallels between the Medieval Quarter as we know it today and twelfth-century Victoria as it appears in the novel."

"That's right," said the archaeologist, clearing his throat. "The book is astonishingly accurate, as though almost a thousand years ago the author strolled the streets we live on today. Right here, next to the former entrance to the palace, on the stairs we know as San Bartolomé, was the medieval site of the South Gate, one of the entrances to the walled town. . . ."

"He doesn't know who the author is," Alba whispered in my ear, which warmed at the touch of her lips.

"What's that?" I murmured.

"The publisher doesn't know who the author is, either. He hasn't said his name once, and he hasn't referred to him by his pseudonym. He has no idea who he is."

"Or he wants to keep us in suspense for the next event."

Unconvinced, Alba looked at me as though I were a child.

"I'd swear that's not true. He's as lost as the rest of us."

The archaeologist continued, "I don't know if you're aware, but we're next to what would have been the palace's original defensive wall, built well before the foundation of the city. Can you see it? It's this one," he said, pointing to the stone wall to his right. "Thanks to carbon dating, we know it was already in place by the end of the eleventh century, one hundred years earlier than we had previously thought. That means that we're seated exactly where the novel takes place. In fact, one of the characters in the book dies nearby along the line of the wall. Many of you are probably wondering about Spanish fly—*la mosca española*, or cantharis. In the novel, the substance appears as a brown powder that is administered to this unfortunate character. And that's true. Or rather," he said, correcting himself, "it's feasible."

He raised his head.

"Spanish fly is an aphrodisiac, the medieval version of Viagra," he went on impishly. "It's a powder made from the crushed shell of the blister beetle, which is common to Africa. It was the only aphrodisiac proven to sustain an erection, because it contains cantharidin, a chemical compound and stimulant. Although it dilates blood vessels very effectively, it fell out of use because, as Paracelsus tells us, 'the dose makes the poison.' Two grams of Spanish fly would kill the healthiest man in this room. It stopped being used in the seventeenth century, after the so-called Richelieu caramels caused the death of half the French court during their orgies. Not to mention the fact that the Marquis de Sade was accused of murder when two women died after he administered the substance to them without their knowledge."

I looked around. Those who had remained for the archaeologist's improvised talk were listening closely to his medieval tales. Deba was asleep beneath her grandfather's beret, held securely in his giant paws. Nieves was following the speaker attentively, Alba was stroking my thigh, and Estí was staring at the roof beams. In short, everything was fine.

Forty minutes later, the Malatrama publisher placed a pair of battered half-moon glasses on the end of his enormous nose and announced: "I would like to end this event by reading the opening paragraphs of *The Lords of Time*:

> "My name is Diago Vela. I am known as Count Don Diago Vela, to be more precise. I began to set down the events described in this chronicle on the day I returned, after two years' absence, to the ancient village of Gasteiz, or, as the pagans call it, Gaztel Haitz, or Castle Rock.
>
> "I was traveling back through Aquitaine, and after crossing lower Navarre—"

Suddenly the door behind me was flung open. Curious, I turned around and saw a white-haired man who looked to be around fifty hobbling in on a crutch.

"Is there a doctor? The palace is empty, and we need a doctor!" he shouted.

Estí, Alba, and I shot to our feet in unison and went over to the man.

"Are you all right?" asked Alba, ever the leader. "We'll call an ambulance, but you have to tell us what's wrong."

"It's not for me. It's for the man I found in the restroom."

"What happened to him?" I pressed, taking out my cell phone.

"He's lying on the floor. It's difficult to kneel with this crutch, so I couldn't really get close to him, but I swear he isn't moving. He's either unconscious or dead," said the man. "In fact, I think I recognized him. I think he's . . . Well, I'm not sure, but I think it's—"

"Don't worry about that for now. We'll take care of it," Estíbaliz cut in, demonstrating her legendary impatience.

Everyone in the room was staring at us. I think the publisher had stopped reading, but I'm not sure. I glanced quickly at Grandfather, who nodded, confirming that he would take Deba home and put her to bed.

Estí and I ran to the stairs leading down to the restrooms. In our haste, we both stepped on the glass panel covering the medieval woman's remains. I didn't even think about it. I arrived in the restroom first to find a very tall, well-dressed man lying motionless on the floor. His face was frozen in an expression of pain so severe that I could almost feel it, too.

The restrooms were aseptically white and spotless. Each stall displayed a photomontage of Vitoria's four towers.

I pulled my cell phone from my pocket, turned on the flashlight, and held it an inch or so from the man's face. Nothing. His pupils didn't react.

"Damn it." I sighed, placing my fingers on his carotid artery and hoping for a miracle. "His pupils aren't contracting, Estí. No pulse, either. He's dead. Don't touch anything. Tell the DSU so she can set things in motion."

My colleague nodded and was about to call Alba when I stopped her.

"It smells like rotten eggs," I said, sniffing the air. "He's wearing expensive cologne, but it still smells awful."

"It's a men's bathroom. What do you expect?"

"It's not that. It smells like those stink bombs they used to sell in Casa de las Fiestas when we were kids. Remember?"

"You think he was poisoned?"

I wasn't sure. But I am a cautious man, and I don't like having to be sorry for what I've failed to do, so out of respect for the dead, I whispered my prayer.

"This is where your hunt ends, and mine begins."

I studied him closely, then turned to Estí.

"I think our witness was right. There aren't many photos. He had a very odd physique, and I always thought . . . I think it's a case of arachnidism."

"What does that mean, Kraken?"

"This man suffers, or suffered, from Marfan syndrome. Long limbs, protruding eyes. Look at his fingers. At his height. If this is who I think it is, there's going to be hell to pay. Stay with the body. I'm going to ask Alba to seal the exits. We have to take statements from at least two hundred people. If this man just died, the killer is still inside the palace."

2

THE NORTH GATE

DIAGO VELA

Winter, the Year of Our Lord 1192

My name is Diago Vela. I'm known as Count Don Diago Vela, to be more precise. I began to set down the events described in this chronicle on the day I returned, after two years' absence, to the ancient village of Gasteiz, or, as the pagans call it, Gaztel Haitz, or Castle Rock.

I was traveling back through Aquitaine, and after crossing lower Navarre, I took care to avoid entering Tudela. I had no wish to give my report to the aged king Sancho. Not yet. I had handed over his daughter Berengaria to Richard, known as the Lionheart. That monster had no honorable reason for marrying her, a fact that became clear after meeting him. And, more importantly, I was anxious to discover what was happening inside the walls of the town I could already spy in the distance.

I would soon be back with Onneca. . . .

My exhausted mount struggled up the steep hill leading to the North Gate, which protected the town against anyone approaching from Arriaga.

We crossed the bridges over the two moats. I was uncomfortably aware that a rider had been following me for three moons now, all the more reason to spur on my horse and finally reach the safety of the town wall. It was an unpleasant night, pitch-black, and the winds promised to bring the first snows of a harsh winter. A wildcat-skin cloak was all that prevented me from freezing to death. This was not a good moment to be arriving in Victoria. The gates of Villa de Suso were closed at dusk right after curfew. I was bound to be asked for an explanation, but I was desperate to get inside the walls as quickly as possible.

There was no moon, so I carried a torch as I rode. On my left I could make out the old cemetery of Santa María. It had been a market day, and there were fish bones on the tombs. The nocturnal creatures that were feeding on them scuttled away as soon as they sensed my presence.

"Who goes there at this hour? Can you not see the gate is closed? We don't want any vagabonds inside the walls," shouted the lad on the battlements.

"Are you calling your lord Don Vela a vagabond?" I shouted, looking up and raising my voice at the foot of the gate. "Is that not Yñigo, the son of Nuño, the furrier?"

"Lord Don Vela died."

"Who says so?"

"Everybody here. Who denies it?"

"The deceased. Is my sister, Lady Lyra, at home?"

"I think she has refused to attend the wedding ceremony. She must be in the forge yard. My cousin is holding a torch for her. I'll go to find her, but on my oath, if this is a trap for my lady—"

What wedding ceremony? I asked myself in bewilderment.

"Don't swear an oath, Yñigo. I will receive the payment for your blasphemy. Do you want to make me richer?" I laughed.

"Were it not that your grieving and dearly beloved brother, Nagorno, announced your death, I could swear you are my lord. You are tall and strong as he was—"

So that was the explanation. Nagorno. Always Nagorno, the man who was everywhere.

"Go and find my sister, I beg you," I interrupted him. "My loins are going to freeze."

When he left, I dismounted and stretched my icy limbs. Was it snowing already? Victoria suffered from a bleak climate. The townspeople had hides as tough as leather.

I had rarely yearned for a hearth as much as I did on that night.

And Onneca . . . perhaps she was asleep?

Only a few hours more, I told myself. *Be patient, Diago. All in good time.*

I was looking forward to finishing my task and getting back to living my own life.

Some moments later, the lad returned.

"Our lady Lyra says we are to open the gate for you. She says you are alive, my . . . my lord. You will find her in the yard outside your forge."

At last I was coming in from the cold. The silent, empty wastelands were behind me. I looked back one last time.

"Yñigo," I instructed the boy, "if tonight or at dawn someone else asks to enter, come and tell me, but do not open the gate. Warn the guards at the South Gate and at the Armería Gate as well."

Nodding, the lad ran off to tell the other guards. My steed and I rounded the burial ground and headed for my family home in Rúa de la Astería.

The seat of our Vela lineage had stood on the northern side of the hill for five hundred years, before the area even became known as Gasteiz.

Our smithy had withstood the passing of centuries. Two hundred years earlier, it had gone up in flames and been reduced to ash during a Saracen raid, but we had rebuilt it, strengthened the walls, replaced the timbers, and carried on.

My family always carried on, no matter what the years threw at us.

We built the first walls to protect our backs. It took ninety men working for almost a decade to construct them. And the village grew: The Thursday market opposite our smithy attracted merchants, peasants, and laborers from the surrounding areas. Then the Santa María Cathedral, also backed up to the town wall, was built.

The town was silent after curfew. The black sky was filling with white feathers, the flakes from a gentle snowfall that was not yet settling on the roofs. I entered the forge yard, looking for my sister.

Several torches fitted into columns provided dim light to the yard, so I saw her from afar. Lyra often trained in fencing, trying to compensate for the weakness of her small body with the curved blade of her *scaramax*. Tonight, though, she was hurling a pair of battle-axes at a scarecrow, the way the Norsemen do. This raised my suspicions: Could it be possible that my trusty Gunnarr . . . ?

I felt a pang of regret at the two years that had passed since I last saw her. I dismounted and hugged her from behind with all my might.

"My dear sister, how I've missed your embrace—" I managed to say.

I did not expect what came next: pecking and claws that tore out several clumps of my hair. A ferocious animal had come out of nowhere—or rather, from the roof over the courtyard.

"Munio, stop it, I beg you. You'll be the ruin of me!" cried a voice that was not my sister's.

The girl I had hugged was not Lyra, although they shared a similar build and were equally small. I couldn't spot any particular differences, though; I was too busy trying to prevent the hell bird from gouging out my eyes.

Then she gave a whistle uncharacteristic of her sex and extended her arm. The huge white owl left me and settled on her, but not without giving me a last warning hiss.

"I'm so sorry, my lord!" the girl cried.

She couldn't be from town, because single women in Victoria had their hair cut short, except for two long locks by the ears. Nor was she wearing a married woman's wimple. It was an interesting enigma; the long blond hair falling to her shoulders was not a common sight in our parts.

"Munio and I have been together since we were born," she explained apologetically. "He was raised with me, and he's in love with me. This happens with some domesticated birds. He considers me his wife, and he's very jealous. He doesn't allow any male to come near me."

"And what is your name, my lady?"

"I'm Alix, the blacksmith."

"The smith? When I left, our master blacksmith was Angevín de Salcedo."

"My deceased father, sire. My older brothers also died of scrofula, so I returned from the convent at Leyre. My father had sent me there years earlier, even though I loved the forge. Molten iron flows through my veins."

"So, in a sense, you are a warrior nun," I said with a smile as I eyed the battle-ax.

"I was a novice, but someone had to defend the convent against the evildoers. They were pretending to be pilgrims on the Jacobean route."

"I brought her here, my beloved cousin," came a booming voice from the darkness. "Lyra asked me to bring Alix home after her brothers died and there was no one left to help her with the forge."

"Gunnarr . . . ? That's you, isn't it? I thought you were ferrying pilgrims along the English Way," I said, rushing to embrace him.

A giant with white eyebrows emerged from the shadows, laughing. He picked me up as though I weighed no more than a sparrow, even though I was head and shoulders taller than anyone in all the courts I had ever been in. Gunnarr Kolbrunson was from the Danish lands, descended from a northern branch of our family—although many in Victoria secretly wagered that he was a descendant of the *jentil*, giants who had inhabited our mountains since time immemorial.

"I knew you weren't dead. How could you have died when you're going to outlive us all?" Gunnarr whispered in my ear, his voice choked with emotion.

"Who says I'm dead?" I asked for the second time that night.

"You must ask your brother that. In fact, I came to Victoria for Nagorno's betrothal. They have already said their pledges, Diago. Nagorno has given her the coins," he said. His words were cautious, as though he was offering me his condolences. "Now they are betrothed. Nagorno and the father of the bride have insisted on witnesses for the test of her virginity. Lyra had no wish to attend, and I did not go, either, out of respect for your memory. And because, even though I am celibate, I don't want to sleep with aching balls tonight. You decide what you'd like to do. They went in some time ago."

My sister appeared then, torch in hand, her face smudged with black. She had on the same leather apron she'd worn on the day we said goodbye. There had been many nights in the East when I missed the times we spent sitting quietly by the fire.

"That's right, Brother, I am not going," said Lyra, her expression circumspect.

I feared the worst. It was something I could never have imagined, precisely the opposite of what I'd been hoping for when I guided my horse toward Victoria.

"Where?"

"I think you know already—the Count de Maestu's mansion, in the territory of Armería. Swear by the goddess Lur that you won't make me regret telling you," said Gunnarr.

"No heads will roll, if that's your concern."

"Yes, obviously that worries me. Swear it."

"I swear."

"By Lur," Gunnarr insisted.

I sighed.

"By Lur. But do not accompany me—you always end up defending Nagorno."

"I'm not going with you, Diago. I know your word is law, but don't ever make me choose between you and Nagorno. He saved my life in the Danish lands, and I became a man by his side in the East. You know I owe him for what I am today."

A quarrelsome, unreliable merchant, my beloved Gunnarr. That's what my brother made of you. I kept silent. It was useless to revisit old arguments.

I turned on my heel and headed for Rúa de las Tenderías and the home of the man who should have been my father-in-law, the good Count Furtado de Maestu.

"Alix, go with him!" Lyra ordered the young woman behind my back. "Make sure my brother doesn't do anything stupid. I'll put Munio in his cage."

A few moments later, I heard light footsteps behind me.

"I don't need a wet nurse. Go back to your tasks," I said, glancing at her out of the corner of my eye.

She had raised the tail of her petticoat over her head, using it as a hood to cover her hair.

"When my lady Lyra is absent, I serve Gunnarr, sire. But since my lord Diago is now lord of my town, in the absence of Gunnarr, it's you I serve." She showed me the battle-ax concealed in the folds of her robe and waved her hand in a conspiratorial gesture. "If you decide to chop off heads, I'll be right next to you to keep you from losing yours."

Tired of arguing, exhausted after the long journey from Navarre, I allowed my new squire to follow me along the dark cobbled street. I had no difficulty finding Count de Maestu's mansion. Its windows were filled with warm candlelight, in contrast with the darkness of the neighboring dwellings.

I came across one of the count's servants in the doorway. He was so intoxicated, he had to lean on the doorframe to stay upright.

"Who goes there?" he mumbled.

"Your lord, Count Don Vela," I replied, weary of this constant questioning.

"At this very moment, Count Don Vela is busy with other, much more pleasant tasks a floor above our heads," he said with the ridiculous vehemence God bestows on drunkards.

I trapped his neck against the door with my elbow, applying just enough pressure for him to take me seriously.

"I am Diago Vela, Remiro, and if you don't recognize me, it's because you're too drunk to be on guard outside your master's door. Let me through before I tell the count about your habit of pilfering his Rioja wine," I growled.

Remiro tried to get some air into his lungs and finally recognized me.

"Yes, it is you. Come in, my good lord. You've been greatly missed in Victoria."

"Where?" I growled, sick of finding every door closed to me.

"They are in the bedchamber."

My squire followed with a worried look as I climbed the old wooden stairs that creaked beneath us. I reached the bedchamber—I had been there before. A dozen guests prevented me from seeing what was happening behind the bed's canopy.

I elbowed my way through. Some of the people recognized me, reacting as though they had seen a ghost. More than one crossed themselves. I paid no attention. I was trying to determine what was going on behind the curtain.

It was my brother, Nagorno, copulating with someone, seemingly oblivious to their audience. The Church in Rome had condemned any sexual congress in which the man was not on top of the woman, and it also forbade nudity in bed. But Nagorno had stripped off his shirt, and I could see his shining dark back and the many scars he had gained in combat.

A pair of white thighs protruded from either side of his body. The woman still wore her nightgown, but her face and her groans left no doubt that she was deriving pleasure from the act.

It had been two years since I had seen that beloved face: those golden eyes, pale lips, and hair as black as mine. Onneca was enjoying herself to the astonishment of the witnesses, who were accustomed to seeing terror-stricken maidens.

My God, Onneca! If they've forced you to have witnesses, you ought to make a better pretense of being a virgin, I thought.

I was concerned for her. She was coupling with my brother, but even so, I was concerned for her.

Neither spared their cries of pleasure until my brother had finished. He rolled away from her, unashamedly showing his naked, muscled body to the witnesses. A dozen curious heads crowded closer to see the result. The three chosen matrons pulled aside the curtain and examined the bed. There it was: the bloodstain her father had been hoping for.

I sighed with relief. For a moment, I had forgotten Onneca's resourcefulness. She would never leave something so important to chance.

We both knew how to simulate lost virginity. It was common practice to conceal chicken entrails in the bride's intimate parts to ensure there would be blood on the groom's member. Years earlier, when we were planning our betrothal, Onneca and I had laughed about it in my bed, realizing that her father would ask for this proof of her maidenhead.

I don't think she recognized me. She was too busy maintaining her dignity, trying not to reveal too much to our insatiably curious vassals. But my brother saw me. It was only for a second. We locked eyes, and then he pressed his lips together and smiled contentedly.

Instinctively, one of my hands reached for the dagger concealed beneath my cloak. A smaller hand prevented me from unsheathing the weapon.

"Count de Maestu, my lord," she warned me.

Furtado de Maestu was still an imposing figure, even though he had aged since I'd seen him last: his shiny hair was now gray, and his smile looked weaker. Still, he made a fine figure—he had always dressed as if it were his daughter's wedding day. It was obvious that he owed his fortune to trading in the rough cloth that was so much in demand among the citizens of Castille. Thanks to de Maestu, the weavers' guild had become the largest in Nova Victoria, the parish of Sant Michel that was surrounded by the wall. Nova Victoria had become part of Villa de Suso a decade earlier when King Sancho the Wise confirmed our charter. On paper, the two districts formed a single walled town, the town of Victoria, coveted for its location on the frontier and known as the key to the kingdom. But the fortifications and the three gates divided more than streets and neighborhoods.

"How is this possible, my dear Diago? You're alive!" the count whispered, peering around him anxiously.

"I always was," I retorted. "You owe me an explanation or two, my dear friend. We said farewell with the promise of a betrothal. You were going to be my beloved father-in-law, and now what am I? The brother of your daughter's husband?"

He motioned for me to say no more and led me up a staircase, trying to make sure no one saw me. With a glance, I commanded Alix de Salcedo to stay in the bedchamber with the others. She clearly did not like the idea, but she obeyed.

"You never said farewell, my good lord," the count said, challenging me when we were alone. "You simply disappeared."

"I had my reasons. I don't owe anyone an explanation."

"I'm not asking for one. Believe me, my grieving daughter waited for you, and I kept my promise of betrothing her to you. But then a letter arrived announcing your death," he said, wiping the remains of the banquet from the corners of his lips with his sleeve. He handed me a letter that he had drawn from a velvet-lined chest.

I read it, then asked, "Who gave it to you?"

"A messenger, I suppose."

"And why did you believe it?"

"Why not? It's full of details about how your boat was wrecked off the coast of Sicily."

Whoever had written the letter knew what few others did: that I had journeyed across the Alps to Sicily and that a storm had separated us from the other ships. What else did he know?

"It's true there was a voyage and a storm. It's also true that my ship was driven off course until we found ourselves near Sicily. But the ship didn't go down, and no one was killed. Not even me, as you can see. So because of a letter brought by an unknown messenger, you hand over my promised bride to my brother?" I said, my voice rising in anger.

"Shh! Don't cause trouble. You're in my house, and most of the guests haven't recognized you, so we need to see how we can resolve this mess. To answer your question, I believed the letter because it bore the royal seal. I didn't see the need to keep the envelope, so I can't show it to you. But here's the pattée of his signature."

I read to the end of the missive, and then had to clear my throat. "The king is Don Sancho the Wise?"

"He governs us now. Do you know of any other king in the lands of Navarre?"

It can't be. He wouldn't destroy my future so cruelly after all I've done for him, I thought, forcing myself to remain calm.

"Get some sleep, good lord. It's late, and it's plain to see you're tired from your journey; you still have blood in your hair. If you stay here there's bound to be a scandal. Let your old friend celebrate his daughter's betrothal in a fitting manner, and tomorrow we'll see how we can resolve this situation. I fear you're likely to face more urgent problems than the fact that your brother has stolen the woman who was supposed to be yours. Nagorno, who is now Count Vela, leads the nobles who recently arrived in Nova Victoria with a firm hand, and, according to those who have spent their entire lives in Villa de Suso, he favors them too much. And if my good-for-nothing eldest son continues playing at the Crusades and manages not to have any children, today's marriage agreement stipulates that Onneca's descendants will become the Counts de Maestu. That means this marriage will unite my fortune with the one that was once yours, and Nagorno and Onneca will be the lords of everything contained within our walls."

3

THE ROOFTOPS OF SAN MIGUEL

UNAI

September 2019

I hurried back up the narrow stairs to the main hall where Alba was waiting.

"We have to bring in more police. And we need it done as quickly as possible!" I told her, perhaps a bit too loudly. "They need to seal off all the exits. We have a dead man, and it may be a poisoning."

Alba took out her cell phone and began to make calls. The doors to the Martín de Salinas room were still closed. The audience for the book launch was inside, unaware of what had transpired a few yards away.

At that moment, I thought I saw a shadow heading upstairs.

"Stay here," I whispered to Alba. "I think I just saw a . . . a nun."

I ran past an enormous French window that looked out on the back of San Miguel Arcángel Church and then climbed to the third floor, trying not to make any noise.

"Stop right there!" I shouted.

Yes, it was a nun, dressed in a white habit and black wimple. She ignored my warning and ran toward a security door that led out of the building. It took me several seconds to react; I didn't expect her to be so defiant or so agile. I followed her out onto a terrace that ran alongside some stairs by the roof of the nearby church. The nun was leaping from one roof to the next, getting away.

"Stop!" I shouted again. I realized I wasn't going to catch her, so I adjusted my strategy.

The nun was reaching the far end of the church and would be forced to jump into one of the narrow passageways separating it from the palace. There was no way out. The alleys, lined with lavender bushes, sloped up to the restored medieval wall. I jumped into one of the alleys and hid in the shadows, waiting.

The nun jumped from several feet up and rolled when she hit the ground.

Now I've got you, I thought.

I ran toward her, but she scrambled to her feet and sped up the slope. I gave chase, but when I rounded the bend . . . she had vanished. Into thin air.

There was nowhere she could hide. The lavender bushes were not tall, and the slope ended at the wall.

"Stop!" I shouted a third time.

My shouts were in vain, as were my searches of the passageways and the gardens.

I dialed Alba's number. "Alba, tell the janitor I'm stuck in a passageway between the palace and San Miguel Arcángel Church, below a restored stretch of wall."

"I'm coordinating the operation. What are you doing there?"

"Take statements from everybody in the palace," I told her. "Ask if anyone saw anything that caught their attention. We also need to close off the Plaza de Matxete and interview all the people working at the medieval market."

"What are we looking for?"

"A nun. But don't ask any leading questions, and don't mention her unless the witness does. I don't want anybody inventing things."

4

THE SOUTH GATE

DIAGO VELA

Winter, the Year of Our Lord 1192

A woman's cry interrupted what had been a sleepless night. Dawn was shedding its first light on the battlements. I had been unable to find consolation in my old bed: it was empty, covered in hoarfrost. The fire in my chamber had gone out before daybreak, and the early-morning chill had kept me awake. At least I didn't dream of shipwrecks.

Voices shouted from Rúa de las Tenderías. "They've found the count! They've found the count!"

Opening my old chest, I chose my most respectable clothes. I didn't want to be taken for a vagabond again. I washed my face with water from the basin and ran downstairs.

I didn't need to ask where the count was found. I just needed to follow the throng.

Near the South Gate, then, I thought. I was soon at the foot of the wall near the gate. Beyond the town rose the spire of Sant Michel, indifferent to the tragedy.

A few heads were pressed close to the corpse. I managed to push my way through, but by the time I stood over him, his body was already cold.

The man who had been destined to be my father-in-law, Count Furtado de Maestu. He had not looked in the best of health when

I left him the previous evening. He seemed worried and careworn; one of his sleeves smelled of vomit where he had wiped his mouth. At the time, I had blamed the excesses of the banquet and the profusion of wine.

But I had seen a corpse like this before.

I needed to be sure. How could I confirm my suspicions in the midst of this crowd?

I bent down to examine him. His dark clothing hid the stain very well. I could just make it out.

This man urinated blood.

It was then that I saw her. Alix de Salcedo, but without her aggressive white owl. Her hair was hidden beneath a three-pointed wimple—an unusual detail—but I saved my curiosity for later. I jerked my chin, motioning for her to come closer.

"He was a just man. I was sure he would die of old age," she said in an undertone, her eyes fixed on the stiff body.

"Can you get me a rabbit?" I whispered.

"Alive or dead?"

"I need the skin."

"I don't think they'll let anyone out of town right now, but the butcher's son keeps a few of them in his yard. Shall I buy it or steal it?"

I slipped a couple of coins into her weathered fist. She had the calloused hands of someone who wielded a hammer or a weapon.

"Where shall I take it?"

"To the count's mansion, we'll meet there."

Before I could turn around, she had disappeared.

"All of you, back to your work," I shouted. "Somebody bring a cart and a mule. We need to return the good count to his home."

"Is that you, my lord, Don Diago Vela?" asked a man holding a crossbow on the rampart.

"That's right, Paricio. I know you were given news of my death, but I have returned. Before I can take charge of what I left in Victoria, though, we have to deal with this emergency. Tell everyone I am back, and that I will listen to their concerns as I always have."

"But your brother is in charge of that now. Which of you are we to turn to?"

I feigned calm and smiled.

"To me, without doubt. You will go to him once I am truly dead and buried."

Everyone laughed with relief.

The count's body was transported to his home, carried up the ancient staircase to the main floor, and laid out on the bed where only a few hours earlier his daughter had been betrothed to my contemptible brother.

"Is the smith here?" I asked, as they were undressing the dead man.

Just then Alix de Salcedo appeared, carrying a white rabbit.

"Everyone is to leave," I commanded.

Remiro, the count's elderly servant, and the two neighbors who had accompanied me to the mansion descended the stairs, which creaked and groaned under their weight.

Alix did not obey. Rather, she gestured as if to say, *There's no way I'm leaving here.*

"As you wish. Do you know how to shave?"

"I used to shave my father and brothers. I have a steady hand."

"You only have to shave the rabbit."

"My lord?"

"If you don't, I will, and you can slit open the body. We have to hurry before anyone returns to stop us."

Alix asked no more questions. She took out a dagger and moved to the window for more light. I raised Furtado's tunic, cut open his stomach, and removed his viscera.

I carefully lifted the organs with a piece of cloth in order not to touch them and placed them in the washbasin.

"Bring me the skin, Alix. I have to rub it against the viscera."

"What are you trying to achieve?"

As I rubbed the skin against the count's organs, blisters appeared and part of the skin appeared to be scorched.

"Just this. Years ago, a doctor in Pamplona showed me this technique. This is the effect of the blister beetle when you take more of it than you should."

"Is that the brown powder the soldiers use in brothels when their manhood fails them?"

I smiled.

"For a novice, you know a great deal. From your brothers, no doubt?" I asked, avoiding the mystery of her three-cornered headdress and its implications for now.

"Yes, my brothers. May I avoid pretending at least in front of you that talking about these things makes me blush? Being a good Christian woman can be exhausting."

"There's no need to pretend; not many things scandalize me. Did the old count live with a woman?"

"It's said that since his wife's death, he shed tears on her tomb and preferred to pray at a cold altar than to share a warm bed."

"So he had no need for powders."

"In all truth, I can't imagine a man less interested in carnal desires."

"Then we need to find someone who knows about poisons," I muttered as I put the viscera back into the count's body and rearranged his tunic. "Could you clean away the blood, dispose of the rabbit, and keep quiet about what you've seen here?"

No sooner had I asked her than it was done. Although her response to my requests was rapid, Alix did not give the impression of being docile. In fact, she seemed rebellious, much like my indomitable sister, Lyra.

Speaking of poisons. I found another venomous being in the small workshop next to the family forge. Nagorno could have been Victoria's most reputable goldsmith if he hadn't been born into a high position.

He was using a delicate hammer to make a gold-and-enamel brooch, depicting an eagle twisting to fend off a serpent wrapped around its neck.

"Is that jewel for your bride? In recent years, the Church has begun to oppose ostentation," I said.

"Come in without asking, Brother," he replied evenly, his voice the same snakelike hiss I remembered. "The door is always open to you. Pope Celestine the Third just banned prosperous merchants from wearing furs, precious stones, or elaborate buckles. Since my wife isn't one of the newly rich, she won't need to conceal my gifts. I'm pleased you are alive, my dear Diago."

"You seemed happier yesterday, when you thought I was dead," I said, sitting on the workbench.

Nagorno sighed and stopped fashioning the jewel.

"Are you bitter? I did it for our family, Diago. Somebody had to rescue us from the anarchy you left behind two years ago."

"By marrying the woman promised to me?"

"You vanished with no explanation, saying only 'I will return.' As the months went by, your promise seemed less likely. Are you going to tell me why you left?"

"I cannot do so, Nagorno. Suffice it to say that King Sancho the Wise employed veiled threats to entrust me with a mission that I could not refuse. My journey became much more complicated than intended. In fact, I have not been to the court at Tudela for fear he might send me on another dangerous errand. Perhaps in a few years' time, I'll be able to tell you what happened, but not now," I lied. I needed to find out just how much he knew.

"As you wish," Nagorno replied. He knew when not to insist. "Are you so upset that I married Onneca? It was quite a sacrifice for me. You know I can't bear to be a married man. How often have I found myself a widower?"

"Too often," I murmured.

"If I'd known you were alive, if I had been sure of it, I would never have married her. But she had rejected two marriage proposals, and you know that, in keeping with the laws of Navarre, she was obliged to accept the third."

"Who made those two proposals?"

"The Lord of Ibida, Bermúdez de Gobeo, and Vidal, the Lord de Funes's son."

"An old man and a dimwitted babe in arms. No wonder the count rejected them."

"Onneca rejected them. Don't underestimate her."

"I never have. But their lands wouldn't have brought her father much. Lowborn relatives, petty gentry—"

"Can you see now that I've done you a favor, Brother?"

"You seemed to enjoy it."

"Every sacrifice deserves a reward. I'm impatient to discover how our lady behaves in private, when there are no witnesses. . . . But you can tell me about that, can't you?"

"As you said, that's none of my concern now," I said with a smile. I would need to get used to this pretense.

"No. . . . It's not that. You saw that my lady cares for me, and it is gnawing away at you. I know you. You've never doubted your prowess, but now . . . I can spot all the shades of your anger, and it's lurking there . . . the doubt, after what you saw yesterday."

I ignored the jab. Nagorno was probing for my weaknesses, like a blunt broadsword striking the shoulder, the thigh, the back, searching for the spot where the open wound was concealed.

My sleepless night had healed that wound.

The blow Onneca's betrayal had dealt me was no more. If the world knew how it had affected me, that would undermine my position—and I could not show my enemies that sort of weakness.

Yes, there were enemies, but how close were they?

"You know you'll have to give her an heir." Now I was the one probing old wounds.

Nagorno didn't react, a sure sign I had hurt him more than I dared hope.

"Yes, of course, that is expected of me."

"And how do you propose to do that, Brother?" I challenged him.

"All in good time, *Brother*."

"Fine. I don't doubt your ability to deceive; you'll find a way around it. But I must speak of a different matter. What do you know about the letter containing news of my death?"

"The messenger was a phantom. The guards told contradictory stories about him. I asked who he was, but nobody could say what he looked like. Two of the guards swore they had seen him at dusk near the South Gate. I had them follow his trail, but they lost it after crossing Cauce de los Molinos."

"*You* should have pursued him! *You* wouldn't have lost his trail!" I shouted, my patience at an end.

"It was meant for Count de Maestu. You know I have a good eye for forgeries—"

"Because you're a master in the art."

He smiled. He was tempted more by some sins than others, and pride had never troubled him.

"My point is that I managed to get a good look at the royal seal, Diago."

"Everything can be forged."

"Everything can be forged," he agreed. "I taught you that. But it was a letter from King Sancho the Wise himself, and counterfeiting a letter from the king is high treason and punishable by hanging. You have to admit, it's not likely anybody would do that. So what was I to do, Brother, if not weep for you and then assume responsibility for everything our family has achieved?"

I seized him by the neck, tired of his playacting. I wanted a real conversation with my brother.

"Don't for a minute imagine I'm willing to believe you thought I was dead. You and I have been in enough tight scrapes to know it's not easy to get rid of us," I said, and he finally let his mask slip so we could speak the truth. "I have to find out who sent that letter."

"You really don't believe it was the king?"

"I can't see any reason why he would do that."

"I know you don't believe me, but I did not do it."

No, I don't believe you, Nagorno. You're the lord of lies. How can I believe you when I've known you all your life? I thought this but said nothing. There was no point. I changed the course of our conversation again.

"There's something else. You brought our beloved Gunnarr here."

"That's right."

"Why?"

"The usual reason. There's a demand for unicorn horn at the Tudela court."

According to many reliable sources, unicorn horn was the best love potion for men unable to sustain an erection, and it was impossible to find. From his voyages in the northern seas, Gunnarr had found a convenient substitute, and nobody could tell the difference.

"Is narwhal tusk the only aphrodisiac requested at court?"

"It's more expensive, and the only one worth bringing here."

I did not offer my suspicions about the blister beetle. It wasn't an insect found in Navarre. The beetle had to be brought from its home in faraway warmer lands. But Victoria was a town of merchants: Could Nagorno, and perhaps Gunnarr, have anything to do with its trade?

A nearby church tolled the bell that marked the passing of a townsperson.

"You'll have learned of my father-in-law's death?" asked Nagorno.

"It's impossible not to in this town. How is Onneca?"

Nagorno looked aslant at me. "She's suffering," he muttered, as if he, too, was grieving.

Surprised, I looked away. So Onneca was important to him?

"The count's funeral will start at the hour of the Angelus," he went on icily. "I've paid for a chorus of mourners. I imagine the entire town will visit the count's mansion for the traditional nod of the head. . . . It would be good for us to be seen together there."

"You've hired mourners?"

"And a keener to compose a lament. The count deserves all the homages I can afford. He was a man of honor. Onneca is keeping vigil over his body. We must all be seen together there. The bailiff, the mayor, the constable, the lieutenant, and the clergy from Santa María Cathedral will be present. I've arranged for him to be buried in our cemetery. He is part of our family and will rest consoled by our blood, among the other Velas."

I nodded. For once, I agreed with Nagorno.

As we left the small workshop, I couldn't help but notice that he put the brooch for Onneca in a concealed pocket of his surcoat.

We headed for the Armería district. The streets were crowded with market stalls and scavenging pigs, and we had to avoid water-sellers and vendors. A few houses farther on, a crowd of neighbors had come to pay their respects to the count's family. Everybody was there, from Nova Victoria, from Villa de Suso, and even from outside the walls, where the cutlers lived.

The nod of the head was an ancient tradition, in which the family of the deceased waited alongside the body of their loved one for the locals to arrive and offer their condolences. The family then nodded in acceptance of the tribute. It was a lengthy, wearisome custom, but it had been established in Victoria centuries ago, and it was impossible to abandon.

"Won't the count's other children be present at the funeral?"

"I doubt it. His good-for-nothing eldest son is in Edessa slaughtering infidels. And the two little girls have been immured."

"Both of them?" I asked, somewhat surprised.

Nagorno did not even deign to reply. He was too busy thinking about the funeral ceremony he had to preside over. He stood at the entrance to the count's mansion, watching the people who were going in.

I knew the family tradition of walling up young girls. When they had too many daughters, the Counts de Maestu sent their daughters to be bricked up alive in some nearby parish. A partition was constructed, and the girls devoted their lives to prayer, immured in a tiny space. Some went willingly, others not.

I was about to enter the doorway when Nagorno took me discreetly by the arm and whispered, "You haven't asked me yet. Does that mean we have a truce?"

"No, I haven't asked if you were the one who did away with the good count, even though you have the motive and the means, and you've never lacked imagination."

"So it's a truce?"

"Yes."

"Why?"

"Because you haven't asked me about it, either," I replied.

We entered the mansion in silence. Those who had come to pay their respects were gathered at the foot of the narrow wooden staircase; some were going up, others were coming down.

This was going to take all morning.

I pictured Onneca sitting next to her father's body, a body I had desecrated. I felt a pang of guilt.

But at that very moment, an inferno of wood collapsed around our heads. The ancient staircase had given way under the weight of so many bodies. There was a deafening crash as the planks splintered, and we were buried under a pile of bloody arms and legs, crushed beneath the weight of the dead.

5

LA CALLE PINTORERÍA

UNAI

September 2019

Needless to say, that night neither Alba nor I got any sleep.

The initial autopsy report didn't take long; it had been given top priority to make sure it came in before the weekend.

But the victim . . . the victim made headlines throughout Spain. The privacy he had worked so hard to maintain during his lifetime swirled down the mortuary sink.

It was Antón Lasaga, the owner and founder of a clothing empire started three decades earlier with a small store on Cercas Bajas.

Scarves.

It had all started with wool scarves.

Tired of depending on his suppliers, Lasaga had set up a drab-looking factory in the Ali-Gobeo industrial park. At the time, the Vitoria City Council had more than enough land for expansion and was trying to attract industry to the city. After scarves came jackets and coats made of quality cloth. Within a few years, Lasaga was established nationally. The public knew nothing about him and little about his family. Some said he lived in Madrid and took a private jet every morning to be at the factory in time for breakfast. He and his family were shielded from the press. The photograph that had appeared in the newspapers was the only one that existed, and it was twenty years old. No one would have recognized Lasaga on Calle Dato if he had stopped for a coffee.

We had spent the few hours since his death investigating his wealth. He was a born accumulator, like the Jay Gatsby of northern Spain. He owned land in Álava, Viscaya, Cantabria, Guipúzcoa, and Burgos. He had vineyards in the Rioja Alavesa and Navarre. Although he was sixty-seven at the time of his death, Antón Lasaga showed no intention of giving up control of his business.

The pathologist had promised she would send us the test results by midafternoon, but Estíbaliz, with characteristic impatience, dialed Doctor Guevara's number from Alba's office well before then. Estí put the call on speaker.

Outside the office window, the sun tinted the leaves a golden brown, and a slight breeze stirred the banners on the avenue.

"Doctor Guevara, thanks again for handling this so quickly," said Alba. She gathered her long black hair in a tight knot, a gesture she repeated twenty times a day. "What do you have for us?"

"Good afternoon, deputy superintendent. I knew the victim: I was a lifelong friend of his wife's. She died less than six months ago. This is such a shame. He was very cultured and devoted to his family."

"Have you been able to determine the cause of death? Inspector López de Ayala and I thought we noticed a rotten, artificial odor in the restrooms where his body was found," said Estíbaliz. "Did you discover anything unusual in the course of the autopsy?"

"Indeed, we did: his esophagus was severely blistered, as was his bladder. He must have felt quite ill in the hours prior to his death. He would have experienced difficulty urinating and dizzy spells, and he probably vomited at least once during that last day."

"And yet he went to the event," I broke in.

"Because of his condition, he would have been in a lot of pain throughout his life. He must have thought it was only indigestion and possibly a urinary tract infection and decided to go about his activities as normal."

"What was the exact cause of death?" I asked.

"Rupture of the aorta. His heart gave out."

"Based on what you've said, it sounds as if he swallowed something that corroded his internal organs."

"That's my suspicion, but I'm still waiting for the lab to send the toxicology report," the pathologist said. "It shouldn't take too much longer—in fact, I was expecting to hear from them an hour ago. I've never seen such catastrophic damage to organs before. It must have been a very corrosive substance. I didn't want to risk telling you my hypothesis before I had all the information, but Inspector López de Ayala called me yesterday and asked me to compare the results with one particular substance. If he's right, it could save us hours of work."

"What substance, Unai? Care to share your thoughts?" asked Estíbaliz.

"Of course. I wanted to tell you earlier, before we got to the office, but there was so much going on that I got sidetracked."

I said the name of the substance out loud, but I have to admit, it didn't sound as convincing as it had inside my head. Estíbaliz looked at me as if I were hopeless. Alba shrugged. I ignored their doubts. I was used to it. They never believed in my initial theories, but that didn't stop me. It was part of my process to cast my lines widely until I got a bite, then I hauled it in.

"Even if Unai is right about what caused his death, if toxicology confirms that he was poisoned, we'll have to determine what his last few meals were. We need to know where he had breakfast, lunch—even a snack—on the day he died and the preceding twenty-four hours," said Alba.

"And we need to know who he ate with," added Estíbaliz.

"I'd like to confirm something with you," I said to Doctor Guevera. "The victim was born with Marfan syndrome, wasn't he?"

"That's right. Long, slender limbs, concave chest, scoliosis, flat feet, small jaw, coloboma of the iris—that is, a hole or a defect in the iris—and a weakened aorta. I don't know what he swallowed or was forced to swallow, but he couldn't tolerate the resulting dilation of his heart. People with Marfan syndrome are usually kept under close medical observation. The victim would have known about his condition. I'll wager we find traces of medication in his blood."

"Anything else, Doctor Guevara?"

"Well, yes, but it's a bit off-topic. I have the DNA results from the blood found at the scene of the Nájera sisters' disappearance."

"Tell us," Estí urged.

"All of the blood we found on the bedroom carpet belongs to the younger sister. I don't know if that helps you at all. We took DNA samples from the girls' parents, and forensics brought me both the sisters' dirty laundry. The blood matches the DNA we found on three pieces of the younger sister's clothing. That's all I have for now."

Just then, Alba's cell phone began to vibrate. She looked at the message and frowned.

"Doctor Guevara, please let us know when you have more information for us. And thanks for everything."

She shot Estíbaliz and me a worried look.

"It's Superintendent Medina. He's calling an emergency meeting. That can't be a good sign."

We left the room in silence. We now had two cases on our hands, and there was too much to process, too much to resolve.

We walked into a dark room. A projector cast photographs of the two sisters onto the wall. Estefanía looked shy and was slightly overweight. Oihana had extraordinary hair that reached her waist. It was her defining feature. Her image was the one featured on the posters plastered on every wall in the city. The superintendent waved his hand brusquely, indicating that we should take a seat. He remained standing.

"We've been working on Operation Frozen for two weeks, and we've had no success. Now we have a new death to investigate. You can imagine how quickly the brass wants us to clear up the mystery surrounding Antón Lasaga's death. Was it natural causes, suicide, accident, or homicide? So let's go over everything case by case: first, bring me up to speed on the disappearance of the two girls?"

"We're looking for two minors," Estíbaliz replied, stepping in. "Estefanía and Oihana Nájera. Sisters—sixteen and twelve years old, respectively. The older one is a responsible girl. The younger one is still very much a child and rebellious. Their parents are young, and both of them teach at the Jesús Guridi Conservatoire. Bassoon and cello. They own their own home on Calle Pintorería, middling income. The father says his daughters got along well. However, the mother admits the two girls argued a lot, which she attributes to differences in age and personality. On the night the girls disappeared, the parents went out for dinner with their *cuadrilla* and left the younger one in the care of her older sister. They returned home at twenty past one, and the girls were gone. Nobody came through that entrance between the time the parents left for dinner and the time they returned. We've checked all the security cameras in the nearby shops. I don't know how to explain it, and I know you'll say it's impossible and you'll tell us to watch the footage again, but we've already gone over it multiple times—"

"Before you ask your next question," I butted in, "there wasn't much traffic in the street. The girls disappeared at the end of August, on a weeknight. Vitoria was empty: most people hadn't returned from their holidays. There are no vehicles blocking the doorway—we had a clear view. When it comes to the home itself, that's where things start to seem strange. When the parents got back to their apartment, the second on the right, the front door was locked from the inside. That isn't odd, they always did that when they left the girls on their own. And the windows were closed. Also, Estefanía's cell phone was switched off at 10:38, which seems strange for a teenager, unless she went to bed early, but her parents didn't think that was likely. The younger sister didn't have a phone. But the most worrying thing of all is the trace of blood on the carpet in the older girl's bedroom. Doctor Guevara has just confirmed that it's Oihana's."

"How much blood?"

"Barely twelve milliliters. Not life-threatening, if that's what you're wondering. She didn't bleed to death, at least not in the apartment. Forensics also inspected the stairs and the entrance to the building, but they didn't find any more blood. No money or clothes were taken. The parents don't think the girls ran away. They were good students, no drug problems, and there was nothing unusual in the older daughter's social media accounts. The idea that this was a kidnapping for ransom grows weaker as more time goes by: No one has tried to contact the family. Both Inspector Ruiz de Gauna and I have been in constant communication with the parents, and we don't think they're lying. We've also been tracking them, and Officer Milán Martínez is monitoring their bank accounts. There are no transfers that imply that they're receiving money behind our backs or asking friends for help. That trace of blood makes me fear the worst. An assailant could have hit Oihana on the head to subdue her and keep Estefanía in line, or the two sisters could have argued. It's difficult to reconstruct the events, and we can't establish why they disappeared. We're not convinced that it was a kidnapping for ransom or that the two of them ran away: they would have nowhere to go, and no way to earn money."

I listened to Estíbaliz walk the superintendent through the investigation. I was extremely concerned about the direction our suspicions were leading us.

"What do you think, Inspector López de Ayala?" the superintendent asked. He sat on the table in front of the projector's light. The girl's pictures flashing across his body were disturbing.

"We need to let the crime scene speak." As soon as the words left my mouth, I knew I sounded crazy. Sometimes I talk through things as though I am alone.

"What's that?"

Alba looked at me as if to say, *Please don't rile him up.*

"The scene is staged," I corrected myself.

"Can you explain?"

"On one hand, it's a typical locked-room mystery. The doors were locked from the inside, and the victims vanished into thin air. . . . On the other hand, we have the younger sister's blood, which suggests a struggle, violence of some kind, and also points us toward the older sister, leading us to believe that she may have hurt the younger one or accidentally caused her death. But we've inspected the furniture, the walls, and the floor, and there's no trace of the girl's DNA on any other surface. Nor have we found a weapon. It must have been a weapon of convenience, something with enough weight to open her scalp. That's why I'm saying the scene is staged to confuse us—it takes us in two completely different directions."

"So what do you suggest?"

"We keep looking for them, alive or dead. But we must avoid committing to any theory about what happened until they turn up or their bodies are found. The scene of their disappearance is deceptive; it's designed to distract us from what's really important, which is finding them. But we're not going to be distracted. We're going to continue Operation Frozen."

We were interrupted by a timid knock at the door.

"Milán, you don't have to knock," Alba told her for the umpteenth time. "You're part of the team."

Officer Milán Martínez had been with us for three years. She was still a clumsy giant who covered her desk in garish Post-it notes. She had become close friends with Estíbaliz and Alba. The three went hiking in the hills every weekend to try to forget the strain of their jobs. Deputy Inspector Manu Peña adored Milán—treated her like she was a goddess of love, sex, and romance—but she had dropped him. Now I often found myself consoling the violinist over drinks in the city center.

Milán slipped into the darkened room without opening the door all the way and took an orange Post-it out of her pocket.

"I've got a message," she said, doing her best to read it even though none of the lights in the room were on. "Cantharis. The toxicology lab just called Doctor Guevara and confirmed that they found two grams of *Lytta vesicatoria* in the victim's body."

"Meaning what, exactly?" the superintendent pressed.

"The victim was killed with cantharis, also known as blister beetle, or Spanish fly."

6

THE OLD FORGE

DIAGO VELA

WINTER, THE YEAR OF OUR LORD 1192

When I regained consciousness, a beak was pecking at my head.

"Stop, for heaven's sake! That's enough," I shouted.

"You're alive!" Alix de Salcedo said.

"Can you get this beast off me?" I begged, pushing aside the timbers that had fallen on top of me.

I looked at the confusion all around: people were moaning and crying and trying to help each other.

"How did you find me?"

"It was Munio. He remembers you from yesterday," Alix said in a concerned tone. "I can see you're as blue as ever, so I know you're all right."

"I'm blue? Like a dead person?" I asked, puzzled.

"No, it's not that," she explained hastily. "It's just . . . well, don't tell anyone, they'll think I'm mad, but . . . my senses are linked: colors have a smell, and sounds have a taste. To me, everyone has a distinct color. I've always been this way."

"And I'm blue?" I asked, smiling. I reached up to feel a huge lump forming on the side of my head.

"It's as though you have a slice of the sea in your eyes. The blue anchors you and weighs you down, but also defines you. It's so strange that you come from a town in the interior."

"What about the others? Or am I the only walking rainbow?"

"Gunnarr is white. Your cousin Héctor, the Lord of Castillo, is earth-colored. Count Nagorno is red—do you want me to go on?"

"I would, you know," I said, as she helped me to my feet, "but first let's determine who's alive and who's dead, and help the wounded if we can."

I was still slightly dizzy, but I tried to assist everyone I could. As I was tending the injured, I overheard enough to make it clear that some people from Nova Victoria were blaming those from Villa de Suso for the accident.

"We hear such things every day now." Alix sighed. "Whenever a misfortune strikes, we all accuse one another."

Four locals died, and news of the calamity spread so rapidly along the road to Pamplona that the next day the inhabitants of nearby villages came to the funeral carrying candles.

A procession of priests and nuns entered the North Gate, accompanying García de Pamplona, a protégé of the Count de Maestu and the youngest bishop ever appointed. He was only seventeen, but his diplomatic skills made him welcome at any court. I had met him in Tudela and thought highly of him. We considered ourselves cousins. He felt the same way about Onneca, and we could all see that the affection was mutual when she flung herself into his arms the moment he dismounted. Even though the snowfall had brought a chill to the air, the bishop wore only a chasuble. He didn't seem to need anything more. The nuns accompanying him on their donkeys looked at him adoringly.

"So much misfortune all at once, cousin! I came as soon as I heard. I will officiate at your father's funeral and the ones of those who perished here."

"I thank you, cousin," she replied, maintaining her composure.

The funerals over, I called in at the family forge on the way to my home in Rúa de la Astería.

Alix was giving orders to apprentices who were unloading ore from our mines at Bagoeta. Lyra ruled her blacksmiths with a firm hand.

"You haven't yet told me all that's going on in town, Lyra. It seems quite different now. The two neighborhoods are at each other's throats."

She nodded and motioned for Alix to come over. I kept a close eye on Munio; the owl glared at me threateningly but didn't move from the courtyard roof.

"My brother wants to know about the town, Alix. Tell him what worries us as inhabitants of Villa de Suso."

"In your absence, the noble families from the surrounding villages have taken control of the town gates," Alix explained, taking a break from her hammering. "The Mendoza family, whose tower is at Martioda to the north, have just won the right to charge a tithe on fruit, despite opposition from the deceased Count de Maestu. Your brother, Nagorno, in his capacity as Count Vela, won over the council. People are angry here because on Calle de las Pescaderías, they're now only allowed to sell fish from the sea. To avoid paying the toll, the women must sell river fish in the Santa María Cemetery outside the walls. You left a well-governed town, but I'm afraid that the Victoria you missed so much no longer exists."

7

ARMENTIA

UNAI

September 2019

"What does that mean?" asked Superintendent Medina.

"Antón Lasaga ingested a lethal dose of a substance that has been used as an aphrodisiac since the Middle Ages," Alba explained. "We'll open a new line of inquiry with that in mind. What else, Milán?"

"Boss, the victim's two sons are at the front desk. They're eager to speak to Inspector Kraken."

I sighed. To my chagrin, I had been the visible face of the Criminal Investigation Unit for three years, since Tasio Ortiz de Zárate had uploaded my photograph onto the Internet. As a result, anyone who had a problem with the law, or something to report, or even a suspicion turned up at police headquarters at Portal de Foronda and asked for Inspector Kraken. Estí concealed a smile, the rat.

"I can see you've got your work cut out for you. I expect you'll have some answers for me soon," said the superintendent, leaving the room, cell phone in hand.

"Have them sent up. Let's see if they have anything interesting to tell us. Estí, Milán, you come with me," I said, dragging them downstairs.

"So we have a dead man with an erection," said Estíbaliz.

"He didn't have an erection. That only happens with hanged men," I retorted.

"Yes, but he wanted to get one. He took a medieval Viagra."

"That's what we're going to check. I'm not convinced."

"Why not?"

"I'm worried about the statistics. Most homicides that target women are sexual attacks or incidents of domestic violence. When men are killed, it's usually the result of a physical assault, a settling of accounts, or . . . God forbid, a random predatory attack."

"No one wants to see predators in Vitoria. If it turns out that Antón Lasaga was a random victim, it's going to make it impossible for us to find a link that leads to the perpetrator."

"My fear exactly, Estí. What we saw in the restrooms in Villa Suso . . . the victim hadn't been restrained, immobilized, or even hit. He went to the bathroom of his own accord," I said. Just then, we arrived at the small interview room where the Lasaga brothers were waiting for us.

They were both much shorter than me and appeared to be in their early thirties. The one with the darker complexion—curly hair, business-school handshake—took the initiative.

"Inspector Kraken, I believe?"

"Inspector López de Ayala, in fact. I'm sorry for your loss. I imagine you must have a difficult day ahead of you."

"Indeed. And because of that, I'll come straight to the point. I am one of four siblings: five, counting my sister. The others are handling the funeral arrangements. My brother and I came because . . ."

He tapped me on the arm in a gesture that implied a trust we didn't yet share. "Why don't you sit down? That way we'll be more comfortable."

"Of course." I glanced at Estíbaliz and nodded. "This is my colleague, Inspector Ruiz de Gauna. We were the ones who found your father. You already know Officer Milán Martínez."

"That's why I wanted to talk to you." He cleared his throat and ignored Estí and Milán, who remained on their feet behind him.

The other brother also sat down, silent as a statue, his face solemn.

I turned to the more talkative brother. "Take it away . . . ?"

"Andoni. I'm Andoni Lasaga, Antón's eldest son."

"I see. I'd love to hear more about why you were so eager to talk to me, but first, maybe you can tell us a little bit about your father and the rest of your family."

"Well, my mother died a few months ago. She and my father were close. We're a traditional family, and they had an old-fashioned marriage. My father was devastated when she died."

I nodded. I believed he was telling me the truth—at least, that's what the wedding ring we found on a chain around the victim's neck implied. If a recently widowed man wanted to use an aphrodisiac before a date, wouldn't he take off his dead wife's ring? It seemed like a counterintuitive way of moving on.

"What I'm trying to say is . . . everything is happening very quickly. First my mother, in a car accident. Then my father . . ."

"What are you suggesting?"

"Not to trust her," he breathed in a whisper that cracked like a whip.

"Andoni!" his younger brother exclaimed in horror.

"It's true! They need to know, don't they?"

"Who is 'her'?" asked Estíbaliz.

"Our sister, Irene, the middle child. She was our father's favorite, his only daughter, always purring on his lap. She brainwashed him. She's a fortune hunter; she wants it all for herself."

"Andoni, this is too much! I thought you wanted me to come to the police station with you to ask about our father, not so that you could accuse our sister. My God, you're really obsessed!"

"She's brainwashed you, too. That's what she does. She's a born manipulator, a psychopath. You're an expert in psychopathy, why don't you talk to her, Inspector Kraken?"

He tapped me on the arm again in that friendly gesture. It was as fake as everything else about him.

"We will be carrying out routine interviews with everyone connected to your father. But let me repeat what you just said, so I can be sure I've got it right. You're insinuating that your father's death was not the result of natural causes or an accident. You're accusing your sister of being involved in his death in order to gain control of his fortune, is that right? Because if that's your formal statement, you'll have to sign it."

"Come on, Andoni. Think about it," his brother whispered to him. "You're upset right now, but this isn't a casual conversation you're having in a bar. You're accusing Irene of something serious. Don't do this to us. Papa doesn't deserve it."

The eldest son clenched his fists and sighed in frustration.

It took another ten minutes to get rid of them. Once they left, I sat staring at the white door.

"A dynasty at war."

"Come back to the twenty-first century, Kraken. We need you here," said Estíbaliz.

"I'll put it in modern terms: there's going to be hell to pay over the inheritance."

"What did you think?" Estíbaliz prompted Milán.

"Andoni Lasaga is domineering and impulsive. He's not intelligent. He talks about his father in the past tense, which is striking. His cell phone is expensive, but it's several years old and the screen is cracked. He wears designer shoes, but the soles are worn. He's dressed in formal mourning clothes, but the sleeves and collar of the suit are frayed. By contrast, the younger brother is not nearly as ostentatious, but both his cell phone and his clothes are new and of good quality."

I nodded proudly. We had trained Milán and Peña, taught them to observe closely, and at this point, I doubted whether we had anything more to teach them.

"In addition," she went on, "Doctor Guevara told me she knew the family, so I asked her for more information on them. Andoni used to work for his father's business, but he was useless and was eventually dropped from the board. He used to, and possibly still does, receive an allowance from his father, but he has an expensive lifestyle and he spends money like there's no tomorrow, so he's always short on funds. The remaining children are discreet; they form a united front. They all have university degrees and have been trained to take over the business, but their sister is the real brains of the family: top marks, MBA, positions abroad. She's been working for her father for more than ten years. She started at the bottom and worked her way up. She has experience in every department. But it doesn't look like Antón Lasaga was in any hurry to step down. I think we're going to have to go to Armentia."

"To Armentia?" asked Estíbaliz.

"That's where our fashion king lived. He owns several properties but lived in a villa in Armentia."

Just then, Peña came in carrying a thick folder.

"I was looking for you. I think I've identified our nun. I've collated all the information we got from the witnesses who were in Villa Suso yesterday: a hundred and eighty-seven people. Only six say they saw a nun. All six say she was a woman, good-looking, thirty or forty years old. Between five feet and five feet six inches tall. One witness thought she was short. The other five didn't notice anything unusual about her height. Two state she was wearing a white habit and a white wimple; the other four say the habit was white but the wimple was dark, either black or dark brown. It was night, it's impossible to know."

The principle of false memory, I thought. Witnesses never turned out to be as reliable as they believed themselves to be.

"Then . . ." Estíbaliz chimed in, "we're looking for a woman?"

"A Dominican."

"A Dominican?"

"Yes. I've spent the entire morning researching nearby religious orders. If we accept what most of the witnesses and Inspector López de Ayala say, the suspect is a Dominican nun, likely from the convent of Nuestra Señora del Cabello in Quejana."

"That's in the Ayala region. Kraken, weren't your ancestors the lords of Ayala?" said Estíbaliz.

"Of course; I have a castle there, and lands as far as the eye can see. . . . But seriously, from what I've read in the newspapers, that convent is empty, and the order moved to San Sebastián a few years ago. Besides, the half dozen or so nuns left at the time were in their nineties. I did not chase a ninety-year-old across those rooftops, I can assure you."

"Unless she experienced an extremely long youth or was exceptionally healthy," my colleague retorted. "In any case, if the convent closed years ago, maybe the habit has nothing to do with the Dominicans. White habit, black wimple. Someone who wants to disguise themselves as a nun could easily choose that combination. But let's not get carried away just yet. We still have to interview everybody who works at the medieval market to find out if anyone there was dressed like a nun. Peña, I need you to coordinate that with a couple of uniforms."

"Milán, we need you to get online and start looking at the black market," I said.

"What am I looking for?"

"Someone who bought Spanish fly recently. Search the IP address and see if you can trace where it came from. If it is cantharidin, it's a banned substance. Let's see what you can find."

"If there's anything, I'll find it," she said.

Estí smiled. This was a tic, a kind of mantra that Milán had. Our colleague always repeated that phrase whenever we asked her to conduct a difficult search in the backwaters of the web. And she usually succeeded: I hadn't needed to consult my outside computer experts, MatuSalem and Golden Girl, for three years. I preferred doing it this way; it isn't a good idea to ask the devil for too many favors. He just might drag you into the flames.

When we entered the gates to the huge private property in Armentia, in the south of Vitoria, I suppressed a whistle. The villa was imposing, but so was the garden. A woman around thirty-five, with short hair and long bangs hanging over one eye, approached us. She was carrying a rake and wearing gardening gloves. She looked extremely sad. Her handshake was as firm as her elder brother's.

"I imagine you must be Irene. Our condolences."

To Estíbaliz's astonishment, I went up to Irene and kissed her on both cheeks. I noticed she was wearing a gray scarf and had on a perfume that seemed familiar.

"Inspector López de Ayala, and my colleague is Inspector Ruiz de Gauna," I said.

"Thank you, Officers. I came to the villa this afternoon: He likes to rake the lawn, he says it relaxes him. With the gusts of wind we had a while ago, I thought the garden would be covered in leaves, and . . . I had an almost physical sensation. When I saw what it was like, only a few hours after his passing . . . I just know that my father would want someone to tidy up," she said in a low voice. "You must know—how long does it take until you start referring to someone you lost and loved so much in the past tense?"

Five days on average, I thought. But I didn't say it—this wasn't a day for statistics.

"It depends on the person, I'm afraid," I replied quietly.

"My mother six months ago, and now my father. It makes your head spin when you learn that you're an orphan, even though I think somehow he prepared me for it. Maybe I shouldn't mention that. Everything seems to come pouring out, and I'm trying to stay strong with you two here. I suppose I'm a walking cliché: an only daughter spoiled by her father."

"You don't seem like a spoiled daughter," I said. "I heard you could have worked in your father's business from the beginning, but that you didn't want to."

"I wanted to gain experience so I'd be able to help as much as possible. I didn't consider a job my birthright, simply because I was the boss's daughter. I've only just realized that now I'll no longer be that. I won't have my office next to his."

"Tell me about your brothers," Estíbaliz interrupted.

"We're a close-knit family. We have our ups and downs, but you won't find rifts between us."

"What if there were rifts?" my colleague probed.

"What do you mean?"

"A couple of hours ago, two of your brothers showed up at our headquarters. Andoni accused you of being manipulative and asked us to investigate you in connection with the deaths of your parents."

Irene stopped raking the leaves. Despite her apparent strength, she was so upset that she had to lean on the rake's handle.

"I must say, I didn't expect that," she said. "It's a little disheartening, especially on a day like today. I don't want you to think I'm a saint or a fool, because I'm neither, but I'm not going to stir things up. I won't say anything against my brothers, although it hurts—it hurts a lot—that they could say that about me. But if you're here, you must not believe my father died of natural causes. If somebody did something to him and you think it could be one of his children, I think you're mistaken."

"Is there anyone who might have wanted to hurt your father—an associate, or ex-associate? Can you think of any motive they may have had?"

"I don't think you realize how large my father's fortune is. In our family, discretion is considered a question of survival. In the dark days of ETA violence, nobody in the Basque Country could afford to flaunt their wealth. Anyway, do come in."

Irene invited us inside. The living room was dominated by a bookshelf that stood twenty feet high. In the right-hand corner, an armchair that probably cost my annual salary plus expenses stood waiting for an owner who would never return. How many hours had Antón Lasaga spent there?

"What kind of books does he like?"

"He adores the Middle Ages. Especially Álavan medieval history."

"Do you know if he read the novel *The Lords of Time?*"

"He was always reading something. He forced himself to read at least a hundred pages every night, no matter how much work he had. It was his own time, and this was his sacred space. He concentrated so hard that he never heard anything going on around him, not even five children jumping on his knees. I suppose he must have read that novel, like everybody else. But the truth is I never talked to him about it specifically."

"Well, obviously your father loved books. Did he write any himself?"

Irene looked puzzled.

"Not that I know of. He is . . . he was very private in his ways. He wrote ideas on sheets of paper or in notebooks, but I always thought that they had to do with his business. Is that important?"

"Forget my question; I just got carried away when I saw this huge library," I said with a smile.

I went over to the only shelf that didn't contain books. On it were framed family photographs: his five children at different stages in their lives, his black-and-white wedding photograph, sepia photos, the eighties in full color with Antón sporting a mustache, and the nineties when he had a more sober look. None of them highlighted his daughter, which was interesting, since it contradicted the eldest son's theory. If she was indeed her father's favorite, he was careful not to show it.

Irene didn't seem to mind our thinly disguised inspection of family mementos. She seemed lost in her own recollections. When she stood behind me and looked at the photos, I could almost hear her sighing.

That smell. . . .

"Could you send me a list of fifteen of your father's closest friends?" I asked, stepping back into the role of inspector.

"Fifteen?" she asked with surprise. "Yes, of course. Let me think about it."

I gave her a card with my contact information.

"And finally," said Estíbaliz, "there are some questions we have to ask. Don't take this the wrong way, it's our job. Where were you yesterday between ten o'clock in the morning and half past seven in the evening? Did you have breakfast, lunch, or tea with your father?"

"I was in my office and had several videoconferences. I'll ask my secretary to send you my schedule. Everyone I met can corroborate where I was during those hours. I didn't see my father yesterday. It was a workday, and we were both very busy."

"What happened to your mother?" asked Estíbaliz, seemingly out of the blue. This was something she did occasionally, to catch her interviewee off guard.

I simply watched.

More sadness. True sadness.

"A traffic accident. Carlos was driving."

"Carlos?" I asked.

"Our driver. He's always been with us—he was like an uncle. He worked for the family for decades. They both died after several days in the ICU. It was a violent crash."

I looked around me. This was the most luxurious house I'd ever seen in Vitoria.

"Your father was diagnosed with Marfan syndrome, wasn't he?"

"He was. It wasn't public knowledge, but we talked about it within the family, everybody was aware of his illness. His cardiologist has it . . . had it . . . under control. At his age there can sometimes be problems with the aorta. The syndrome makes the walls thinner."

"Thank you so much, Irene. We won't bother you anymore. Do send us that list of friends and have your secretary send us a copy of yesterday's schedule. We're sorry to have met you under such sad circumstances."

"It's no trouble. I'll show you out."

Estíbaliz and I found a secluded bench on our way back to the car and sat for a while. It took some time to gather our thoughts.

"Do you think it was her? Do you think she was in a hurry to inherit?" Estí prompted me.

"No, her grief is genuine. She was wearing a scarf that belonged to her father. She must have found it in his bedroom. It was soaked in that expensive cologne we smelled yesterday when we bent down to check his pupils. The first thing she did today was a pointless but sentimental task: clearing the leaves out of his garden. No one is going to see it, and more leaves will fall tomorrow, but she did it for him."

"Or she could be a born manipulator, as her eldest brother claims."

"That's hard to tell after one interview, but she might have manipulated us. Even so, it's not her, or any of her brothers. And Antón Lasaga didn't take the Spanish fly voluntarily, either. He loved his wife, even though the children aren't his. Carlos, the driver, was their father."

"I beg your pardon?"

"Where would you like me to begin?"

"With why they're not his children? That would be a good start."

"Five children, all of whom have a father with Marfan syndrome.

Did you get a good look at the photos? All five are of normal height; their photos show no evidence of the syndrome. Each child had a fifty percent chance of inheriting the illness. None of them did. Statistically, that's almost impossible."

"What are you suggesting?"

"As Grandfather would say, he raised someone else's litter."

"And yet you're sure none of them gave their father Spanish fly."

"None of them. They all knew he had a weak heart, and Spanish fly is a vasodilator. Whoever poisoned Lasaga gave him a two-gram dose, a lethal amount for a healthy person. That reveals the murderer's intent—and it's our best clue. Any of the children, Irene included, would have wanted us to believe that their father took Spanish fly as a stimulant. With Antón's condition, even a normal dose would have killed him. But the killer didn't have that information, which rules Lasaga himself out as well. If he took medication for his heart problems, why run the risk of using an aphrodisiac? And why give himself a lethal dose? I don't believe it was a suicide, either. Symptoms of Spanish fly poisoning are dirty, painful, and uncomfortable, and he didn't stay at home that day. He was seen in public. A private man wouldn't have been walking around after poisoning himself, and he wouldn't expose his family to such a dreadful scandal. The murderer must have been in his orbit. So the way I see it, there are two options: either the killer was an acquaintance, or he chose his victim at random. When I saw Lasaga's house, I thought of one of the mortal sins: greed. We want what's in front of our faces. But now I'm not so sure, and it scares me, Estí. The idea that he may have been a random victim scares me a lot."

"Because if that's the case, we won't be able to find a link between the murderer and the victim. There won't be one." She finished my train of thought, as if she could read my mind.

After so many years of working together, we had developed a sort of hive brain.

Back home that evening, I sat in an armchair looking out over the Plaza de la Virgen Blanca, the heart of the city. Deba had fallen asleep on my lap, and I had put her to bed. Alba lounged on the sofa while I read the copy of *The Lords of Time* that she had given me.

We had exchanged copies of the novel with inscriptions.

It was something we had started doing as a couple who enjoyed reading. If we both liked a novel, we gave a copy to each other, and we competed to see who could write the most memorable, most passionate inscription . . . whatever occurred to us at the time.

On the first blank page of *The Lords of Time* she had copied a poem by Maya Angelou that her mother used to recite on stage: *You may kill me with your hatefulness, But still, like air, I'll rise*. In the copy I bought for her, I'd written a phrase by Joan Margarit: *A wound is also somewhere to live*.

"You're very pensive, Unai. I don't know whether I find it sexy or worrying."

"Do you mind if I think out loud? Tonight, not even you will be able to disperse the storm clouds."

"Go on then. What are you so worried about?"

"Here are a few questions from Profiling for Beginners: Why did someone do it like that? Why here, in this city? Why now? Why Spanish fly? Why in Villa Suso? Why during the launch for a novel that has three things in common with his death: the place, the trade, and the MO?"

"And what's your answer?" she asked.

"That the universe is lazy."

"Lazy?" she repeated, scratching her head.

"Yes, lazy. It doesn't try to arrange coincidences—that's why they so seldom occur. What I mean is that I don't believe there can be three coincidences in this case: a leading figure in the textile industry dies using the same modus operandi employed in a novel that is being launched the same day and time as his murder. No, the killer wants to send a message, and he's made this death public because he wants us all to understand: 'This murder is related to the novel. Investigate that.' And that is what I plan to do."

I looked at her and said, as if I were delivering judgment, "It's time for me to talk to the publisher."

8

ÁLAVA-ESQUIVEL PALACE

UNAI

September 2019

I was destined to meet one of the most unusual and exceptional people I'd ever encountered during my career as a criminal profiler. But when Estíbaliz, Milán, and I walked to the Álava-Esquivel Palace, we had no idea what lay in store for us.

The building was doing its best to withstand the ravages of time, but the façade was still covered in mesh to protect it from falling masonry. The gardens lay on the border of the San Roque and la Herrería districts, and behind their incongruous palm trees rose a dilapidated white stone building. Inside lived the last courtiers of Vitoria: families paying a pittance to endure the damp and peeling stucco walls.

I stepped under the doorway's rounded arch and pressed the intercom.

A deep voice answered: "Who's there?"

"Prudencio, this is Inspector Unai López de Ayala. Could you open the door?"

It took him a couple of seconds to reply. "Of course, Inspector. Straightaway." With that, he buzzed me in.

Estí, Milán, and I skirted a colorful tricycle and climbed a bowed staircase to the third floor.

"Milán, were you able to find any trace of Spanish fly on the black market?" I asked as we climbed.

"Nothing," she replied with a smile and a shrug, but it somehow sounded like a yes. "There are lots of products being sold as Spanish fly, but they're actually made from L-arginine and vitamin C. They're all fake. No one asks for genuine Spanish fly. What's the point? There are thousands of varieties of Viagra available at every price imaginable. There is nothing to indicate that anyone is selling authentic Spanish fly. There's no supply and no demand. I don't think anybody buys it on the Internet."

"Well, then . . . ?"

"He made it himself. The insects, the blister beetles. He crushed their shells to get two grams of pure Spanish fly."

"Are you saying you found somebody who bought the insects?" asked Estíbaliz.

"No, but I found something better."

"What do you mean?" Estí probed.

"I came across a report around the end of August about a robbery at the Natural Science Museum. Someone stole two hundred Coleoptera that had just been delivered to expand the insect collection. When I remembered the report, I thought, *What if the blister beetle was one of the insects taken?* If you think it's worth checking out, we could visit the museum after we speak to the publisher."

"Fine, you do that," I said, casting a sideways glance at Estíbaliz to see how she was doing.

My colleague pulled up the collar on her military jacket. She looked detached. The Natural Science Museum was located in la Torre de Doña Otxanda, so we would have to walk past the esoteric bookstore that had once belonged to her murdered brother, Eneko. Had Estíbaliz been able to move on? Even though several years had passed, can you ever move on from the loss of a brother, even one who was an irresponsible drug dealer?

"What's worrying you, Estí?"

"The investigation into Lasaga is taking time away from our

search for the two sisters," she muttered, without looking in my direction.

"What if they left home of their own accord?"

"What do you mean?"

"Estefanía didn't get along with her younger sister. Maybe they argued; maybe Estefanía hit her harder than she meant to, then got rid of the body and ran. In that case, there would never have been a kidnapping and, therefore, no ransom demands. What if there's no predator? What if it is as simple as the ancient story of Cain and Abel?"

"You must have little faith in the human race! Sisters killing sisters. . . . I can't even think about it," Estí snorted, staring at a pair of tiny, egg-shaped windows.

"Look where we work. Do you really want to talk about faith in the human race?" I winked at her to dissipate the growing tension hanging in the air. "But let's say I'm wrong. What could have happened to them, Estí?"

"A sixteen-year-old girl wouldn't run away with the body of her twelve-year-old sister. She wouldn't be able to carry a burden like that," she insisted. "Estefanía is just a kid. Something had to have happened. Besides, we found a trace of Oihana's blood."

"We've been going around in circles for two weeks without a break in the case. No matter how hard our investigations get, we have to make progress where we can. And that brings us to—" I stopped outside the door of the third-floor apartment.

"Good morning, Prudencio," I greeted the owner, who was standing at the doorway.

"Pruden, call me Pruden. And don't stay out there. Come in."

We crossed the threshold into Malatrama, the publishing house. The office had an open floorplan, with several slender columns rising to a white, vaulted ceiling with wooden beams. All four walls were plastered with images of frightening goddesses and apocalyptic science-fiction landscapes. The art had a dizzying effect. It made me feel tiny. And apparently I wasn't the only one who was affected.

"Can you really concentrate with these images around you?" Milán blurted. "They're so—"

"So striking, so full of life, so imposing?"

"That's right."

"They're a tribute to the publishing house's biggest successes . . . until now," said Prudencio. He was barefoot on the warm wooden floor, wearing a pair of white linen pants and a white smock that strained under the weight of his enormous belly. With his white hair and curly beard, he reminded me of a druid about to devour a roasted boar.

Even though it wasn't a particularly hot day, Prudencio wiped sweat from his chubby cheeks with a small handkerchief. He held a large watering can in his other hand.

"I was watering the plants," he said, noticing my gaze. "I think I saw you at the book launch."

We followed him through a set of double doors that opened onto a narrow inner patio. When I leaned cautiously over the rail, I could just make out a pleasant communal courtyard several floors below. Tidy geraniums coexisted with the damp laundry that hung on the line under a flimsy canopy. I could hear the everyday sounds of the building: saucepans being pulled out of drawers, TV sets blaring the morning debates. I felt like I was peeking behind the curtain, catching a glimpse of the small intimacies of life in central Vitoria.

The scent of potatoes and chorizo wafted from the first-floor apartment on the right, where a grandmother was cooking breakfast. Estíbaliz tried to cover the rumbling of her stomach.

"I like to think about the fact that I live in a place people have been living in for a thousand years, before this palace was even built. And you," he said, pointing at me with a guffaw, "you're a López de

Ayala, so what a coincidence that you live right next to the entrance to La Correría."

I cursed under my breath. Did everyone in this city know where I lived? There was no way to remain anonymous here, not since I'd been shot three years ago and a crowd had filled my doorway with candles.

"In the fifteenth century, when warring factions were struggling for control of the city," Prudencio continued, "your ancestors controlled several strategic gates into the town of Victoria. The Ayalas gathered at the doors to San Miguel Arcángel Church. The Calleja family met at Portal Oscuro, which is close by at the end of the Anorbin district, or Angevín, as it was called in medieval documents. The Ayalas protected the interests of the city's first inhabitants. Does the apartment on the Plaza de la Virgen Blanca belong to your family? That would be an interesting coincidence."

"No, it's a rental I got for a real bargain."

"It's curious, though—an Ayala is still watching over that part of the city."

I liked the idea of being the custodian of my neighborhood, but it meant nothing. Try telling the two missing girls or the murdered father of five that I was keeping Vitoria safe.

"Let's not digress," I said, clearing my throat. "To your earlier point, yes, I was at the launch. I went hoping the author would sign my book, just like everybody else. But he seems to be very elusive."

"Private, I would say."

"Do you know who he is?"

"I wish I did."

"But you have your suspicions," said Estíbaliz.

"Why don't we sit down? I haven't offered you anything to eat or drink."

"Don't go to any trouble. We won't keep you long; we have a

thousand and one things to do today. We're here because we have begun an investigation into Antón Lasaga's death. His body was found in the restrooms at Villa Suso."

Prudencio stopped in his tracks, a quizzical expression on his face.

"So, it wasn't a natural death. I wondered why you wouldn't let us leave, and why you questioned so many people. The officers said it was routine, but it seemed odd."

"We can't confirm the cause of death. We're in the early stages of the investigation, and we're following several lines of inquiry. We don't wish to alarm you, but we do have to determine whether Lasaga's death was related to the book launch, so it's important to know the name of the author of *The Lords of Time*."

"The ghostwriter, you mean," Estíbaliz whispered in my ear.

"Well, I won't lie to you. I do have my suspicions," Prudencio said, turning to stare at one of the murals. "I know what you're going to ask me. How can I not know who he is? Have I never met him, never spoken to him on the phone? Didn't we meet to sign the book contract?"

"Yes, those are some of the questions we have," I said.

"He communicated with me through e-mail, and he always used the pseudonym Diego Veilaz. This is a small publishing house, and we don't normally publish fiction. We produce graphic novels, and we do contract work for exhibition catalogs, usually financed by museums or local councils. . . . But when he sent me that manuscript, how could I refuse? It was pure gold. This business is largely a series of gambles; you never know how the market is going to respond to anything. But I was willing to take the risk for this novel, even though it took us out of our comfort zone. After all, I had my bookstore distribution network, a couple of salesmen, contacts with the printers, and a warehouse to distribute the book. I had all the necessary infrastructure. And finding a good illustrator for the cover was the least of my worries—I work with them every day.

"In any event, our business was conducted by e-mail. Of course, I insisted we meet in person. I always want to get to know my authors. We end up having a close relationship, because there are lots of creative decisions that must be made throughout the publishing process. But with him, the relationship proved impossible. Still, I couldn't let the opportunity to publish that book slip through my fingers."

"You said you have your suspicions," I prodded.

"And I do. Look, you'll understand better if I show you something," he said, leading us over to his computer screen.

"I have two e-mail addresses. The first appears on the publishing website. That's the one used by the artists and institutions that want to work with us. It's public, so you can't imagine how many e-mails I receive. The second is my personal e-mail address, which I only give to authors after we've signed a contract."

"How many authors do you have?"

"Not many, twenty-eight."

"You're trying to tell us that the author of *The Lords of Time* got in touch with you directly via your personal e-mail, not through the e-mail address listed on your website. That's why you have your suspicions," I suggested.

He looked surprised, tugging the curls of his beard.

"You're a quick study, aren't you? Yes, that's exactly what I wanted to show you. Either the writer has already published with me, or, and this is impossible to know, someone gave him my e-mail address. But honestly, there are very few graphic novelists, and that world is extremely competitive. They have a hard-enough time finding a publisher; they aren't going to share their contacts with their rivals. I doubt any one of them would hand out my e-mail address, at least not without asking my permission first or mentioning that someone they knew was going to contact me about publishing a novel."

"So we have a list of twenty-eight graphic novelists who could also be our author," said Milán, a gleam in her eye. "Could you give us access to your contact list?"

"Of course. I have no desire to obstruct a criminal investigation. Although you must understand that this is confidential information."

"We understand," I said. "It won't leave our hands. But I got the impression you had one or two specific people in mind."

"I'm going to take a look at your computer," said Milán, who was already seated on the publisher's huge throne. "I'll leave it the way I found it, but I want to trace all of these addresses and determine where these e-mails were sent from. Could you pull up your correspondence with the author for me?"

"No problem," he said, and typed *Diego Veilaz*.

We looked on eagerly as Milán got to work. A few minutes later, the magic happened: a spot in the Valdegovía Valley appeared on a map of Álava province.

"That's strange . . ." the publisher mused.

"What is?"

"That was one of my bets."

"I went to an exhibition there a few months ago," Estíbaliz broke in.

She stepped back and began searching for something on her cell phone.

"Your GPS is pointing to the Nograro Tower, in Valdegovía Valley, isn't it?" she asked, still staring at her cell phone.

Milán nodded, and Estí motioned me over discreetly.

"One of the rooms there was displaying a habit worn by one of the Dominican nuns from Nuestra Señora del Cabello. Take a look, Kraken," she whispered, showing me a photo of a slender mannequin wearing the same habit as the one I had pursued across the tiles of San Miguel Arcángel's roof.

"Pruden," I said, "did you hire any actors to liven up the book launch?"

"Actors? I don't know what you mean. I can assure you, the archaeologist who was with me worked on the excavations carried out by the Santa María Cathedral Foundation."

"No, not the archaeologist. I want to know if you hired a Dominican nun."

"It never even occurred to me. The novel is a bestseller, so what would've been the point?" He blew out his cheeks and wiped the sweat from his temples once more.

Dead end, I told myself. We would have to search for our nun on other roofs, because there was no sign of her here.

"Let's go back to your bet. You said you weren't surprised the e-mail was sent from that spot in the Valdegovía Valley."

"Ramiro Alvar Nograro, Lord of Nograro Tower," Pruden replied somberly, as though the name should mean something to us.

"Who?" asked Estíbaliz, her interest aroused.

"The twenty-fifth Lord of Nograro," he explained. "A young man, not yet forty, but a real scholar. He's very shy. He was educated like a nineteenth-century lord and has an encyclopedic knowledge of his family's noble history. I remember he told me about someone being buried alive. I can assure you: he was born, brought up, and will die without ever stepping foot outside his tower. His ancestors have been the lords of that valley since the Middle Ages. The eldest sons inherit the name Alvar, and their brothers take it as a second Christian name, in case the heir dies without children. That's how they've done it for more than a thousand years. I think it's the only heritage in the province that's been wisely administered for a millennium. They still lease all the homes and all the land around the tower. Back in the day, they ran the forge, the mill, and the church, like the Mendoza, Avendaño, and Guevara families. Ramiro Alvar once told me, somewhat shamefacedly, that he had done the calculations and he was so rich that his descendants wouldn't need to work for the next five hundred years. Yet I doubt whether a young recluse like him, no matter how brilliant or well educated, will have descendants. When we were working together, he never came to me. I always had to go there."

"What were you working on?" Estíbaliz asked.

"The catalog for an exhibition about the Valdegovía Valley organized by the Ugarte Town Council. It was some time ago. Ramiro Alvar wanted to promote the exhibition in order to attract tourists to the region. He's always been a local patron, discreetly."

"That must have been the exhibition I went to," said Estíbaliz. "Do you have a copy of the catalog?"

The publisher nodded and went to look for it on one of the shelves.

"Does Ramiro Alvar fit the profile?" I asked.

"Honestly? I thought it could be one of several male and a few female authors, but yes, I've always wondered whether it was him."

"You say he's extremely shy."

"He's a bookworm. Apprehensive and unaccustomed to dealing with others, other than the woman the local council hired to lead tours of the tower. That said, he's well loved in the town. The mayor and town councilors say he's easy to work with; locals and even his own lawyers go to see him when they have a question about their lease. He's like a relic from another time, though. He doesn't even have a cell phone; he says he doesn't need one. It's true, he uses a landline in one of his offices. I got the impression he never leaves the grounds. He lives on the top two floors of the tower. The first floor houses a permanent exhibition of family heirlooms: antiques, army uniforms, ancient matchlock guns or harquebuses, saddles, books from his ancestors' library. . . . There are all kinds of people in his family tree: soldiers, priests, men of letters, local mayors. Similar faces are repeated in engravings and photographs throughout the house: first daguerreotypes, then black-and-white photos, then sepia, and finally full-color portraits."

"If he did write *The Lords of Time*, that could explain why the author doesn't give interviews or appear in the media," said Estíbaliz.

"That's true, but there are quite a few authors like that. It's one thing to write, but not everyone feels equipped to deal with the press or speak in public. They're two different skill sets, and people aren't necessarily good at both."

"What about the contract you signed? What was the name on it?"

"Diego Veilaz, Ltd. There was a bank account number, but it belongs to a popular NGO. He wasn't interested in making money, and we didn't expect it to be such a huge success."

"So he's not interested in money . . ." Estí repeated, her mind clearly working overtime.

Or he's not interested in making money off the book, I thought. If Ramiro Alvar is so rich, would he be concerned with royalties?

Just then Peña called, and I moved away from the others.

"Kraken, we just got a report from a building site in the Medieval Quarter. Are you there now?"

"Yes. What's it about?"

"We don't know exactly, but there's a bad odor coming from an apartment they're refurbishing between La Cuchi and Santa María. No one can figure out what's causing it. There's absolutely nothing in the space other than the floor and the walls. Anyway, I'd like to take a look."

A cat caught in the pipes, I bet. I'd have smiled if it weren't something we had to deal with at least twice a year. Usually we called the fire department, but if they heard about it first, they sent it to us. The hot potato was passed back and forth, depending on which department received the first call from a neighbor with a sensitive nose.

"Are you coming or not?"

"Estíbaliz and I are going to Valdegovía. We'll be back in an hour or two. We're with Milán." I looked at her, and she turned away. Ever since she had broken up with Peña, it was difficult for them to conceal how uncomfortable it was to work together. I didn't like to force them, but the bashful Ramiro Alvar Nograro had piqued my curiosity. Meeting him would be interesting, whether or not he was the author. "Milán will catch up with you in the Santa María district."

"Milán . . . As you wish. Tell her I'll meet her in ten minutes," he said with a sigh.

Estíbaliz took the wheel and headed out of Vitoria. I leaned back in the passenger seat and watched the beeches' golden canopies speed by as we got into the hills and the highway turned into a dirt road.

I hadn't been back to Villaverde, my grandfather's village, in days. I was spending too many hours on these cases. I missed the fresh air when I was walking in my hills, trudging through muddy leaves as I wandered between the oaks and boxtrees.

We passed the small village of Ugarte, a delightful place that still looked as it did in the Middle Ages, fuchsia plants in every window. We took the narrow lane leading to Nograro Tower, which was no more than four hundred yards from the town.

The grounds consisted of a rectangular tower with battlements and machicolations at each corner. There were a few windows at each cardinal point, and a small wall around the perimeter that concealed a moat. A pointed arch with a small window led to the entrance.

"So you've been here before," I said to Estíbaliz as she parked the car.

"Yes, but the exhibition took place after the guided tours had ended. I had no idea the old lord of the tower lived in the same building."

"Old lord? The tower might be a hundred years old, but its owner is not, at least not according to Prudencio," I said, as we clambered out of the car.

We crossed the drawbridge and entered through the gateway. It was like stepping back in time. An immense cobblestone compass rose spread on the ground in front of us, a pair of Roman scales stamped with the date 1777 hung above our heads, and several worn statues lay scattered on the ground. Pure Middle Ages. It was wonderful.

A very tall young woman with a cleft chin and a long side ponytail greeted us at a small ticket window. We assumed she was the guide the town council had appointed to lead tours of the tower.

"Good morning," I began, "we came to—"

"Did you call? I didn't have any visits scheduled for today," she said in a soft voice.

"Criminal Investigation," said Estí, flashing her badge. She was already impatient and wanted to dispense with the small talk. "Could we please see the lord of the tower?"

"Of course. I'll tell him you're here," the woman said, and pressed a button on the intercom next to the polished wooden counter.

The tour guide's office held an old-fashioned computer, a display case filled with catalogs, and little else. I imagined she spent endless hours there, bored, surrounded by wheat fields in a forgotten paradise.

"Ramiro Alvar, there are people here to see you," she said vaguely.

"I'm not here," came the reply.

"I think you should meet them," she insisted.

"This is Inspector López de Ayala, from Criminal—"

"A López de Ayala. So they still exist. . . . Come on up. I'll see you." The young man spoke with an authority I often wished I possessed.

"Go up to the third floor. He's in the Tapestry Room office," the woman informed us.

"So the count has several offices," said Estí, half impressed, half resentful.

Rich people always had the same effect on her, and she wasn't good at hiding it. Estíbaliz was brought up poor, in a decrepit shack fifty kilometers away.

Ignoring her comment, the guide opened a door that led to a wooden staircase. We climbed to the third floor and entered a room hung with tapestries depicting a hunt: a pack of hounds pursuing their prey.

The lord of the tower walked into the room, intent on making our jaws drop.

He strolled slowly and confidently in front of his ancestors' pictures, hands clasped behind his back and a mocking smile at the corner of his lips. He looked like a mischievous boy showing off his playroom, or his tree house, or a tent he had set up on the back lawn.

Ramiro Alvar Nograro was wearing a cassock and a delicately embroidered scarlet chasuble. I couldn't tell if he was a priest, a chaplain, a bishop—but whatever his title, he was the most attractive man of God we had ever laid eyes on. I say "we" because in another life I would have killed to have Estíbaliz look at me the way she was ogling him.

When we were young, Estí and I would run into each other in the old city's bars. She was going through her punk phase, and it drove me crazy. She was so free; she didn't give a damn about anything. I was constantly striving to accidentally bump into the diminutive redhead. One night, I told her best friend, Paula, the sad story when I was drunk on *kalimotxo*, and Paula comforted me. Later on, we went for a coffee in El Caruso, then another and another, until the Grim Reaper's scythe put an end to our love story on the Avenue of Pines.

I shook off the past and took a good look at the curious man standing in front of me.

Ramiro Alvar had intelligent, darting blue eyes, and his stylishly slicked-back hair revealed a prominent forehead and eyebrows that seemed to stare down at us from an imaginary pulpit.

"Would these kind souls care to accompany me to lunch?" he asked. "I can offer you rooster-comb stew, my favorite dish."

I was about to refuse politely when my cell phone interrupted the awkward moment. Alba's face flashed on the screen.

"Unai, my mother has had an accident. I'm on my way to the hospital now."

9

EL CAUCE DE LOS MOLINOS

DIAGO VELA

Winter, the Year of Our Lord 1192

I swear I didn't want it to happen, but I now believe that what took place on that icy dawn was just the beginning of the many deaths and misfortunes that later befell us.

I came across her walking barefoot on the blue-tinged snow, a pair of skates across her shoulder. Onneca was striding along as if the cold didn't bite at her feet, as if there were no layers of frost on her heels.

Broad-shouldered, flat-chested, head erect, she was absorbed in whatever intention she harbored, barely conscious of the world around her. She took no notice of the howling wind, the white winter birds searching for mice on the icy ground, the branches of the oak trees weighted down with snow. . . .

An armed band could have attacked the old mill, and she would have been none the wiser. Nor would she have been afraid. That is the way Onneca was.

She hadn't seen me arrive at Cauce de los Molinos. It was my favorite spot, a secluded area east of the town wall. The tranquil blue sky reflected off the white land like a mirror, as if a calm sea were set out before me.

A dense wood of holm oak offered me the privacy I sought. I approached the ivy-covered ruins of the old mill. Once the mill had been important, but it lost its value when the road to the Arriaga Gate became popular. The millrace that used to flow under the enormous wooden wheel was no more than a trickle, the blades merely dripping icicles. The mill now looked like an old woman whose tears had frozen on her cheeks.

I was sitting on a tree stump, staring at the frozen river. Onneca appeared in the distance, skating, her eyes fixed on a point on the horizon that only she could make out.

All of a sudden, she became aware of my presence. At first she was startled, but she relaxed when she recognized me. She came over to me, ignoring the snow that crunched beneath her bare feet.

"Where are your shoes?"

"I left them on the bank of the pool," she replied, as though it didn't matter.

"I'm sorry about your father's death," I said, in part to test her reaction. How should I behave now toward my sister-in-law?

"I've come here every week over the past two years," she said, her red-rimmed eyes fixed on me. I thought I saw sadness in them. Much sadness. "Thinking about what it was like before the *gallicantus*, when we used to meet behind my father's back. Come, I want to show you something."

There was so much I wanted to say that I decided to stay silent. Besides, nothing could be more eloquent than the gazes we exchanged.

I followed her until she stopped near the mill's north wall. It had become a ruin; perhaps it was an indication that whatever we once had was never to return.

"What's this?" I asked, confused.

She bent and brushed the snow off a small, engraved stone on the ground.

"Your tomb. The lavender has survived. I planted it to keep you company, so you wouldn't feel alone. It was silly of me not to understand that it was a sign that you were alive. It was right in front of me."

"You had a tombstone made for me?"

"What does it matter now that you're alive?" she exclaimed. "How can I live now? How can I sleep with your brother tonight, when I know you are breathing only a few yards away?"

"I'll move out."

"You're breathing!" she repeated, coming closer. "You're breathing, I can scarcely believe it. So many sleepless nights I thought you were decaying beneath the waves. I was worried about your body, about how cold and damp your bones must've been."

She was staring at me as if I were a ghost, with the same mixture of disbelief and respect for the incomprehensible. She raised her hand and brushed my cheek. I caught it. Her fingers were hot, much hotter than I expected.

"Am I not even allowed to touch you now, dear Diago?"

"You know what happens to wives who are unfaithful. Nagorno will be following you. We shouldn't meet alone."

"So I must make do with your countenance, the polite words of my brother-in-law?"

"That is the way it will have to be."

Because of a single accursed day, that is the way it will have to be, I thought.

"At least tell me there was no one else, that I was the only woman in your thoughts for these past two years."

I sat on my own tombstone, shading it from the bright sun.

"Yes. That's the truth."

"There were rumors . . ." she began.

"They were just that. There was nothing."

"The silent, devoted Berenguela."

"I brought her to Richard with her virginity intact, just as her father charged me. Do you think I'm so foolish as to give the kings of Navarre and of England a reason to chop off my manhood?"

"I was hoping for a more romantic explanation, one that had something to do with me."

"Everything has to do with you. I don't need to repeat it or dress it up, you already know it. You have never been a woman who seeks praise. You have no need for it. A polished mirror and the knowledge of what the chronicles will say of your dynasty is enough for you. Who told you of the mission King Sancho gave me?"

"As you always used to say, I'm the eyes and ears of Nova Victoria. Did you really think I wouldn't find out why you galloped off to Aquitaine one night with no warning?"

"Who told you, Onneca?" I insisted. "Not even your father knew."

"Who was close enough to the Tudela court to be privy to the preparations being made?"

I rose to my feet, thinking.

"Ah, now I understand. The good bishop García, your father's protégé."

"He took pity on me when he saw my desperation. He feared the worst. Don't blame him. It was a confidence between cousins. He didn't even tell Father. It remains a secret that only the three of us know."

"That is how it must stay. The king put his trust in me, and my life would be at stake if my mission were to become public knowledge. I couldn't even tell you about it, Onneca. Will you ever forgive me?"

"A message, Diago. A message would have sufficed. Nothing more. If you trust me to stay silent now, why not then, when I was betrothed to you?"

"So that's it! You're angry with me."

She pursed her lips, and the color drained away.

"Angry?" she cried. "I'm furious! They were about to hand me over to the Lord of Ibida, that hunchbacked widower, and then to de Funes's young son, a man known to all the sailors in San Sebastían. If it weren't for your brother—"

"Don't say any more about Nagorno," I roared. I stepped closer and covered her mouth so as not to hear her say his name. "I cannot bear it."

We collapsed on top of what would have been my tomb—and still would be—holding each other like the passionate lovers we had once been. When I felt the weight of her body on top of me, her lips searching until they found mine, I felt alive for the first time in two years.

"Onneca, let's go inside the mill," I whispered. "We'll freeze to death out here."

So we slipped into the milling room, as we had so often done in the past. It had partially collapsed, but there was still an area that was protected from the snow, and the old wooden boards gave the winter morning a little warmth.

Onneca was not in as great a hurry as I. She removed her white headdress, which identified her as a married woman, unbuckled her leather belt, and let the tight yellow woolen tunic fall to her feet. I don't know how many nights I had cherished the memory of her naked body. She sat on a stone that had grown tired of grinding grain into flour a century before and motioned for me to come to her.

I removed my hose and was about to enter her when she stopped me.

"No, I want you to be naked as well."

I obeyed. What else could I do?

Once we were both stripped bare, we embraced.

My two years of celibacy ended quickly. We groaned with pleasure as we always had, our bodies recognizing each other.

"Do you believe me now?" I asked in a choked voice.

"You were telling the truth. You waited for me." She laughed.

I lay in silence, deep in thought. Then I slipped her tunic over her head.

"I felt your absence," I whispered. "But I thought that someday we would have our wedding ceremony, that once I was freed from my duties, once I completed my voyage, we could pursue our plans for Victoria. I can't imagine governing two districts at war without you by my side."

Onneca sat by the grain trough, her back to me.

"You have wheat in your hair, and your braid has come loose. Let me comb it for you," I said. "And wear my boots until you find yours, or they're going to have to cut off your frostbitten feet."

Smiling contentedly, she put on my boots, then leaned back against me and allowed me to neaten her hair.

"The men of the Church aren't going to like the fact that you don't completely cover your hair," I said.

"Bishop García is like a brother to me. If Bishop García speaks, everybody else in this town stays silent. And if Bishop García permits something, everybody keeps their accusatory fingers in their pockets. Yesterday at my father's funeral everyone saw him give me, in my headdress and braid, his blessing. No one will reproach me or say a word against me for letting my hair show."

That is how Onneca was. She always managed to get her own way and to protect herself. I admired her pragmatic approach to life.

"When I saw you on that bed, the pleasure you seemed to be taking from him," I said regretfully, "I thought we had lost what we once had. That it had become a remnant of the past, and that it couldn't be recovered. I find it so hard to accept that a single day kept our spirits apart. That if I had returned just one day earlier, you would still be unmarried and we could have canceled the wedding."

"Cancel it? You think I would have canceled it?" she asked, surprised. I felt a sudden distance between us.

I let go of her braid and walked over to sit facing her.

"You would have married Nagorno even if you knew I was alive?"

"Nagorno is a great man. He has always been attentive, friendly, charming."

That's not who he really is. It's just one of his many masks, I wanted to tell her. But how could I explain? Where to begin? *He wants to take advantage of the power you have over the weavers; he wants your estates; he wants everything.*

"And he's implementing great reforms in town," she continued.

"Great reforms? The Mendozas already control the road to Arriaga, and now Nagorno has allowed them to collect a tithe on fruit. And what have they done? They've squeezed the traders even more. Yesterday I passed the Santa María market. There are hardly any apples, turnips, or leeks for sale. If the townspeople of Victoria can't buy fruit or vegetables at the market, they'll go elsewhere. That's not what we want. We don't want the nobles living a life of ease simply because they've increased the vendors' tariffs. Victoria has always been a town of artisans and traders."

"Strange words for a count."

"Before we were counts, we were blacksmiths. That's how we all began. And the lords of the town must protect Victoria. That's why my ancestor Count Don Vela had the walls built when Alfonso the First, the Battler, was king. So that Victoria's inhabitants could feel secure and to allow any visitors to the area to find security. If the market empties, the people will leave, and there will be no one left."

"You sound like my father," she said in a low voice.

"And he was found dead—"

"We all have to die," she said, handing me my boots. "He was an old man. His time had come."

He was a vigorous man, not yet forty-five. It wasn't his time, Onneca. But I said nothing; for I had no evidence, only suspicions.

"The town has grown since you left. When I was a little girl, the king granted us a charter and the San Michel district became Nova Victoria. Eventually, the same thing will happen to the cutlers' area in the east—some king will build walls around that area to protect them. We need to control the town's gates. The Maturanas now live close to the Portal Oscuro at the end of the Angevín district. My father didn't want to give them the right to collect taxes, and he rejected the idea when it was raised by the council. But Nagorno is not against it, and I support him."

"What are you saying? You want to put families that control other villages in charge of our gateways and let them charge tithes, imposts, taxes? What right do they have to do such a thing?"

"You know they're not happy with King Sancho's laws. The inhabitants of Avendaño are still moving to Nova Victoria, abandoning their villages, and so are people from Adurza, Arechavaleta, and Olárizu. Their lords would like to take up arms against us. The Lords of Avendaño have already attacked us on two occasions. They set fire to two roofs on Rúa de la Ferrería, and the baker's wife, Anglesa, was badly burned. Why don't you look to the future: we give control of the gates to the families who ask for it, and we make them our allies."

"Not if they abuse their power, Onneca. What do the women vendors say?"

These women kept the town supplied with necessities in the same way a good housewife keeps her larder well stocked. If the town were running out of salted fish for Lent or if the harvest seemed likely to fail, they anticipated it months before and could bring seaweed bread or wheat seedlings from the Baltic so that no one would suffer from hunger. Oil, fish, candles, sardines . . . The council controlled the prices and punished those who didn't supply the town adequately. And Onneca roamed the streets, walking among the stalls and chatting with the guild wives by firelight. In that honeycomb of streets, gateways, and walls, she knew which women worked hard and which were lazy. She spoke to them all: the silent ones, the nosy ones, the astute and the simple, the cheerful, the talkative, and the melancholy. Among them, they wove the fabric that kept Nova Victoria together. Onneca knew who drank, who went whoring, who dipped their wick outside the home, and which sister-in-law was about to grab another's wimple, an offense punishable by a fine of fifty days' pay. Onneca knew everything that went on within the town's walls.

"They won't complain as long as they're making money," said Onneca.

"That's not what they told me. Why did they banish Joana de Balmaseda?"

"She committed fraud with some candles."

"I was aware of that, but why did she do it? She was a widow with two small children. Why would she risk losing everything? I don't think people are as satisfied as you say they are. I don't like it, Onneca. I don't like what Nagorno is permitting, and your father didn't like it, either. He told me so the night he died."

"Father is no longer with us. And until my brother returns from the lands of the infidels, I am the head of the de Maestu family. I suppose you will reclaim your title, and Nagorno will no longer be Count Don Vela."

"That's right. Tomorrow the notary will prepare the documents, and the lieutenant, the mayor, and the royal bailiff will serve as witnesses."

"So in the end I'll only have been Countess Vela for a few days." She sighed.

"Nagorno has been Count de Maestu since yesterday."

"That too," she said.

"That too."

This was how we had always ended our discussions, both of us refusing to budge.

"Our heir will be a de Maestu and a Vela. If you remain unmarried, who knows, perhaps the son I have with your brother will be Count Don Vela."

I had no more interest in talking. Perhaps two years had been too long. Perhaps Nagorno had been too much.

As we left the mill, a squall rained hailstones on us, so we hastily took cover again. As we were doing so, we heard a horse whinnying and turned to look. Nagorno was staring at us from the door to the mill. He wasn't alone. He had a magnificent animal with him, the finest mare I'd ever seen. A short coat, with a metallic sheen. Her coat's pure gold was reflected Onneca's eyes.

"It began to snow so we sought refuge," Onneca lied.

"I know," said my brother calmly, smiling.

"He didn't see us," Onneca whispered in my ear. "He doesn't know what we did."

This is Nagorno, dear Onneca, I wanted to tell her. *Believe me, he knows what we just did better than either of us.*

10

NOGRARO TOWER

UNAI

SEPTEMBER 2019

"What happened to your mother?" I asked, pressing Alba for more details as I stepped into the corridor of Ramiro Alvar's apartment.

"She fell down the stairs at home after she dropped Deba off with Germán. They're operating on her now: I think she broke her hip."

"I'll come right away."

"Where are you exactly?"

I told her about my visits to Malatrama and the Nograro Tower.

"Well, finish your interview and come after that. Deba is with your brother, and Grandfather is on his way from Villaverde. He'll arrive before you do. I'm going to the hospital even though she won't be out of the operating room for another three hours. Pick up Deba when you get to Vitoria. I'll call with any news. There's nothing you can do right now."

"All right, I'll finish things here and then we'll head back. Estíbaliz will want to see your mother as well."

"I know. See you soon."

"Alba . . ."

"What is it?"

"Don't worry. Your mother is strong, and we'll take good care of her."

I went back into the room. Taking advantage of the cell phone still in my hand, I took the opportunity to snap a discreet photo of Ramiro Alvar. The lord of the tower was opening the windows, and I could feel a cold draught blowing in. He didn't seem to notice, but Estíbaliz automatically raised the collar on her military jacket.

Ramiro Alvar sat in a white leather armchair behind an enormous desk. He studied us with twinkling eyes.

"So what brings a López de Ayala to the home of the Nograros?"

"I'm here in my capacity as a Criminal Investigation inspector. We'd like to ask you some questions. This is Inspector Estíbaliz Ruiz de Gauna. . . ."

"Ruiz de Gauna . . . Even better. Did you know that *Aestibalis* is Latin? It refers to the villas where the Romans spent their summers."

"Wow. No, I didn't know that," Estí answered.

Ramiro Alvar must have liked her candid response, because he gazed at her as though she were a precious sculpture.

"I'll ask you again: What brings you two here? I can't think of anywhere less appropriate for two guardians of the law. Everything here is in order. Always. The girl the bailiff occasionally sends in and I are the only ones in the tower."

"The woman employed by the local council, you mean," I corrected him. Ramiro Alvar didn't appear to know what century we were in.

"Mere details . . . But you still haven't answered me. The rooster combs will be getting cold, unless you'd care to join me."

"Really, there's no need," Estíbaliz cut in. "We came to ask you about a novel, *The Lords of Time*. What can you tell us about it?"

"*The Lords of Time*? I haven't read it. Why did you come all the way from Vitoria to ask me that?"

I watched his reaction. The question barely interested him; he was already growing bored with us, or at least with me.

I took a copy of the novel out of my pocket, the one I had hoped to have autographed the night before. Was I now facing the person who should have signed it?

"I like the cover. I see the Carnicerías district and the guilds' streets," he said, inspecting it carefully. "But I still don't understand why you're asking me about it."

"Are you Diego Veilaz?" Estíbaliz asked him, point-blank.

"Me, a Vela?" he asked. He looked as though he were sucking on a lemon. "Why on earth would I want to be a Vela when I'm Alvar Nograro, the twenty-fourth Lord of Nograro Tower? Vela's dynasty died out, but mine continues. Would *you* want to claim an extinct noble line?"

"Not at all," replied Estíbaliz.

"What is the novel about?" he asked, staring at the book on his desk as if it were a strange insect.

"It's set in the twelfth century," I explained. "Count Diago Vela has just returned to the chartered town of Victoria, and the novel takes us through his clash with Count Nagorno—"

"Forgive me for interrupting, young man, but I fail to see what a historical novel has to do with your work."

"Well, lots of people die in the book," I began.

"It was the Middle Ages, that's to be expected . . ." Alvar said absentmindedly. His attention had already wandered; he was leafing through the novel, pausing at certain pages, as though reading passages at random.

"We're investigating the death of a local businessman. He died a few days ago, under circumstances similar to one of the deaths in the novel."

"What were the circumstances exactly?"

"He died near the back wall of Villa Suso palace. As I'm sure you know, that was the original medieval wall, built in—"

"You're saying that this man died close to the fortifications," he said, interrupting me again.

"And that's not the only similarity. Have you heard of cantharidin?"

"Spanish fly? Caesar's wife, Livia, used to give it to her guests. She added it to the dishes in her banquets, let Mother Nature take its course, and then threatened to destroy their reputations. Given the turn this conversation has taken, I'll no longer insist that you eat with me," he said, winking mischievously at us.

"As I said, we're working," Estíbaliz insisted.

"So the man died in sin, or with the intention of sinning."

"No, we don't think so," I explained. "The dose he ingested leads us to believe the cantharidin was used as a poison, not as an aphrodisiac."

"Then I'm pleased, for his soul's sake. But you really must explain what the Nograro Tower has to do with your investigation."

"We know that you have collaborated with Malatrama, the publisher of the novel. We have evidence that indicates that the author hiding behind the pseudonym Diego Veilaz contacted the publisher from this tower. All of which leads us to believe that you published that novel under a pseudonym, for whatever reason."

"And why would I want to publish a book? To earn a living?"

"It's possible."

Alvar rose from the heavy armchair and motioned for us to follow him to the large window that dominated the room.

"Have you seen my estate?"

We could see wheat fields that had been harvested, poplars planted with geometric precision, vegetable gardens, a cemetery, a large backyard, and some houses in the nearby village of Ugarte.

"My family has overseen these lands for centuries. At one time they also owned the mill, the forge, the toll bridge, and the church. I don't want you to assume I suffer from the deadly sin of pride, but trust me, my family does not need to work."

"Don't you even celebrate Mass?" asked Estí, who had moved to stand beside him in order to enjoy the view.

"Oh, please. . . ."

Alvar was pretending to take everything we said in stride, but he was clutching the novel, marking a spot in the book with his finger. I assumed a particular passage must have caught his eye.

"Can you see the moat, Estíbaliz?" he asked her, seemingly out of the blue.

"Yes. It's funny, I thought they only existed in fairy tales and period dramas. I didn't think I would ever see one filled with water."

"It's the setting for one of my earliest memories. When I was a child, our whole family used to get into a little boat and row all the way around the tower just for fun. Would you like to try it?"

"Oh yes, I love the water," replied Estíbaliz, doing a good job of feigning enthusiasm.

We exchanged glances for half a second. *I'll take care of him; you handle her*. I nodded.

"I won't join you," I said, although it hardly seemed necessary, since I hadn't been invited. "I'm going to ask the guide to show me around the . . ."

But Alvar was no longer remotely interested in what I had to say. He was leading Estíbaliz through a door camouflaged by the wallpaper, and I was left alone in the strange, old-fashioned room. I nosed around the library, which was full of heavy volumes with ancient leather bindings.

Eventually, I went back the way I had come in. I walked over to the small office on the ground floor, where the guide was pretending to work on the computer.

"I don't know whether this is possible, but I'd love a tour of the tower?"

She gave me a rather timid smile and picked up a bunch of keys.

"Let's go to the exhibition room. You can ask me any questions you have. It will have to be quick, though. I need to close in twenty minutes."

"Let's get started then, shall we?"

She agreed, and we entered a room that served as a gallery. Portraits of past lords were displayed in glass cases.

I paused to study them. Some of the men's faces were similar to Alvar's, young and attractive. Others were quite different, with heavy mustaches and darker skin. There were also family scenes, including an old photograph of several women and small children in a small boat being rowed by a priest.

"Only the sons named Alvar could inherit," the guide reported. "They also had to respect a code of honor that Fernando the Fourth put in place when he bestowed the family title."

Then she showed me a large canvas with a painted tree trunk bearing tiny, handwritten names. Different generations branched off to the side: the younger sons' entire families. I counted around thirty generations in a thousand years.

"I was expecting to see a mannequin dressed in a nun's habit," I said.

"A mannequin? We haven't ever used clothes in our exhibit, at least not that I know of," she said, puzzled.

I showed her the photograph Estíbaliz had sent me, and she looked at it in confusion.

"Yes, that does look like this room. It must have been a temporary exhibition. I haven't been here for that long, but I know they change the display so the pieces don't get damaged. I don't think I can help you. I'm really sorry. Ask Ramiro Alvar, though, he's the one who takes care of things."

She proceeded to show me more of the tower's collection: shotguns, rifles, revolvers, rusty cartridges, riding crops, and red-velvet saddles worn with use. There was also a significant collection of holy relics, as well as fire pokers, oars, and—

The guide's phone began to ring.

"I'm sorry, I'll step aside to take this," she apologized.

The priest and my colleague appeared before my eyes, laughing conspiratorially as they reached inside the glass case and stole the oars. The impish Alvar also took a pretty white-embroidered parasol from the wall. I don't think they even noticed I was there; like fish in an aquarium, they were oblivious to being watched. Estí and Alvar slipped out of a door behind the cases and disappeared.

Ten minutes later, I said goodbye to the guide at the tower's pointed arch. I didn't want to call Estíbaliz in case she was obtaining useful information during her tête-à-tête with the intriguing Alvar.

I was crossing the tower's lawn when I saw them.

It was like staring at an old print—the scene so anachronistic that it didn't seem possible that it was happening in present-day. A boat, gliding along the moat, powered by Estíbaliz's lazy rowing, and a resplendent priest holding a parasol. Estí was laughing, enjoying the outing.

When they saw me, her rowing grew stronger, and the old-fashioned craft floated alongside me.

"I'm afraid we have to get back to work. Many thanks for the trip," said Estí, stepping out onto dry land.

"That's how we'll leave it then," Alvar said, smiling gently.

The fact that Alvar did not have the copy of *The Lords of Time* that I had lent him did not escape my notice. I waited for his promise to return it, but he said nothing, so I filed away the information and we said goodbye.

At that moment, my cell phone rang. I took it out, without considering that we were still close to Alvar.

"Peña, what is it?"

"You have to get here quickly, boss. The two sisters . . . I think they've been walled in."

Hearing that made my blood freeze. I shouldn't have repeated the information out loud. I know I shouldn't have. But you're a person before you're a cop, and sometimes horror catches you completely unaware.

"What do you mean, the two sisters are walled in? Did you find the bodies . . . behind the walls?" I finally managed to ask.

Estí looked quizzically at me. I walked away from her and Alvar. My world had been turned upside down.

"No, no! They're alive. Milán and I have been in the apartment ever since we responded to that call about the bad smell. There's a brick wall in the unit that appears to have just been built. When we came in, a girl's voice began crying for help. She identified herself as Oihana Nájera, the younger sister. The fire department and an ambulance are on their way. We're going to knock down the wall."

"Call forensics as well," I ordered. "Hand out gloves and shoe covers to anybody who goes near the apartment. This is a crime scene: a kidnapping, maybe even an attempted murder."

"Understood. How long will it take you to get here?"

"We're in Ugarte, forty kilometers away. But you have permission to demolish the walls. Our priority is to save those girls' lives."

11

LA CUCHILLERÍA

UNAI

September 2019

We drove back to Vitoria as quickly as we could within the speed limit. Both of us were tense, immersed in somber thoughts, yet we were hopeful. Finally being able to remove the photos of the missing girls from our wall would be a weight off our shoulders.

I had to break the wall of silence.

"What did you get out of our young pope?" I prodded Estíbaliz.

"Absolutely nothing; he's very evasive. He wouldn't tell me anything he didn't want to. I tried asking direct questions, but he simply changed the subject or didn't answer. We're not going to get anything out of him as long as he's comfortable and confident, in his own element. He's in his natural habitat, where he has full control of the situation. We're only there as onlookers."

"So what do you suggest?" I asked. "His publisher says he never leaves his tower."

Estí shrugged.

"We'll have to lure him out of his lair."

"Can you do that?" I wanted to know. "Do you have something in mind?"

My colleague said nothing for a while.

"What are you thinking about?" I insisted. I'd had enough of her silence. It was especially maddening because I needed her to distract me. I didn't want to think about having to face the terrified sisters stuck between the walls.

"The Nájera sisters," she lied, clearly avoiding a topic she didn't want to discuss. "Thank God, they're alive. What kind of animal traps two girls behind a brick wall?"

"Haven't you read the novel, Estí?"

"There you go again. No, Kraken, I haven't had time."

"You'll understand what we're dealing with a lot better if you do. It's top priority. Start reading it tonight if possible. Will you do that?"

"All right, but can you leave the damn fiction aside and concentrate on the two cases we need to solve?"

What if it's only one case? I thought. I considered asking, but didn't. How could I explain my fears to her? It was too soon.

"I don't think he wrote the novel," she said eventually.

"I'm not sure he did, either. Of course, he could easily have done the research using his library. But did you notice how he reacted when we asked him about the book?"

"Yes, it was odd," she said. "At first it didn't interest him. I could've sworn he was on the verge of getting rid of us. Then he came across something in the novel—he marked a page with his finger. When we came downstairs to pick up the oars, he left the novel on his desk, stealthily putting a letter opener in the book to mark the spot. That's why I don't think he wrote it. If he had, why keep our copy and why mark a passage? He would have had more than enough copies, or drafts, or manuscripts, whatever you call them."

He hadn't kept just any copy; he kept my copy—although that gave me a good excuse to return.

"Okay, let's say he isn't the author," I conceded. "Something still attracted his attention."

"Yes, and then he concentrated on me, because there was no

chemistry between the two of you. So he tried to seduce me, or whatever that was, to worm information out of me."

"And did he succeed?"

"He asked me the dead businessman's name, but I didn't tell him. I want to see if he keeps asking, how important it is to him. Besides, he could find out by reading the paper. It's not a secret. So let's suppose he's the killer, not the author. Does he have the right profile, Kraken?"

I had been expecting this question for some time. "I can't create a profile based on a single meeting."

"But you can share your initial impressions."

"He has narcissistic tendencies. He believes he is superior to others culturally, socially, and intellectually, at least according to his own values. He even reinforces his power by calling us 'young,' when he's younger than we are. He keeps the real world at a distance. My guess is that he doesn't feel the need to relate to anyone. He's a hedonist, he surrounds himself with beautiful things, and he loves food. He enjoys and seeks the company of women, and he has the means to pursue them. He's arrogant, and I saw no empathy in him."

"So he fits the profile of a narcissist. I've been working with you long enough to know that a small percentage of narcissists can eventually cross the line and become criminals if their conscience is anesthetized and someone gets in their way. But why would he want to kill anyone?"

We were always asking ourselves this question, as though there were a single answer. There wasn't. Not a simple one. Not a logical one.

"Narcissistic psychopaths get bored," I recited from memory. "They tire of people and things easily, like spoiled children who throw away a new toy after a few minutes. They don't think about the consequences. Their only concern is how to manipulate those around them to achieve what they want. But we're assuming too much. Alvar has narcissistic traits, but there's a whole world of possibilities between that and him being a psychopath. Psychopaths have no empathy. Although they're incapable of understanding someone who's suffering, they're very good at presenting the emotions they're supposed to have in almost every situation. They're emotional chameleons. We'll need to have many more conversations with Alvar to reach any conclusion about whether or not he's a psychopath."

"I'm going to do something you're not going to like," she said, her eyes fixed on the road.

"Yes, you mentioned it already. You're going to lure him out of his tower."

"He intrigues me. You don't meet someone like him every day."

I raised an eyebrow and looked across at her.

"Are we still talking about work?"

"Why? What did you notice?"

"The electricity in the way you two looked at each other . . . He deliberately brushed against you three times. Twice he touched the back of your hand, and then he grazed the nape of your neck while you were standing at the window next to him."

"I'm watching him, okay?"

Your pupils were saying something else, I thought.

"I know, Estí. I've seen you deal with dozens of seductive men over the years. You wanted nothing to do with Ignacio Ortiz de Zarate, and you weren't reeled in by Tasio or by Saúl Tovar's charisma. You're not easily swayed."

"I'm glad you noticed," she said. "But to change the subject, he doesn't have a cell phone. He uses a landline."

"The publisher suggested that might be the case. It's useful information. I'll ask Milán to look into it."

"I can't help asking myself why someone who is uninterested in the outside world would complicate his life by killing a prominent businessman?"

"Antón Lasaga owned lots of properties in this region. Maybe there was a dispute over land."

"Yes, that's possible. Here we have two extremely rich men: one with no family, the other with five children who aren't his. But I'm struggling to find a motive, a link. Even if he did write the book, we need something more than cantharidin and the crime scene, and I can't see it."

"You can't see it because we haven't conducted a full investigation. We need to find out what properties they own, if there were any land disputes . . . and one other thing."

"What's that?"

"We need to find out if the fashion king is part of a family that was considered important in the Middle Ages."

"Why's that?"

"His name was Antón Lasaga Pérez. In Álava, many people called López, Martínez—any of the patronymics—lost their double-barreled surnames generations ago because of parish priests' errors on their birth or marriage certificates. Get Peña to talk to Lasaga's daughter and collect all the information he can about the family name and its origins. Then ask him to contact a genealogy company in Vitoria specializing in Álava surnames. We need to uncover a motive, and everything seems to point toward this region's past. But you haven't asked me the most important question: Where is Ramiro Alvar?"

"Didn't we just meet him?"

"No, Estí. That wasn't the person the publisher told us about. Prudencio described a timid Ramiro Alvar, who wasn't going to have any descendants, so where is he?"

"Why are the descendants so important?"

"Because Prudencio can't have met the Alvar we just met, at least not while the man was wearing a cassock. If he had, he wouldn't have mentioned the possibility of offspring. Besides, the man we just met presented himself as Alvar, the twenty-fourth Lord of Nograro, not as *Ramiro* Alvar."

I had further suspicions, but they were still too vague, and I didn't want to share them until I had checked a couple of things over the course of the next few days.

"Understood." Estí left it there. She pretended there was nothing more to discuss, but she had probably filed it away for a future talk.

The car pulled up at the first set of traffic lights at the entrance to Vitoria. Now was the moment. "There's something else. . . . Nieves fell down the stairs at my apartment."

The light turned green, but Estí didn't move.

"What did you say?" she asked anxiously. "Is she all right?"

"She's being operated on. Alba says it'll take three hours and that there's nothing we can do at the hospital before she gets out."

"We'll be there in fifteen minutes. I'll go to the hospital, that way I can at least keep Alba company," she said resolutely. "You go to the apartment and coordinate the operation: the superintendent will be beside herself if all three of us are at the hospital when there are two girls trapped behind a wall."

"I'd rather be the one to stay with Alba," I said.

"You'll be more useful at the crime scene. You can cover her back. You'll still have time to go to the hospital before Nieves is released."

I didn't like the idea, but Estíbaliz knew as well as I did that if I went to the hospital Alba would just be angry that I hadn't gone to check on the two sisters.

When Estí dropped me off near La Cuchillería, it was easy to spot the apartment I was looking for: an ambulance and several police cars had blocked off the street from pedestrian traffic and the doorway was cordoned off.

Curious onlookers were crowding around the barrier, but if they had known what lay at the top of the stairs, they would have run home and hidden under their beds. I flashed my badge and went up.

The apartment was being remodeled. There were sacks of cement and other building materials everywhere. I stepped past several buckets full of rubble and found the room Peña had mentioned. The firefighters were about to take a sledgehammer to the wall.

"Why didn't you start earlier?" I asked Milán.

"We heard Oihana's voice, but it took us some time to figure out where we could knock down the wall without hurting the girls. The firefighters didn't want to use a battering ram in case there's not enough room on the other side. They were afraid they might crush the girls. We haven't heard their voices for twenty-three minutes. It doesn't look good. We have paramedics standing by. I just hope we're not too late and that we don't end up hurting them even more."

Two of the firefighters called out to the sisters, but there was no reply. They started to hammer at the wall, and with each strike, my nerves frayed a little more.

Come on, you have to be alive, I thought, as though my eagerness to rescue them could help us get to them any faster.

The blows echoed throughout the room.

Bits of brick cascaded to the ground near my feet. I should have moved away, but I was desperate to get to the sisters. I wanted to leap through the hole and get those poor girls out as quickly as possible.

I couldn't stop thinking about what I had read recently on the so-called vow of darkness. Who could have thought of something like that?

I had studied the worst aspects of the human soul for years as a criminal profiler, but there had been no case of immurement, or walling in, in the recent global history of criminology. There was no mention of it in terms of a modus operandi, or a macabre act, in the past hundred years. Nobody killed like that. Why now? Was it a copycat effect from the novel?

It couldn't be. That was impossible: the dates didn't fit.

The Nájera sisters had disappeared several weeks before the novel was published. That fact was tremendously helpful for a profiler. It ruled out everyone who had read the book after it was released. If the crime *was* linked to the novel, the suspect pool could only include the much smaller number of people who might have read the manuscript before publication.

Finally, I could no longer bear it. The damned noise. The damned slowness.

I picked up a hammer and went to help the firefighters. I don't know how many voices called for me to stop, told me not to get involved, that it was dangerous for the girls, that . . . To hell with it.

Nothing could have prepared me for what I saw.

There was a body smothered in red dust at my feet. Once a starving girl, it was now a corpse in an advanced state of decomposition.

The stench was unbearable. The apartment suddenly stank like rotten eggs, the unmistakable odor of cadaverine. She had probably died several days earlier. I ran to the unfinished bathroom and threw up. Not even the strong scent of camphor could trick me into thinking the smell of death wasn't everywhere.

Despite my revulsion, I took a deep breath and went back to the hole in the wall. The two firefighters were still busy chipping away. A doctor had arrived, but there was no need for him to take the dead girl's pulse.

It seemed there was some good news, though. The flashlight's beam fell on a girl in the corner. I thought I saw her move.

I ran toward the shape huddled against the wall. She seemed to be made of nothing but clothes and thick, matted, waist-length hair. She was trying to cover herself with a couple of rough plastic sheets. It was Oihana, the younger sister.

We pulled her from the crypt filled with excrement and urine. The paramedics began resuscitating her right there on the floor of the apartment, while the seven of us looked on in horror. The bundle of bones was not responding to our efforts to revive her. It seemed we were too late.

But then a miracle happened.

The skeletal little girl, covered in red dust from the crumbled bricks, began to cough and breathe very softly, almost imperceptibly. The paramedics fitted her with an oxygen mask and lifted her onto the stretcher. She was so thin that any one of us could have picked her up with one hand.

After she was carried out, we were left with a thick silence and the smell of her sister's body. There we were, half a dozen desolate professionals, with almost no strength left to keep working in that tomb.

12

LA ROMANA INN

DIAGO VELA

Winter, the Year of Our Lord 1192

Fascinated, Onneca walked over to the magnificent golden mare. "I've never seen such a beautiful animal. How did she get to Victoria?"

"I breed these horses in the lands of the Almohads. I had Olbia brought here as a wedding gift, but I couldn't give her to you on the day of your father's burial. I awoke at *hora prima* and your bed was already cold, so I guessed that you were trying out the skates Cousin Gunnarr gave you."

"Olbia . . ." whispered Onneca, stroking the mare's glistening mane with an air of respect.

Nagorno smiled with satisfaction. Until then I hadn't considered what brought them together, other than a convenient marriage.

"There's a story as well," Nagorno continued, in his most seductive voice. "Do you remember the Scythian colony Herodotus mentions in that chronicle I gave you? It wasn't just a city. Olbia was the name of an Amazon, like you, my lady. She was a bloodthirsty leader. She used a small bow when she galloped into war, and she also wielded a whip and an *acinakes*, the curved sword of the Scythians."

"Don't get so excited about the idea of war, Brother," I interrupted him. "Onneca won't have any need to brandish a sword."

"She doesn't look very much like our northern horses," said Onneca, ignoring my comment.

"She's an *Argamak.* They have been bred in the remote lands of the Turks since before the coming of Christ. This one is a direct descendant of Alexander the Great's horse."

"Of Bucephalus?"

"That's right," replied Nagorno proudly. "She's yours now. If you like, ride her back to Victoria; I'll follow on foot."

"We could both ride her."

"Take a good look. She is nothing like the other steeds in Victoria. She's a queen and should be treated with the respect she is owed, thanks to her lineage." Nagorno shot me a sideways glance. A silent warning.

I nodded. Why deny it?

"I'm on my way to La Romana Inn," I said.

"Going whoring, brother? Are you so starved for affection?"

I smiled but said nothing. I needed answers, so I had set up a meeting with one of the few older relatives I trusted with my life. In fact, I had often put my fate in his hands.

Onneca was also waiting for my reply, but to no avail.

"I'll find you in the council chamber later, Nagorno. I've summoned the notary, and the mayor and several others will attest to the fact that I am still drawing breath. Today, I will recover the title that you took such care of in my absence . . . and God knows how grateful I am to you for it."

"My beloved sister-in-law." I saluted her, lowering my head. Then I adjusted my hose and headed north across a path of virgin snow.

La Romana was a stopping place for pilgrims from Guipúzcoa, Aquitaine, and Navarre who were traveling to Santiago. The inn also catered to those interested in less charitable but more lucrative activities. As a result, it had changed hands several times. Arguments sometimes grew violent, and not even the innkeeper was safe from a furtive stabbing.

I had outlawed prostitution in Victoria before I left on my mission for the king, so I presumed a warm reception was not awaiting me.

I walked past the stables, where a peasant was seeking relief leaning against the wall, an obese girl on her knees in front of him. Apparently he was in too much of a hurry to wait until they reached the bedrooms.

Inside the inn, a woman with no nose and a receding chin was cleaning tables.

"Wine?" she asked, barely glancing at me.

"I'm expecting an old friend. Is anyone upstairs waiting for me?"

"Go on up, he's paid already."

"So be it. Leave us alone for a time. Although . . . perhaps you could help me. Do you know where I could find some Spanish fly?"

The woman continued scrubbing the table, possibly with even more energy.

"I think you're mistaken. Here we provide only good food and drink. You are Count Don Vela, aren't you? The resuscitated?"

"To be that I would have to have died first," I repeated for the hundredth time. "But since you know who I am, I shall rephrase my question: Has my brother visited you recently?"

The innkeeper looked the other way, biting her lip. Had Nagorno threatened her?

"I'll make it easy for you. My brother comes here every Friday, and he always takes three girls upstairs. He pays you handsomely. Has he ever asked you for Spanish fly?"

"If what my sisters tell me is true, your brother is a man who doesn't need it. Do you know if he'll be back to see us now that he's a respectable married man?"

"Don't worry, he's a gentleman of habit."

Nagorno had a long tradition of worshiping the goddess Venus with three women. Three was a sacred number to him. He had a pagan soul. And, like the person writing these lines, Nagorno clung to his rituals like ice to a tree trunk.

I climbed the stairs, my hand on the dagger at my belt. I clasped the hilt as I knocked on the door. The floorboards creaked, and I could hear rapid footsteps coming my way. I stepped back a little as the door opened.

"Diago!" exclaimed my cousin Héctor. Before even letting me through the door, he embraced me warmly. I returned his affection.

"I knew you weren't dead. But if you had taken any longer to reappear, I would have gone in search of you."

"I know."

Héctor Dicastillo was the lord of one of the villages to the south of Victoria. The ties between our families went back a long way. Unlike many of the other nobles, Héctor was content to live quietly in his small castle in Castillo. He had no wish to move to Victoria.

"Have you brought what I asked?" I urged.

"Yes, but you'll have to tell me what is going on and why you didn't want to meet in town."

"I didn't want you to encounter Nagorno before I told you what has transpired."

"I want you to know that I didn't go to the wedding ceremony out of respect for you. The woman you were betrothed to—"

I interrupted him. "That's in the past. She is his wife now. I asked you to meet me in this out-of-the-way place because I want you to tell me whether this letter from King Sancho is a forgery."

I handed him the document, and he took a couple of scrolls out of his bag, saying, "These are royal letters establishing the imposts and other taxes on the inhabitants of Castillo."

"Is my letter written by the same hand?"

Héctor unrolled his papers on the straw mattress. I did the same with the letter announcing my death.

"The Chi-Rho is identical. The cross with the bar and the letter *P*. Also the letters *alpha* and *omega*. That is the heading used in the court of Navarre."

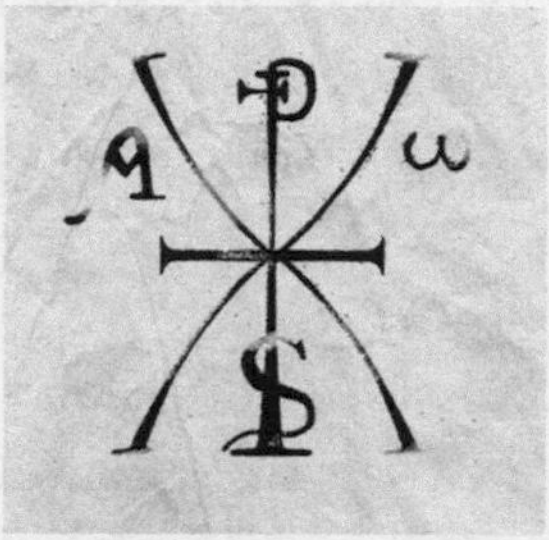

He continued comparing the two documents.

"*In nomine omnipotentis Dei, Ego Sancius Dei gratia, rex Navarre. . . .* It's the same formula. Who signed it, I wonder?"

He looked at the bottom of the letter.

"His loyal notary, Ferrando. *Ego quoque Ferrandus domini regis notaries eius iussione: han cartam scripsi et hoc signum feci.*

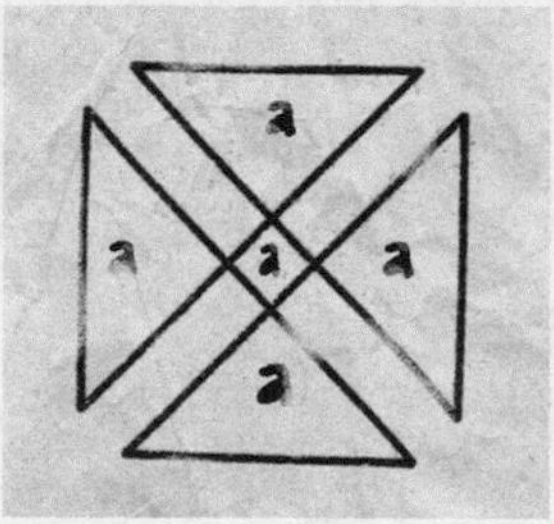

"Diago, that's the signature of King Sancho the Sixth, the Wise. Can you think of any reason for him to claim you were dead?"

"I don't know, but I have no wish to go to Tudela to ask him, at least not now."

"Why?"

"First, I fear he may send me off again on some mission to a distant land or off to the Crusades, and I want to live quietly here in Victoria. Second, I do not know what is happening here in the town. It's not the prosperous Victoria I left. The streets are filled with rumors. Third, I am not sure who killed Count de Maestu."

"Are you insinuating that because Nagorno profited from it?"

"No, I didn't say that. I don't think even my brother would stoop to marrying the count's daughter and poisoning him on the same night."

Héctor stood up, ill at ease.

"You know I've always defended Nagorno, but I don't agree with what he's been doing in Victoria since you left. There are complaints on every road into town. Laborers who left Villafranca de Estíbaliz to settle in the Sant Michel district before falling out with the monks are now overwhelmed with taxes. Some have no idea if they'll be able to pay the rent in March."

"I know. Something is brewing. People who have lived their entire lives in Villa de Suso are eyeing new arrivals in Nova Victoria with suspicion. And the wealthy families are pushing merchants through the gates as though they were moving chess pieces. We have to stop them before they leave both neighborhoods empty. I am going to need allies, Héctor. Lyra is with me; she just wants peace in the town, as do I. As always, Gunnarr won't commit himself, nor will he betray Nagorno."

"You are brothers, the same blood runs in your veins," said Héctor. "I'm with you for now, but don't forget it is a town. Neighborhoods will be won and lost, created and abandoned. The chain of violence stretches back to the first age of man, and we've never been able to stop it. But family endures."

"I never forget that, Héctor."

He got up from the tattered bed and gathered the scrolls.

"Well, then, let's go before they accuse us of being sodomites."

Leaving the inn, I saw a young lad with a receding chin and a mop of blond hair throwing a small hatchet at a bale of straw. It was the second time that day I had seen a chin like that.

"You're the son of the innkeeper, aren't you?"

"I'm Lope, my lord. My mother, Astonga, runs the inn. Do you want to know her story as well?"

He continued to throw the hatchet while he spoke. He had good aim. He reminded me of Gunnar, before he grew into a giant.

"What story?" I asked, though I was not particularly interested.

"The story of how they cut off her nose. Everybody asks me."

"Let me guess. It was as punishment for thievery. I've only seen such a harsh penalty used on Camino del Santiago. In Castile and Leon, the punishment is less harsh, and the thief only loses a hand. But the Roman Church doesn't want word to spread that the pilgrims' road is dangerous, so the punishment is more severe."

"You're a man who has seen much of the world."

"Is that what happened?"

"Do you want to know the truth?"

"Yes, always. Tell me the truth. There are too many lies of late."

"It's a story of the poor: You'll have heard more than enough of them. My grandparents had an inn on the pilgrims' way, but they were young when they died of anthrax, leaving seven girls. My mother, the eldest, was twelve when she had to start looking after her sisters. She was an innocent. A drunken Navarrese lord and his soldiers finished off all the inn's provisions and then refused to pay. He also took liberties with my mother's youngest sister. My mother wanted him to face justice, but he accused her of being a thief. Naturally, the trial was decided in his favor. My mother's nose was cut off, and my grandparents' inn was burned to the ground. The sisters swore never to separate. They tried their luck in Pamplona and finally ended up here at La Romana. They keep the inn running. Important men come here," he said with a seriousness that belied his young age. "I'm sure that I'm the son of an important man. When she's old, my mother won't have to work."

A poor whoreson whose father was unknown. Given the fact that he was still alive, and hadn't been left in the woods to die from exposure, his father must have been a married man from the town who paid for the boy's well-being.

"How will you make sure your mother doesn't work?"

He smiled, like he knew how to keep a secret, and motioned for me to come closer. I did so, although I raised my hand to my dagger in case he was laying a trap.

"Do you need something for your manhood? You left without making use of my aunts."

There I was, searching inside the inn for the supplier, when he was outside all along.

"Are you the one who can provide it?"

"I have powders that can solve your problem."

"Unicorn horn, or Spanish fly?"

"I can see this isn't your first time," he said. "I don't sell unicorn horn. It's so expensive that only lords can buy it, and it's useless anyway. Thanks to unicorn horn, I was bitten by a snake and almost lost my right hand. It swelled up and turned black. I almost went to hell because of that damned thing."

"Someone from the town threw a snake at you. Who would do a thing like that?"

Lope squirmed nervously, then went over to the bale and wrenched his ax free.

"You know, Ruy's son. Smooth cheeks with veins as red as vine shoots on his nose. The one who looks crazy."

"Who?"

"Ruiz de Maturana."

"Maturana, the young lad."

Apparently in my absence, he'd grown into a man. Even as a youngster, he'd had a bad reputation. He chased after cats that were later found disemboweled. His father took liberties with the women in town, and according to rumor, Ruiz was a bastard by one of his father's maidservants, whom Ruy, the animal, would beat.

"Yes, but I have to put up with him. He bought three pinches three nights ago."

"Three pinches of what?"

"Spanish fly."

"One is enough for a bull."

The lad shrugged.

"He must want to be hot the whole winter. I don't ask questions, my lord. If they want to buy for one day, I give it to them. If they want some for an entire army, I'll sell it to them if I have it. So, are you going to buy one of the powders?"

13

"LAU TEILATU"

UNAI

September 2019

We had put Deba down for the night. Her bedroom was warm, like a bear's den, but outside our little apartment, it was bitter cold, and the windowpanes had fogged up.

"How could he . . . ?" I said, thinking out loud.

I was sitting on the wooden floor in the living room, leaning against the wall next to the doors to the balcony. Alba was sitting across from me. We would often sit in symmetrical positions, sometimes talking, sometimes silent, both attuned to life inside the apartment and alert to the outside world below us, in the heart of the city.

Alba was cropping the family photo we had taken on the evening of the book launch. She had bought a wooden frame and was determinedly working to fit us within its borders.

But I could tell that she was distracted. I knew she was worrying about her mother; they'd recently become closer, to the point of being almost inseparable. The surgery had been a success, but Nieves needed to recover before she could return to Laguardia.

Earlier that Thursday evening, a few *cuadrillas* had crossed the square heading for the bars on Calle Cuesta—the Cuchi, or the Pinto—looking for some diversion as they tried to cut the week short. I'd personally wished the week had ended on Monday morning. Instead, there'd been one piece of bad news after another. The younger of the two missing sisters, Oihana Nájera, had survived, but the doctors warned us that it would be at least a week before she was strong enough for us to interview.

In the meantime, the only thing we had to work with was another crime scene. Muguruza, our head of forensics, told us the floor in the empty apartment had been swept and scrubbed. There were no footprints, and whoever built the wall had used gloves. We hadn't found the gloves, or any other clues, in the empty apartment.

We concluded that the sisters had been transported in the two plastic bags found at the scene, after strands of the girls' hair were discovered inside them. The bags resembled those commonly used on construction sites. There were no other objects in the apartment. Someone had bricked up the two sisters and left them to die of thirst and starvation. Murder once removed, but still an incredibly cold-blooded thing to do to two young girls.

As I puzzled over the case, I fiddled with a three-dimensional model of the city's Medieval Quarter. It was a typical souvenir—a clay trinket depicting the city's buildings and orange rooftops. I ran my fingers over the miniature churches, streets, and districts of the old neighborhood.

I tried to imagine how a minor deity might see the case from the heavens.

"You son of a bitch, how the hell did you kidnap two girls from their home, transport them to an empty apartment that was under construction, and seal them inside a wall—without being seen?" I whispered, caught up in my thoughts.

Alba shot me a dejected look.

Her day had been doubly difficult. On top of Nieves's operation, Alba had to tell the girls' parents that they'd been found. She conveyed bad news better than most could. Her composure and her confidence gave the parents hope that we would find the monster who took their children. The mother had hugged her, while the father smashed his fist against the door, cutting his knuckles on the wood. His blood had gotten everywhere.

When I got home, her white coat was on a hanger in the shower. She had cleaned it, but the bloodstains wouldn't come out. Her favorite coat looked like a painting by a sadistic Expressionist. Rubbing at the stain had only managed to crease the fabric.

Now she would always carry a reminder of the day. I thought that maybe she would be better off getting rid of the coat and the memory now embedded in its fibers.

Don't let this affect our family. Don't let these bastards ruin what we have, I repeated for at least the hundredth time. It had been my mantra since Deba was born. I did not want to let these cases impact our life.

Besides, we had paid the piper many times over. So, we tried to discuss our work as little as possible at the end of the day. But I couldn't help but wonder whether it would ever end or whether our life would be entangled with each new case until we finally turned it over to the magistrate?

I was still turning the model of medieval Vitoria over in my hands, touching its rooftops and the four church spires, when Alba's cell phone rang and I heard "Lau teilatu."

It had been a long time since we had first listened to that song together, on the roof that was now just a few yards above our heads, during our first Fiestas de la Virgen Blanca before we were officially a couple.

Since then, we had gone to the roof only once or twice, and once Deba was born, we'd let the tradition slide completely. We couldn't leave her alone in the apartment while we climbed onto a roof, and even when Grandfather, Nieves, or Germán were babysitting, we didn't have much time to ourselves.

Then it struck me: "Lau teilatu." Four rooftops.

The Nájeras' apartment was in Calle Pintorería, and the girls were found in Calle Cuchillería. The roofs were connected.

Many buildings in the Old Quarter's narrow guild streets had skylights in the stairwells to let in light.

I used my cell phone to search for a more recent aerial view than the one I had on my medieval replica. Google Earth had what I needed.

Alba turned around. She looked relieved.

"That was Milán. She insisted on staying at the hospital so I could get some rest. She says Mom is loaded up on painkillers. She's fast asleep. I think I'll go to bed early and visit her first thing tomorrow. You can go running at six if you want, and when you get back, I'll head out and stop at the hospital on my way to work."

I breathed a sigh of relief. My mother-in-law was a tough woman who'd been through a lot. A tumble on the stairs wouldn't stop her, but she was older and it would take longer for her to recover her mobility.

Alba remained pensive as she sat down opposite me, her back against the wall. She saw the glint in my eyes.

"What's up, Unai?"

"I know how the kidnapper got in. 'Lau teilatu.' Four rooftops. He got in through the skylight, and he left with the girls the same way. It was the end of August, so a lot of people were away on holiday. Nobody saw him. He carried them over the rooftops and then lowered them through another skylight into the building where we found them. The apartment was being remodeled: He had probably already started building the wall. He left a space big enough to push them through and then sealed it up. Remember our mysterious nun? She escaped over the roof of San Miguel Arcángel Church, and she was very agile. What if our culprit is familiar with the rooftops in Vitoria, either because of his profession or for some other reason?"

"There are a few holes in your theory. It's still a locked-room mystery. Don't forget their apartment was locked from the inside. The windows, too. Honestly, even with years of experience, I still can't get my head around how somebody could do such a terrible thing to two young girls."

"No, not two young girls. To the perpetrator who was carrying them, they were just two garbage bags. By the time they were inside the wall, they were completely concealed in plastic," I pointed out.

"Call it whatever you want, but forensics confirmed that the girls were alive when he abducted them."

"True. But I think that the killer's use of the bags shows a degree of compassion. He doesn't want to acknowledge the fact that he's killing two girls, so he places them in bags because he prefers to think of them as bundles."

"And what does that tell us?"

"That he has empathy, so he's not a psychopath. Killing them is a means to an end. He derives no pleasure from the act, but it's part of his larger plan."

She frowned at me.

"And is that good or bad?"

"Bad. In fact, it's really bad," I said, "because it means that his plan has been set into motion."

Alba didn't welcome my assessment. The idea that we might be in for a series of bizarre murders committed by a killer whose modus operandi seemed to be based on medieval crimes, like poisoning people with Spanish fly or bricking them up, was enough to make anyone nervous.

But that wasn't all. There was something else. Alba was distracted, far away.

"What's wrong? You've been distant for a while now. I feel like I'm living alone. We're going to have to talk sooner or later."

She folded her arms and gazed out at the monument to the Battle of Vitoria.

"I'm thinking of going back to Laguardia to help my mother."

"You mean when she gets out of the hospital?"

"Yes, she won't be able to manage the hotel on her own, and her staff and their families depend on it staying open. I grew up handling the bookings and the paperwork so I could easily run the place when she retires, and that time is not too far away."

"Hold on a minute. . . . We're not just talking about you spending a few days in Laguardia when she gets out of the hospital, are we? What are you trying to tell me?"

Alba took a deep breath and plucked up her courage. She looked me straight in the eye as she said, "I don't know if I want to keep doing this job, Unai. I don't know if I want to continue being a DSU, exposed to so much tragedy, to the ugly side of humanity, day in and day out. I see things differently now that we have Deba. I only have one life, and so does she: one life, one father, and one mother. You're always in the line of fire, all of Vitoria knows who you are. Deba is Kraken's daughter, or worse—" she broke off.

"Worse?" I echoed. "What do you mean? I'm not sure I'm following. Is this about you and your job, or is it about Deba's future? And what exactly are you saying? Do you want to ask for a transfer back to the Laguardia police force? You'll be giving yourself a demotion. You don't need me to tell you how difficult it was for you to break through that glass ceiling. You're a living legend on the force, the youngest woman ever to be made DSU. Everyone respects you. And now you're talking about taking an indefinite leave of absence to help your mother run a hotel?"

"Yes. I'm talking about living near the mountains, a slower pace of life. I'm talking about coming home to dinner without being splattered with blood, about closing my eyes without seeing a teenage girl's rotting corpse. My mother is on her own, and she's going to need me more and more. We're closer now, and I want to spend the future with her. I want Deba to grow up with her and with her great-grandfather. If we move to Laguardia, we'll be closer to Villaverde. You know Deba and your grandfather are inseparable. She'll give their lives renewed meaning."

"And what about her father? Don't you want Deba to grow up with her father? Where do I fit in?"

Alba looked up at me. At some point during our conversation I had gotten to my feet. Now I was standing over her as she sat on the floor. And I must have raised my voice, because Deba appeared in her mouse pajamas, eyes wide as sunflowers.

"Can I sleep with you?" she asked in her baby voice.

"Of course, you can, sweetheart. Papa's going to bed right now," I replied. "Alba, I'll go for a run at six, and we'll see each other at work." I planted a kiss on her lips, but she barely reacted. Then I clasped my daughter around the waist and carried her off to our bedroom, as though she were a small gift.

Whenever I had an awful day, watching Deba sleep would comfort me. It reminded me that I must have been very good in a past life, because I got to hold this small miracle in my arms, her tiny galloping heartbeat giving me all the warmth I needed.

But that evening my daughter was wide-awake.

"Papa, is *twenny-two* a lot?" she whispered.

"That depends: Twenty-two what? Twenty-two hugs isn't very many. I give you way more than that every morning. Twenty-two roasted chestnuts is a lot for you; remember the time you ate a whole packet?"

"*Twenny-two* dead people," she said.

In my daughter's tiny voice, those words chilled me to the bone.

"What do you mean by twenty-two dead people, darling?"

"I heard a grown-up at school say it when I was going pee-pee. She said my papa has twenty-two dead people behind him. Can I see them?"

Goddamn. Now I understood what Alba meant. To some people,

Deba was Kraken's daughter. But others saw her as the daughter of a man who had murdered twenty-two people.

"They found out! How?" I parried, making my voice lighthearted.

"What did they find out, Papa?"

"About my Halloween costume. I'm going as a zombie hunter. I carry a sack on my back with twenty-two zombie dolls in it . . . but it's a secret. How did they find out?"

"Was it the people in the fancy dress store, Papa?"

"Why didn't I think of that! Of course. We won't go there again, Deba," I said. I stroked her soft blond hair, which usually made her fall asleep within minutes.

"No, Papa. . . . We won't," she murmured, her breathing becoming steady.

Alba had been listening in the doorway, arms folded.

She didn't have to say a word.

Three years earlier, Alba and I had made a promise, one that united our family against the world. We would stick with one story, forever, no cracks. It was the only way to keep Deba safe from the inquisition of others.

14

LA HERRERÍA

UNAI

September 2019

I had a rough night, trying to come to understand what Alba was saying: she needed more than just a few days back in her village to unwind. Alba and Deba were the only things that mattered to me. I loved them. What Alba was suggesting was a major change—for all of us.

I was still lost in thought, familiarizing myself with the shadows on the ceiling, when the clock struck five. I showered, slipped on my sneakers, and snuck back into the bedroom to kiss the two ladies in my life before hitting the pavement. The early dawn welcomed me with its icy breath. I put on my headphones and began to run to "Cold Little Heart."

I was on the Plaza de la Virgen Blanca, heading for the verdant arches of Florida Park, when I saw curious figures on Calle Herrería.

Curious, because one of them was wearing a cassock—at six o'clock on a Friday morning, that was surprising to the say the least. I knew the other figure's shock of red hair all too well. They were giggling, but they didn't look drunk.

"Good day to you, López de Ayala! Are you out on your dawn rounds? Are the town's inhabitants safe and sound?" Alvar asked with genuine delight, finally recognizing me when we were practically face-to-face.

I shot Estíbaliz a quizzical look. I had no idea what was going on.

"Good day to you, Don Alvar, or should I say good night?" I retorted.

"Last night we went to see the vestment exhibit at the Museum of Sacred Art in the New Cathedral, and then I decided to give Alvar a taste of Vitoria's nightlife," Estíbaliz answered for him. She looked at her phone as though it were broken. "Surely it can't be ten after six already?"

Estí was the only person I knew who could get away with taking a priest in a cassock out on the town. In under twenty-four hours, she'd managed to lure Alvar out of his tower. It was pure instinct, and I knew she'd been watching him while she plied him with drinks. Not the most conventional approach, but, with two bodies in the morgue and a young girl in the hospital, it was certainly good enough for me.

"Did you know Calle Herrería used to be called Calle Ferrería? Alvar knows the names of all the old places in the Medieval Quarter. For example, Zapatería was actually Çapatería, and Calle Correría used to be Calle Pellejería because the traders sold pelts there, and . . ." She trailed off as I leaned toward her.

"Read the novel, Estí. Now," I whispered in her ear. Then I shook Alvar's hand and resumed my run.

Estíbaliz's feigned enthusiasm was designed to nurture Alvar's inflated ego, but she and I both knew that she was a skilled huntress, and that she would place her bait wherever she needed to. She had taken him outside his comfort zone all night and doubtless probed his behavior to learn more about him—all of which she would later put in a report.

My colleague was still working the Thursday shift.

By midafternoon, I had visited my mother-in-law at the hospital. I was relieved to discover that she was on the mend. Then I drove out to Valdegovía again. I wanted to check a couple of things at the tower.

To my surprise, the wooden gates were locked, and no one, not even the guide I had met the day before, answered the visitors' number. Instead I was invited to leave a message on the answering machine.

I resorted to knocking on the door. I assumed Alvar was in his apartment, because while I was parking the car in the lot near the moat, I had seen someone close the study window. I thought it was Alvar, but the curtains had obscured him.

I kept banging on the door until the hand-shaped knocker grew warm in my palm. I was ready to camp outside, when the door finally opened and I heard a soft male voice I didn't recognize murmur, "Here I am, here I am. . . ."

I was expecting to meet a mysterious new resident, but instead I saw Alvar wrapped in a thick blanket that trailed on the entrance cobblestones behind him.

He was wearing a pair of black horn-rimmed glasses with thick lenses that made his blue eyes look smaller. But they couldn't disguise the puffy shadows from his night on the town. His blond locks were no longer slicked back, in fact, he seemed oblivious to the wavy strands that drooped over his forehead and covered his right eye.

"May I help you?" he asked.

Again, I was stunned by his voice. It wasn't just that he whispered, as if he were afraid of waking a sleeping mother. His tone was also higher and he sounded younger than I remembered. The ravages of a hangover, I supposed.

"Good afternoon, Don Alvar. Forgive me for bothering you, I came to retrieve something I left behind—"

"I'm sorry, do we know each other? Are you from the village?"

"Er . . . No, I'm Inspector Unai López de Ayala. I came here yesterday with my colleague Estíbaliz Ruiz de Gauna. Are you feeling okay?"

"Yes, I'm fine. Actually, I'm a little tired. I must have had a bad night. Won't you come in? Claudia doesn't seem to be here today. I suspect there weren't any tours booked for this afternoon. So it's just you and me. You said you're an inspector. How can I help you? Isn't that the phrase?" he asked, pulling the thick blanket closer around him.

I took a few seconds to react. I was astonished, but I couldn't waste this golden opportunity.

"Actually, you can help me," I said. "Shall we go inside where we can speak more comfortably? It's a bit chilly down here, don't you think?"

"Yes, of course. I am sorry. I hope you don't think me rude. Let's go up to my apartment."

I followed him through a different door. This one was on the right side of the entrance, and he led me through it and up a flight of stone steps to the third floor. Every landing was cluttered with objects: worn-limestone corbels, broken columns, even a huge overturned baptismal font that blocked the bottom step.

"The most recent renovation," he explained. "I have no idea where to store all these discarded objects."

"Why bother? A lot of people would kill to live in a museum like this."

He turned and smiled a little self-consciously. "I have to admit, I love it, too. I adore the past, and this tower is a piece of living history. I strive to be worthy of my ancestors' legacy, but it isn't easy."

The man seemed cripplingly shy. I looked at him with something verging on tenderness.

He guided me through the tower's maze of corridors. Some I recognized, but others opened into rooms we hadn't seen the day before. There were tiled chambers, long-abandoned nurseries, and dining rooms with fully set tables.

When we reached the third floor, he walked resolutely to the end of the corridor, perhaps to another study I hadn't seen. But as we passed the tapestry room we had been in the day before, I walked in without waiting for an invitation.

"My book! I hope you enjoyed it. Actually, it was a gift from my wife, which is why I came here to get it back," I said. Without giving him a chance to protest, I crossed the room and picked up my copy of *The Lords of Time.*

"Ah . . . so it's yours. Be my guest," he said, eyes glued to the cover as he watched me slip it inside my jacket. He was staring at me like I was stealing a Fabergé egg. "Thanks for the loan. I'll certainly buy myself a copy. I only dipped into it. But tell me, Inspector, what really brought you here?"

"Is there somewhere we can talk that's a bit warmer than the corridor, Alvar?"

"Ramiro. Ramiro Alvar. Come into my study. Heating the entire tower is an impossible task, although, as you may have noticed, I'm terribly prone to the cold. And yet I wouldn't live anywhere else."

I followed him into his den, which couldn't have been more different from the room he'd taken Estíbaliz and me into the day before. The tones were dark red and gray; the style more modern, yet welcoming, suggesting the decorator had impeccable taste. A sumptuous armchair invited hours of peaceful reading, an oasis in that isolated tower. Several large books lay on the huge desk. *Notes on the Seven Divisions* by Alfonso X lay alongside Marcus Aurelius's *Meditations*. The walls were lined with bookshelves that stretched to the ceiling. There were also framed pieces of parchment.

I walked over to one of them.

"Those are the privileges and concessions granted to Lord Nograro by Ferdinand the Fourth in 1306," he explained. "You see that metal insignia? That's the royal seal: a quartered shield emblazoned with two castles and two lions rampant. On the back is a figure in relief. It's difficult to see, but it's the king on horseback. It's only a copy. Documents this old are extremely valuable, so the originals are kept in the Historical Archives of Álava, in Vitoria."

I tried to decipher the text.

"Is this Spanish? I can't understand a word of it."

He smiled timidly.

"It takes practice. For example, this passage says: 'To guarantee the lineage will pass to men of honor, I may be neither imprisoned nor condemned.' This is our private family library. It's where I keep all our records: wills, prenuptial agreements, dowries, concessions, proof of nobility, lawsuits, disputes, and grievances. But enough of that. Will you tell me the reason for your visit?"

"I'm friendly with the editor at Malatrama. He told me you two collaborated once. An exhibition at the Town Hall in Ugarte or something?"

"Yes. They needed permission to reproduce some images, and he asked for my help. Pruden publishes a lot of this kind of material. Did something happen to him? Is that why you're here?"

"On the contrary, he's in perfect health. No, Alvar, that's not why I'm here. I'll be honest with you. The author of *The Lords of Time* sent Pruden the manuscript under a pseudonym, and, because you are well versed in the medieval period, he thinks you might be the author. What do you say to that?"

"It's Ramiro. Ramiro Alvar," he corrected again. "And I can assure you, I didn't ask him to publish that novel. I swear on my family's honor that this is the first time I've seen this or any other copy of the book. I don't deny having read some of it today or that I'm familiar with the events, and some of the characters, described. But I didn't write it. What makes him think it was me? There are hundreds of authors or historians who could have written the book."

"I'm going to be up-front with you again," I said, "because I don't like lies. Pruden received an e-mail with the manuscript attached, and our technical team traced the message to this tower."

"What?"

I could see his incredulity, his bewilderment. His expression bordered on primal fear.

"Did you send him the manuscript?"

"Of course not. I didn't write the novel, much less ask him to publish it. I don't—"

"Yes, I know, you don't need the money, that much is clear," I cut in.

"That isn't what I meant, it's not about money, that's not my excuse." He sighed in frustration. "It's just that I would never publish that particular story. You have to believe me."

He shrank back into his blanket. I wanted to fire a barrage of questions at him: Don't you remember going out last night with my colleague? Why aren't you wearing a cassock? Why are you suddenly sensitive to the cold? Of all the lies you've told, which weighs heaviest, which is the most ludicrous, which is filling you most with guilt?

Yet I chose to leave him be, to let him contemplate whatever it was that had scared him so much. I wanted him to guide me through his labyrinth of lies. I wanted to see what questions he chose to ask me.

"Inspector Unai . . ."

"Unai. Call me Unai," I said.

"Why would a police inspector come here to ask me about the authorship of a book? Has someone made a complaint? Is there a problem with the copyright?" he ventured.

"I don't think you understand. I'm with the Criminal Investigation Unit. I'm a profiler."

"You're a profiler. . . . Are you also a psychologist?"

"I have a degree in criminal psychology, but I'm not a psychologist."

"I did a correspondence course in psychology. I also hold a number of degrees—in history, law, and economics. They are subjects I thought might help me in handling my family legacy. I try to manage the day-to-day running of the estate. And I think I do a good job. I enjoy it. But that's not why you're here. Criminal Investigation? What happened?"

"A few days ago in Vitoria, a businessman was killed. The cause of death was very unusual: he was poisoned with cantharides, a medieval aphrodisiac. Yesterday, two missing sisters were discovered walled up in an apartment in the Old Quarter of Vitoria. The elder sister died of starvation. Her younger sister is in intensive care."

Ramiro Alvar doubled over, clasping his stomach.

"Two young girls? I don't understand. Why would anyone want to kill two young girls?" he whispered. The question wasn't even directed at me. "I'm sorry, death sickens me. You'll have to bear with me a moment. . . ."

"Naturally."

I waited patiently. For a few seconds, he was lost in grief. I would have sacrificed all twenty-two of my daughter's teddy bears to see inside his head just then. I wanted to take his picture, but I couldn't think of an excuse to pull out my phone.

"So someone is murdering people using medieval methods," he said at last.

"That's one angle we're pursuing," I conceded.

"All I can tell you is that I didn't write the novel, I didn't contact the publisher, and I didn't kill anyone. I imagine you'll need me to provide an alibi, which could be difficult. I basically work alone here. I don't know when the deaths occurred, but Claudia will be able to account for my whereabouts during the times she was here. I have occasional visits from relatives, who might also be able to assist with your inquiries. Then there's the mayor, the councilors, and my neighbors in Ugarte. . . . I don't know. You're welcome to whatever you need."

"All right. I'll come back in a few days, and we'll clear up all these questions. That's all for today."

He nodded with relief, and we went downstairs in silence. He seemed to be carrying the weight of the world on his dark-red blanket.

"Unai," he said when we reached the entrance, placing his hand on my forearm. It felt more like a cry for help than a gesture of complicity. "I'm sorry, deeply sorry about these deaths. I wish you good luck with the investigation."

This Ramiro Alvar bore little resemblance to the impish priest Estíbaliz had gone carousing with. His mouth was taut, his lips pressed together to suppress secrets he feared he might blurt out during our casual conversation.

He had day-old stubble when the day before he had been clean-shaven. And that soft voice—it apologized for existing, for taking up space. I thought I saw a pleading look when I left, as though he were saying, *Don't abandon me here alone.* I'd never seen anyone so vulnerable.

To this day, I'm still not sure if what I saw in those blue eyes was a cry for help or a warning.

As I walked back to my car, I was aware of his eyes on my back. He was watching me from his lookout. I sat behind the wheel and dialed my partner's number.

"Estí, are you okay to talk?"

"This isn't the first time I've stayed out all night. I'm at the hospital with Nieves and Grandfather. She's doing fine. She asked about you."

"I'm on my way. Can you step outside the room for a minute? We need to talk about work."

I heard the sound of the door closing and Estíbaliz's agitated breath as she walked along the hallway.

"Okay, I'm alone now. Where were you this afternoon? You weren't picking up your phone. Did you have any interesting interviews?"

"Very. I've been with Alvar in his tower. But first I wanted to ask, did you get anything out of him last night? Did he take any drugs?"

"Not as far as I know. I only lost sight of him when he went to the bathroom. And he didn't seem to know anybody, so it's clear he doesn't normally go out in Vitoria."

"Did he drink?"

"A few glasses of wine. To appease me more than anything."

"Just a few?"

"Just a few," she repeated.

"Is he a habitual drinker, do you think?"

"No. He drank lots of water and made several trips to the bathroom. I think he wanted to be in control at all times, although he played along whenever I offered to buy him a drink. But I never saw him drunk or even tipsy. He was always in control. Constantly on alert, observing everything."

"Just to be clear," I forced myself to ask, "you did this for work, right? Are you luring him out of his comfort zone to see if he's behind these murders? Or is this personal? Should I not butt in?"

"Are you?"

"Am I acting like your big brother? No way. You can take care of yourself, and I'm not going to question your taste. I realize he has . . ."

"Charisma?"

"He's the king of charisma, and he's also handsome, seductive, attractive," I said.

She snorted. "Should I book the two of you a room with a view?"

"Don't be stupid. All I'm saying is that I can see why you might be attracted to him."

"I didn't say I was."

"No, you didn't."

"Will you tell Alba?" she asked.

"As a friend, she'd understand. As your boss, she might think you were being unprofessional because we're in the middle of an investigation. But no, I don't want to give her more to worry about, she's got enough on her plate with Nieves, and the case."

"So you'll keep my secret for now?"

"Even if it means lying to my boss, my partner, and the mother of my child?"

"Yes," she said vehemently, although there was a touch of guilt in her voice. Guilt was present in our whole conversation. We both felt it.

"You already know the answer. Yes, of course I'll keep your secret," I said eventually. "But only because it's you. I don't want to lie to Alba, but I'll do it for you. Just don't make a habit out of putting me in this position, because I hate this feeling."

"You still haven't told me what you were doing at the tower."

"Finishing what you started, observing him in his own territory after you enticed him away. What would you say if I told you he doesn't remember anything about last night, or yesterday? In fact, he didn't even recognize me."

"You're kidding me!" she exclaimed.

"He wasn't wearing his cassock. He looked dreadful, puffy eyes, five-o'clock shadow. He said he was tired. I swear he thinks he had a bad night's sleep. And he was puzzled about the novel. He didn't remember me leaving it behind yesterday; yet he seemed reluctant to return it. I almost felt sorry for him, because he kept looking at it like it was a holy object. He became quite upset when I told him about the deaths, but, curiously, he didn't ask the victims' names.

I'd say the incident with the two sisters bothered him the most. Oh, and by the way—he's a genius. He has degrees in law, history, economics, and . . . psychology. Interestingly, he said everything he studied helped him manage the family's legacy."

"Hold on, Kraken, stop bombarding me with information. I'm a little slow today. I can't take it all in. Are you saying our suspect is an amnesiac?"

"I have no idea, Estí. No idea whatsoever."

15

SAINT AGATHA'S EVE

DIAGO VELA

Winter, the Year of Our Lord 1192

Night was falling by the time I passed through the North Gate and hurried toward one of the oldest houses on Rúa de las Pescaderías.

People were making merry amid the hustle and bustle of the snow-sprinkled cobbled streets. Young maidens wearing cone-shaped wimples collected eggs from the chicken coops to place in their baskets.

The young men laughed as they rehearsed their songs, tapping their long hazel canes on the cobbles, as if the sticks they'd plucked from the hills would give them the courage they needed for Saint Agatha's Eve. They were even more excited and eager than the young women.

I rapped on the old, studded wooden door with the knocker, but there was no answer. When I grew tired of waiting for someone to bid me enter, I pushed the door open and whistled. She would already know it was me. I'd climbed those stairs many times. I shook the snow from my boots and stepped inside.

The corners of the stairwell were full of shadows, and once again my hand went to the dagger at my waist, an involuntary gesture from my time as a soldier.

She was sitting in a corner next to the window, watching the celebration in the street below. Her toothless mouth curved in a smile when she saw me.

"Grandmother Lucía . . ."

"Diago, Diago, my boy," she murmured.

Her voice was faint and it trembled. She had aged over the past two winters, and that worried me. Each time I saw her, I wanted to believe time had stood still, but that wasn't true. I remembered her with gray hair and crooked teeth, but both her hair and her few remaining teeth had fallen away, like leaves from a walnut tree after the first frost.

Her back was even more bowed, forcing her head almost to her stomach. She was spinning on a finely crafted wheel made for her by Lupo, the cabinetmaker. The sum of her possessions were the wheel, a narrow bed, a chair, and a trunk where she kept her meager trousseau—a summer petticoat perhaps, or a pair of sandals for when she wanted to venture out.

I went over to the empty chair Grandmother Lucía always kept next to her.

The townsfolk of Victoria visited her almost every day. They brought her apples and turnips, and she listened patiently and sympathetically as they shared their problems and disputes, sins they wouldn't speak of even in the confessional. They knew that she had seen too many things in her hundred and fifty years to pass judgment.

"I've brought chestnuts from Héctor. I'll roast them while we sit," I said, drawing near the hearth. I leveled the coals with a poker, pulled out my dagger, and began to prick the chestnuts before placing them on the embers.

"I'm the only one who never believed you were dead," she said joyously, her mottled hands holding mine in a firm grip.

"The warmth feels good, Grandmother," I declared, sitting back down beside her.

She wasn't my grandmother, yet she had always been there for me. There wasn't a single person in Villa de Suso who didn't think of her as Grandmother.

"Are those lardy cakes I smell?" she asked, cooing as though I were a child.

Instinctively I raised my head. The sweet aroma of yeasty dough wafted up the staircase, reminding me of all the comforts I had missed in my two long years away.

"It's me, Grandmother Lucía!" a voice called from downstairs.

"Tell her to come up. I get hoarse if I have to shout."

The feeble light coming from the hearth and the candle at the window weren't sufficient to illuminate the shadow bearing the delicious-smelling cake.

"Are you roasting chestnuts?"

"Alix de Salcedo?" I asked, looking at the three peaks of her wimple. One steeple was for married women, two were for those twice widowed. Three were for women who had buried three husbands.

I rose to offer her my seat, and she accepted.

"Don't tell Grandmother that I sometimes remove my wimple," she whispered, smiling as she walked past me. Then she spoke up so the old woman could hear: "Sire, will you join our feast? They say the more the merrier."

How could I decline? I pulled up the trunk and sat opposite them.

"Is Grandmother Lucía really your grandmother?" I asked.

"My grandmother's grandmother, actually. She says she was a girl when they built the town walls, during the reign of Alfonso the Battler. By my count, she is more than a hundred and sixty years old."

"Jaun Belaco, your great-grandfather," Grandmother Lucía began. She smiled, and I could see the cake in her toothless gums. "He paid for the wall using money from the forge. He hired two stonemasons from Estella, along with forty laborers and ten women.

Carpenters, herdsmen, journeymen . . . They were hired by the day. Those who brought a beast earned twenty-two ducats; those who didn't were paid only seven. I brought water from the well, and they paid me four ducats for it, as a maid. The wall took ten years to complete. Many of the workers settled here, and Villa de Suso swelled in numbers—Graciana de Ripa, Pero de Castresana, Bona de Sarasa . . . Some of the youth who'll court you tonight are descended from these men, Alix. What a pity the count died in his prime. I was a mere slip of a girl, but I was in love with him, and I wept bitterly when he passed. He cared for everyone; in those days there were only two hundred of us in the village, and we were all related. You look just like him, Alix. The same blue eyes, and the same nose."

Alix lowered her gaze, holding back a smile when Grandmother mentioned her nose. If this was a joke, it was lost on me.

"Why do I have no recollection of you before I left town two years ago?"

"I was sixteen, sire, and a late bloomer. I've changed a good deal in two summers."

"Two summers and three spouses?" I said without thinking, and regretted it instantly. "Forgive me. You must be weary of speaking about such matters."

"Indeed, I know what they say about women like me: 'A healthy widow should be married, buried, or immured.' "

"I've never approved of that saying. What fool mocked you for losing three husbands?"

"More than one, but no matter. And I suppose I'd prefer to tell you myself before you hear it elsewhere. I was married to Liazar Díaz, a young man my age. He owned the bakery on Rúa de las Tenderías and insisted on weighing out the sacks of rye himself, even though we hired a boy to do it. He was full of vigor, never grew tired. One morning I found him in the grain store, writhing on the ground as though he were possessed by a demon. It was Saint Anthony's fire.

I tended to him, and told no one but Grandmother Lucía. Then he started to see ships sailing in the streets and trees climbing Los Montes Altos. Your cousin Gunnarr tried to comfort me, explaining that the rye in the grain store must have been contaminated with ergot. He said he had seen some Norman warriors ingest it to become frenzied, have visions like the saints, and strike fear into the hearts of their enemies." She gritted her teeth.

Grandmother Lucía could tell the memory still pained Alix and clasped her hand.

"I was heartbroken when Liazar died. I kept myself busy by tending the ovens. But I was with child, and when his brother, Esteban, came a-courting two years ago this very night, on Saint Agatha's Eve, we soon wed. I continued with the bakery. Another tragedy followed on the heels of the last, and the sweating sickness took him. He became bedridden until finally he could no longer breathe. The shock caused me to lose the child, and I almost lost my love of baking as well. But then Ximeno Celemín came along. He was a blacksmith at Lyra Vela's forge. We both lived with ovens—I baked bread while he made nails and horseshoes. But six months ago a fire broke out. Some say the straw was set alight on purpose by the Mendozas, who live on Rúa de la Çapatería, and left to spread in the south wind. Ximeno was burned alive. Afterward Lyra asked me to be head blacksmith, like my father before me. Since then I've been in charge of the forge."

"Whenever tragedy strikes in this city, someone points the finger at those outside the walls," said Grandmother Lucía wistfully. "Those accursed walls. Why don't you undo your grandfather's labors and pull them down?"

"The walls protect us."

"From whom?"

"Enemies on the outside."

"But we've never been attacked."

"When the Vela family first came here, all we had was the forge, the well, and the big house. After the harvest, the Saracens would raid the settlement and carry off everything they could. The Velas would abandon their grain stores, take their children and the elderly, and hide in Los Montes Altos until the marauders left. Then one year the Saracens burned the houses to the ground. The Velas rebuilt everything. Where once the houses had been made of wood with straw roofs, they were now built with stone and were taller and stronger. But the walls were still necessary. The Saracens may no longer be a threat, at least while we have a king who believes in diplomacy, nor are the Castilians a threat under Alfonso the Noble, who respects our treaties. But this town needs a wall."

"And who will save us from killing one another, young Diago? Old Gasteiz against Nova Victoria? The nobility with their tariffs against the traders who only want to sell their wares in peace?"

"No one is killing anyone, Grandmother."

As she gazed out the window, the strands of hair on her head glinted in the glow of the torches.

"If you insist," she replied. Yet I heard *They are, and you know it*.

I turned away from her uneasily, and went to salvage the chestnuts from the fire. Alix rose to assist me.

"I wanted to ask you about the night I returned," I said in a hushed tone, as I poked the chestnuts with the fire iron. "Who was Count de Maestu entertaining at the wedding ceremony? I couldn't see their faces, and I was . . . distracted."

"The petty noblemen, the Ortiz de Zárate brothers, and Ruiz, Ruy de Maturana's son. Although the exchange seemed less than convivial. They've clashed a good deal at town council meetings lately."

"Ruy de Maturana was given a title?" I asked, bewildered.

"Only because he had seven sons in wedlock—the last was born shortly after you left. But almost all of them have died, only Ruiz is left."

"I'm grateful to you for the information and for the supper," I said, stooping to remove the chestnuts from the embers.

"I saw you enter the North Gate and head for Grandmother Lucía's house. I wanted you to feel joyful, if only for a moment. At Count de Maestu's funeral, you reeked of sorrow, so I resolved to prepare a little something to lift your spirits."

I looked up, surprised and embarrassed.

"You needn't trouble yourself on my account. I've wandered down many dusty roads, but now I'm home at last, surrounded by my family."

"And yet your heart is broken. I stood next to you at Onneca and your brother's marriage. I've never seen eyes as sad as yours. The eyes of a widower, like mine when I lost Liazar."

I stood up, ill at ease.

"I'm no widower, my dear Alix. And I wish my brother and his spouse a long life."

I put a few roasted chestnuts in her palm; her hand was accustomed to the heat of the forge and she didn't flinch. On the contrary, she drew closer, as though she had noticed something. A puzzled look flitted across her face.

"You've smelled of lavender ever since I met you, but today it's stronger than usual. Have you been rolling in it?"

I remembered the lavender next to my empty tomb, beside the abandoned mill. I remembered falling backward under Onneca's weight, and I buried the memory.

"Come on, Grandmother's still hungry," I said, attempting to change the subject.

"Wait, it isn't just lavender. I knew it, you smell of flour, rancid flour. And of—oh, my dear count!"

"What?"

"You have a woman's smell about you." She shook her head, as if I were beyond all hope.

She took another handful of chestnuts and returned to Grandmother Lucía's nook.

"I may have to console your brother with a venison pie," I thought she said as she walked away.

The old woman watched the youths milling outside as she gummed a piece of lardy cake.

With a mysterious smile, she opened her trunk and pulled out a skein of red wool. Then she produced a tiny knife from the folds of her skirt, cut three strands from the skein, tied a knot at one end and began to weave them together, holding the threads between her knees.

Alix and I said nothing about it. We three finished the chestnuts and discussed the recent snowfall.

We fell silent when the bells of Santa María began to chime. The din was to scare away the *gauekos*—the spirits of the night that even now spread its blanket over us. I had asked the parish priest, Vidal, a thin, biddable young fellow, to present the young bachelors with a pitcher of wine, as was the custom.

The youths began to sing. Every year, on Saint Agatha's Eve, they formed a circle around the well in the churchyard. As they began tapping their canes on the gravestones, the onlookers fell into reverential silence.

Alix was reluctant to go to the window, even though her grandmother's house was the first to be serenaded. We heard the earnest voices of the young bachelors:

"With God's approval
And that of the mayor,
We are out serenading
Doing harm to no one."

When the canes stopped tapping, a deathly silence filled the air. The bachelors were awaiting their reward.

"Would you take these chorizos down to them?" asked Alix.

"Won't you allow them to serenade you?" I responded, puzzled.

"I have no wish for another husband. I have renounced marriage."

"And yet you're still so young."

"I may be young in years, but I am old in grief. I have buried more husbands than most women in this town. If there were rumors after the second, by the time the third had died, many men began to look at me with fear and distrust. There was talk of branding me as a murderer, but many in Villa de Suso depend on the forge for their livelihood, even though some resent it. It kept me safe. Were I to marry and be widowed a fourth time, how long do you suppose it would take them to hang me? No, you go down to them while I stay here with Grandmother."

"Don't worry, I'll go. I was planning to join them, anyway," I added hurriedly.

"You? Are you sure?"

"Am I not a bachelor?" I grinned. "But I do need a favor from you. Come with me to the yard. I'll give them the chorizos. They won't see you."

"If that's all you're asking . . ." Alix said timidly. She shrugged and accompanied me downstairs, where I searched among the shadows for a stick that might serve as a cane.

We observed the young men from the dark stairwell. They waited outside with their torches. Mother Moon was full and the snow-laden streets reflected enough light to reveal their faces.

"Ruiz is the one with the bulging eyes, is he not?" I whispered in Alix's ear. I had not seen him since my departure.

"That's him, doubtless expecting to reap his reward in some hay barn tonight," Alix murmured, without looking at me.

A dozen or so youths were giggling in the street, debating whom to serenade next. Would it be María Bermúdez, or Sancha de Galaretta, the hosier's eldest daughter?

I stepped outside and presented the basket of chorizos. Several youths emptied the links of cured sausage into a large hamper, which by evening's end would be brimming with more sausages, bread, eggs, and rabbit meat.

"I'll join you," I declared, positioning myself alongside Ruiz de Maturana.

"My Lord Vela, I'm pleased that you've returned. Your absence was mourned by many here in the town," he remarked with a broad smile. Too broad, and too tense.

"I knew your father, a good man."

"Yes, he was a good man," he agreed, somewhat halfheartedly.

We gathered at the next house to sing, our canes keeping time, tapping the ground and leaving circular hollows in the snow.

"On Saint Agatha's night
When the bell doth ring,
We young men delight
To dance around and sing.

"As in days of yore
They were wont to do,
Going from door to door
Their promises to renew."

A ruddy-faced girl and her mother leaned out of the window on the first floor. It was Milia, the layer-out, who fetched candles to illuminate the church for the dead and brought bread for the offerings. She always had work, especially in the winter. Despite her grim occupation, she was a cheerful sort and seemed to find amusement in everything she did. Milia's daughter threw a loaf into the air, and the youths vied with one another to catch it and to thank the maiden for her contribution.

"Your father and I dealt with each other on occasion. Will you be taking over his affairs, I wonder?" I murmured in Ruiz's ear. We followed the serenade, laughing along with the others.

"What sort of affairs?"

"Questions of manhood. . . . I won't mince words: Do you have a pinch of Spanish fly?"

"I have but one."

"And I need two or three."

"Then I suggest you pay a visit to La Romana Inn."

"I've just come from there." I stopped in the middle of the street, while the other youths flocked toward the South Gate, unaware we were lagging behind.

"In which case I fail to see what you want from me," he said, shrugging. He began to whistle a tune unfamiliar to me.

"I want you to tell me what became of the other two pinches you purchased."

"I used them with a married lady whom I cannot name, lest her cuckold of a husband take a whip to me."

"You're lying. A single pinch is enough to fuel a man's ardor for two days and nights. Tell your next lie carefully, lad, for this is a grave matter."

"What do you care about my use of such powders?"

"I care very much if it transpires that you slipped the two missing pinches into Count de Maestu's goblet, causing his bowels to rupture."

A sinister smile spread across Ruiz's face. Indeed, the fellow seemed to have a continual smirk.

"You have no proof."

"I've seen it for myself. If necessary, I will open him up again for the council to see."

"Very well," he finally conceded. "I'm guilty of two sins: lust and greed. The truth is I do have two pinches in my possession; the third is at home. I simply did not wish to share them, lest tonight lead to further pleasure in the days to come. But you are my liege lord, and your sharp mind is legendary. I have failed to deceive you. I shall give you one of the pinches I have with me, and you can reward me generously later. Tonight I feel ready for anything. I doubt I shall need powders to bed the cutler's daughter."

He bade me hold his torch as we veered off toward an orchard that belonged to the yeoman Pero Vicia. Ruiz pulled a small leather pouch out of his doublet, drew closer to me, and whistled.

Too late, I understood the reason for his whistle.

He handed me the pouch. Although I was wary, I did not foresee his next move. Just as I discovered the pouch was empty, the accursed youth raised his cane and struck me in the groin.

I doubled over, winded, as two figures emerged from the shadows and began to beat me viciously. Once I was on the ground, Ruiz kicked me in the head. His two cohorts vanished behind me, while Ruiz fled toward the town wall. I lay sprawled in the middle of Rúa Tenderías.

I managed to stand. The wet snow had quenched the flame of the torch in my hand, but that same snow guided me to Portal de la Armería.

I followed Ruiz's path as best I could, my head spinning. One hand clutched my side, but the other grasped my cane; I was more than ready to use it.

I'll hunt down your father's killer, Onneca. The promise pushed me forward. My mind dwelled on Onneca, the powders, and Count de Maestu.

I could hear the reveling youth in the distance, but I took care to descend into the Armería district as silently as I could. I stayed alert to the slightest sound. I knew Ruiz could not have gone far.

The huge gate leading out of Villa de Suso to Camino de la Cruz Blanca and the village of Ali was shut, and no sentries were on the walk. They must have joined the young serenaders. I could expect no help from that quarter.

I approached the stairs to one of the gate's towers, and there Ruiz's footprints ended. As I lunged at the darkness with my cane, a dim figure emerged from the shadows and aimed a kick at my head. This time I ducked. The figure fled up the two flights of wooden steps along the side of the wall.

I set off in pursuit, despite my aching ribs and throbbing head.

"Stop, Ruiz!" I shouted, but he ignored me and ran along the ramparts until he reached the farthest tower.

Someone must have heard my pleas, for a sentry appeared, blocking Ruiz's way with his pikestaff.

Ruiz wheeled around, only to realize that he was trapped between us.

"Very well, I surrender!" he cried.

But as I drew near, he took a running jump and leaped from the wall.

It was a twenty-foot drop. Even though Ruiz could survive the fall, my injuries prevented me from following him. I raised my cane like a lance and aimed it at the rogue, who had rolled down the mound and risen to his feet.

Mother Moon came to my aid once again as I launched the wooden staff. It hit him square in the back and he fell forward, the breath knocked out of him.

"Open the gate quickly and come with me!" I ordered the sentry. "We must arrest Ruiz de Maturana and take him directly to the prison."

"On what charge, sire? Has he forced himself on yet another young girl this night?"

"You'll have to ask the townsfolk about that. No, I am accusing him of the murder of Count Furtado de Maestu."

16

SANTIAGO

UNAI

October 2019

"Oihana didn't make it," Estí announced as soon as I picked up the phone.

"She didn't?" I repeated, stunned.

More than a week had passed since we'd pulled Oihana out of the wall. I was on my way to the hospital to interview her. I'd been counting on her testimony, hoping she would be able to tell us something about her kidnapper.

"She fought to stay alive, but her body was too damaged. She suffered multiple organ failure. She was so dehydrated by the time she was discovered that there was a considerable chance she would've had brain damage if she survived. The doctors say the carbon dioxide she inhaled while immured killed her. I can't describe how helpless I feel right now," said Estíbaliz. Her words were heavy as stone.

I didn't have to see her to know how angry she was.

"Where are you?" I managed to say. I wasn't really in the mood to talk, either.

Two young girls trapped inside a wall.

The sick bastard.

"I'm in her room at Santiago Hospital. I stopped by to see how she was and found . . . this."

"Wait for me. I'm close by," I said. I didn't want to discuss this over the phone. "Send me a WhatsApp with the room number."

I quickened my pace on Calle Postas. Eventually, I made it to the hospital, a building with white arches and checkerboard tiles. Then Alba called.

"She's dead, Unai. I'm at the hospital," she whispered. She sounded strangely agitated; for once, she was more affected than I.

"I know, I know. I just found out. I'm downstairs. What's the room number?"

"They moved her into 317."

"I'm on my way up. I'll be right there."

We were all shocked when the victims turned out to be children. But this was the first case we had worked since Alba and I had become parents. No amount of training can give you the tools to deal with a child's death. I suppose you simply have to harden your heart.

I entered the room, expecting to see Estíbaliz and the girl's parents, but instead Alba was alone, sitting on a green leather sofa. She was devastated.

The body in the bed wasn't Oihana. It was Alba's mother, Nieves.

A pale lady, at peace with death. She died that way.

"What happened?" I asked.

"She had a massive stroke. There was nothing they could do." Alba pronounced the words slowly. She was repeating them, practicing, so she didn't forget. They would become her shield in a performance worthy of her mother's talents.

"Come here, I'm . . . I'm s-s-sorry. S-s-sorry." Something in my brain was short-circuiting. My Broca's aphasia was reappearing, like a nightmarish flashback.

I held Alba, moved by her indomitable strength. We had no need for words. We were two orphans on the front lines now, as Grandfather used to say. We were truly alone. Motherless and fatherless—alone.

I held her for a long time, but Alba was already far away.

Very far away.

What felt like lifetimes later—though my cell phone said it was only twenty minutes—Alba surfaced again. I listened to her frantic thoughts with the patience spouses have for each other.

"Do you know what my last conversation with my mother was about? She told me this hospital was founded by María Sarmiento, the wife of Fernán Pérez de Ayala. It was originally called Hospital de la Virgen del Cabello. The couple inherited a protective instinct for the city. Like you. You can't help it. If there's a murder in Vitoria, you won't be able to sit around twiddling your thumbs at the police station in Laguardia. It would drive you crazy. Do I have the right to ask you to renounce your identity? I don't want you to be frustrated with your life. I believe my mother found what made her happy in life. When I was little, she used to tell me, 'Be who only you can be. Do what only you can do.' No one else can do what Kraken does; no one else could have solved the double crime of the dolmen after twenty years—or the Water Rituals case. It's who you are; it's what you do best."

"Are you leaving me?" I whispered.

"No, but I can't force you to back my decision."

"I will back you all the way, Alba. How could I not? We're a couple. You aren't alone in this. Will you take Deba with you?"

She nodded. "If it's okay with you, I'll pick her up from the nursery and take her with me. I have a few days' bereavement leave. I'm putting Estíbaliz in charge of the investigation. You have your work cut out for you here: three murders, little evidence, and no obvious motive."

"I know."

"Will you come to see us every day?"

"It's only a fifty-minute drive. A fifty-minute drive won't keep us apart."

17

THE NEW CATHEDRAL

UNAI

October 2019

Midday. Nieves's funeral had just finished. I won't give any details. I'll keep Alba's suffering to myself. Estíbaliz was so upset, I had to stop her from kicking a derelict grave. Luckily, Alba didn't see. Alba read Maya Angelou's famous poem, "Still I Rise." Then she and Deba left for Laguardia. I headed to Vitoria with a specific destination in mind. I made my way to the steps of the New Cathedral, looking for a young skateboarder.

I counted nine of them, a big gang. Caps, hoods, piercings.

No sign of MatuSalem.

Matu was my unofficial IT consultant. He was my go-to person, only—and I mean *only*—when it was absolutely necessary. I would use him only if Milán ran up against a brick wall.

MatuSalem was prickly, morose, and foul-mouthed, and I had the greatest respect for him—not only because he was a young genius but also because his worldview was more sensible than that of most adults I knew. He'd managed to turn his life around after a foray into credit-card fraud landed him in jail at eighteen. There, Tasio Ortiz de Zárate, who had been convicted twenty years earlier for the double crime of the dolmen, had taken him under his wing. He made sure that no one touched the boy while he was in prison. MatuSalem had been loyal to Tasio ever since.

Matu was reluctant to do me favors, but he was the only hacker I had. My other contact in the hacking world, Golden Girl, had disappeared after the Water Rituals case was solved.

I sat on a bench next to an enormous yew in Florida Park, watching the skaters. The location brought back sad memories. I was on the verge of leaving when he appeared at the front of the cathedral. I hadn't seen him in more than two years, but he still looked like a kid. He was twenty-something now and still small, skinny, and smooth-faced. He looked like a manga cartoon, with his doe-like eyes and blue hair hidden under his signature white hoodie. I recognized his skateboard, too, with its image of the biblical patriarch Methuselah. Matu was also a good street artist and belonged to the Brush Brigade, a band of volunteers who decorated the city's walls with murals.

He noticed me from twenty yards away, even though I thought I was in a discreet hiding place. For MatuSalem, paranoia was an occupational hazard. He gestured at me, warning me not to approach.

I complied and sat on my bench watching pigeons strut around until I heard his youthful voice behind me.

"El Jardín Secreto del Agua."

Meekly, I obeyed. I was feeling amenable that day. I'd just buried my mother-in-law, and I was in no mood for an argument.

I crossed the park at a leisurely pace. People cycled and strolled past me: older residents with pushcarts, dogs taking their owners for a walk through the park's maze of towering trees. The world kept turning, indifferent to the hole Nieves had left in the lives of the handful of people I loved the most.

I entered the Jardín Secreto del Agua, a secluded garden. Hundreds of plants formed a mosaic at my feet.

After a while, MatuSalem appeared in his white hoodie, glancing over his shoulder.

"How many times have I told you I don't want to be seen talking to a cop?" he scolded in a whisper.

"I know, and I'm sorry to bother you, Matu, but I need you to find a name for me. It'll take you five minutes, and my team is taking forever."

"I wish you'd stop asking me for help. I always end up doing something illegal," he muttered.

"It's about the two girls."

"Which girls? The ones who were abducted?"

"I work for the Criminal Investigation Unit. What other girls could I possibly mean?"

"What happened to them? The only details in the news were that Estefanía was found dead and that her little sister died yesterday. I saw Fani around; my girlfriend sometimes hung out with her *cuadrilla*. It's all they talk about these days."

"Yes, of course, everybody here knows everybody else. Some bastard trapped them behind a wall in an apartment on Calle Cuchi. While you and I were going out for drinks, they were screaming for help just a few yards above our heads. But no one heard them—not you, not me, not even the neighbors. Certainly not Estefanía's friends, who probably walked right past the entrance to the building, right below the room's window. Oihana watched her big sister die of hunger and thirst and then had to live with her corpse in a twenty-square-foot space for days. When we found her, she was already too far gone. She couldn't talk. Only you can help us shed some light on this crime."

The harsh truth affected him, despite his characteristically cocky indifference. He swallowed hard a couple of times, and his chin was quivering.

"You think I could find this asshole?"

Could—the conditional. Matu was starting to entertain the idea of helping me. I turned up the pressure a notch.

"With a keystroke, I'm sure. Please, employ your superpowers to help poor Oihana and Fani."

Matu thrust his hands into his pockets and began kicking at some stones uneasily.

"What's it about?" he finally asked.

"The e-mail that triggered this inferno was sent from a specific location. I want to know everything about the sender. I want to stop him. I don't want more white coffins."

"You're messing with me, Kraken. I told you I don't want to get involved, but you make it impossible. You come here, flatter me, use me, and then go. I realize it's for a good cause, but you're the one who chose to be a cop, not me."

"What do you want?"

"You don't get it. I'm not playing hard to get, and I'm not bargaining with you. I'm not for sale. I'm saying no. I don't want this in my life."

"Me either. But sometimes people get killed, and if we all refuse to get involved, every psychopath who decides to hurt other people will have carte blanche. I won't let that happen."

Matu stood, stomped on the tail of his skateboard, and looked at me as though I were trying to sell him bad dope.

"No, Kraken. Don't ask me again. You choose to inhabit this dark world, but I don't. *Agur.*"

"*Agur,*" I replied, gritting my teeth.

It was amazing. This boy genius was giving me life lessons that I probably wouldn't learn on my own, even if I lived to be a hundred.

Frustrated, I left the garden and took the tram to the Lakua headquarters. I had a meeting I couldn't miss.

Half an hour later, we closed the door to the conference room. Estíbaliz had asked Milán, Peña, Muguruza, and Doctor Guevara to join us. Estíbaliz seemed to have regained her composure since

Nieves's funeral. She motioned for me to sit down, and then she kicked things off.

"As you're all aware, DSU Salvatierra is on bereavement leave and has left me in charge of our ongoing investigations. I've called this meeting so we can share our progress on Antón Lasaga's poisoning and on Operation Frozen, which has taken a devastating turn. Let's start with Antón Lasaga. Agent Peña, tell us what you have."

"The judge signed a warrant that lets us monitor Lasaga's five children, including their cell phone usage. We've traced their movements and the calls they made in the days before and after their father's death, and we found nothing suspicious. We paid special attention to Andoni, the eldest son, because of the accusations he made against his sister, Irene, but he has no prior drug convictions, nor has he had any contact with known criminals. He's just a playboy who has run up a few debts. Irene's alibi also checks out—she was working all day. We spoke to the dozen or so close friends on the list she provided, but, again, nothing out of the ordinary came up. Lasaga was focused on his work and occupied with his routine."

"Sergeant Martínez," I asked Milán, "was he involved in any land or property disputes in Valdegovía?"

"I checked. There's nothing on him or on his company. His children confirmed it."

"Did you also look into his surname?" I asked.

"I didn't have to; his daughter gave us a copy of their family tree. There are no distant ancestors from Álava, and none of the surnames that appear in the novel are in their genealogy, if that's what you're asking, Inspector. However, I did find something else interesting. I spoke to the director of the Natural Science Museum in la Torre de Doña Otxanda. It looks as if the thieves didn't just steal the two hundred insects, they had also tampered with other display cabinets. The museum staff is taking inventory to see if other specimens are missing. The director sent the delivery notice for the stolen insects." Milán placed a document in a plastic sleeve on the table. Attached to it was an orange Post-it note with the word *here* written in capital letters next to a big arrow.

"*Lytta vesicatoria,*" Estíbaliz read aloud. "Blister beetle. So we know that a couple of weeks ago, someone stole the raw material for a rare poison that was used to kill Antón Lasaga. It might give us a lead, but I doubt the judge will agree that it's solid evidence. Whoever stole these insects isn't necessarily our murderer. Also, when we investigated the theft, we didn't find any suspects. Doctor Muguruza, your team cross-referenced the prints you found at the scene and there were no matches with our database. Isn't that correct?"

The head of forensics nodded.

"In other words, this case is still wide open. We've made zero progress."

"I might have a line we can follow," Peña offered, raising a tentative finger.

"Go ahead," said Estíbaliz.

"A couple of hours before the book launch, an event for Álava-based businesses took place at Villa Suso Palace. Antón Lasaga's PA confirmed that his boss attended. I'm just waiting for the organizers to send me a list of the other guests. The most interesting part is that they were served cocktails and canapés."

"That's significant. The timing matches when we suspect he ingested the cantharides, and his stomach contents are exactly what you'd expect: smoked salmon, caviar, porcini mushrooms . . ." Doctor Guevara said, reading the list from her report out loud.

"So it's possible someone laced one of the canapés with poison," said Estíbaliz.

"In a mushroom vol-au-vent, for instance," the pathologist said, nodding. "He could have bitten into it and swallowed, even though the sauce tasted unpleasant."

"Ugh!" said Milán, wrinkling her nose. "You know what it tastes like?"

"There aren't many references to it in forensic literature, but I dug up a fragment of an account that mentions Germana de Foix, Ferdinand the Second's second wife. Historians depict her as a passionate eighteen-year-old. Maybe she just wanted the aging king to give her an heir before he died. Germana refers to 'those nauseating black powders the king takes in his beverages.' That suggests it tasted bad but was not intolerable."

"We still don't know whether the poisoner specifically targeted Antón Lasaga, or whether killing any of the entrepreneurs would have suited his or her purpose," I said. "What we do know is we have three murders with an unusual modus operandi. The similarities between these crimes and the ones described in the novel are too obvious for us to ignore."

"What if the killer targeted a random businessman, but at a specific time and location?"

"Very good, Peña," I said encouragingly. "Why might that be?"

"To link the death to the novel, of course."

"Who could have laced the canapé with poison?" I asked the room.

"Any of the kitchen or catering staff hired for the day," said Estíbaliz.

"One of the cleaners, or the janitor at Villa Suso," suggested Milán.

"Someone dressed as a nun?" said Peña.

"And why would someone dress up as a Dominican nun?" I prodded.

"Because the medieval market offers the perfect excuse to come in a disguise, and with a wimple, no one would be able to see their face," he replied.

"Good, but let's not make assumptions yet. Any of the other guests could have laced the canapé," I pointed out. "We need a list, Peña."

"Didn't you go to Nograro Tower to ask about the nun's habit?" interjected Milán.

"We did, but the costumes were part of a temporary exhibition and are no longer on display," said Estíbaliz. "But I'll go back to the tower and ask the owner about it again. And, since I'm sure you've noticed that the e-mail sent to Malatrama's publisher came from Nograro, you should know that both Inspector Ayala and I interviewed Alvar several times. He denies sending the e-mail, just as he denies having written *The Lords of Time*."

"Martínez, did you find out if Ramiro Alvar de Nograro has a cell phone registered in his name?" I asked.

"I checked all the service providers. He's probably the only person on the planet who doesn't have a cell phone," she said.

"What about Diego Veilaz, Ltd.?" asked Peña.

"It's a joke. The publisher signed without checking the register. It doesn't exist. The tax number is fake."

"Then we can assume that the author has no interest in making money from the novel. The aim was to publish the text," I said. "Inspector Gauna, when you next speak with the lord of the tower, ask him if he donates to the Museum of Natural Sciences."

"I will," she nodded. "We're going to keep looking into him, but we need to focus on other lines of investigation as well. We need something we can bring to the judge. Okay, now let's move on to the two sisters."

"One last thing," said Milán. "Malatrama's publisher gave us a list of the twenty-eight graphic artists he usually employs. I've run background checks, and I'm currently getting their alibis for the afternoon of the book launch. Nothing so far."

"Thanks, Detective Martínez. Great work," said Estíbaliz. We all suppressed a smile when Milán blushed. "Moving on. Doctor Guevara, what can you tell us about the autopsies on the Nájera sisters?"

"We found no evidence of sexual violence. The older sister died six days into their captivity, and her body wasn't moved postmortem. She died where we found her. The younger girl had a cut on her arm, made by a knife or another sharp object that wasn't found at the scene. The blood found in the family home probably comes from that wound."

"Then we can safely say that they were trapped behind the wall at the end of August, before the novel was published," I said. "This isn't a copycat killer who was inspired by the book. And it isn't someone who abducted the girls after poisoning Antón Lasaga and decided to improvise by walling them up to make it look like the work of a serial killer. This is the best indication we have so far that the killer knew what was in the novel before it was published. That rules out the average reader as a suspect. But it doesn't help us move forward."

"I have something interesting to report," Peña piped up. "I spoke to Oihana's father yesterday, after he was informed of her death. He wasn't as upset as when we found his daughters, probably because he was either prepared for the worst or just emotionally exhausted. He told me he had a family locator app on his phone so he always knew where his elder daughter was. Remember, we found her phone in her bedroom. Either her kidnapper left it behind so she couldn't be traced, or the girl did so her father wouldn't know where she was going that night."

"Or how they vanished from the apartment," I said. "Don't forget, the big mystery here is how they got out through the main entrance when there's no sign of them on the CCTV footage from either the local stores or the forty-three traffic cameras covering the area. Here is an aerial photograph of the Medieval Quarter," I said, putting a Google Earth image on the projector. "Crime scene one, where the girls were abducted, is on the same block as crime scene two, where they were found. Look closely and you'll see that both buildings have a skylight. Perhaps the kidnapper took them across the roofs to avoid being caught on camera. I want you to contact the construction company hired for the La Cuchillería job and ask for a list of employees who have worked on the apartment. Find out if the company does any construction on tall buildings. We can't rule out a sexual motive just because the girls weren't assaulted, so do a background check on the employees who have experience using harnesses. Have any of them been reported for harassment or sexual violence? It's possible the culprit intended to rape them in the apartment, but things got out of hand, maybe they screamed or fought. There were two of them, after all. He may not have intended to kill them. Walling them in may have been an afterthought. And we can't get too caught up in the case's similarities to the novel. We need to focus on the physical evidence: the plastic bags, for instance. What can you tell us about them, Doctor Muguruza?"

"There's no evidence that the bags were dragged across a roof, but the girls were certainly put inside them. We're cross-checking other bags found at the site; interestingly, these two are different. They're white with a red stripe at the base, but there are no other identifying features from a manufacturer or a sales outlet."

"Milán, Peña, I want you to check with all the companies that supply materials to DIY stores and construction firms," said Estíbaliz. "Anything you find, send to forensics so they can run a cross-check. Someone had to make them, and someone had to sell them."

Two days later, I got an unexpected message: *Send me all the info. But this is the last time you involve me in your work.*

MatuSalem. He'd backed down. Within minutes I had e-mailed him everything he needed. The case was stalling, and I knew we had to make progress somehow.

Twenty-four hours later, he got back to me: *I know who sent it. This evening at 7:00 in the New Cathedral crypt.*

I was feeling optimistic, so I was as punctual as a suitor on his first date. I descended the deserted steps to the crypt and scanned the polished pews for my contact. He hadn't arrived yet.

I paced restlessly between the bare altar and some bouquets of wilted flowers nearby. They smelled faintly of death. Dead flowers always reminded me of funeral wreaths.

Time passed. My phone remained stubbornly silent. Finally it began to buzz, and I half expected to hear Matu apologizing, even though that wasn't his style. But it was Estíbaliz. Since I was alone, and there was nobody to chastise me for taking a call in a place of worship, I answered.

"What's the matter, Estí?"

"Bad news, Kraken. A boy's been found."

"A boy?"

"Yes, in the River Zadorra, near Gamarra," she said. "He's inside a barrel that someone threw into the water. But that's not the weird part: the barrel also contained a snake, a dog, a cat, and a rooster. What the hell is going on?"

"Dammit, you haven't read the novel yet. What the hell are you doing every night? I told you it was a priority."

"Are you listening?" she shouted. "I'm telling you a child has been drowned in a river, in a barrel with four animals, and you say I should read a book."

"Yes, Estíbaliz! Yes! If you'd read the novel, you'd know that this boy is the victim of a medieval punishment called *poena cullei*—'penalty of the sack.'"

18

THE COUNT'S CHAMBER

DIAGO VELA

Winter, the Year of Our Lord 1192

"He's burning up, and the fever shows no signs of weakening. The wound on his side is festering. I doubt he'll survive. They say it is the Vela's fate to die young," the elderly physician whispered to a woman holding a candle who was peering down at me.

I awoke in my bed, dazed, with a searing pain in my back.

Onneca waited for the physician to leave, then sat on the bed we had often shared in happier circumstances.

My chamber was large and the fire in the hearth kept the stone walls warm. But when I looked into her eyes, I found coldness.

"We were together in the old mill, you had every opportunity to tell me and yet you said nothing about my father having been murdered."

She was reproaching me. She sounded angry and hurt.

"They were suspicions, nothing more," I managed to say, even though I could barely speak and knew I was on the verge of delirium. "I was on my way to La Romana Inn to make inquiries when I bumped into you."

"There was a time when we shared everything, even our suspicions. Especially our suspicions."

"We were betrothed then, nothing stood in our way. You are my sister-in-law now, and Nagorno will always come between us."

Onneca rose and pummeled the wall with her fist.

"I've had no word from my sisters since Father died. I wrote to inform them of his death, hoping they might leave their immurement, but they didn't attend his funeral. I am alone, Diago. Without my sisters, and without you. I have no one."

Just as I was mustering the strength to respond, Nagorno walked in.

It was hard to tell how long he had been eavesdropping. He was as stealthy as a reptile.

"How determined you are that I should become Count Vela, Brother," he offered as a greeting. "Are you planning to face many more attempts on your life?"

I closed my eyes, too weak to give a worthy rejoinder.

"Leave us alone, dear wife, this is no place for you," he ordered Onneca.

Onneca rose to her feet again. She was taller than my brother, and one of the few women who did not submit to him when he raised his voice.

"On the contrary, I'm staying. Your brother has a lot of explaining to do. What's this about my father being poisoned, Diago?" Onneca drew closer, holding my gaze.

I was incapable of sitting up. My body was burning with fever and my head was spinning as if I were on one of Gunnarr's ships.

"I recognized the signs as soon as I saw the body. I know it was a sacrilege, but I hope you will forgive me. I cut him open and rubbed the skin of a rabbit against his viscera. The beast's skin immediately blistered. Your father was killed with two pinches of Spanish fly. He was butchered."

Nagorno cast Onneca a sidelong glance. She clenched her fists and turned to hide her face.

"Have you proof?" she asked, still averting her eyes.

"The rabbit is in that trunk. It will be much decayed by now, but it will still serve. If necessary, we can disinter your father to confirm my story. Given the recent frosts, his body will be well preserved."

"I trust that won't be necessary," she murmured.

"We'll need witnesses at the trial," I continued. My voice was a whisper, but I think they could hear me. "Alix de Salcedo assisted me during the experiment and will support my findings. Nagorno, go to La Romana Inn. The landlady's son sold Ruiz three pinches of Spanish fly some days ago."

"Will the boy talk?"

"I expect so," I replied. "Ruiz has mistreated him and his aunts. Besides, Lope knows his clientele will grow once the townsmen hear that his powders work."

"Did you see your attackers?" Nagorno asked. "I assume there were more than one, for I've seen you in a fight."

"This was no fight. We were serenading on Saint Agatha's Eve. I was not expecting the scoundrel to set upon me, and my guard was down. But you're right, he whistled and two men appeared. They attacked me from behind. All I could see were their boots and sticks, and then Ruiz kicked me in the head."

"Whoreson!" my brother hissed. "And I defended him at council meetings."

"So I was told," I replied, "but I wanted to hear it from your own lips. Why did you do that when the family has such a bad reputation?"

"He's a nobleman. A petty one, but a nobleman all the same. A town made solely of artisans and traders cannot thrive. We need noblemen from the surrounding settlements to build their homes here, to spend their money. Without that, our walled town will be forgotten, lost to the mists of time."

"You should choose your allies more wisely, Nagorno! Look where your association with him has led," I shouted, wincing from the pain. "Look what they've done to your wife!"

"They did this because, like you, Count de Maestu sided with the artisans and traders. Pure folly. Now they've turned their sights on you. You must tread carefully."

"I refuse to tread carefully on the streets I helped pave. We must speak of the trial. What have you to say, dear sister-in-law?"

Onneca listened to the daughters of the Mendozas and the Iruñas as they sat spinning in her parlor, discussing openly what men dared not. Women pacified, poured water on the fire, before tempers became inflamed.

"The traders believe God should decide whether Ruiz is to burn and are demanding trial by boiling water or red-hot iron. Tempers are frayed. Before your return, my father was their main champion on the council."

"That is impossible," I said. "Eleven years ago, King Sanchez outlawed trial by ordeal in the jurisdiction of Victoria."

"Is my father, your faithful friend, to receive no justice, then?" cried Onneca.

"Justice will be done. You have my word, sister-in-law. However, we must uphold the law, for the king's lieutenant and one of his coroners from Tudela are sure to attend the trial, and they will report back to him. We cannot take the risk."

"My brother is right, dear wife."

"What will the sentence be, a simple reparation, blood money?" asked Onneca, agitated. "My father's life was worth more than five thousand ducats."

"There is another matter," interjected Nagorno. "According to our charter, any man who unsheathes his sword inside the town with the intent of wounding a fellow citizen shall forfeit his right hand."

"I saw no sword unsheathed," I said.

"Judging from that stain on your cloak, I beg to differ."

I was unaware of the blood oozing from my side. It was soaking into the white bearskin cloak Gunnarr had brought me from Friesland, turning it red.

Nagorno raised the cloak, exposing my bruised, naked body, which was swathed in a bloody bandage.

"Onneca, help me lift him. I want to examine the wound on his back."

Onneca and I looked at each other uneasily.

"You won't see anything you've not already seen, Wife. This isn't the time to play the pious lady. Help me lift your brother-in-law, and let us take a look beneath these bandages."

Merely being upright increased my lightheadedness, and just before I toppled over onto Onneca, I smelled the delicious aroma of meat stew. Alix de Salcedo had appeared in the doorway holding a meat pie, and she hurried to help my brother and his wife so that I would not fall to the floor.

"What are you doing? I thought the count was on his deathbed! Whose idea was it to make him sit up like this?" Alix asked, bewildered.

"You two, slip your arms under his shoulders," Nagorno ordered, undaunted, "while I remove these bandages."

"Will nobody cover this man's shame?" protested Alix. "I was told the priest from Santa María is on his way to give extreme unction. If he finds the three of us with the count naked, we'll be accused of fornicating."

"All the more reason to make haste. Besides, you wear a three-coned wimple, so this can't be the first pair you've seen," my brother rejoined.

I was in too much pain to feel discomfited by the fact that I was naked and being propped up by two women—Onneca on my right and Alix on my left.

Nagorno began to peel away the bandages, which had stuck to my skin in places. He wet a new piece of cloth in the washbasin and dabbed my swollen flesh.

"You see people's colors. What shade am I now?" I whispered

to Alix. My brother's ministrations were causing me to see stars and the firmament.

"You are still blue, but a deathly blue. Life is draining from you. Eat some of my wild boar and lavender pie. It will give you strength," she whispered, as Onneca pretended she wasn't listening.

"I'm too weak to eat."

"Grandmother Lucía insisted I kill a wild boar and bake this pie for you. She said she would feed it to you herself if you refused."

"You killed a wild boar?"

"My third husband was a blacksmith, he made traps. He left me enough to kill an army."

"Well, if Grandmother Lucía has ordained that I should live, then I must force myself," I said, smiling as best I could.

"Here's the proof," my brother declared in his hoarse voice. "A long, straight gash. This isn't the work of a dagger. This cut was made by a sword."

"Serenaders on Saint Agatha's Eve, armed with swords? Who would be so foolhardy as to violate the decree against unsheathing them within the city walls?" asked Alix.

She looked at me, alarmed. She was struggling to hold me upright and had draped my arm around her shoulder. Her face was pressed against my chest.

"What if the two men weren't serenaders, Diago? What if they planned to attack you all along?"

19

THE RIVER ZADORRA

UNAI

October 2019

When I arrived at the Gamarra Bridge, the area was already cordoned off, and forensics had started to process the scene. I had no idea who had called the press, but two reporters were talking in front of a camera about a case I hadn't even figured out yet. A boy. It felt all wrong.

Peña greeted me, his hand shaking like he was playing a tambourine. I guess murdered children made him sick, too. A boy in a barrel thrown into the river didn't sound like manslaughter to me. If this wasn't premeditated, then God should take another look at the world. But God wasn't paying much attention during those autumn days, it seemed. He was too busy blowing dead leaves around the city, strewing the path to insanity.

The stone bridge was raised on cement blocks that spanned the River Zadorra, like towers on top of a wall made of water. The river was flowing quickly, its green waters reflecting the weeping willows on its banks. Their fronds drooped to waist level, partially obscuring the scene.

Two police divers had taken the boy and the sodden corpses of several animals out of the barrel. The bodies lay on a piece of plastic sheeting.

"I've never seen anything like it, boss," whispered Peña. "A drowned boy. He was dead when they took him out of the barrel. He was stuffed in there with a dog—"

"A cat, a rooster, and a snake," I cut in.

"How did you know?"

"Read the book, for fuck's sake! *Poena cullei*. 'Penalty of the sack.' It was used in Navarre in the twelfth century."

"What kind of person would kill someone like that?"

"Don't ask me questions you know I can't answer," I said with a sigh. "Do we have an ID on the kid?"

"You'll have to ask Muguruza. There's a lot to process, and forensics hasn't finished yet. The judge and the chief clerk will be here any minute to move the body. They took the boy out of the barrel in case he was still alive, but . . . Anyway, someone reported seeing a barrel sink into the river. They said they heard barking. No screams. I understand the dog was the last to drown."

I went over to the soaking wet body of the boy, who was sprawled out in a white hoodie.

I genuflected discreetly in front of my colleagues, who were busy numbering and photographing dozens of footprints around me.

"This is where your hunt ends, and mine begins."

I raised my head. The sight of dead children sickened me. The boy's face was covered in scratches, and his hair . . . his hair was dyed blue.

It was worse than being punched in the stomach.

This wasn't a boy. It was MatuSalem.

The killer had murdered MatuSalem.

They buried him in El Salvador cemetery, an area surrounded by fallow wheat fields. Four of his skater friends served as pallbearers, sailing on their boards through the sea of graves, the casket next to them. The Brush Brigade had painted a portrait of Methuselah across the coffin, and I caught glimpses of his face as it glided among the cypress trees. I imagined that the hacker community had paid homage to him in their forums, too.

A group of girls was consoling a young woman with a round face and blue hair. She looked about twenty years old and was stricken with grief, clutching her waist as if to keep herself warm. Maturana's girlfriend.

I remembered what he'd said to me every time I asked him to help me on a case. For the first time, his words registered. I had never really thought of Matu as a person with a family, a girlfriend, friends. He had simply been a resource: a rare, precious resource I had to handle delicately, like a bomb disposal expert.

I'll never forget the way that girl looked at MatuSalem's coffin.

Her disbelief.

I wanted to feel the same way.

Because if I could only look at death that way again, it would mean I wasn't accustomed to loss, to living without all those people who had passed on: my parents, my grandmother, Paula and the twins, Martina, Jota, Nieves.

I took a deep breath and approached her after the others walked away.

"My condolences. You're Matu's girlfriend, aren't you?"

"And you're Kraken," she managed to reply.

I thought I saw a hint of bitterness in her puffy eyes, although I could have been projecting my own guilt.

In any case, her response surprised me. I had always assumed MatuSalem treated our relationship with the utmost discretion. Although I suppose at that age, most people share all kinds of things with their partner that they shouldn't. Still, I felt bad—awful, in fact.

I nodded and moved away. She seemed to be the epicenter of everyone's grief. My heart ached for her.

Did MatuSalem die because of me, because of what I'd asked him to do? Or was he just another victim of the sadist bent on re-creating *The Lords of Time*? Had his surname, Maturana, doomed him?

Estí, Milán, and Peña, sitting in a vehicle in the parking lot, were filming people entering and leaving the cemetery. They stood out like foxes in a chicken coop. Despite the work we had to do, I was pretty shaken, so I stopped analyzing my surroundings and focused on getting through the service as best I could.

"What's going on, Kraken?" Lutxo said, walking up to me after MatuSalem's coffin had slid into its niche. "Anything you want to share?"

"Now's not the time, Lutxo," I whispered.

He didn't seem to be listening.

"Yeah, yeah, I know. Since the double crime of the dolmen, every murder investigation comes with a gag order. You guys tell us nothing. Well, too bad. The public wants to know what's going on and whether they should be worried. This kid's death has set off a lot of alarm bells. . . ."

"How did you find out?" I asked.

"That's irrelevant. But if you must know: Some people from Gamarra saw an ambulance, they stuck around, the forensics team arrived, and the cordons went up. Anybody with a cell phone can take a picture, they share it on WhatsApp, and the information filters through to us. These days, everyone is a potential source."

All very vague, very Lutxo. I wouldn't get anything out of him, but nor did I want anything. I turned around, desperate to get away.

"As an investigator, there's nothing I can tell you. The investigation is ongoing. If we issue a press release, you'll hear about it."

You could have poisoned the water supply of several cities with the look Lutxo gave me. I walked off, leaving him in my wake. I'd had enough of cemeteries.

That was when I saw him.

He was sitting on a tombstone. I think he'd been waiting for me. Tasio Ortiz de Zárate.

The guy who had spent twenty years in jail for the double crime of the dolmen. The guy who had maintained his innocence but who no one took seriously until I decided to listen to him. The guy who had fled to the States after his release.

He was hiding behind a pair of expensive shades and a tailored suit. He motioned for me to join him. I don't know why, but I instinctively felt for the gun holstered inside my jacket. I felt like I was like walking straight toward the angry animals from Matu's barrel.

"I thought you were in Los Angeles," I said, sitting beside him. We were perched on a tomb, the final resting place for someone who had died several decades ago.

The granite was freezing, but I didn't want him to have the territorial advantage. We stared at MatuSalem's colorful procession, refusing to even look at each other.

"I had to come for Samuel Maturana's sake," he said. His gravelly voice took me back to our prison meetings a few lifetimes ago.

"When did you get in? You must have bought a last-minute flight. . . . Or were you already here?"

He smiled, and I had the sense that he was expecting questions.

"Are you interrogating me?"

"Not yet. I'm just saying that I'm impressed you made it in time for the funeral."

"I did it for Maturana," he repeated, his face stiff with anger this time.

"Is there anything you can tell me that might help with the investigation? You knew him better than I did."

"We kept in touch. He wasn't getting into trouble anymore. He had reformed; he'd learned to appreciate the life he created for himself outside prison. I think he'd grown up. I tried to be a sort of father to him, to make him feel like he could depend on me, for money, moral support. . . . Clearly it didn't help. What happened, Kraken?"

"If I knew, I wouldn't be so upset," I admitted.

"Does this have anything to do with you? Did you get him mixed up in something? Did you go to him for help?"

I looked away in frustration. When he understood what my silence meant, he exploded.

"Damn you, Kraken! If his death is your fault . . ."

"What? What are you going to do to me? Do you think I wanted to see him dead?" I retorted. "You dare to say this to me when you destroy everything you touch?"

I glanced around. I'd raised my voice on hallowed ground, and people wouldn't take kindly to that. Thankfully, no one was near us. There were only headstones and, far off in the distance, a few people were leaving.

"Well, I see we have unresolved issues. You're still angry with me about Deba," he muttered.

"You keep away from her," I exclaimed.

"Or what?"

"Or nothing, Tasio. I'm not stupid enough to threaten you. All I'm saying is if you really care about her or you think you might grow to love her, then leave her alone. Don't destroy her life. I've had enough of this. I'm sick of spending my time with scum, going to funerals—I'm sick of the public expecting me to produce miracles. I have no idea how many times a person can rebuild their life, but I imagine it's a finite number."

"Look, I realize this isn't the best time, Unai, but I want to point out that until now, I've respected your wishes. After what happened to DSU Salvatierra during the Water Rituals case, I stopped bothering you. I thought you'd both been through enough."

"Your absence was duly noted."

And much appreciated.

I had always wondered why Tasio had stopped insisting on a paternity test. It had been two long years, and we hadn't heard a word. His lawyer had been in touch a couple of times about the TV series he wanted to write based on the double crimes of the dolmen, but I'd asked Germán to deal with it. I wanted nothing to do with Tasio. I wanted him out of our lives. And yet here he was, back in Vitoria.

"Couldn't I see her, just for a little while?"

I wasn't sure whether he was pleading or probing.

"What for, Tasio? So you can get close to her? It's better if she knows nothing about you or Ignacio. As you said, we've suffered enough."

"You don't have a restraining order against me. You wouldn't be able to stop me," he said sharply.

"Her mother just passed away," I snapped.

"Who?"

"Alba's mother. She died a few days ago. Deba and I are the only family she has left other than my family, my brother and grandfather. . . . Don't destroy that, Tasio. We're broken enough as it is; we need to prop each other up or we'll fall apart completely."

"At least you have a family. After twenty years in prison, I have nobody in Vitoria besides my brother. My friends, my *cuadrilla*, my relatives—the dead and the living—they've all vanished into thin air. They don't want to know anything about me. Most of them refuse my calls. A few have agreed to meet me for coffee, but then they can't wait to get away. Women are nervous around me; they avoid me. At least in Los Angeles, I'm just an anonymous guy working in the industry, an intriguing European screenwriter. I've lost Vitoria, Kraken. It's gone. I just want to have something pure left."

"I'm sorry about the injustice you suffered, Tasio. Remember I was the one who caught the guy who did this to you, at no small cost to myself. But solving the problems of the adults around her isn't Deba's job. She doesn't deserve to be brought up as the daughter of a serial killer. You have to stay away. Why can't you rebuild your life, start a family of your own? Why do you need Deba? I don't understand."

"No, you don't. How could you? I'll never be able to get close to a woman again. I'll never have a child of my own."

"Maybe not here, but you said it yourself: in Los Angeles, people know nothing about you."

"You still don't get it. I can't have sex with a woman. Prison destroyed that for me, too." He lowered his head. He had murmured these last words, as though afraid that someone might hear.

"What do you mean? You've gotten over your time behind bars, haven't you? You're yourself again."

"They castrated me." He removed his dark glasses. His eyes were bloodshot. He kicked the leaves strewn on the ground.

"What?"

"My first year in prison, some of the inmates . . . they castrated me. To them, I was a monster who'd killed eight kids. What they felt for me . . . it was deeper than hatred. No one tried to stop them; the other inmates and the guards looked the other way. They stopped me from bleeding to death to avoid a scandal, but no one felt sorry for me. It changed me. I became a true monster. For a long time, I frightened myself. But I had this burning desire to survive, to get out of there. That's why I protected MatuSalem when he arrived. I couldn't bear to see the other inmates destroy him the way they had destroyed me. He was young; he'd get out in no time. I knew that if they ruined him, though, he might end up doing a lot of harm on the outside. He was impressionable. I did my best to influence him, to keep him safe, both inside and outside prison. But in the end, I couldn't protect him. Now do you see why Deba is so important to me?"

I stood up, reeling from what I'd heard.

"Before you take the next step, think about the lives you'll destroy if you pursue this. I hope I never see you again, Tasio Ortiz de Zárate. I hope I never see you as long as I live."

20

K, +THN1

UNAI

October 2019

A few hours after MatuSalem's funeral, I forced myself to find Doctor Guevara. I wanted to see Matu's autopsy report. I would have to make myself look at the photographs of his corpse, the clinical data on the weight of his organs, the cold facts about the cause of death.

I owed it to him.

I owed him for the favors he'd done for me over the years, for agreeing to get involved, for immersing himself whenever I'd asked him to make my cause his. What a poor mentor I had been. As disastrous as Tasio. Between us, we'd failed to protect the boy. If I were being honest with myself, I'd simply used him for his brainpower.

The guilt was killing me.

"Inspector." Doctor Guevara's voice brought me back to the world of the living. "Just the man I wanted to see. I have something to show you. It was overlooked when he was first found because he was fully clothed."

I sat down, facing her, and looked at the autopsy file as if it were toxic. I finally forced myself to open it and study the crime scene photographs.

"I want you to test everything you found on the riverbank. He must have fought back, left some trace of what happened there," I said.

She showed me a photograph of the left arm. It was still hard to believe that the bluish corpse had once been Matu.

"That's why I wanted you to see this. The victim scratched it on his arm after he was placed in the barrel with the animals."

Horrified, I stared at the image. I could only make out a few barely legible, jagged symbols.

"What do you think it says?" she asked me.

"It looks like *K+THNI*. K plus thni?" I ventured. I wasn't convinced.

"I think there's another mark. Was he was trying to write something else, do you think, and didn't finish it? Or is it just a random scratch, like the ones on his face, neck, and hands?"

"No. It's a comma," I said. "I think he wrote *K, +THNI*, or *THN1*. . . . I can't tell if the last mark is an *I* or the number one. In any case, did he write it or did his killer?"

"No, I'm confident he did it—and you'll never guess how. Look, these are the photographs of the animals put inside the barrel by the maniac who did this."

"It's *poena cullei*, one of the punishments in the novel," I said.

"A cruel, terrible way to die. The animals panic when they're stuffed into the barrel. It gets covered and then thrown into the water. The person trapped with them suffers all kinds of injuries. Snake bites, too, if the snake was alive."

"It wasn't, though, was it? Snakes hibernate this time of year."

"It was taxidermy. A prop," she replied. "But I'm afraid the other animals were still very much alive. Look at the victim's right hand. It's far more scratched than his left. The boy grabbed the rooster's spur and wrote these signs with it. See, these tiny wounds were left by the animal's beak and claws when it defended itself. It couldn't have been easy. The dog and cat bit and scratched his legs, which were partially protected by his clothes. The animals tried to claw their way out; the cat's paws were torn and full of splinters."

"Will you send over the toxicology report? We should find out if he had any drugs in his system."

"Of course. Although if he reacted the way we think he did, he was in full possession of his faculties. That suggests he wasn't drugged in any way."

You don't know what this kid was capable of, I almost said.

MatuSalem had sent me a message.

A warning. To me.

Of that I was certain. He knew he wasn't going to make it out alive. And he knew I'd be at his autopsy.

The *K* was me: *Kraken*. But what was he trying to tell me with *plus THN I*? Or was it *Kraken, plus THN1*?

What had MatuSalem found in Ramiro Alvar Nograro's tower?

Then it dawned on me. I knew what the warning meant.

It was what I'd been thinking since I last visited the Nograro family home: *Kraken, more than one.*

That was the message. Matu had reached the same conclusion as me: maybe Alvar wasn't one person, but several.

21

LA PLAZA DEL JUICIO

DIAGO VELA

Winter, the Year of Our Lord 1192

A lame donkey brought Ruiz to the Plaza del Juicio from his prison cell near the Sant Viçente fortress. By royal decree, the court of mediation's trials were held at the town gates, so the townspeople congregated beneath the South Gate next to the old cemetery at Sant Michel Church.

The artisan families—rope makers, tinkers, cobblers, grocers, and millers—stood on one side. On the other, watching the accused anxiously beneath the tower stairs, gathered the petty noblemen and aristocrats: the Ortiz de Zárates, the Mendozas, the Isunzas, along with a few other noblemen from the outlying villages, including Avendaños and his son.

Some were on horseback. Onneca sat sidesaddle on Olbia, ignoring the admiring stares of the townspeople.

Ruiz's probable fate was a summary execution. The boughs of the old oak at the foot of the Sant Viçente fortress were sturdy enough to bear a hanged man.

A couple of goats, oblivious to the noise below, had scaled the tree to nibble its frozen shoots.

"Lorenço, get those goats down! This isn't grazing day," the mayor ordered, his belly protruding beneath his long, bushy beard.

Embarrassed by the crowd's jeers, the goatherd, a young lad soon to be ten years old, whistled to the animals. Bleating, they climbed down from the tree.

The mayor, Pérez de Oñate, disliked being the focus of attention.

Mendieta, the executioner, a giant of a man with red hair and a flowing beard, tugged on the reins of the bony donkey, turning the animal to present the prisoner riding it to the town authorities. Ruiz's hands were tied behind his back. As he drew closer, I noticed something about his face that alarmed me.

I walked up to him. Although my wound had stopped bleeding and the physician had applied a fresh bandage to my back, I was not completely recovered. Still, I needed to attend the trial.

I could see that Ruy's son was no better off than me. There was blood caked around his mouth. Fearing the worst, I parted his lips.

"Good God!" I cried. "They've cut out his tongue! Who was on guard duty at the prison?" I asked the lieutenant.

Lieutenant Petro Remírez, a fellow with a droopy mustache, stormed over.

"When did this occur, and why wasn't I told?"

The two guards escorting the prisoner cowered.

Petro went up to one of them. "Bermudo?" he asked the leaner of the two, seizing the man's chin and forcing him to make eye contact.

"It happened the night he was brought to the prison. It was Saint Agatha's Eve, and we were out carousing with everyone else. We left him locked in the cell while we went out, and we found him like this the next morning."

"How did it happen if he was locked in?" asked the mayor.

"It's not as strange as you might think," replied the other guard. "Somebody beckoned Ruiz over, and when he got close enough, they grabbed him through the bars and did the deed. How were we to know? Nothing like that ever happens here."

"Well, it has now!" the lieutenant shouted. "While you were

gobbling eggs and smoked sausage and sloshing wine all over Villa de Suso, someone cut out this poor wretch's tongue."

"A poor wretch he may be, but innocent he is not," the other guard interjected. "Ask him which parts he likes to cut off cats, foals, and rabbits. His fondness for knives is well known."

"All the more reason to believe he did not poison Count de Maestu," a member of the Isunza family piped up.

"Let Count Vela outline the charge," the mayor said, intervening. "He called for the trial, and he must pass sentence."

I remembered that I had yet to reclaim my title. The document signing had been held in abeyance, as had the restitution of my property, my inheritance, and all my other worldly goods, which at present my dear brother, Nagorno, was enjoying. Currently, it didn't seem as though there would be any point in trying to regain my title. The stench from my wound worsened each day, and the upheaval around this trial was taking its toll.

I strode forward, attempting to disguise my stumbling gait.

Do not reveal your weakness, I told myself.

I did not yet know who had cut me, or whether they had paid somebody else to do it, but I felt sure that whoever it was stood nearby, watching me closely. The attack had taken place after curfew had sounded and the gates had closed, so my assailants must have been townsfolk.

"I shall call a witness who can confirm that, five nights ago, Ruy's son purchased three pinches of Spanish fly. An unusually large quantity, as this same witness will affirm, since a single pinch lasts two days and nights, and those who avail themselves of such powders do so with caution, as excessive use renders it poisonous and causes an agonizing death. Yet, on Saint Agatha's Eve, two nights after procuring the powders, the accused himself confessed to me that he had only one pinch left, despite not having shared his cache with a soul. By this reckoning, if he took one pinch himself, he would have two remaining. I ask, therefore: What became of the remaining powder? Alas, I believe it found its way into the deceased Count de Maestu's stomach. As a learned physician in Pamplona once taught me, this proves the count was poisoned," I declared, holding up the white rabbit's blackened, blistered skin. "Imagine what the Spanish fly did to the good count's insides, dear neighbors, and the agony of his final hours."

"What has the accused to say in his defense?" demanded the mayor.

Ruiz gave a few grunts and waved his arms. Many of the townsfolk began to jeer. They hated him; for years, they'd listened to their daughters' complaints and dealt with his violent incursions into their farmyards.

"Since the accused is unable to defend himself, will anyone speak for him?" the mayor asked.

"Let's speak frankly," Mendoza said, urging his horse forward. "We all agree that he could have been the culprit, but I suggest he pay blood money for his crime. Because of what was done to him in prison, I propose that the incarceration tax be waived."

"Is that how the matter is to be settled?" An excited voice rose from the ranks of artisans. "Those with money get away with wretched murder? They murdered our protector, and they've all but murdered Count Vela."

I tried to step forward again, intending to make an appeal for calm, but as I started to walk, the hanging tree toppled over onto me, or so I thought. The world grew suddenly dark as I collapsed to the ground in the center of the Plaza del Juicio.

When I regained consciousness, the first thing I saw was a three-coned wimple. Alix de Salcedo was sitting by my bed, holding a cold compress to my brow.

"What happened?"

"You fainted during the trial. The wound in your back reopened and you started to bleed again. Here, eat these pig kidneys. Grandmother Lucía says they replenish the blood."

I raised myself slightly, and Alix passed me a knife to slice the kidneys. The sauce smelled of rosemary and red wine, and when I swallowed the food, it warmed my insides. By the time I wiped the bowl clean with a morsel of bread she had given me, I could feel strength flowing back into my body.

Alix watched me in silence, but her lips were pressed together and she kept looking toward the window, as though she were in a hurry to leave my side.

"You could have called me as a witness, yet you chose not to," she said at last.

"Tempers are running too high. I didn't want to risk it."

"I would have come forward. They almost killed you, but you're stronger than I thought. Half the people in Villa de Suso have been praying for your soul, and the other half are wagering that another Count Vela will die before his time."

"What about you?"

I sensed Alix's unease as she stared into the warm embers, avoiding my gaze.

"Why, I did both. The mayor has followed your advice. Ruiz will be executed. But there is much ill-feeling in Nova Victoria. Are you sure he deserves such an ignoble punishment?"

"What execution is preferable to hanging? It's quick, and it will deter his supporters."

"Sire . . ."

"Sire? Why, only the other day you called me Diago. And you've now seen me naked as the day I was born. Haven't we earned the right to dispense with such formalities?"

"Diago it is, then. Ruiz will not be hanged. He has been

sentenced to *poena cullei*. You recommended it in a letter to the mayor, and he has carried out your wishes. You said it was the most fitting punishment."

"What letter, Alix?"

"The council received a letter signed by Count Don Vela, or so I heard."

I was on the verge of saying that I had written no such letter, but I decided to keep my counsel.

"Has the punishment been carried out yet?"

"Those who wanted to attend left for the River Zadorra a good while ago."

"You did not wish to see it?"

"I wouldn't say that. I simply thought that with the town half empty, the gates open, and you so weak, I . . ."

She pulled a dagger from the folds of her gown.

"You stayed behind to protect me. . . . Was this Grandmother Lucía's idea as well?"

"She sends me to fatten you up with my pies and tarts. I didn't tell her about your recent bout of fainting. I didn't want her to fret."

I shook my head.

"She will have heard about it from a hundred different sources by now." I struggled to get out of bed. "With or without your help, I will attend the execution."

"Are you sure?"

I nodded weakly.

"As you wish. I don't want to witness any more cruelty," she murmured. "I hope you sleep well tonight."

With that she disappeared through the door, as if she were fleeing the devil himself. I could tell she disapproved, yet she had stayed behind to protect me. I knew tongues would start to wag if her visits continued.

Her ministrations must cease. I would speak to her after the execution, and to Grandmother Lucía. With each day, I was gaining more and more enemies. I was not a proper companion for a thrice-widowed young woman.

Half an hour later I reached the River Zadorra. A thaw had set in over the past few days, but the waters would still be icy.

I followed the muddy tracks and ruts left by the feet, hooves, and wheels that had passed earlier. By the looks of it, few people planned to miss this execution. *Poena cullei* was a rare punishment indeed. There were rumors that it had been used by powerful men who had accused their wives of adultery, but no one here had ever witnessed such a spectacle.

When I reached the point where the river slowed, I spied Mendieta, the executioner, struggling to push a stray dog into a wine barrel.

Half the town's population watched expectantly from the near bank: smithies, cobblers, fishmongers—I even spotted two of the grocer's wives nursing infants. There were more than fifty people cheering on Mendieta. But over by the somber, gray poplars on the other side of the river, petty noblemen on horseback and local aristocrats looked on gravely, forming a stark contrast to the villagers' laughter and heckling. They hadn't wished to miss the execution, either.

Mendieta opened a sack containing a yowling cat, then tossed the beast into the barrel. Then he extracted a rooster and a coiled snake from two other sacks. The snake looked drowsy. They had doubtless sent a young lad for it, and he had fetched it from beneath a rock up in the hills.

"You came to stop it," Nagorno said, edging toward me on his steed, Altai.

I was too distressed by the spectacle to look at my brother. Ruiz's desperate cries as the executioner threw the barrel into the water hushed more than one jeerer, and the excitement and applause soon gave way to an uneasy, then barbed silence.

"You sent the letter," I whispered.

"I still bear the title Count Don Vela," he replied in a low voice. "And if you had intervened, you would have undermined the mayor's authority. Pérez de Oñate was chosen by the very residents of Villa de Suso you so cherish. If you oppose them, you will find yourself in no-man's-land. You've already gained enough enemies among those on the far bank. They won't forget this slight. It's too late to stop the punishment now, and, besides, Onneca will despise you if you do."

"I know that."

My first consideration had been Onneca. She would never forgive me if I were to show leniency to her father's murderer.

"Nagorno, have you considered the possible consequences for the town?"

"What do you think? I was always a better strategist than you."

I swallowed hard. I could hear Ruiz's screams from the barrel. Tello the tanner cupped his hands over his little boy's ears, then picked him up and set off wordlessly along the muddy path toward town. Others followed in a silent stream, heads lowered. But the noblemen stayed until the bitter end, until water seeped into the wooden barrel and it began to sink into the Zadorra.

"This is a game of chess, then," I retorted.

"Yes, it's been a game since you vacated your seat. I'm obliged to you for the two-year head start."

Very well, I thought. We'd played this game before, with more pawns, more lives. We both ended up losing, but he didn't care. And therein lay my brother's strength and my weakness.

"One question, Nagorno. When will this round begin?"

It was my way of asking whether I must immediately prepare for the battle he was staging, or if I might live a little first.

"Don't you see what is unfolding before your very eyes? You, who have always been the shrewdest of the Vela siblings? The game begins today, you fool."

As he spoke, the remaining residents of Villa de Suso abandoned the scene with a bitter taste in their mouths. Ruiz's cries had been drowned in the riverbed, and the barks and mewling had ceased as well.

The mayor and the executioner pronounced the man and the animals dead and then cast a length of thick rope—supplied by the rope maker, Sabat—into the water. After several failed attempts, they managed to snare the barrel, and between them hoisted it onto his cart, its deathly cargo inside. Nobody had the courage to open it. Even Mendieta, who had seen nearly everything in his many years as executioner, was forced to withdraw behind a poplar tree, where he noisily purged his stomach of its contents.

Onneca was the only one left. The others had all headed back to town, but she sat steadfastly on her horse. She approached us, dismounted, and spoke to Nagorno.

"Leave us, dear husband. I need to speak with your brother alone."

"I prefer to stay."

"Nevertheless, I wish to speak with him on my own. Wait for me in our bed, for I shall need your embraces to comfort me after what I have seen."

Nagorno held my gaze, but in the end obeyed.

"You've risked a great deal to avenge my father," said Onneca, once my brother was out of sight.

What could I say to her, if one day she were to discover the truth?

"What do you want, Onneca? You were unwise to stand up to Nagorno. You must save that for when it's truly needed."

"Don't concern yourself with my battles with my husband. I'll fight them on my own terms. I need to speak with you because I'm worried about my sisters. I sent word again this week about the proceedings against our father's murderer, but I've had no response. Your family has always administered the affairs for Santa María Cathedral. My father decided my sisters should be immured there, in a section of the granary. Can you think of any reason for their silence?"

"Our family built a simple chapel there before the king decided to erect a church, but there is little to oversee, apart from the schedule of masses and collection of the wheat tithes, along with a few other religious matters. When I left, your sisters were two little girls, and your father doted on them, so his decision came as a shock to me. I'll find out who is looking after them. Is there anything else you need from me, sister-in-law?"

"No, thank you, Diago. You should rest. You look weak."

I stayed on the riverbank until all the others had left: Onneca on her golden horse; the cart bearing that travesty; the spitting, cursing noblemen on the far side of the river . . .

And I saw how the town had been rent in two. From that day on, no one was safe within its walls.

22

ARKAUTE

UNAI

October 2019

I drove the short distance from the cemetery to the Police Academy in Arkaute, on the outskirts of Vitoria. I had done my training there years ago, first as an *ertzaina* and then as a criminal profiler. I used to go running on the roads around the compound, where new recruits had cohabited for nine months before the word *partner* acquired a more professional meaning.

I wanted to talk with my mentor, Doctor Marina Leiva. The psychiatrist had guided me from the outset along the dark labyrinths of the mind, helping me understand psychopaths, psychotics, and the most heinous serial offenders, my specialty.

I flashed my badge at the academy's entrance and was allowed through the barrier.

I checked the time. Well acquainted with the doctor's routines, I knew better than to look for her in the lecture halls where she taught profiling classes.

I entered the wing that housed the indoor swimming pool and saw her swimming in the otherwise empty lanes. She was wearing a red bathing suit, and a rubber cap covered her blond hair.

I stood in the chlorinated water, boots in my hand, and waited patiently for her to finish her laps and notice me.

"Unai, I didn't expect to see you here!" she said, clambering up the metal ladder.

"I owed you a visit. I'm afraid it's long overdue."

"Of course. You flew the nest a while ago, and you're doing well, I hear."

"Not that well, Marina. I've solved a few cases. But I've run up against something—someone—who has me completely stumped. And I need your help."

I motioned for her to sit with me on the bleachers.

"Why do you need me?" she asked, leisurely toweling herself dry. Marina was petite, calm, and easygoing. She just sat and listened, sometimes nodding, never making you feel uncomfortable or as if you were being analyzed. I'd forgotten what a soothing effect she had on me.

"Let me explain. Remember when you told me about your first collaboration with the police? It involved the rapist called Bigmouth."

I had been a teenager at the time. The national newspapers didn't pick up the story, and there was no social media back then to spread the news.

He'd earned the name Bigmouth because he talked to his victims throughout the crime, even during the rape. He demanded they tell him their fantasies and sexual preferences. All the women described the rapist as talkative with an Eastern European accent. The police got lucky, obtaining semen samples from a few of his victims.

They ran a search targeting sexual offenders who held passports from the relevant countries, but it led nowhere.

Around the same time, there was a second rapist active in the area, one who was extraordinarily cruel. His victims described him as Spanish and said he never spoke—a completely different profile from Bigmouth. But then an anomaly occurred: DNA from a victim of the second rapist matched the DNA on file for Bigmouth. The perpetrator was arrested. He was indeed Spanish and turned out to be one of Doctor Leiva's patients. The police turned to her for help. She had been treating him for dissociative identity disorder, or DID.

"Dramatic cases like that are few and far between," she reminded me, folding her towel carefully before placing it on her lap. "In fact, most of my colleagues are skeptical of the disorder, because there are so many false cases. In the fifties, 'multiple personality disorder,' as it was called then, became well known thanks to a movie, *The Three Faces of Eve*. The movie and subsequent books were very popular, and a lot of felons feigned symptoms, hoping to persuade forensic psychiatrists to diagnose them with DID in order to avoid prison. Many offenders also claimed to suffer from amnesia or dissociative fugue disorder. Now, we have clinical tools to help us determine whether the disorder is genuine. We don't have precise numbers about how many people in the general population are afflicted with DID, but it's certainly a rare disorder. Most psychiatrists will never encounter or diagnose a case. I have only treated a few during my thirty-year career. Why do you want to talk to me about that case?"

"I want to describe someone to you. We'll call him Alvar."

"Okay."

"He's a priest in his late thirties," I explained. "He arguably fits the profile of a narcissist: extroverted, self-assured, charismatic. He insists on being addressed formally. He runs hot and is content to wear nothing but a simple cassock whether he's indoors or out at night. He's the scion of a wealthy aristocratic family, landed gentry whose members have held a privileged position in society for more than a thousand years. He also has a superiority complex. And he's a rich snob."

"I think I get the picture."

"The day after I met him, the same man introduced himself as Ramiro Alvar. He didn't recognize me and had no recollection of what he'd said and done the previous day. He is introverted, doesn't wear a cassock, and is always cold. Unlike Alvar, he wears prescription glasses. He is rather informal and doesn't stand on ceremony. His timidity doesn't lend itself to narcissism. I suspect he's highly intelligent: he holds degrees in history, economics, law, and psychology that, curiously, he claims he studied to be worthy of his family inheritance. However, he made no mention of having studied theology. He manages the family estate efficiently and seems like an old soul. I suspect he prefers the company of books to people, but I also get the sense that he is driven by trauma. He's obviously afraid of something. It is apparent from the moment you meet him. He keeps a well-thumbed copy of Marcus Aurelius's *Meditations* close at hand. His fondness for the Stoics is all the more remarkable because the day before he had described himself as a hedonist. His voice is several tones higher than Alvar's. It's astonishing, you have to hear it to believe it." She smiled, as if that didn't surprise her. "I could have sworn they were two different people."

"Is there more?"

"Yes, one other puzzling detail: he says he's the twenty-fifth Lord of Nograro, whereas Alvar says he's the twenty-fourth. I suspect Ramiro Alvar may suffer from agoraphobia. The few people who have met him say they've never seen him leave his estate."

"A quick throwaway question before you go on. Are you absolutely sure you're not describing two different people?"

"I am. They have the same build, the same body odor, and identical iris patterns. Both have attached earlobes, which is a recessive trait. Also, the morning after Alvar stayed out all night carousing, Ramiro Alvar came to the door unshaven with bags under his eyes, claiming he hadn't slept well. Oh, and one last thing: The day I met him, Alvar must have literally just divested himself of Ramiro Alvar and his glasses. I managed to take a photo of him, and when I blew it up, I could see the telltale indentations on the bridge of his nose. I bumped into him on the street later that day and he didn't recognize me until I was standing right next to him—a sure sign he's nearsighted."

"Okay, so we have Alvar the twenty-fourth, the priest, and Ramiro Alvar the twenty-fifth, the bibliophile," she said, as though it were the simplest thing in the world.

"That's correct."

"Ramiro Alvar is the apparently normal personality, or ANP. Alvar, our priest, is a typical alter identity. Alters are habitually dramatic, larger-than-life caricatures. He's a creation from Ramiro Alvar's mind, which has chosen those strong traits for a specific reason. His alter isn't like you or me; he isn't a person in his own right. His personality lacks nuance, rather it's made up of broad brushstrokes—"

"How do you know that?" I cut in.

She smiled and shrugged. "This alter is abusive. He has Ramiro Alvar under his thumb."

"Is that how it works? People with DID create alters that abuse them?"

"Alters are a defense mechanism. An individual with this type of personality disorder has a 'split self.' I try not to use the term *multiple personality*. I prefer to talk about alternating identities, fragments of the patient's personality that haven't been properly integrated."

I motioned for her to continue.

"At home with your family, you're Unai. At work, you're Inspector López de Ayala; sometimes you have to be tough on suspects and behave in ways you never would with your loved ones. With your friends perhaps you regress, you play the fool like you did when you were a teenager. To the media and the people who don't know you, you're Kraken. They ascribe traits to you that you may or may not like, but these traits certainly don't correspond with the Unai you are with those you're closest to."

I stared at a pool of water on the floor. Being dissected like this made me feel uneasy.

"Generally speaking," she went on, "this is true for all of us. We're the mother, the friend, the daughter, the lover, the boss. Our behavior changes depending on where we are, whether we're at work, with our family, in a social situation, or in an intimate moment. Most of us have integrated these different facets of our personality into one whole. We call on them as and when we need them. Individuals with DID can't do this, and that's where amnesia comes into play. Their general memory isn't affected, but parts of their life disappear—like, for example, they can't remember what their alter did the day before. They bury those actions through amnesia and dissociative fugues. As a result, they are highly mistrustful and paranoid. They don't trust themselves, or rather they are suspicious of what their alter gets up to. That's why most of them live solitary lives. They're incapable of forming relationships or holding down a normal job without being discovered. This is a highly disabling condition that the majority of sufferers spend their entire lives disguising and hiding from those around them."

"You said these are defense mechanisms. What are they defending against exactly?"

"Previously, DID was believed to be the result of early trauma or disorganized attachment experiences in the person's childhood and adolescence. When confronted with unbearable levels of stress, the self splits, and the patient develops alternate personalities: the savior, the persecutor, and the victim. One of these personalities suppresses the memory of trauma in his or her everyday life, while the alter or alters fixate on those experiences and take defensive action. Some clinicians suggest that people with DID have an aggressive, an evasive, and a submissive side. I'm not sure I agree, nor do I believe that childhood trauma is necessarily a factor, although it's certainly common among those who have the disorder. I do believe, however, that DID can be triggered or aggravated by a stressful episode, particularly if that episode has particular significance to the patient."

"If I bring him to you, do you think you could give me a diagnosis, or at least tell me if he's faking? I need to find out what's going on, Marina. I have evidence but not enough to satisfy a judge. Everything I have points to him, but it would be enormously beneficial to have your professional opinion."

"He sounds like an interesting case, and with therapy, the prognosis for integration is good. You'll need to discuss it with Ramiro Alvar. His alter, Alvar the priest, will be dead set against it."

"Why wouldn't he want to get better?"

"I don't think you quite understand, Unai. Alters will do whatever it takes to survive. Believe me, he'll do everything in his power to prevent integration from happening."

23

THE LADY OF THE CASTLE

UNAI

October 2019

I arrived in Laguardia early that morning. My two ladies were on the hotel terrace, peacefully eating their breakfast. Alba was relaxing, her head resting against the back of her chair in order to absorb more sunlight on the balmy autumn day.

I glanced at the newspaper an early riser had left behind and prayed that Alba hadn't read it.

"Will you come up to the tower with me?" I asked after kissing them both hello.

I lifted Deba onto my shoulders, and we climbed the octagonal spiral staircase to the ramparts and then stepped outside.

"What's going on?" asked Alba. She seemed suspicious, as though afraid of more bad news.

I pulled three pieces of red silk from my inside jacket pocket, waving my arms like a magician. I had woven each of us a wristband using slipknots. I knew the circumference of their wrists, so they would fit perfectly. They looked slightly disappointed, though.

"I want *chessnuts*," whined Deba, before a dragonfly distracted her.

I perched on the tower's wall and sat her on my lap. "I'm going to tell you a story that my grandmother told me," I said. "You see Mount Toloño? Well, that's where you come from. You and your mother stayed with the god Tulonio for a few days, and Mother

Earth took care of you. She's another goddess, the most important goddess of all, actually. People here used to call her Lur. You see, Lur is a spinner, and she likes to spin at night by the light of the waning moon. She spins threads of destiny."

"What's *desty-nee*?" asked Deba, suddenly interested.

"It's what brought the three of us together; it makes us a family," I explained. "You can tie knots in these threads to make them longer or shorter, but they can never be broken: Lur won't allow it. Now we're each going to put on our wristbands, and we'll be joined by these threads forever. You can wear it every day, and if you feel sad, you can touch it and remember that Dad and Mom are wearing theirs, and that we are all looking out for one another. That is what families are for."

Alba looked at me and smiled. I think she was touched. I tied their bands on their wrists, and it made me happy to see our three matching bracelets.

"How do you manage to make me emotional this early in the morning?" she whispered in my ear.

Deba clapped her hands when we kissed; it had become a noisy habit of hers. I found it adorable.

"Let's go downstairs," Alba said cheerfully, "I have a thousand things to do. I'm organizing some events with the Laguardia Town Council, and we have a meeting this morning. I want to offer guided tours of the underground bodegas, with a glass of wine at the hotel to follow. I also want to set up Segway tours of the vineyards, and I think we should participate in this year's Medieval Tapas Contest."

I followed them down the stairs. Alba had the same energy and focus she always did, but she'd never smiled this much at the police station, and I'd never felt the positive energy she was exuding since she had moved to Laguardia.

The bubble burst a few minutes later. I was in the kitchen slicing an apple for Deba when Alba came in with the newspaper.

"What's this?" she asked, pointing at the headline above a photograph of Tasio and me sitting on the tombstone at the cemetery.

KRAKEN AND TASIO:
THE KEYS TO THE *LORDS OF TIME* MYSTERY?

"Hey, Deba, why don't you go to your room and get your coloring books? I want to see what you've been doing," I suggested.

Deba happily obeyed. As soon as she left the kitchen, Alba came over to me. I thought I saw fear in her eyes.

"Tasio Ortiz de Zárate is back in Vitoria and you didn't tell me?"

"I wanted to let you mourn in peace," I explained. "It would only have scared you. I don't want you to live in fear."

"It's too late. How can I not be afraid when Tasio has made it clear that he wants to be a part of Deba's life?"

"He came to Samuel Maturana's funeral. He had every right to be there. They were close. But this nonsense in the paper has nothing to do with the case. We just talked. I told him to stay away from Deba, and I hope he takes me seriously." I sighed.

Alba had been clutching the newspaper without realizing. She was furious. She turned around, went over to the window, and stared out at the garden.

"It's happening again," she finally said.

"What's happening again?"

"You're endangering the lives of those around you by associating with murderers."

It would've been so easy.

To cut her down. To wound her deeply.

To remind her that her instincts had failed her in the past, that she had, at one point, become a cliché: a police officer who consorts with a killer. But I didn't. These small decisions show us where we want a relationship to go—they trace its trajectory with laser precision. I didn't want to be the kind of partner who went for the low blow when we argued.

Winning an argument by reminding her of those failures would've been taking the easy way out—and I didn't do easy.

I took a deep breath, trying to imagine water flowing from a mountain spring. It took me far away, but also anchored me.

"We get to set our own limits," I said. "And if you can't accept that part of me . . . Look, Alba, I want us to be together. I know that you're grieving, but I want to be with you even though you've set out on your own and taken Deba with you. I know she's enough for you, and I'm not demanding your affection or your company. I want us to be a family, and I haven't given up on that. But I need to know that you don't want to go on without me. It's your decision. I'm going to work."

I needed to work, to clear my head, to swap one obsession for another, to fall into my own patterns. That was *my* emotional trigger. I knew myself well; I'd learned to accept my faults.

And so to work.

I took Alba's copy of *The Lords of Time*, the one I'd given her with the line from Joan Margarit.

I moved my hair over my scar, a habitual gesture I repeated a hundred times a day. I felt naked if I didn't cover it.

Heading upstairs, I sneaked into one of the empty bedrooms in the hotel. I think it was the Love and Madness room. Definitely two things that should be kept apart. I installed myself in a wingback chair and started rereading the novel, a pen and a pad of hotel stationery beside me.

I was looking for parallels—surnames, professions, motives—for what drove that dark world. Who was the magician behind the curtain, the unseen character pulling the strings? Was he right in front of me, hiding in plain sight?

Soon afterward, Alba entered the room. She sat on a corner of the bed and studied me.

"I thought you were working," she said at last.

"That's exactly what I am doing," I replied, scanning the novel.

. . . And then I found it.

A familiar name, a surname that had caught my attention the first time I read it.

But it was more than just a name. I'd found a character: Héctor Dicastillo. He was the Lord of Castillo, one of the settlements surrounding the ancient town of Victoria. My attention had been drawn to what he'd said to his kinsman: "There has always been a chain of violence going back to the earliest ages of mankind."

I'd heard that expression before.

A close friend had said it when we were immersed in the Water Rituals case. "There's a chain of violence going back to Paleolithic times." Was it a family saying that had been handed down, generation to generation? Whatever it was, I had nothing to lose by making a call.

I rose from the armchair and climbed the spiral staircase that led to the tower. I needed to make three calls.

The first call.

"Inspector, what a pleasant surprise! How are you?" he said in his calm voice.

"Hello, Héctor, what's new in Cantabria?"

"Actually, my brother and I are in London, on family business. What can I do for you?"

For several years, Héctor and Iago Castillo had been joint directors of the Cantabrian Archaeological Museum, the CAM. They'd worked with me on a couple of past investigations.

"I'm not sure where to begin, so I'll get straight to the point. Have you read *The Lords of Time?*"

"I'm sorry?" he asked, puzzled.

"The novel. *The Lords of Time*."

"I'm not sure what you're talking about, Unai. Can you explain?"

"It's a historical novel that came out recently. It's gotten rave reviews. I assumed you'd heard about it in Santander."

"My brother and I have been abroad for several months. We're not really in the loop. Why do you ask?"

"Well, because it's set in Vitoria, or rather the town of Victoria," I explained, "at the end of the twelfth century. It chronicles the power struggles between the kingdoms of Navarre and Castille, and also features prominent families in Álava. It was published under a pseudonym, by someone calling himself Diego Veilaz."

"Did you say Diego Veilaz?"

"Yes, and the protagonist is also Diago Veilaz, the legendary Count Don Vela. It's written in the first person. Since it was published, there have been several murders in the city, all of them using a medieval modus operandi like the deaths in the novel: poisoning with Spanish fly, immurement, and the *poena cullei*."

"Good heavens," he breathed, seemingly in shock.

"Exactly. I'm calling you because I think one of the characters might be an ancestor of yours: Héctor Dicastillo, the Lord of Castillo. You once told me a branch of your family came from Álava, and I know you're an expert on northern Spain's ancient and medieval history."

"Yes, that's right," he replied. He sounded distracted. I'd have given anything to read his mind right then. "Who published the novel?"

"An independent local publisher called Malatrama. The editor received the manuscript over e-mail and doesn't have a clue who the real author is."

"I'm going to hang up and buy a copy of the novel. My brother and I will read it, and I'll call you back later. That's all I can tell you for now, okay?"

And he hung up, leaving a somewhat angst-ridden inspector standing alone on a tower overlooking a mountain.

But I had no time to give in to anxiety. There was still so much to do.

The second call.

I dialed a landline and waited as it rang.

"Yes?"

"Hello, this is Inspector López de Ayala. Is this Ramiro Alvar?"

"Speaking. What is this con . . . concer . . . What can I do for you?" he said, clearing his throat.

"I'd like to stop by the tower today, if that's convenient."

"Of course. I'll be here. Has something happened?"

Oh, nothing much, just that someone killed MatuSalem using a medieval punishment.

I had other plans for Ramiro Alvar. Introducing him to Estíbaliz, for example. I wanted her to judge for herself.

The third call.

"Estí, I'm in Laguardia. I'm going to Nograro Tower, and I'd like you to come with me. I want to show you something."

"Pick me up in Vitoria in an hour," she said.

We parked next to the moat, crossed the drawbridge, and found the huge wooden door wide open. The tower was taking visitors. The guide's voice filtered down from upstairs, and by the time we walked in, we saw her propelling a group of older people down the first-floor hallway. I waved at her and motioned that I was going to use the intercom to call Ramiro Alvar's apartment.

"What is it you want to show me, Unai?" asked Estíbaliz. She sounded slightly uneasy.

"You'll see in a minute."

"Come on up, come on up." The arrogant voice rang out from the speaker.

Goddamn it, I don't believe this, I said to myself.

But it was true. Alvar had tricked me. *He* had answered my call earlier, pretending to be Ramiro Alvar.

He was waiting for us in the tapestry room, immaculately groomed, sporting a green-and-gold embroidered dalmatic.

"*Aestibalis*, I was sure we would meet again," he said, smiling beatifically.

"Hello, Alvar," I said, greeting him, although he scarcely acknowledged me. He only had eyes for my colleague.

"Nice to see you again, too," said Estíbaliz. "We're here to check some facts that we've recently uncovered during our investigation."

"I've already told you that I'm at your disposal."

"I know," she replied. "We were wondering if you have or have had any dealings with the Natural Science Museum."

"Why on earth would I want to visit a fake medieval tower when I live in a real one?" he declared, astonished. And his astonishment was genuine, there was something rather childlike about his response.

"I'm asking whether you've ever worked with the museum, as a donor for instance," she explained.

"You've come to my house to bombard me with tedious details about which I know nothing," he replied coldly.

"Let's talk about your family, then," I interjected. "Do you remember the Dominican nun's habit that was in one of the display cabinets on the first floor?"

"It belonged to my great-aunt, Magdalena de Nograro. She took the veil at the Quejana convent. You're boring me again."

Alvar turned his back and stared out the window at the overcast sky. I watched him, wondering if he could see the stand of golden poplars below or if they were a blur without the glasses he wore as Ramiro Alvar.

"*Aestibalis*, can you ride?" he asked.

"Yes, I was brought up on a farm at the foot of Mount Gorbea," she responded buoyantly. Estí loved riding. She often spent her weekends at the equestrian center. "We had cart horses, not thoroughbreds, but—"

"We have several magnificent animals in our stables," his mellifluous voice cut in. "And the weather is perfect for riding. Would you honor me with your company once more?"

There it was again. The brush of their hands, the penetrating gaze. Neither one seemed to notice when I announced my departure. I left the room with the distinct feeling that I had become the invisible man.

I crossed the moat and decided to look around the village of Ugarte. It was just over a half mile away, along a stretch of road that had only an occasional building. The one nearest to the tower was an abandoned outhouse, the entrance opening onto a side path overgrown with weeds.

I kept walking until my ear picked up something that sounded utterly incongruous with the surroundings. Albinoni's Adagio. I glanced around, puzzled.

I followed the trail of the violins and came to a charming villa with an enormous garden. A woman in her fifties was pruning some shrubs. She wore gardening gloves. A slightly older man carried two pails of water out of the garage.

"Hello," said the woman, removing a glove and smoothing her short burgundy hair. "Are you lost?"

"No. As a matter of fact, I was planning to take a stroll around the village. Is that music coming from your house?" I asked.

"Yes. My Fidel and I keep a few free-range hens at the bottom of the garden. The music calms them. We play it when we feed them outside."

"Lucky hens," I said. "I've just visited the tower. What a strange place. Did you know the Nograro family?"

"If you mean the parents, Inés and Lorenzo Alvar, they died twenty years ago," said the woman, turning the pruning shears over in her hands.

"How did the locals feel about them?"

"The father? He had many faces, so I suppose it depends on whom you ask," said the husband, shrugging and looking away.

"They had money. In our house, we never had a bad word to say about them," the woman added hurriedly. "Of course, they didn't live in the village; they had the tower. But they employed a lot of locals, in the forge and at the mill, and, of course, some families in Ugarte were tenant farmers. The Alvars were polite, educated people, and the mother was charming. Inés was her name, like I said. Good people, and they adored those children."

"Children? The guide only mentioned Lord Nograro, Ramiro Alvar?"

"He's the younger brother. Alvar was the elder, but he died young. Such a handsome lad. He went to Vitoria for his studies. He returned after his parents were killed in a car accident. His brother was still a minor, so Alvar took care of him, although he was already quite ill by that point. Come to think of it, we never saw him. We heard that he'd died, but they didn't hold a funeral or even have a Mass here in Ugarte." She finished explaining and looked up at me. "My name's Fausti, Fausti Mesanza, by the way."

"Pleased to meet you, Fausti. Tell me, do you know if the two brothers got along?"

"They adored each other. Ramiro Alvar was such a polite, charming lad. Very timid, even then. But nobody ever lays eyes on him now. There was a lot of love in that family. Lorenzo Alvar couldn't have been prouder of his firstborn, Alvar. The boy managed all his father's affairs. If the illness hadn't taken him the way it did—"

"You only saw his good side, just like all the other women," her husband snorted.

"Don't you start; he couldn't help being handsome," Fausti said, elbowing her husband in the ribs. "Besides, you shouldn't speak ill of the dead."

"How old was Ramiro Alvar when his brother died?" The Adagio the hens had been listening to gave way to Pachelbel's solemn Canon.

"I believe it was in 1999," said Fausti, "so Ramiro Alvar must have just turned eighteen, because he went to Vitoria on his own. He was a responsible boy, grown-up for his age. He's been in charge of the estate since then, and he seems to be doing a good job. I never hear any complaints from those who rent his land. He continues to employ locals one way or another, even using local boys as stable hands or gardeners. And the old forge is now used for agritourism and as a glassmaking workshop."

"What about the abandoned outhouse?" I asked.

"You mean the old bodega," said Fidel.

"Bodega? But there are no vineyards around here. Did the Nograro family own it?"

"Yes, but they used it solely for their own consumption," explained Fausti. "They used to bring truckloads of grapes from La Rioja Alavesa, but that was years ago. All that remains of the old bodega are bits of machinery and some other equipment. Would you like to see it? There's a path at the back of our chicken coop that leads through the poplar grove. It's very pretty."

"I'd love to," I said.

We walked past the hens, who were pecking at the grain strewn on the ground in time to Pachelbel, and ended up on a path bordered on either side by tall poplars.

The contrasting yellow leaves and silvery bark instilled a feeling of serenity that I hadn't experienced in days. The poplars' perfect symmetry infused the decades-old plantation with a mystical atmosphere.

It was an immersive woodland experience, a place for calming the nerves, where you could stop and listen to the breeze murmuring through the autumn leaves. My companions smiled sympathetically when they saw the effect it had on me. Unconsciously I felt for my red-silk wristband. I needed to bring Deba and Alba here so they, too, could see this little time capsule.

No matter how relaxed I felt, I reminded myself that I was working.

"Fidel, why did you describe Lorenzo Alvar as a man of many faces?"

"He was a polite fellow—and yet, during Carnival, he often appeared in the village dressed in his mother's or grandmother's clothing. He was a laughingstock—"

"Not every year," his wife cut in. "Sometimes he dressed as a soldier."

"A soldier," I repeated.

"Yes, in one of his ancestor's uniforms. You can still see them on display at the museum. He came fully decked out with a shotgun and a haversack."

"Like I said, he was the life of the party during Carnival," her husband went on. "Everyone would try to guess what costume Lorenzo Alvar Nograro would wear next. Some folks claimed they saw him sneak out of the tower, in disguise, at other times as well. Apparently his exploits weren't limited to Carnival."

"That was just village gossip," insisted Fausti.

"Yes, from a village full of bastards," he said under his breath.

"Sorry, what did you say?" I asked.

"Don't mind him, he got up on the wrong side of bed this morning, that's all," Fausti said quickly, giving her husband another obvious jab. "Did you know the people of Ugarte used to be known as the frog silencers? Not anymore, of course, but we like to tell villagers the old story."

"I'm all ears," I said, pretending not to notice her clumsy attempt at changing the subject.

"Many years ago, back when Lorenzo Alvar Nograro's great-grandparents ruled over the land, the lords of the tower would summon the inhabitants of Ugarte to the moat to silence the frogs with sticks, because the croaking annoyed them. And the nickname stuck, although I've never seen anyone do anything like that to a frog."

We now emerged on the other side of the poplar wood. A sagging fence ringed the old building.

"Here we are. As you can see, it's just a derelict old building," said Fausti. "I'm afraid I have to go; I have a book club this evening."

"Sounds interesting. I'm an avid reader, too."

"So is everyone in the village. A group of us meets in the bar on Wednesday and Friday evenings."

"Which book are you reading right now?"

"*The Lords of Time*. It's all the rage. Have you read it?"

"I'm in the middle of it," I lied. I had spent hours poring over the text, and practically knew the story by heart. "Actually, I'd love to have the chance to discuss it with other readers."

"You should join us. Our book club is open to everybody. We're very informal."

"Maybe another day," I nodded. "Thanks for the walk; I'm going to stroll around the woods for a while."

We said our goodbyes, and I waited for the couple to disappear before taking a look around. The old bodega was a long white building with a gray slate roof. It wasn't inviting, and the last thing I wanted to do was venture into the surrounding area, but I nudged open the metal door anyway.

Light slanted through the high windows and illuminated the dust particles suspended in the air. At first, I was overwhelmed by the strong odor of musty wood and fermented wine.

Hundreds of big wooden casks were stacked on either side of me. Some were sealed; others had no lids.

I walked up to a barrel that caught my eye. I had seen one just like it before. But that wasn't the only thing I found. Piled in a corner were some plastic bags. They were white with a red stripe along the bottom.

I took out my cell phone and called Peña.

"Tell forensics to come to the old outhouse near the Nograro Tower. I think I've found out where MatuSalem's killer got that damned barrel. I found one just like it, as well as some plastic bags that are identical to the ones the Nájera sisters were put in."

24

CARNESTOLENDAS

DIAGO VELA

Winter, the Year of Our Lord 1192

Despite our resolve, there was nothing we could do to protect her sisters.

In any case, there was much to lament that Maundy Thursday.

I waited for Héctor outside the town gates. The fruit vendors had been setting up their stalls there for weeks, directly opposite Rúa de la Pellejería, Rúa de la Çapatería, and Rúa de la Ferrería. It was their way of letting the Mendozas know that they refused to pay the increasingly exorbitant levies being demanded for permission to sell produce inside the town walls.

The sounds of rattles, mortars and pestles, and cowbells soared above the ramparts. Early-morning Mass at Santa María had ended, and the townsfolk, dressed in their costumes, came in carts from their barns.

It was tradition to greet friends and kinsmen from the outlying settlements at the town gates, so when I spotted an impressive woolly mammoth, I set off down the hill.

Héctor was wearing a long brown cloak of unspun wool; a tiny skull with two curved tusks sat on his head. Nagorno had gifted it to him after returning from his travels in the far north, beyond even Gunnarr's birthplace. The Dicastillo coat of arms was a mammoth in an ocher field. The celebration of Carnestolendas—*carnis tollendus* in

Latin, or abstaining from meat—was a perfect excuse for each family to display its crest. Nagorno, however, usually wore a cape made from the skin of a gigantic serpent, which he'd purchased from the barbarians living south of the Saracens.

Glancing around uneasily, Héctor said, "I'd heard rumors that the fruit market had moved outside the walls. Is the rift in town really this great?"

"Victoria has become a town of walls, gates, and boundaries. Since Ruiz's execution, his kinsmen have been stirring up trouble during late-night meetings at Portal Oscuro. I fear the Mendozas, the Isunzas, and the Ortiz de Zárate brothers are plotting something. Keep your eyes open, Héctor, and warn me if the atmosphere of this Carnestolendas appears more heated than before."

"I will," he said, nodding. We entered the South Gate in search of our kinsmen.

Carnestolendas was a time for mockery. Artisans dressed up as noblemen, their coats of arms painted on coarse sackcloth. We passed one mimicking the limp of the Mendoza family patriarch, another the hunchback of the youngest Ortiz de Zárate, and a third the bulk of Johannes de Isunza.

Alix de Salcedo did not escape ridicule, either. A young lad wearing a charred robe and a three-coned wimple carried a sack embellished with a skull and filled with traps.

We saw Nagorno arrive in his snakeskin cape, his face painted with red scales. Beside him walked Gunnarr, wearing a snow-white bearskin on his head like a berserker. He had also removed his shirt and daubed his body. He'd tried covering himself in white chalk as part of the disguise, but his sheer size immediately gave him away.

Onneca was dressed as a lamia. Her dark tresses were concealed beneath a flaxen wig held in place with a golden comb that Nagorno had surely made for her. A robe of green moss and webbed feet completed her otherworldly costume. Sitting atop Olbia, she was as beautiful as a sunset. I had been avoiding her for some time.

I wanted nothing more to do with Onneca.

She had chosen my brother.

And I had little respect for anyone who could make such a bad decision.

We entered Rúa de la Astería. A group of young men, merry with wine, were throwing air-filled pigs' bladders at small children.

"Have you come disguised as . . . an old man?" Onneca asked me, puzzled.

"As the old man *and* the old woman, in fact." A few disguises were common during Carnestolendas. The Bear and the Judas were most popular, but it wasn't uncommon to see a youth dressed as an old crone carrying a straw effigy of an old man on their back.

"And where's the old woman? Haven't you forgotten her?"

"I'm on my way to fetch Grandmother Lucía now. She's waiting for me to give her a ride. Have you ever known her to miss a bacchanalia?"

I headed toward the corner of Rúa de las Pescaderías.

What I saw as I went worried me. The townsfolk were throwing handfuls of flour at all and sundry. Some were dressed as herdsmen, with bells around their necks, their faces blackened like sheep. It was hard to tell who anybody was, and many seemed to be using their anonymity to mock others; one youth rode on the back of his companion and pummeled those near him with an inflated pig's bladder. His wig of carrot fronds imitated the unruly locks of Mendieta, the executioner.

What gave me most cause for concern, however, was the straw effigy of Judas that the Mendozas had erected on their cart. The figure dressed in black was surrounded by a string of apples, turnips, carrots, chestnuts, and other produce rather than with the traditional eggshells. A group of nobles amused themselves by pelting the figure with rotten leeks. It was a crude reminder of the animosity they felt toward the fruit and vegetable vendors who'd refused to bow their heads and pay the excessive tariffs.

The noblemen had dressed up as cutlers, ironmongers, and bakers. Some nobles sported hunched backs, blackened teeth, or fake bellies in a mockery of the poorest townsfolk. I stood outside Grandmother Lucía's house, ill at ease as I watched the crowd. Alix de Salcedo was leaping and prancing at the head of her band of blacksmiths, who were wearing dresses and capes with *eguzkilores* pinned to the front. They gave out buns stuffed with chorizo that the local children wolfed down with gusto. I drew near as she came past me.

"How wonderful not to have to wear my wimple!" she cried with a sigh of relief. Yet I could sense anxiety in her voice.

"Is something worrying you?" I asked.

"A good deal more firewood has gone missing from the forge this year than in years previous. It's a youthful prank, but this time they've gone too far. I won't report it, but it reminds me of what I'm seeing in Villa de Suso today. It seems to me there's too much anger, too much ill will."

"Why *eguzkilores?*"

"Our guild protects Victoria. We provide arms for the townspeople when they need them. Here," she said, "take a bun. We made extra to celebrate Maundy Thursday."

The bun she handed me tasted like heaven.

"I'm here to fetch Grandmother Lucía, to carry her around the celebrations for a while."

"If you see danger, take her straight home and come find me."

"I will. Can you spare an *eguzkilore?*"

"What do you want it for?"

"An old ritual," I said, shrugging.

I spent the morning capering around town with Grandmother Lucía on my back. She giggled like a little girl, overjoyed to be outside and on the streets once more. I told her my plan as we approached Santa María Cathedral, where we came upon Vidal, the young priest, in solitary prayer. Although the Church of Rome denounced pagan festivals, in reality it turned a blind eye. It was impossible to prevent the townsfolk from celebrating. Priests did not often join the festivities, perhaps because there was always a pot-bellied drunken cleric mounted on a donkey among the disguises, and self-ridicule wasn't a virtue commonly found in men of the cloth.

"May we climb the bell tower?" I asked the young priest.

He startled when he saw me, a response I attributed to my disguise and to the unexpected presence of Grandmother Lucía. And yet he gave me a fleeting look of horror, too.

"Are you not Count Don Vela—the man who rose from the dead?"

"So folk say. Will you lend us the key?"

"What do you intend to do up there? I've already rung the Angelus."

"I yearn to view town from above, my child," Grandmother Lucía said. Her dulcet tone would have melted even the devil's heart. "Surely you won't refuse an old woman's fancy?"

The priest handed us a heavy iron key, and Grandmother Lucía took his hand and clasped it in her tiny fist.

His eyes met hers before darting away, as though burned. Then he abandoned the little church, leaving us to puzzle over his curious behavior.

I mounted the narrow spiral staircase with Grandmother Lucía still clinging to my back. The bell was suspended from a wooden crossbeam at the top of the stairs. Grandmother Lucía and I exchanged glances like a couple of mischievous children. I managed to find an old nail in the beam and pulled it loose. Grandmother Lucía took out Alix's *eguzkilore*, and I nailed it to the crossbeam with a stone I found lying at my feet.

"Let us pray this will suffice to keep the *gauekos* from entering town," she said, looking uneasily beyond the confines of the bell tower.

"I am more afraid of the evil within our walls than of spirits of the night, Grandmother."

With a roguish twinkle in her eye, she produced a length of red wool. "I braided this for you. Wear it always," she declared solemnly.

Red wool. I had come across spinners in other lands who claimed to thread together people's souls with skeins of red wool. I looked back at her, moved. This gift created a stronger tie between us than even the spilling of our red blood; it made us kinsfolk.

"Go ahead, put it on. Should you lose it, you know what will happen."

"I will never take it off. I swear on the goddess Lur."

"The goddess Lur," she echoed, speaking as if from her pagan soul.

I set her down, and she turned toward the north.

Suddenly she began to sniff the air, then she looked at me.

"What are they burning, Diago my boy?"

I looked out across the town and could see smoke rising from beyond the walls. The Mendozas had set fire to the Judas effigy. Joined by other nobles, they were dancing around the cart and jeering at the burning figure, which represented the vendors.

"We must go, Grandmother. It's time I took you home," I said, alarmed.

She nodded, and we descended to the chapel in silence. As we passed the door to the sacristy, she stopped me.

"Do you smell what I smell?"

"What does it smell like, Grandmother?"

"Like the priest, when I held his hand. Like rotten eggs."

I left her on the altar steps and approached the sacristy. The door was closed, but I pushed against it with my shoulder until it gave way. Grandmother Lucía was right, except the smell wasn't quite that of rotten eggs, although it was similar.

It was an odor not easily forgotten.

A dead animal, an abandoned battlefield left to the crows, an exposed mass grave after an execution—I covered my nose with my sleeve and looked for the source of the stench.

I found it coming from a tiny, shuttered window that stood at waist height. At that moment, I understood.

I left the room to breathe in fresh air.

Grandmother already knew, too. She looked at me with ageless eyes and lips tight with grief and rage.

"Take me home. You must take care of it."

"Grandmother, don't tell anyone. I need you to keep quiet."

"I will."

25

THE LORDS OF CASTILLO

UNAI

October 2019

Héctor called me the next day, and there was an unusual urgency in his voice that I'd never heard before.

"Iago and I would like to meet you in Vitoria as soon as possible. We read the novel carefully and are caught up on the events that have shaken your city these past few weeks. We have something to show you, but it's a valuable object that needs to be kept safe."

"You can come to my office at Portal de Foronda, in the Lakua district. There's no place more secure."

"I don't think I'm explaining myself properly," he said. "We don't want any security cameras or any record of this. There must be no paper trail. I've known you for many years, Unai, and I trust you to be discreet. The information we have will help your investigation, but we don't want our names in any reports. Is there somewhere else, somewhere more suitable, where we can meet?"

"Come to my apartment, then. Number Two, Plaza de la Virgen Blanca."

I greeted them on the landing. Although I hadn't seen Iago del Castillo for years, he looked pretty much the same: tall like me, dark hair, light eyes. He was carrying a hefty briefcase fitted with high-tech security locks. His older brother, Héctor del Castillo, was following behind him; Héctor was even-tempered and always weighed his words before speaking.

"Unai, good to see you!" Iago said, entering my apartment. "Héctor told me about the Broca's aphasia. Be sure to take care of that brain of yours. It has to last the rest of your life."

I hugged him; I was just so delighted to see them both.

The trust and affection that Iago and I shared had developed gradually. After completing my studies in criminal profiling, I was transferred to police headquarters in Santander for a few months, where I met Iago. A series of troubling homicides had put the brothers' private museum of archaeology, the MAC, at the center of an investigation led by Inspector Paul Lanero—a lovely man we called "Paulaner."

At the beginning, Iago and I had clashed because I thought he was concealing information. As time went by, though, my opinion changed. Iago was extremely smart—almost too smart—and he knew it, but he was also an honest man, and in the end, we solved the case.

"Don't worry about my brain," I said, "I doubt it'll atrophy with all the serial killers keeping me busy. Why don't we sit down and you can show me this mysterious object of yours. You sure know how to create intrigue."

The brothers exchanged a knowing look and then cast furtive glances at the windows overlooking the Plaza de la Virgen Blanca before sitting down. I put my cell phone on silent. Iago opened the briefcase and then slipped on a white cotton glove.

I leaned in, intrigued by a bundle of yellowing sheets bound in leather.

"What is it?"

"A chronicle that dates back to the twelfth century," replied Iago.

"Can you elaborate?" I asked, mesmerized. Were these pages really . . . a thousand years old?

"This, my friend, is a kind of diary written by one of our family's ancestors, Count Diago Vela," Héctor explained.

"You're descendants of Count Don Vela?"

"The Del Castillo branch were older relatives of the Velas, as recounted in that novel that's just been published," Héctor answered. "We have shared blood, yes. Several variations of our surname appear in documents pertaining to King Sancho the Seventh, Sancho the Strong, as well as in some of the cartularies in the General Archive of Navarre: Dicastillo, Deicastello, Diacastello, Diacasteyllo, Dicastello . . ."

"Count Don Vela's Christian first name also holds an indelible place in our family," Iago added. "It's no coincidence that our family baptized me in the ancestral tradition: Diago, Diego, Didaco, Didacus, Tiago, Santiago, Iago, Yago, Jacobo . . . They're all recurring names in our lineage. They come from the Greek *didachos*, meaning 'learned.' Names are important, don't you think? They define our lives. But to go back to what brings us here, this chronicle is a family heirloom, as I'm sure you've already deduced."

"May I take a look?" I asked, awestruck.

Iago smiled.

"Of course," he said, reverently turning the first page.

The ancient document was speckled with brownish spots, a process of deterioration called foxing. I examined the text, but I could not decipher it.

"I don't understand a word," I confessed.

"It's the written variant of the dialect used in this area. Suffice it to say that its beginning closely resembles that of the novel. Moreover, based on what we've read, *The Lords of Time* appears to parallel this chronicle throughout," Iago added.

"Would you be able to transcribe it?"

"I'm able to read the text," replied Héctor, "but Iago is the medievalist expert. He has studied it in depth and knows it well, which is why I asked for his help when you called. To be honest, I haven't even read it in its entirety," Héctor admitted. "It is, after all, a private diary, something intimate. I feel uneasy intruding on the thoughts of a man who loved, suffered, and grieved while writing it."

"Are you saying that the events described in *The Lords of Time* actually happened? That the novel is based on your ancestor's thousand-year-old diary?"

"No, not exactly."

"Then you'll have to explain, Iago."

"From what I've been able to read, the novel's author has taken our ancestor's account and rewritten the events, using modern language and employing a similar narrative structure to the chronicle," he clarified. "It is our opinion that the events depicted did take place. Carbon dating suggests the manuscript was written between AD 1190 and 1210, so the timeline matches as well. But there are slight variations in some events and characters."

"For example?" I prompted.

"Some of the deaths in the novel aren't mentioned in the chronicle, nor in any other historical documents from that period. But what I'm trying to tell you is that this manuscript is unknown. It has never been published. In fact, it has always remained exclusively in our family's possession. In other words, whoever wrote the novel must have accessed either a copy of the text or the original document written by Count Vela himself," said Iago.

"So there's another manuscript, identical to this one, that hasn't been published, either?"

"Exactly."

"Do you know where it is?"

"If only." Iago sighed. "It was lost in 1524 in Vitoria, when Diago Vela's palace burned to the ground and all the possessions belonging to his descendants were destroyed. Their family coat of arms, which hung in the San Miguel Arcángel Church, was also obliterated, even though they helped build the church, the walls—the entire neighborhood."

"Who destroyed them? Who demolished all that heritage?"

"At the time, several rival families were fighting over Vitoria. The situation worsened during the Revolt of the Comuneros."

"What are their surnames, Iago? Are any of these families present in Vitoria today?"

"Yes, many of them are: the Maturanas, the Isunzas, the Ortiz de Zárates, the Mendozas . . . Others, like the Calleja family, died out in the seventeenth century."

"Is it possible that the missing copy is in the private library of a direct descendant of one of those families?" I asked.

Héctor and Iago exchanged a swift, wordless glance.

"Well, clearly someone with the necessary knowledge gained access to the document, read it through, and created their own version of the diary," Iago concluded.

"For the record, and you know I have to ask: Did either of you write this variant or version of the chronicle?"

"No, obviously not."

"Is there any chance it was stolen and then returned without your knowledge?"

"Look," Héctor explained, "ever since the theft of the Cabárceno Cauldron three years ago, we've increased security at the museum. We keep this chronicle, along with other items of value, in a vault in the basement. Only Iago and I have the access codes. There's video surveillance, which are only erased after three weeks have gone by—that's standard in most security systems. But we always review the sped-up footage first, and believe me—no one broke in. In fact, no one other than my brother and I even knows the vault exists, not even the museum employees. And that's not even the strangest part.

There are only a few documents that have endured since the twelfth century, and if you've read the novel, you should know this chronicle is a firsthand account of events that occurred in Vitoria between AD 1192 and 1200. The missing copy alone is worth several million euros."

"Or dollars," interjected Iago. "There would be significant interest from American and European universities, private collectors, and museums. Have you ever been to the Conjunto Monumental de Quejana?"

"No, I haven't."

"What a shame," he said, shrugging as he closed the chronicle. "The lord chancellor built an altarpiece next to the tomb he and his wife, Leonor de Guzmán, occupy. That piece is actually a re-creation. A group of Dominican nuns sold the original to an English antique dealer in the early twentieth century. It was then purchased by an American tycoon, whose daughters donated it to the Art Institute of Chicago, where it's currently on exhibition. Do you see what I'm getting at? It seems absurd that someone who either has, or has access to, such a valuable document is content to forego wealth in favor of rewriting the chronicle to reflect their own version of events. I'm not sure if showing you this has helped the investigation or given you a bigger headache."

I smiled, too excited to speak.

"You have no idea how much clearer things are now," I said. "But I have one final question: Are Alfonso the Tenth's *Notes on the Seven Divisions* written in a language similar to this?"

"Yes. Alfonso's notes appeared in 1256, so they're later than the chronicle," replied Iago. "But grammatical structures and expressions didn't change as quickly back then as they do now, so the language is very similar, although the notes possibly use a Toledo variant."

"Thank you," I said. "You've been extremely helpful."

"Look, Unai . . . I know we can count on your discretion. If what we've told you proves helpful to your investigation, please keep our names out of it," Héctor repeated as we all rose to our feet.

"Don't worry, I'll find a way to avoid mentioning you. If it's discretion you want, though, you'd better show yourselves out of the building. All the neighbors know who I am, and they might put the pieces together."

"We'll do that. If there's anything else we can do, you know where to find us," added Iago as he gave me a firm handshake on his way to the door.

I waited until they had gone downstairs. I needed to organize my thoughts, but an idea was already forming. Who could have inherited the purloined copy of the chronicle? Who didn't need that money and, in fact, would have spurned it? Who had the skills necessary to read a document written in the twelfth century?

Just then, my phone vibrated in my back pocket.

I picked up as soon as I saw the name on the screen. "I have a bone to pick with you, Lutxo," I said.

You're the reason I argued with Alba, I thought.

"Are you downtown?" he asked hurriedly.

"Yes, do you want to meet for coffee at the Virgen Blanca?"

"Okay, I can be there in ten minutes," he said, agreeing.

"Fine."

I went downstairs to the café next to my building and waited at the most secluded table I could find. The other customers stirred their milky coffees and munched on tapas as they stared dreamily at the square through the café's plate-glass windows. Lutxo stubbed his cigarette out in the doorway, ordered at the bar, and then sat next to me.

"Hey, what's up?" he said.

"You do realize I'm pretty pissed off with you?"

"Look, Kraken—"

"It's Unai. My name is Unai. I'm one of your oldest friends. You've known me since we were children, remember? I'm not the celebrity your headlines are turning me into."

"Whatever. Look, Unai, I'm just doing my job. I saw you and Tasio Ortiz de Zárate together, locking horns. How could I let that story go? People need to know that he's back and that he has something to do with these murders."

"Watch it, Lutxo. Who said Tasio had anything to do with these murders? Have you already forgotten that the guy was falsely convicted and spent twenty years in prison? Are you going to turn public opinion against him again? Okay, he's an asshole, a real asshole, but if you make him out to be more than that, you are no better. What's this all about? Do you have some sort of problem with me? You don't even know what he and I were talking about. Our conversation had nothing to do with this investigation, or these murders. You've put your foot in it now, Lutxo, big time. Tasio is going to be furious with you. Now he can't even come to Vitoria to attend a funeral without being accused of murder. What kind of a life is that?"

"So tell me. Explain what he was doing so I won't feel obliged to speculate."

"So now you're blackmailing me: either I tell you what you want to know, or you use my image to spread vicious rumors. Don't you see how that might interfere with how I do my job? Or maybe you do see, maybe the problem is that you don't give a damn."

"Do you honestly think I'm going to stop doing *my* job just because we belong to the same *cuadrilla*? I don't see you treating me with more consideration because I'm your friend. So what's the difference? Because I don't see one."

"The difference is that every time you sneak behind a cypress tree to secretly take my picture in a cemetery you wreck my life—you steal another piece of my privacy in Vitoria."

"There's an easy way out of that," he said, shrugging as he stirred his espresso.

I sighed. There was no arguing with him.

"Things are going to end very badly between us, Lutxo, and it won't matter that you're in my *cuadrilla.* I'm going to ask the judge to extend the gag order on this case so you won't be able to publish anything remotely related to it."

"You wouldn't dare. And you know why? Because if you do, I'll just keep writing about your personal life."

I suppressed my urge to unleash the Kraken inside me and throttle him right then and there. Instead, I fired my parting shot.

"Exactly when did you sell your soul, my friend?"

As I stood up to go, I heard "Lau teilatu." Alba was calling. I'm not sure how well I managed to conceal how eager I was to speak with her, how much I wanted to bring her up to speed. I walked away from Lutxo and his ridiculous goatee, leaving his anger behind.

To find some privacy, I descended the wooden stairs to the bathrooms. I glanced around; both doors were open, so I could share my news discreetly.

"Estíbaliz has been calling me because you won't pick up," she said. "Forensics has confirmed that the samples of the wood from the barrel MatuSalem was found in match those taken from the casks in the abandoned bodega. French oak, used for aging wine. Rare nowadays. We're still waiting for the test results on the bags."

"I have news, too," I said, my voice hushed. "I think I know who wrote the novel and murdered all those people."

"What?"

"I can't tell you much right now. What I can tell you is that *The Lords of Time* is a retelling of an unpublished twelfth-century chronicle by Count Vela. The person who wrote it must have a copy of the original text penned by the count, which is worth several million euros—"

"Estíbaliz is in charge of the investigation. Why don't you tell her?" Alba cut in.

Because I'm afraid Estíbaliz has fallen in love with our mysterious author's murderous alter, I wanted to tell him.

But I kept quiet.

I had other plans.

26

ANP

UNAI

October 2019

I dialed the number for the tower and Claudia, the guide, answered.

"Good morning, I'd like to visit the tower," I said. "What time are your guided tours?"

"There's one in an hour, and another at six this evening."

"Perfect, I'll come at six."

"Please try to be punctual."

I drove to Ugarte and parked next to an abandoned lot. I walked toward the tower, keeping an eye on the time. As soon as I saw people milling around the entrance, I joined them. Claudia was ushering visitors through the inner courtyard. I indicated that I was going up to the apartment.

As I pressed the intercom, I said a quiet prayer.

"Hello?"

"Good evening, Ramiro Alvar. It's Unai, may I come up?"

"Of course, please."

I was in luck; the person waiting for me in the blue hallway was Ramiro Alvar. He was wearing slacks and his glasses. He looked tense.

"I don't want you to think I'm not pleased to see you, but is something the matter?" he asked in his wispy voice.

"Why do you ask?"

"Well, you've been coming here quite a bit," he replied with a shrug.

"Could we go into the library?" I said.

"Of course, the library is my favorite room."

"If I had one like yours, it would be mine, too."

He sat in his reading chair and gestured for me to take a seat next to his walnut desk.

"So, what's this all about?"

"Let's not play games," I began. "Something strange is going on around you."

"Please explain."

"After you wrote a novel based closely on a twelfth-century diary, people have started to die in the same ways as the characters in your book."

I hadn't arrived unprepared. My gun was in my shoulder holster, and the safety was off. I leaned forward so I would be able to reach it more easily.

But Ramiro Alvar simply stared at his hands as if they were someone else's.

"So you've figured out that much. . . . I tried . . . I did my best to keep everything under control, but obviously I failed."

"Of course, you're free to call your lawyer, but if you want to make a confession, I'll have to take you to the police station."

"That won't be necessary. I don't intend to confess to anything, Unai. I didn't kill anyone. I'm incapable of violence. I literally couldn't hurt a fly. Call me soft, if you'd like, you wouldn't be the first. But yes, I admit: I did write my own version of Don Vela's chronicle. It was something private, therapeutic. I never intended for it to be published, for obvious reasons."

"One of which is that Don Vela's descendants might demand you return the copy of the chronicle. Your ancestors stole their property."

Ramiro Alvar lowered his head in shame, as if the ancient sin weighed on his conscience.

"It's true. I was horrified when I saw your copy of *The Lords of Time*. I realized that my manuscript had been stolen and published under a pseudonym."

"So the novel is your manuscript, word for word?"

"Yes, it's unchanged."

"Can you prove it?"

He went over to the desk and turned on his laptop.

"Here, see for yourself."

I approached cautiously and stayed well out of his way just in case he tried to poison me with a medieval powder.

He opened a document and showed me the date of his last revision. It was over a year ago.

"Writing this was cathartic, and for a while I thought the therapy had worked. At one point, I printed a copy, but I destroyed it because I wanted to move on. I have no idea who hacked into my computer and stole the manuscript. Of course, it should be intellectual-property theft, but because I never registered the manuscript, I don't own the copyright. Although I don't want or need the money, this story was never meant to be seen. Now thousands of people are reading it. . . . And four have died. I don't understand what's going on."

"Then help me by telling me what you do understand. You admit to writing the novel, and you insist you didn't publish it or kill anybody. But you must suspect someone. You've also concealed your diagnosis from me. It's time for you to tell me the truth, because I have evidence linking you to every one of the crimes: At the scene of the first murder, there was an intruder dressed in a Dominican's habit like the one from your collection. Samples of wood taken from the barrel that contained the young man and animals drowned in the river match the barrels in your abandoned bodega. We also found plastic bags there that are identical to the ones used to transport the sisters who were trapped in the wall."

Ramiro Alvar looked at me, aghast.

"Do you have fingerprints, DNA, footprints, other evidence . . . ?" he asked.

"Physical evidence linking you to the victims and the crime scene? Not yet. But we're still looking. Tell me: Why did you rewrite the chronicle, and why did you change some of the events?"

"Because I wanted to kill my alter and any others who might follow him! I never meant for anyone to die. I just wanted to cure myself, and I thought I'd succeeded. Alvar disappeared for an entire year, and I was able to live in peace. Then when you came here the other day to pick up the novel and I didn't recognize you, I realized that he must have met you the day before. It meant he was back. I hadn't killed him off after all. Since then, I've been terrified. I have no memory of what happens when he's here, and I'm afraid of what he might do to keep me from killing him."

"So you confirm that you have dissociative identity disorder. Is that why you studied psychology?"

"I'm not the first Lord of Nograro to suffer from this condition. There's something I want to show you."

I followed somewhat warily to the floor below. This was a room I hadn't seen. Stretching across all four walls were blue canvases depicting a magnificent cityscape. The effect was dizzying. Dozens of old photos were displayed on an upright piano.

"Carnival," I whispered.

"Carnival?" He laughed hollowly. "A festival for the villagers, and for the lord of the tower, who could openly dress up as one of his alters: the aging countess, the boy, the abbess, the soldier, the priest. The day was a torment for the rest of the family who stoically endured the silent ridicule. I have fond memories of my parents in their old age. They didn't really have the energy to raise me, but my father was dutiful and affectionate, and my mother gave me all the love and support a child needs. However, my father suffered from the illness that afflicts Nograro men, known as multiple personality disorder back then. Although he saw several psychiatrists, no one was able to cure him. When my parents died tragically, my brother and I had to identify their bodies at the Santiago Hospital morgue. We had to experience the shame of seeing our dead father dressed in a maid's uniform, complete with cap, apron, stockings, and high heels."

"What happened to your brother?"

"He died of a hereditary blood disorder. He was a priest, but after our parents died, he came back to live at the tower. I was still a minor, so he became my legal guardian. We were very close. He was a wonderful brother, quite brilliant. I miss him every day."

"I have a degree in criminal profiling," I said, "and I've been in touch with a specialist in dissociative identity disorder, one of the few people in the country who has successfully treated people with the condition. I told her about you, and she helped me understand DID a bit better. She told me that this disorder is rare, so not many incidence studies have been conducted, but there's nothing to indicate that it's hereditary."

"Really? So what do you think these are?" he snapped, gesturing emphatically at the photographs. "People in costumes? Wake up, Unai. These pictures weren't taken during Carnival. The men in my family dressed up like this every day. The condition always started as a childish prank, but as they grew up, they developed several alters. These men didn't know how to deal with their multiple personalities, so they hid them away from the rest of the world. The family became known for being reclusive. But how could they go out dressed like someone different every day without ending up in an asylum?"

"Doctor Leiva believes she can help you integrate your alter if you agree to therapy with her. You're the apparently normal personality, the ANP, aren't you?"

"I believe so. This is the personality I've had since I was young, and this is how others remember me as well. My disorder came later."

"Why did you rewrite the chronicle?"

"I associate it with them: my father, my grandfather, my brother. It's our family's hidden gem, the spoils of an ancestral feud. It paints a vivid portrait of our forefathers' day-to-day lives, describing how they confronted the events of 1199. We were all familiar with it. I remember gathering around the hearth with my family—my mother, siblings, uncles—and listening to my father read it aloud. He brought his ancestors' voices to life in the very library I showed you the other day."

"So you rewrote it as a form of therapy," I said. "You created a character who reminded you of your alter, changed a few details, and then killed him. Even though, in the real chronicle, in Victoria's real history, that person didn't die."

"I believe Alvar read the book, realized he was going to die, and started to target the people he thinks correspond to the characters in the novel. He's killing them to avoid being killed himself."

"In other words, he's doing what alters do—trying to survive."

"I'm not sure, Unai. It's just a theory. Whenever Alvar appears, he takes over. The next thing I know, there's a crumpled cassock in my wardrobe and a hole in my memory. It's as though he unplugs my consciousness. He switches me off entirely."

"And you think he's the murderer?"

Ramiro Alvar looked at me helplessly.

"Is there really no DNA linking these crimes to me?" he asked again.

"No, which is why I can't present this to the judge. She'd think I was crazy."

All I have is circumstantial evidence. Any defense lawyer would immediately have it thrown out, I thought.

"Besides, you can't be a witness to something you can't remember. I really believe that the only solution is for you to meet Doctor Leiva and start therapy with her. She'll know how to activate Alvar."

He flipped up his jacket collar, as though a shiver had just run down his spine.

"You don't know what you're asking me to do. I'm scared. I'm scared that Alvar is mad at me for writing that novel and trying to kill him off."

"Alvar can't hurt you physically. You're the ANP; without you, he doesn't exist. I have one more question: Did you see us from your window?"

"I'm sorry?"

"I assume you can see the road and the parking lot from your library window. Do you remember seeing Inspector Gauna and me the first time we visited you here?"

"Now that you mention it, I think I remember seeing you both get out of the car. But I have no recollection of meeting her. Did she come upstairs with you?"

Yes, and you stayed out all night with her, Casanova, I was tempted to quip.

"Yes, she did. I suspect it's my colleague, Estíbaliz, who triggers Alvar."

All of a sudden, Ramiro ripped off his glasses as though they pained him. When he spoke, his voice was imperious.

"No more talk of psychiatrists, Inspector. This visit has gone on long enough. Allow me to show you out."

I looked at him, and my reptilian brain, the ancient part of us that alerts us to danger, ordered my right hand to reach for my gun.

"Of course, I was just leaving."

I let him walk out first. I didn't want to turn my back on him. We walked shoulder to shoulder along the faded corridors. With a smug grin on his face, Alvar held his head high, hands clasped behind his back. He was like a child, keeping a secret inside his wooden castle.

"Will you give my regards to your colleague?"

"Naturally. We both have her best interests at heart, don't we?" I asked pointedly.

"Indeed. You can't imagine the ways in which my chance encounter with that extraordinary woman has turned my life upside down."

"Enough to make you leave the priesthood?"

I swallowed hard. I knew I was talking to Alvar, but his gestures were as real as Ramiro Alvar's.

His gaze wandered off, as though he were thinking of a pleasant memory.

"If anybody were worth doing that for, it would, of course, be her."

"We're agreed on that," I said, nodding.

"Put in a good word for me, will you?" he asked, a touch of desperation coming through his golden voice.

I leaned closer. No one could hear us, but I needed to win him over, to create a certain complicity between us, so I whispered, "Come on, Alvar. You know that isn't necessary."

With that I walked down the stairs, away from him. *Okay,* I thought, taking stock. *Alvar monitors the phone and the road, and he's isolating Ramiro Alvar in his tower. That's easy enough to do. Ramiro Alvar has become agoraphobic because he's afraid people will find out about his condition. At the mere mention of Estíbaliz today, Alvar took over. He is alert to when his ANP is present, and he can take over whenever he wants. Ramiro Alvar has no memory of what his alter does.*

I walked back to the village, knowing that Alvar was watching my every move from the library window.

I had another visit to make that day. I headed toward Fausti Mesanza's villa and found her closing the gate to her garden.

"Am I in time for book club?" I asked.

"Yes. I was just leaving. Come with me, and I'll introduce you to the others. The village bar used to be a doctor's office, but we did some remodeling and started running it as a collective. We took turns every month. It was open on Saturday evenings and on Sundays after Mass. But we're getting too old now, and some young people have taken over the lease. We still go there for a glass of vermouth and to play a few games of cards. When it's cold, they light the stove, so it's nice and cozy."

We climbed the steep streets of Ugarte, a beautifully preserved village complete with a medieval drinking fountain next to the church. Although it had fewer than a hundred inhabitants today, it had remained populated for a thousand years. The bar was located next to the fronton court and the outdoor bowling alley.

Peering through the window, I could see a bar with a wooden counter, a well-worn pool table, and several teenagers playing foosball. The evening had grown chilly, and the warmth of the blazing fire was welcome. It enveloped us as soon as we stepped inside.

An elderly lady in a wheelchair observed us from the corner of the room near the stove. She scrutinized me, a sardonic smile on her face. I'd seen a similar expression on others who had lived a long time and were past caring what others thought. Her sunken eyes took in every detail as we went over to say hello.

"This is my mother-in-law, Benita," said Fausti. "Best not to tell her anything since nothing escapes her. She's sharp as a tack."

I pulled over a chair and sat next to Benita. She sounded like the perfect accomplice.

"That's Cecilia, the pharmacist," Fausti informed me, filling me in as more neighbors entered the bar.

"Apothecary," Benita corrected her. "She and Aurora, the woman who just walked in, hate each other. Aurora ran the dry-goods store, but she's retired now and bored stiff."

A young man, around twenty-five, came in carrying a bunch of cans.

"That's Gonzalo, he runs the bar."

The man smiled at us. His T-shirt had a picture of an animal with the body of a goat, the head of a lion, and the tail of a serpent, along with the words *I'm a chimera.* He came over to ask if we wanted anything to drink. Fausti asked for "the usual," and I ordered a bottle of water.

"Txomin is a cabinetmaker. He grew tired of living in the city and set up his workshop here in the village. It's worth a visit; he has some beautiful things," Fausti said.

"I'll stop by," I said.

Within ten minutes, I knew the names of the twenty locals in the circle. Their copies of *The Lords of Time* were all open to the same page.

"We have a new member," Fausti announced. "He isn't from Ugarte, but we welcome him nonetheless. His name is Unai, and he's—"

"I'm an inspector with the Vitoria Criminal Investigation Unit, but I'm here as a reader." I smiled. My announcement came as a surprise to everyone, including Fausti.

Everyone stared at me, intrigued. I studied their expressions, making mental notes.

After they'd recovered, a young woman with curly hair began to read aloud in a leisurely way. I'd been told that her name was Irati, and she ran the glassworks and the Ugarte agritourism business.

I watched the fire crackle, letting myself become hypnotized by the flames as I listened once again to the story I already knew so well.

27

THE SACRISTY

DIAGO VELA

WINTER, THE YEAR OF OUR LORD 1192

I met Gunnarr on Rúa de las Tenderías. When he saw my expression, he led me away from the festivities into Pero Vicia's garden.

"I can tell something's going on, Diago. What do you need?"

"Your strong arms and two maces."

"Then we'll go to the forge."

We set off in silence, skirting the crowd, the flour, and the ashes. I looked over my shoulder every once in a while. I could sense that we were being shadowed, but I couldn't make out who was following us. All I saw were colored streamers, dunce caps, and faces painted black and red.

When we arrived at the church, the doors were wide open, but nobody came out to greet us. It was strange that the priest hadn't returned. As we entered the sacristy, Gunnarr held his nose.

"You are right, I fear," he murmured.

Neither of us was in the mood for conversation. We didn't speak as we hit the sacristy wall with our maces. Soon the mortar between the stones began to crumble, and eventually the hole was big enough for one of us to climb through.

"Do you want me to go in?" Gunnarr asked, burying his nose in the crook of his arm.

"No, just bring me a candle from the candelabra," I replied.

At that moment, Nagorno and Onneca appeared in the doorway.

"Is it true, Diago?" Onneca cried. "Is what Vidal told me true?" Her green-painted face was streaked with tears—it frightened me to see her like this.

"What did the priest tell you?"

"That you forced him!" she screamed, pummeling my chest with her fists. "You ordered him to stop giving them food and drink."

"You believe me capable of that?" I replied, aghast.

I snatched the candle Gunnarr had brought and stepped through the hole in the wall.

I have no wish to remember the complete squalor I saw. There were rats with the two dead bodies, as well as Onneca's unopened letters.

I emerged gasping for breath, the stench of death clinging to my skin.

"No one is to go in there—what's inside is not of this world," I ordered, my voice cracking.

Neither Gunnarr nor Nagorno was a stranger to death, but I silently begged my brother: *Don't let her see them.*

"I want to go in. I want to see them!" cried Onneca.

Nagorno stood in her way, but she thrust him aside.

She took the candle from me—as though she couldn't see me, as if I weren't there—and entered her sisters' tomb.

We could hear her sobs. We could hear her speak to them, though they could no longer reply. Her heartrending cries still haunt my nights.

The three of us despaired as we contemplated the scene on the other side of the broken wall.

"Get her out, Nagorno," I begged in a whisper. I wished I could block my ears. I couldn't bear to hear her suffering a moment longer. "Please, Brother. Get her out of there."

Nagorno stood motionless, staring through the hole as his wife clung to one of the bodies.

"If you won't do it for him, then do it for me," Gunnarr added in a hushed tone. "Go inside and fetch her."

"For you, then, Gunnarr. For what we owe each other," he said at last.

He entered as serenely as Death. He whispered something into her ear, removed the flaxen wig, and stroked her black tresses.

I never knew what my brother said to her, what soothing words he used to tear her from that torment.

She emerged a different woman. More terrible, all fury.

She rushed at me with the burning candle in her hand, full of rage.

"Because we're family, Diago . . . !" she roared. "Because your brother has asked it of me, I shall await your trial rather than have you killed this very night. But I shall never forgive you."

I forgot about Nagorno, Gunnarr, even the two dead sisters. She and I were alone with our shared hatred.

"And I shall never forgive *you*, Onneca! For believing me capable of murdering your sisters, for choosing to think that of me . . . after what we were to each other, after I opened myself to you. You knew me. You knew my mornings and my evenings, my happiest days and my most sorrowful. Yet you choose to think me a murderer of children. Do you believe yourself capable of falling in love with a monster?"

We held each other's gaze as the melted candle wax dripped onto the stone floor of the sacristy. All my instincts were on alert, watchful; I felt as though I were on a hunt, waiting for a wounded boar to attack with sharpened tusks.

"Yes, I think I am capable of falling in love with a monster," she replied at last.

I looked at Nagorno and then at her.

"Not my words, but yours," she said.

I turned away from the stench of rotting flesh.

But Gunnarr barred my way, silently imploring me to remain calm.

"Onneca, word of this must not be spread tonight. The streets are awash with drunken revelers, and if the townsfolk were to learn of this atrocity, they would lynch your brother-in-law, or the priest, or whomever they deem to be at fault." Gunnarr's soothing tone was born from time spent calming mutinous sailors aboard a ship.

"My cousin is right," Nagorno interjected in a monotone, as unruffled as ever. "Gunnarr, inform the lieutenant, but tell him to keep his counsel until the morrow. Send guards to detain the priest so that he may bear witness. Seek him discreetly in the barns, or in Sant Michel Church. Close the town gates. The burning of the Judas has enraged the fruit vendors. If we do not take care, we will all end up on the sharp end of a sword before the night is done. Brother, go home and stay hidden. Do you need protection?"

"You know my answer," I said without looking at them.

"As you wish. But sleep with one eye open."

"I always do."

I set off for home.

At midnight I woke from a light sleep to find myself standing in the bathtub with dagger drawn. I had locked the door to my dwelling, and few people knew the key's hiding spot.

Once home, I'd soaked my spirits in the hot water for several hours, staring into the hearth, surrounded by darkness. I'd fallen asleep, only to wake naked and wet with my dagger in hand.

"Diago, it's me. Put away your blade. I came alone," said Alix.

I set my weapon on the ledge above the fireplace and sank back into the water.

"What's the matter with you?" she asked, drawing nearer. She was still wearing her costume, the dress bedecked with *eguzkilores*.

I felt a little safer with her by my side. Her calm presence soothed me, as it had since our first meeting.

"Have you heard anything?" I asked her.

"No, but when I checked on Grandmother Lucía, she was tossing in her bed; usually she could sleep through a war. What happened? What did she see? What did you tell her?"

"The priest starved Count de Maestu's two young daughters to death. He has testified that he did so in accordance with my instructions." I spoke frankly because I had no wish to keep any secrets from her. Not that night, when I felt so raw. "Of course I did no such thing, which means someone forced him to do it and then to lie and say it was me. I can think of only two reasons he might have been tempted do such a thing: the promise of riches or blackmail. Does he have a family?"

Alix sat heavily on the edge of the bathtub, as though her legs were about to give out.

"Does Vidal have a family?" I repeated.

"An elderly widowed mother in Toledo," she replied, blank. "I can't believe they are dead. Bona and Favila . . . I grew up with them. We learned to walk together. I danced with them, prayed with them."

But my thoughts were elsewhere. Did the villain behind this have influence as far away as Toledo?

"You cannot speak of this," I said at last.

"I know I cannot."

"Why did you come, Alix?"

"I came to be here. Just to be here. I realized something terrible had happened when I saw Grandmother. Is there room for me in your tub?"

I nodded in silence.

Why speak.

Words had harmed me enough that day. I was weary of it all.

I wanted only to close my eyes, for sleep to wash away the words of the day. Alix stepped out of her robe and slipped into the tub, the light of the flames sliding over her naked body. She spread her loose hair across my chest and pulled my arms around her, so she was enfolded by me. We stayed like that, staring into the fire, allowing the night to lull us to sleep in each other's embrace.

"What shade of blue am I now?"

"A distant blue, somewhere beyond sorrow. Your eyes are lost in the flames, as if you were gazing at the ocean."

"It's true."

"The blue of abandonment."

"Yes. I smell of death, the odor of their decaying flesh has clung to my hair and my skin. I wanted to wash it away for my own sake, but also because I didn't want you to smell it on me," I confessed, after staring at the flames in silence for a few minutes.

"We mustn't be together. I will not bury a fourth husband, and you've seemed intent upon dying since your return."

"I agree; we mustn't. It is too dangerous for you. They'd find a pretext to accuse you if I were to die. Let's just sleep tonight. Tomorrow we'll be simple neighbors again. Alix . . ."

"What?"

"I shall never forget how well you have cared for me since I returned to Victoria."

28

VALDEGOVÍA

UNAI

October 2019

I was jogging through the Old Quarter the night Peña called. My runs calmed me and cleared my head. Since Alba and Deba were no longer with me, I took to the streets every chance I got.

I took a breather between Calle Zapatería and Calle Correría, sitting on the lip of an open drain in the Carnicerías district to take Peña's call.

The city had transformed its medieval open-air sewage system into well-kept enclosed gardens: el Túnel, los Hospitales, los Rosales, los Tejos, los Acebos . . .

"Kraken, have you checked Twitter?" Peña asked.

"I haven't had time today," I replied. The wind was picking up; it lifted my hair, exposing my scar. I quickly covered it.

"Well, it's going viral as we speak." He sounded concerned. "I'm calling to ask if we should step in."

"Tell me what 'it' is first."

"I'll read you the tweet: '*The Lords of Time* is based on an unpublished twelfth-century chronicle. Its market value, according to an expert, could reach three million euros.' "

"Damn it," I blurted.

"Did you know about this?"

"I just found out yesterday," I replied, heading back home. My run was over. "And other than my source, no one should know. Have you spoken to Estíbaliz?"

"She's not picking up. It's eleven o'clock. She could have gone to bed, I guess," he said.

"We'll have to start without her, then. Did you call Milán?"

"She's already trying to trace the owner of the Twitter account. We think it was created recently just to drop this bombshell. The number of retweets is increasing every minute. Local and even national media are bound to publish the story tomorrow. What concerns me is that if no one knew about this other than you and your source, then somebody could be following you or could have hacked your cell phone."

"I mentioned it to Alba. I was with Lutxo in Café de la Virgen Blanca, but I took her call downstairs in the restroom. I'm pretty sure he didn't follow me, and there's no way he could have heard anything from upstairs."

"Maybe there was someone in the bathroom with you?" Peña ventured.

"No, I checked. Unless . . ."

"What?"

"I suppose someone could have been eavesdropping from inside the wine cellar. That's the only thing I can think of."

Lutxo knew the waitress. Would he have bribed her to listen behind the door? Would she have agreed? Was this leak even advantageous to Lutxo? I wasn't sure. But it made no sense for Iago and Héctor to share that information.

"In any case, the judge knows nothing about this line of inquiry, so we're powerless to take down the tweet," I told Peña.

"You're right, we certainly can't do anything tonight. We'll brief everyone at the office in the morning. Besides, you've been in a bad mood for days, Kraken. You need to get out. Why don't you come with me to Calle Pinto? There's a new bar that has live music, and there's a Celtic band tonight, fiddles and flutes. It might help us forget death and literary intrigue for a few hours. What do you say?"

I forced myself to accept, if only for my mental health. I knew I needed to disconnect and that ultimately a night out would help with the investigation. For weeks I'd been avoiding meeting my *cuadrilla* for coffee, once again putting my life on hold to solve a case.

It was almost three in the morning by the time I said goodbye to Peña and left the bar. He had stayed behind to have drinks with his musician friends.

Peña's pals had ended their Celtic set with "Fisherman's Blues" by the Waterboys. For the first time, I'd managed to relax and forget about how depressing my situation was. But as I stepped outside onto a practically deserted Calle Pintorería, I realized I had missed several calls. At around two thirty, Estíbaliz had left a disturbing voice mail: "*Come to the tower right away, I think . . .* " It trailed off.

I dialed her number a few times, but she didn't pick up. I was worried. Estí always answered my calls.

I ran back into the bar.

Peña put down his drink when he saw the look of alarm on my face.

"I need you to come to Valdegovía," I whispered. "Estíbaliz called me from Nograro Tower. She sounded frightened, and now she's not picking up. I have no idea what she's doing there this time of night, but I have a bad feeling. Let's go see what's happening."

We left Vitoria behind us. The countryside was dark and tree branches formed a tunnel over the car as we sped toward the tower.

"She's still not picking up," I muttered, trying to keep the concern from my voice. "She's not even replying to my texts. But her phone is on. She just isn't answering."

"We're here, Kraken. Should we call for backup?"

"Let's wait until we know exactly what we're dealing with."

I don't want to get her in trouble, I thought.

I didn't know what was going on yet, and I didn't want to expose her by calling anyone. I didn't trust Alvar, but Estí may have gotten him to talk, and I didn't want to risk compromising that.

We parked on the edge of the property and switched off the engine. I knew the path well enough to find my way using only the faint light of the stars. We saw Estíbaliz's car in the parking lot.

We walked over the drawbridge and crossed the lawn. The small window above the arched entrance was open.

This time, instead of dialing Estí's cell phone, I called Ramiro Alvar's landline. I could hear it ringing from inside the tower. I let it ring, but no answer. I pounded on the door. Nothing. Not a sound.

"Shine your light on the window," I told Peña.

It didn't appear forced or broken.

The window's been opened from the inside, I thought. *Ramiro wouldn't leave a window open overnight; he's sensitive to the cold. Estíbaliz called from the tower two hours ago. If she's still in there, someone or something is preventing her from picking up. Alvar or Ramiro Alvar isn't answering the phone, either. She's in danger. Ramiro Alvar never goes out. So he must be inside. What the hell is going on?*

I shone my phone's flashlight on the patch of grass below the window. There were no marks that would indicate a heavy object had been dragged through the area.

They haven't been abducted. They must still be inside, and a third person must have jumped out of this window.

"We'll climb in. I'll give you a leg up," I told Peña.

He placed his foot in my cupped hands using the wall to steady himself, pulled himself through, and disappeared inside the tower. A few seconds later he popped his head through the opening.

"The coast is clear," he whispered.

"Go downstairs and open the door for me."

I had to wait two minutes, each one as long as a bitter winter, until finally, the heavy wooden door opened and I entered the tower.

Everything was dark, except for a beam of light shining onto the inner courtyard. I looked for the source: a lamp in Ramiro Alvar's apartment was giving off a warm glow.

I pressed the intercom several times. Nothing. So we couldn't get into Ramiro's private residences. We could only access the public areas of the tower.

I pulled out my gun. Peña did the same.

I crossed the inner courtyard, planning to climb the stairs.

But I slipped.

One of the cobblestones was wet, and I fell onto something soft, cracking my elbow on the ground. Wincing from the pain, I was going to pull my phone from my pocket—I could use it as a flashlight—when I realized my hands were wet as well. Peña managed to turn on his flashlight first, revealing that I was sprawled on top of a half-naked body, my hands covered with blood.

"The hair . . . Kraken."

"What hair?"

"You tripped over someone with red hair."

No, that's impossible. I refused to believe it.

"Shine the light over here!" I commanded.

I scrambled to my feet, but it was difficult to keep my balance—I was standing in a dark pool of blood.

I looked down at Estíbaliz's pallid face. I snatched Peña's phone and shone it in her eyes.

Her pupils contracted. She was still alive, but she was unconscious.

"Call this in, now! We have an officer down. She's lost a lot of blood. She'll need a transfusion—blood type AB-positive. Tell them to send a patrol car and a forensics team."

"Kraken, there's another body."

Peña shone the flashlight on a second figure. I could just make out an old-fashioned white nightshirt soaked in blood, with a pair of bare legs peeking out from beneath it. Everything outside the light from Peña's phone was swallowed in darkness.

"See if they're still alive!" I ordered.

Peña stepped forward to check while I called for backup. I forced myself to step into my criminologist shoes so I could observe my colleague's injuries. I had no choice; I couldn't dwell on the fact that this broken body lying at my feet was Estíbaliz.

Not you, not you, not you.

"Male, pupils responsive to light!" Peña shouted. "What do we do?"

"We don't know how far they fell, so we can't move them," I said. I shone the light from my phone across the length of the balcony. "They probably have internal injuries and internal bleeding. Describe the man's injuries."

"One leg has multiple fractures. The body is twisted, like a broken doll. I think he fell feetfirst."

"If so, he will have injuries to his pelvis and femurs and possibly fractures of his heels and ankles," I said.

"It looks that way."

"Estíbaliz is almost in the center of the yard, while he's at the foot of the stairs. That means she was pushed or possibly thrown from a greater height. And yet I can't see any damage to the balcony's railing. Maybe somebody picked her up and threw her over? That would take incredible strength, even though she only weighs a hundred and ten pounds or so," I reasoned.

I visualized how this crime could have taken place. Someone broke into the building while Estíbaliz and Alvar were . . . well, enjoying themselves in Alvar's apartment. For whatever reason, one of them came down the tower stairs and fell or was thrown over the balcony. Afterward, the exact same thing happened to the other one. Estíbaliz's slight frame worked in her favor: less weight, slower speed, less energy released on impact, fewer injuries.

Alvar hadn't fallen as far, but they were both unconscious. Only the doctors could assess how severe their internal injuries were.

"As for you, Estí: How are we going to explain what you were doing in your underwear at the main suspect's house tonight?" I whispered in her ear. I knew she couldn't hear me, just as I knew I was going to have to lie for her, as she had always done for me.

But that was the least of her problems. Right now her life was hanging by a thread.

29

EL JARDÍN DE SAMANIEGO

UNAI

October 2019

Dawn had broken by the time I started the drive to Laguardia. It had been a long night. The surgeons were still operating on both Estíbaliz and Ramiro Alvar. I supposed that was one of the drawbacks to being the ANP: when your alter gets into trouble, it's *your* body that suffers.

The medical team told us it would take several more hours—and they gave no guarantees. Estíbaliz was in critical condition.

And that was more than I could bear, so Kraken took control: *What can I do right now? What else needs to get done?*

I focused on what was in front of me. On what was feasible right then.

Driving to Laguardia and back was a better use of my time than climbing the walls in the hospital waiting room. And I knew that Alba deserved to hear the news from me in person.

When I got to the hotel, Deba was dressed and having breakfast with Alba. I watched them from the doorway. It was a tranquil, rather ordinary scene: a perfect moment.

Deba seemed to sense me with her superolfactory powers and wheeled around, happy as a puppy.

"Papa! You look ugly!" she shrieked joyously.

"Deba's right, you look terrible," Alba said. "Long night?"

I was about to respond when Grandfather arrived carrying an assortment of plastic bags. Deba ran and leaped on him as though he were a life preserver.

I knew the feeling. He was my anchor, too.

"Why are you here so early, Grandpa?" I asked.

The old man set down his bags carefully. He scratched his head with his crooked forefinger, the way he always did when he was telling a fib.

"I got a ride with Eusebio's son."

"From Villafría? So you walked along the main road to Villafría carrying those heavy bags?"

He shrugged dismissively. "It's only two kilometers, son. Walking is good for me."

"Grandpa, would you take Deba over to the park? Alba and I will join you in a bit."

"Come here, little one," he said to Deba, picking her up and plonking his beret on her head. "Alba, my dear, I brought you some pots of jam. I thought your guests might like some with their breakfast."

Alba smiled. Grandfather had a soothing effect on her. He seemed to ground her, giving her the same solace that comes from hugging a thick, gnarled oak.

"Thanks, Grandpa. That's a splendid idea."

We watched in silence as they disappeared downstairs. Alba could already sense that my early-morning visit would bring dark clouds.

"Come on, Alba, let's go up to the tower, I need to clear my head."

"Is it that serious?"

"You have no idea."

She followed me up the steep spiral staircase. Outside, a pale sun was shining, but it gave no warmth. Alba shuddered and clasped her arms across her chest; she was used to consoling herself. I suppressed the painfully vivid image of Estíbaliz's body smashed against the ground.

I glanced at the sierra, following its jagged contour until I came to San Tirso. I was searching for something that would ground me.

The tower overlooked a section of the park. Grandfather had taken Deba to the playground, where he knew we could keep an eye on them.

He sat on a bench while Deba stormed a wooden castle. The stairs and low-slung bridges had tiny climbing holds perfect for small hands.

I turned toward Alba, sighed deeply, and began: "Estíbaliz is in critical condition. They're operating on her right now. She fell thirty feet or more. We think she was thrown over a balcony at Nograro Tower late last night."

"Last night?"

"Last night. I wanted to give you the details before you read them in an official statement. We found Ramiro Alvar Nograro on the ground a few yards away from her. We won't know exactly what happened until the forensics team gives us their report, but it seems like Ramiro Alvar didn't fall quite as far, although he's severely injured, too. He fell feetfirst, and one of his legs is broken in four places. Estíbaliz is in worse shape, though. She landed on her side and has multiple fractures. We don't know about internal injuries; the prognosis is pending. When we found them, Estí was in her underwear, and Ramiro Alvar was in his nightshirt. The attacker must have broken into the building. The main door was locked, but a low window had been opened from the inside. We suspect the culprit used it to escape. Estíbaliz and Ramiro Alvar must have discovered him, and then he threw them off the balcony. I've asked forensics to check the library for fingerprints, because I think the perpetrator was looking for the copy of the twelfth-century chronicle. I doubt the thief will be stupid enough to try to sell it on the black market right away. In any case, we won't know if I'm right until Ramiro Alvar can confirm that it's missing. I've asked Peña to get a gag order; the public will link the murders to the appearance of the chronicle. If word gets out that it's been stolen from Nograro Tower and that the owner and the lead officer on the case were attacked during the robbery, the press will focus all their attention on the tower and this fiasco will become even bigger."

"I need to go see Estíbaliz," Alba finally said. "Is anyone with her?"

"Peña and Milán are taking turns. They'll call me as soon as there's any news."

"For God's sake, you left our best friend on her own?"

"They'll be operating on her for several more hours, and the doctors won't tell us anything until they finish. I came here because I didn't want to tell you over the phone. I called Germán, and he's taking the day off so we can drop Deba at his place. We'll take Grandfather with us. Whether we're visiting the hospital or . . . arranging a funeral, we won't be home much over the next few days. Germán and Grandpa can take care of Deba."

Could anyone possibly deal with all this death? Was it even possible for two detectives to raise a family? Had it ever been done? And if so, who gave those everyday heroes the medals and awards they deserved?

I turned to go back downstairs, but Alba put her hand on my arm to stop me.

"Wait. We won't be able to discuss this with Grandpa and Deba in the car. I want you to tell me everything. Don't leave anything out. I'm going to have to come back to work."

"I know. I tried to keep you out of it until now. You deserved some time off to grieve for your mother. Everyone deserves that, goddamn it."

"How long?"

"How long what?"

"You know exactly what I'm asking. How long has Estíbaliz been involved with our main suspect, and how long have you known about it?"

"About them sleeping together"—I checked the time on my phone—"approximately twelve hours."

"Unai . . ."

"I'm telling the truth! I never would have dreamed it would go this far. Estíbaliz never told me how she felt. All I had were suspicions, and I didn't think it was worth bothering you with them. You took yourself off the investigation, and I wanted to respect your decision."

"You should have told me, Unai. My God! Did you know about this inappropriate relationship when I put her in charge of the case?"

"Yes, I knew the very first night. I went out for an early run the next morning and bumped into the two of them. I sensed it."

"Sensed what?"

"What you and I had at the beginning, the way we looked at each other. Estíbaliz couldn't take her eyes off him, and he looked at her like he couldn't believe she was real. I don't know if Estíbaliz was even aware of her feelings at that point, or if she was only pretending to flirt with him. But I knew it, the moment I saw them. I've never seen that look in her eyes before. They gazed at each other like precious objects, like gifts waiting to be unwrapped. What Doctor Leiva would call the 'halo effect.'"

"Is that how you felt about me?"

"With you, it was so much more. You're in control of your life. You've always made your own decisions, and all I can do is choose whether to go along with them. I admire you, and I still find you incredibly sexy. Actually, I'm more hooked now than the day I met you. Does that answer your question? And yet it's even more than that. It's a matter of flesh and blood. Isn't that what we're creating together? Hasn't Deba made us a family?"

"Grandpa's jam is what makes us a family," she replied, fingering the length of red silk I had tied around her wrist a few days ago. "Okay, let's get going. I'll never be able to forgive myself if we leave Estíbaliz alone in Vitoria."

I peered at the park, looking for the bench where Grandfather had been sitting.

And then I recognized him.

Tasio Ortiz de Zárate.

Tasio had approached my daughter. He was holding something in his hand, and he was talking to her. He had intercepted her as she came down the slide, but the castle's wooden sides blocked Grandfather's view. He was still sitting on the bench, oblivious to the danger his great-granddaughter was in.

"Alba, Tasio is talking to Deba. Don't yell for Grandfather. If Tasio panics and grabs her, he won't be able to run after them," I whispered. A shiver ran down my spine, and I broke out in a cold sweat that quickly seeped through my T-shirt.

We flung ourselves onto the stairs, ran outside, and circled the wooden castle, all without saying a word. Tasio was crouching down, timidly stroking a delighted Deba's hair.

"Step away from her, Tasio!" I shouted as I drew within a few yards of them.

When Alba came charging around the other side of the castle, Tasio leaped to his feet and made a run for it. Alba scooped up Deba and whisked her away while I went after Tasio. I couldn't catch him even at a full sprint. The bastard was in good shape. I ordered him to stop several times, but he kept going.

His pace slowed as we reached the bandstand named after the fabulist Samaniego, and I seized the opportunity. I lunged forward and tackled him to the ground. We fell onto grass still damp with the morning's frost.

"Okay, okay! I'm sorry, Inspector Ayala," he exclaimed, putting his hands in the air.

"I told you not to go near her, Tasio."

"There's been a mistake, Inspector! Look in my wallet. I'm Ignacio."

I came to a halt. I hadn't expected that.

"Ignacio? What are you doing in Laguardia?"

"I have a villa here," he cried nervously. "I was walking through the park, and I saw your grandfather and the little girl. I'm sorry, my curiosity got the better of me—I couldn't help myself. I had no idea you'd spoken to Tasio, or forbidden him to talk to her. Please, look at my ID, Inspector. It's in my back pocket."

I kept him immobilized while I pulled his expensive wallet out of his back pocket. ID, driver's license, credit cards—all in Ignacio Ortiz de Zárate's name. It was true.

I loosened my grip. Ignacio sat on the grass beside me.

"I'm really sorry," he said. "I don't want to cause any problems for you or for DSU Salvatierra. There's been enough tragedy already. Tell me where you usually go around here, and I'll make sure I avoid those places whenever I'm in Laguardia."

I clapped him on the back, catching my breath.

"Thanks, Ignacio . . . and sorry I tackled you."

Ignacio nodded, still in shock.

"Actually, I think it was good for me. I felt like a cop again, briefly, except back then I was always the one giving chase, of course."

I smiled at him. He seemed a little more relaxed, but I was still waiting for my heart rate to return to normal.

"Do you ever miss life in the force?" I probed.

He thought about it for a moment.

"I don't miss dealing with scum every day. I spend time with normal people now, law-abiding folks. No violence, no tragedy, no complications. Don't kid yourself, Inspector: a life lived far away from criminals is easier."

"Of course, it's easier to look the other way when you know someone else is going to take them off the streets, stop the bad guys from having free rein. But I'm not sure I could live the kind of life you're talking about without losing my mind."

"You suffer from the hero complex, an overblown sense of duty. I used to be the same, and I paid a heavy price," he said ruefully. "My twin paid an even heavier one. I took away twenty years of his life, and he'll never get them back."

Just then, I felt my cell phone vibrate. It was Peña. Possibly with news about Estíbaliz.

I stood up and extended my hand to Ignacio.

"I need to take this call. Sorry again about the tackle, but could you . . . ?"

"Don't worry, I'll steer clear of your daughter when I'm in Laguardia."

"Thanks. DSU Salvatierra just lost her mother. I'm sure you understand. . . ."

"I do," he said, looking me straight in the eye. He pressed my hand to say goodbye and walked away in his expensive, grass-stained clothes.

I hurried back to where I'd left Deba, Alba, and Grandfather, returning Peña's call on my way.

"Any news?"

"Not yet, they're still operating. Ramiro Alvar is no longer in critical condition."

"Okay. I'm heading back to Vitoria now with DSU Salvatierra. She's going to take over the investigation again. We have a meeting with forensics this afternoon."

"By the way, Milán has been tracking that Twitter account since the tweet about the chronicle appeared. It was set up yesterday in central Vitoria with a burner phone that is currently inactive. There haven't been any more tweets sent from the account. And I doubt there will be."

"We have to make sure the information about the chronicle's theft isn't leaked to the press, or it will obstruct our ability to investigate. We need to get a gag order on that now. Another thing: watch the entrance to Number Two Calle Dato. Tell me if you see Ignacio Ortiz de Zárate today and, if you do, I want to know what clothes he's wearing. I want photos."

30

THE HANGING OAK

DIAGO VELA

WINTER, THE YEAR OF OUR LORD 1192

Fire took her from me, and fire brought her back to me, I thought.

I woke to the sound of shouting. I had fallen asleep in the tub, and the water was cold. Alix was gone, and I felt more alone than ever. I leaped to my feet, draped myself in Gunnarr's bearskin, and looked out the window.

They weren't shrieks of joy; they were shrieks of horror. I made myself presentable, went downstairs, and joined the crowd. Beyond the town walls, several women were on their knees, weeping, beneath the hanging oak.

Swinging from one of the boughs was young Vidal.

The lieutenant was already in the Plaza del Juicio, waiting for a ladder. Seven Navarrese guards who had been on duty at the Sant Viçente fortress had formed a circle around the tree and were keeping the townsfolk at bay with their lances. Was that necessary?

The mayor, the bailiff, and the lieutenant gathered around me. The four of us looked up at the hanged man's feet. Vidal had died with an erection and his clothing was soiled with excrement. It was all crudely on display before the entire town. I could not decide whether he deserved this ignominious end.

"We can no longer conceal what happened last night," I said to the lieutenant. "But neither can we stop Carnestolendas with all these people in the streets."

"Take your men, Lieutenant," I ordered. "Confiscate all the wine in the town and cart it out through Portal de la Armería. Make an announcement: Everyone is to abstain from drinking out of respect for the souls of Count de Maestu's daughters. Mayor, sign a proclamation and have it read to the people this very morning outside the Santa María and Sant Michel churches. Inform the town that the priest acted alone and chose to punish himself for his crimes. And for heaven's sake, cut down that poor lad from the tree, or I'll climb up there and do it myself."

The executioner unsheathed his dagger.

"That won't be necessary. They have just brought the ladder," he said. He propped it up against the hanging oak as we watched closely.

I left the square and made my way to Nagorno's house, which stood next to my own on Rúa de la Astería. I found him stoking the hearth, stirring embers that had doubtless warmed the chamber all night.

He did not turn around when I entered—he knew my footsteps.

"I know what you're thinking: Who stands to gain from these deaths?" he said slowly, still with his back to me.

"Was this your doing?" I asked simply.

"You know it was not."

He took his time standing up, as though he were already tired of the matter. Then he went over to the window and peered outside. I joined him.

"Listen to me, Nagorno. Carnestolendas isn't over yet, but I know all your masks. I won't say a word to Onneca. I'd honestly rather she continue despising me. I also believe she's in love with you, or something akin to love, and until her brother returns from Edesa, you're the only family she has left. So, as long as you are by her side, make her happy."

Nagorno nodded with the languor of a serpent. Then something caught his eye.

"Where is that black smoke coming from?" he asked, puzzled.

I leaned halfway out the window.

"There are fires!" I shouted. "On either side of town. I think the fruit market is on fire, and the Santa María marketplace as well. Are you to blame for this? Have you been stirring up trouble with the Mendoza family?"

"You give me too much credit. I'm flattered, but this time I fear they've whipped themselves into a frenzy."

"Very well," I said, as we prepared to leave. "Rally the townsfolk, tell them to ring the bells in both the churches, and to bring buckets to the Santa María well. The inhabitants of Nova Victoria can fetch water from the Zapardiel to douse the flames at the market."

I ran down the stairs and along Rúa de las Pescaderías. My worst fears were confirmed when I reached the end of the street. Grandmother Lucía's roof was in flames.

They had set fire to the cloth overhang on the stalls beside her dwelling. The flames had reached the first floor.

I hurried to the well, drew a pail of water, and poured it over myself. Then I ripped off one shirtsleeve and wrapped it around my nose and mouth.

The thatched roof was a pyre of black smoke. A few onlookers watched the conflagration, entranced, like mice before a snake. Some men shouted ridiculous orders, bumping into one another and throwing punches as they ran about, while the women either tugged at their sleeves to separate them or handed them pails of water to douse the charred wood that had once been their market stalls.

The front door to Grandmother Lucía's house was wide-open. I filled my lungs before entering and ran toward the stairs.

Crawling up the steps on my hands and knees, smoke burning my eyes, I managed to reach the kitchen. Her straw bed was ablaze. It was giving off so much heat that I could feel the flames on the right side of my face as I passed by.

"Grandmother, where are you!"

"Over here!" Alix shouted.

She was trying to drag the old woman's lifeless body across the floor. Alix's dress and wimple were in flames. She was a moving bonfire.

I hurled myself on top of her. My sodden clothes smothered the flames on her dress, and I tore off her wimple and flung it away.

Choked by the fumes, we descended the stairs just as the joists gave way and the floor caved in. I groped my way, carrying Grandmother Lucía in my arms, but she gave no sign of life. It was hopeless. At this point I was simply rescuing her corpse for a decent burial. No breath remained in this charred, wizened shell. I stumbled and fell headlong down the stairs. I tried to shield her brittle bones, but we collapsed to the ground as the house erupted into blistering flames around us.

I lay sprawled at the entrance. After managing to carry Grandmother Lucía out into the street, Alix came to get me.

By now I was half delirious from lack of air. I didn't want to breathe because I had inhaled so much smoke that each exhalation seared my lungs. Alix emptied a bucket of water over me to soothe my stinging eyes and throat.

And then, as though she had just realized I was too heavy to move, she seemed to give up. She sat beside me in the entrance, surrounded by flames, and cradled my head as though I were a baby. We gazed into each other's eyes, waiting for the inferno to engulf us and end everything.

But that didn't happen. Nagorno appeared in the midst of the flames, and, despite always having been smaller than me, he swiftly pulled me outside to safety. Then he carried Alix out over his shoulder. Her owl, Munio, had apparently hooted to alert him that his mistress was trapped in the flames.

Some neighbors gave us water to drink and carried us away from the fire on a cart.

"And Grandmother Lucía?" I asked as soon as I could speak.

"She's badly burned and has lost her hair, but the physician says she will live."

I was overcome with joy. It was more than I had dared hope for. Laughing between coughs, I fell back on the cart as it rattled over the cobblestones on Rúa Pescaderías, and then I abandoned my scorched body to the care of others.

Alix lay sprawled beside me, breathing shallowly. I was too weak to sit up or even to turn my head to make sure she was still intact. We gazed up at a sky, which had darkened from red, orange, and yellow to gray. I felt for her hand and pressed it firmly. She responded by squeezing tightly.

Thus our tacit pact was sealed: "Given that we shall die soon, we renounce nothing."

Three nights later I had finally stopped coughing up ash and each inhalation had ceased to be a torment. My eyes no longer wept with the brightness of the candle flames, and chamomile compresses had soothed my burns. I made my way to Alix's forge.

It was three hours until cockcrow. Outside the town was dark and deserted, but the torches on the wall lit up the street.

Alix, wearing her new wimple, was hammering a horseshoe on the anvil. In her furnace, the glow from the fire was warming instead of threatening.

"How is Grandmother Lucía?" I asked in a whisper.

"She's sad. Her home has been reduced to four burned posts. She lives with me now."

"I've hired a master builder to build her an identical cottage. May I see her?"

"She's sleeping," Alix replied hesitantly, "and besides, you're not here to see Grandmother."

She set down her hammer, and I went over to her. The last time I saw her she had been covered in ashes.

"What do I smell of today?" I asked as she sniffed my chest.

"Of a decision made," she said slowly. "Close the shutters."

I did as she asked, and when I turned around, she had removed her wimple.

"We spoke of this," she murmured, holding my gaze as she slipped off her leather apron and leaned back against the wall. "We decided it was unwise."

"And it is. But I promise you: I'm not going to die." I grabbed her shoulders. "Believe me, I'm not going to die. You will not have to bury me, and no one will accuse you of murdering four husbands. You've seen how resilient I am."

"You're surrounded by enemies."

"No leader can go through life without having to fight every step of the way. I was born into this, Alix. My life has been one long battle, and my brother has made me pay for each of my victories. I am accustomed to it. You do not see my armor, but I have it, and it protects me always."

"You can take it off with me, for I have no intention of harming you."

I nodded; I believed her.

Then I noticed the piece of red yarn tied around her wrist. It was identical to the one Grandmother Lucía had woven for me.

"I believe we have Grandmother Lucía's blessing," I murmured, showing her my wristband, which had miraculously survived the fire.

"I know, I was waiting for you to realize," she replied.

"Then . . . you consent," I said, kneeling at her feet.

"I consent."

I lifted her robe and caressed the length of her leg from ankle to thigh.

"And do you also consent to this?" I asked.

"For the love of God . . ." She suppressed a moan. "Hush, and don't stop what you're doing."

"But you *do* consent?" I insisted.

"Yes. I consent to everything, Diago. Everything."

31

THE AVENUE OF PINES

UNAI

October 2019

When I got back to the swings, my family was no longer there, so I headed to the hotel. Alba had locked the door.

"Where's Deba?" I asked, anxious.

"She's with Grandfather in Doña Blanca's room. I made her promise to scream if any handsome blond men ever go near her again. Did you arrest him?"

"It wasn't Tasio; it was Ignacio. I checked his ID. He said he didn't know that I told Tasio to stay away from Deba. He promised to keep his distance if he sees you."

"So we can't lodge a complaint or ask for a restraining order against Tasio, because Ignacio wasn't directly involved in the first incident."

"That's right," I said.

"What do we do now?" she asked. I was surprised to hear her say "we." She didn't usually.

"We go to Vitoria. And we never leave Deba unattended. Between you, me, Grandfather, and Germán, we'll be able to protect her. But right now, Estíbaliz is in the operating room, and I want to be there when she wakes up, assuming she does. She stayed by my side the entire time I was in a coma."

"I remember. She needs us now, and we won't let her down," Alba said.

She looked up at the ceiling in the hotel's entrance, saying goodbye.

"This place was beginning to grow on me," she said in a hushed tone.

I know.

I drove slowly. No one said a word; we were all too tense. I didn't like the defeated look in Grandfather's cloudy eyes. He blamed himself for not seeing Ignacio approach Deba.

"Was it the fox himself?" he had asked when I went up to the room and found him and Deba grooming her plush wild boar. It was Deba's favorite stuffed animal because her great-grandfather had given it to her when she got her first tooth.

"No, Grandpa, it was his twin. He meant no harm. We had no real reason to panic."

"Well . . . I won't let her out of my sight again, son," he whispered, lowering his head.

Half an hour later, we were driving down the Avenue of Pines on our way to Vitoria. I always sped through that stretch of the road, where my first family had crashed into the giant tree on the right shoulder.

Since that day, long ago, a kind person had left a bouquet at the foot of the enormous tree every week. It wasn't me. I couldn't bring myself to stop at that accursed place. At first, I couldn't even look at the memorial. I'd step on the accelerator and stare straight ahead. Gradually, with each journey, the familiarity of the road eased my pain, and I started noticing the flowers. Sometimes there were dahlias, other times there were tulips, or occasionally winter roses that had survived the harsh weather in the Alavese mountains. Curiously, they always coincided with the seeds I bought Grandfather to plant in his garden.

I had never asked him. For once, this was a mystery I was in no hurry to solve.

That day, though, as I approached that spot, I instinctively slowed down. I was driving my wife, my child, my grandfather. I was terrified of losing them. And I started to wonder whether my determination to protect the city meant that, in some ways, I was repeatedly crashing them into a tree.

We finally arrived at the hospital. I squeezed Deba's hand firmly as we walked into the building.

Come straight to the third floor, Peña had texted.

We went up, our hearts in our throats.

We found Peña in the hallway. Germán and Milán were also waiting for us.

"The doctors say she's made of rubber. No burst kidneys, no brain damage. Just some broken bones. She has to wear a neck brace, and her arm is fractured in about two hundred places. She'll need physiotherapy and lots of rest. We've lost our best markswoman for a while, but Inspector Ruiz de Gauna is still in one piece," said Peña, grinning from ear to ear.

"Can we see her?" I interrupted him impatiently. Deba, in my arms, kept asking for her auntie.

"They just brought her up from the recovery room, and I think she's still a little groggy from the anesthetic. Forensics wants to talk to us."

"Later, Peña. Not today."

I walked in without asking permission. I felt a pang when I saw her. She was in a neck brace, with her right arm encased in bandages, and she was hooked up to IV bags on a drip pole.

"Auntie *Eztí*! Are you a mommy now?"

Estíbaliz could barely muster a smile. She held my gaze, and her look spoke volumes. She was a soldier returning from battle who recognized a fellow survivor.

The Grim Reaper tested you. You looked him in the eye and came back from the abyss.

"I called you. Alvar had gone out to the kitchen and he hadn't come back. I heard noises and . . ." Estí whispered, but she was having difficulty speaking. Her lips were dry, her tongue sluggish.

"It's okay, Estí. Not today. Today the whole family is just here to see you. They're out in the hallway, worried sick. We can't take another shock."

"I have no family, Unai. Even if you went to Txagorritxu and told him about what happened, my father wouldn't understand. I have no family."

"Yes, you do," I insisted. She was speaking nonsense.

I gently set down Deba on Estí's uninjured side and lay on the bed next to her.

"You see, you do have a family, and quite an extensive one, in fact," I whispered in her ear.

We touched foreheads, in the way animals sometimes do when their guards are lowered.

"Look, Auntie, a red bracelet. I'm gonna give you one," said Deba, proudly showing off her braided wristband.

"And I'm going to give you an *eguzkilore*. It will protect you forever, so you won't fall down the stairs like your auntie," she replied, running her fingers through Deba's unruly curls.

I didn't see Alba standing in the doorway, but she must have been watching.

"Mama! I know what I wanna be when I grow up!" Deba exclaimed when she saw her mother.

"A doctor?"

"No, I'm gonna have a hospital. With lotsa comfy beds."

I smiled and sat up. Deba had started to stamp her feet on the bed, as if to prove the merits of the mattress to her mother and thereby justify her choice of career. I scooped her up and whisked her away from the IV.

"Alba, we need to talk," said Estíbaliz.

"I know, Estí. But not now. Just enjoy the pampering for a few days."

"I messed up, didn't I?"

Alba approached the bed. I knew memories of her mother in that same hospital were painfully fresh, but she put on a brave face. She smiled.

"On a professional level, there will be consequences, yes. Your superintendent wants you off the case."

"How is Alvar? When I saw him on the ground, I ran downstairs. There was hardly any light coming from the upstairs windows."

"And . . . ?"

"The attacker was waiting in the shadows in a corner of the stairs. He tripped me, and I fell to the floor. I tried to fight him off, but he grabbed my neck and legs. Then he threw me off the balcony."

Physically strong. I made a mental note.

"Are you sure you saw Alvar lying in the courtyard?" Alba probed.

"Yes, he had on a white nightshirt, and it stood out in the dark. Why? Do you think I'm covering for him?" she asked, defensive.

"I don't think anything, Estí. I haven't even seen a report."

Furious, Estíbaliz tried to hoist herself up, but her elbow gave way and she fell back on the bed.

"What's wrong, Auntie?" Deba screeched.

"We don't need to discuss work now," Alba said, backing off. "We came here to let you know that whatever happened, we're behind you. We've all struggled to separate our personal and professional lives. I didn't mean to upset you. I'm sorry. You need to rest, get better, and come to terms with what happened. Unai and I are going to leave now, because a lot of people who love you are waiting outside. We love you, too, very much."

She sat beside Estíbaliz and gave her a big hug. They didn't need me, so I took my fidgety daughter and left them.

Peña, Germán, Grandfather, and Milán gathered around me as soon as I came out of the room.

"How is she?" they asked as one.

"Like they said, she's made of rubber."

32

SANTIAGO HOSPITAL

UNAI

October 2019

The days passed more quickly than I had expected. Ramiro Alvar had regained consciousness that morning, but we still were unable to get his statement. Daily visits to Estíbaliz before and after work took up all of our family's time.

Alba had to juggle reacclimating at police headquarters and liaising with the staff at the hotel in Laguardia over the phone. I knew she didn't want to lose the place and would fight tooth and nail to save her fortress, her octagonal tower overlooking a sea of vineyards.

But back in Vitoria, we had urgent business.

Alba walked into my office. The serious look on her face told me she had bad news. I stared out the window. The east wind was not only cold; it had turned the entire day tiresome and unpleasant. But I still couldn't tell whether a storm was brewing. Grandfather was much better at reading the sky.

"Now that Estíbaliz is out of danger, we need to get her statement. Do you want to do it?" Alba asked.

"Yes, leave it to me. She'll hate me for it, but one of us has to play the bad cop. It might as well be me."

"Suit yourself. Let me know when you're finished, and I'll call her afterward," she said, disappearing through the door.

Good idea, she's going to need it, I thought.

Once I was alone in my office, I called Milán. "I need you to find out if Ramiro Alvar Nograro had the tower insured and, if so, for how much."

I went into Estíbaliz's room. In the past few days, she'd improved by leaps and bounds. She now found bed rest challenging and had taken to pacing back and forth with her IV pole. She made my head spin.

"You look serious today," she said by way of greeting.

"We have to get back to the real world, Estíbaliz."

"You make that sound like a bad thing."

I stepped out of her way, standing next to her empty lunch tray—poached chicken and rice pudding.

"We need to take your statement. We need to know what happened at Nograro Tower. We're looking at a possible aggravated robbery. You know how this works."

"Do you really think he stole the chronicle?" She shook her head, incredulous.

"We still don't know whether the motive for the break-in was to steal it. We haven't spoken to Ramiro Alvar yet. He only just regained consciousness this morning. But it's possible that he staged the robbery to shift suspicion away from himself."

"Are you saying he slept with me as part of some master plan?" she demanded angrily.

I was irritated, too. How could she be so blind? I raised my voice. "Is he really worth it? You're telling me you don't feel threatened by Alvar after what happened?"

"*Threatened* is the last word I'd use to describe how Alvar makes me feel. And I know what I'm talking about, Kraken. I grew up with a man who was prone to violent outbursts but was extremely good at convincing other people that he was a loving father and husband. I know the signs. Alvar isn't violent. He's not our killer."

"I need to tell you something. I've discussed Ramiro Alvar's case with Doctor Marina Leiva, the psychiatrist who taught me at Arkaute. She couldn't account for his amnesia and at first thought he might be agoraphobic. But now we're both convinced that he's suffering from dissociative identity disorder. He admitted as much to me the day before the accident, but he said he's never wanted to see a psychiatrist for treatment. He told me he had written a version of the chronicle as a kind of therapy. He hoped it would help him get rid of his alternate personality, or alter. And it seemed to work for a year or so, but for whatever reason, meeting you reactivated his alter. I was going to explain this all to you the night you visited him at the tower. The man you know as Alvar Nograro, the twenty-fourth Lord of Nograro Tower, is an alter ego. Doesn't that scare you?"

"So far you haven't proven your multiple personality theory to me. I know only the Alvar I met. You don't even have a diagnosis. You don't have anything."

How can I explain this to her? How do I make her see?

I sat on the bed. I wished the gods had blessed me with patience when I was born, but they hadn't. I was sick of this.

"Estíbaliz," I said at last, "I think you suffer from hybristophilia."

"You think I'm attracted to criminals? Is that what you're saying?"

"It's common in people who grow up surrounded by violence and crime. Your father was a violent alcoholic. Your brother was a drug dealer. You became a detective, and that choice puts you in contact with people like that on a daily basis. Being around people who live outside the law seems to be part of your pattern, your emotional trigger."

"Says the guy who empathizes with serial killers!" she screamed.

A low blow. I took it in stride and tried to keep my cool.

"It's my job to get to know them. I need to understand how they think," I said in a measured tone, possibly to convince myself more than anything else. "We try to classify them, but no two psychopaths are alike. They're all unique. And the only way I can persuade them to admit their guilt is by gaining their trust."

"Okay, Kraken, so tell me this: What do you call someone who chooses to surround themselves with women who suffer from hybristophilia, like me and Alba?" she protested. "Is there a name for what you are? A fucking junkie addicted to sickos?"

I was barely aware of Alba's presence. She had stormed into the room while Estí and I were arguing.

"Enough! Everybody in the hallway can hear you."

"Weren't you supposed to stop by later?" I asked reproachfully.

"This has to stop. You're out of control, both of you! This happens every time."

"Every time?" I wheeled around, as furious as Estíbaliz. "Is that a criticism? Our division has the highest clearance rate in the country. If you don't believe me, go through the records. There hasn't been a single unsolved case since Estíbaliz and I teamed up."

"But at what price, Unai? You're out of control. All three of us are out of control, and it's affecting every aspect of our lives right now. And you know it."

I took a deep breath. I could feel the dark clouds engulfing me.

"Yes, Deputy Superintendent. Nothing makes sense, but in the guarded room at the far end of the hallway, we have a suspect who suffers from dissociative identity disorder. He refuses to undergo psychiatric treatment, and we can't legally force him to do it. I'm the only person he trusts enough to confide in. And I swear to you, he holds the key to solving this. So, unless you're taking me off the case, I intend to do my job and interrogate your deputy's new boyfriend."

I rose to leave.

"Let me see him," Estíbaliz said suddenly.

"Are you crazy? Have you developed Stockholm syndrome on top of everything else?" I asked her.

"You said he's being guarded, and you and Alba will be with me. Even if he is the monster we're looking for, what could he possibly do to me?"

"Nothing. He's hooked up to a hundred tubes and his leg's in traction," I admitted.

"In that case, show me the guy you insist is so different from Alvar. I want to confront the asshole who slept with me and then left me like this. As for Stockholm syndrome, stop insulting my intelligence and stop making assumptions."

Alba and I exchanged a quick glance.

My look said, *We have nothing to lose.*

But hers let me know, in no uncertain terms: *This is the last time I give in to you.*

"Unai, can you step outside for a minute? I'd like to talk to you," she asked.

I followed her into the hallway.

"It would be incredibly helpful for me to see how Ramiro Alvar responds to seeing Estíbaliz. For the time being, we won't ask him about the theft of the chronicle. We'll wait and see if he brings it up," I said quietly, once we were out of earshot.

"All right," she said, after thinking for a moment. "We need some momentum in this investigation, and this seems like the best way forward. But remember, Estíbaliz's safety is our first priority."

"That goes without saying."

Estí slipped on the quilted, daisy-patterned robe that Grandfather had bought for her, and we all walked down the hallway, Alba and I on either side of her.

Alba spoke to the two officers outside Ramiro Alvar's room.

I reached for the door handle, but Estíbaliz pushed past me, impatient, with IV in tow, neck brace on, and one arm in a sling. I felt sure this wasn't going to be the romantic reunion she imagined.

"Alvar . . . ?" she murmured, perplexed.

Ramiro Alvar was in worse shape than Estí. He seemed smaller, shrunken since the fall. He peered out at us from behind his glasses—someone had retrieved them—as he read a book from the pile on his bedside table.

The glasses were a crucial detail. I'd asked my colleagues in forensics to search for them during their inspection. The glasses were eventually found in his desk drawer. The conclusion was obvious: Alvar slept with Estíbaliz, and Alvar fell down the stairs.

"You must be Inspector Ruiz de Gauna. I'm sorry to be meeting you under these circumstances. I can't even greet you properly," he whispered.

"You really don't remember me?" she asked, drawing closer.

Alba took a step forward as well, to stand beside her.

Ramiro Alvar said nothing. It really did seem as though he were seeing Estí for the first time. A lock of curly hair fell over his brow. Estí was in a state of shock.

"I'm afraid not," he murmured apologetically.

"Even your voice is different," said Estíbaliz.

"I beg your pardon?"

"Your voice . . . It's softer."

"I don't like drawing attention to myself," he mumbled, looking down at his book.

"Aren't you hot in this room? The windows are always open at the tower. Shall I open one here to let in some fresh air?"

"No!" he blurted. "Please don't. I'm sensitive to cold, and it looks like it's going to rain any minute now."

It broke my heart to see Estíbaliz's face. She moved closer to the bed and reached out her left hand. With her forefinger, she touched Ramiro Alvar's arm where it lay on the sheet. She was very gentle. It was such an intimate gesture, I was almost ashamed to witness it.

He shrank back slightly, as if hers were the burning finger of God.

"Alvar, is this an act? Do you want them to leave? Would you rather speak to me alone?"

"No! No. . . . Please don't take this personally, Inspector. I like your company, but . . . Inspector López de Ayala, well, he understands. He's the only person I've ever told about my illness. You may not want to believe that I suffer from dissociative identity disorder, but it's true. Alvar is my *alter*, an alternate personality I've been trying hard to suppress."

"Don't you start with that, too!" yelled Estíbaliz.

The timid Ramiro Alvar held her gaze. Estíbaliz searched in vain for a glimmer of recognition.

"Inspector, I think you activate him," he said after a pause.

"Then why isn't he here now, huh? Why am I looking at this . . . this fucking boring nerd? Where's the most fascinating man I've ever met?" she shouted.

"Estí, stop yelling. It only makes things harder," Alba cautioned.

"Hell, is this some kind of stunt? One of your mind games, Kraken?"

I opened the door and directed Estí out. The two of us stormed down the hallway to her room while the nurses pretended not to watch.

"No, Estíbaliz, this is not a mind game. It's the truth. You fell for a guy who exists only intermittently, and you need to face that. I'm going to do whatever I can to ensure that Ramiro Alvar heals and gets rid of his damn alter. So Alvar's days are numbered. He didn't resurface when I took you to see Ramiro just now, so I think it's possible that this recent trauma has changed the balance of power in that man's mind. No matter who he is, Estí, he's suffering from a mental illness. And, as you well know, we have a piece of evidence from every crime scene that links each murder to the tower."

Estí turned her back to me. She went over to the window and looked out at the storm. It was brilliant: lightning, thunder, the whole damn spectacle. It was coming down hard, raindrops streaking diagonally on the glass.

"How timely, right?" she said without looking at me. "A clue with each crime."

"What?"

"Do you think my involvement with Alvar clouded my judgment? Do you think I haven't considered all your lines of research? That I haven't reread the damn novel so many times, I practically know it by heart?"

"Well, then prove you haven't lost your way. Because you haven't contributed anything to the investigation yet."

Estí winced. The neck brace was bothering her, I thought. Or maybe it was something else.

"Could you just leave me alone for a while?" she pleaded. "Just a few hours or a few days. I need to sit with all this . . . with what I just witnessed."

"We don't deal with easy people in easy situations," I said. "You and I get caught up with complicated people in complex situations." I turned to go, intent on leaving and not bothering her anymore.

"But it hasn't always been that way," she replied. "Paula, Iker . . . They were normal people who led normal lives—and we loved them."

"Perhaps this profession takes too much from our lives. If our job requires us to deal with criminals, to surround ourselves with them, then what type of people are we letting into our personal lives, Estíbaliz? How could we *not* be affected by all that toxicity? Every night we bring home all this hatred, all these unresolved neuroses. How can we avoid being influenced by that?"

"Everyone has neuroses in some form or another," she pointed out. "The world is filled with unresolved conflict. And even if we didn't work in criminal investigation, we'd still be affected. Leaving the force won't bring you peace of mind."

"All I'm saying is that not all countries are at war," I murmured to myself, gazing out at the rain-drenched streets.

Estí looked me up and down, as though inspecting me for the first time in a long while.

"In all the years I've worked with you, I've never heard you talk like this."

"And I've never seen you lying in a heap with all your bones broken. It upset me. Fuck, Estí, I thought you were going to die," I said, frustrated. "You're the one who always protects *me*. I can't imagine my life without you. Now, I feel broken, like the emotional connection between us has snapped—and I'm going to have to carry on the investigation without you. It terrifies me."

"You're frightened."

"Yes," I admitted.

She sat down on the edge of the bed. I rested my head on her thigh and watched the rain. Estíbaliz seemed content to stroke my hair, avoiding my scar.

33

YENNEGO

DIAGO VELA

Summer, the Year of Our Lord 1199

Seven years go by quickly for a man who sees the faces of his son and cheerful wife first thing when he wakes every morning.

Thus passed the seven happiest years of my life.

Should I have heeded the silent warning on the southerly wind—the dreaded *hegoaizea*, said to drive men mad? It greeted us that ill-fated morning as soon as we flung open our shutters.

Alix drew the sheet over her head, fleeing the light. I loved to comb her hair when she wore it loose at home and detested her four-coned wimple as much as she did.

"Where's Yennego?" she asked drowsily.

"His uncle Nagorno arrived at dawn and took him out riding." I cast a sidelong glance at the open window. "I expect they'll have returned from their jaunt by now."

We dressed and set off for the North Gate. When we arrived, Nagorno was dismounting from Altai, and Yennego was holding the reins to a fine-looking colt.

"Father!" he exclaimed when he saw me. He ran into my arms despite his bad leg. "Look what Uncle has given me! A big horse, just for me!"

Yennego was seven summers old now, and had helped thaw relations between my brother and me. Nagorno adored his nephew and treated him as though he were his own son. He indulged his every whim and had taught him to ride a horse and to make jewelry.

I embraced Yennego. He had my dark hair, but he smelled of pastries, like his mother. He was born with a good pair of lungs—a healthy baby—but when he was two years old, an accident on Rúa de la Astería had injured one of his legs, stunting its growth.

All the same he learned to walk, and then he learned to ignore the mockery that came his way, even though at times he was forced to throw stones to defend himself. As a result of the other children's teasing, Yennego preferred to spend all day on horseback, where his infirmity was indiscernible. When he wriggled free of my arms, I saw him grimace.

"Is it your tooth, son?"

"It's coming loose, Father, and it hurts. Grandmother Lucía gave me a bracelet with a hedgehog's tooth in it, but it still aches." He showed me a length of braided red yarn, identical to the ones she had woven for Alix and me prior to our betrothal. The bracelets were the only things we never took off, even between the sheets or on winters' nights when we talked in our bathtub.

"Try walking around Sant Michel Church three times," said a voice behind us. "They say that takes away pain."

It was Onneca, as serious and circumspect as ever. Her unhappiness had grown as the years passed and she waited for an heir that never came. Her brother had been killed in an ambush after he returned from the Crusades, which left her to bear the burden of continuing the de Maestu line. She was finding it difficult. She never showed her nephew any affection, nor did I expect it. I was polite to her whenever we met, but that was all.

But Alix, ever hopeful, never stopped trying.

"Better not, son," my wife interjected, walking over to Onneca and tenderly clasping her arm. "Apparently, a young maid who walked around the church in Respaldiza three times was taken by a demon and never seen again."

"Pray, don't frighten my nephew, my lady. Today is a day for rejoicing, if I'm not mistaken," said Nagorno, who was always in an excellent mood after a ride.

"I know of no reason for jubilation, although I see that you've made a generous gift of Olbia's foal for the boy," retorted Onneca.

"Won't you share your news with us, dear sister-in-law?" asked Nagorno, drawing closer to Alix to caress her belly. "The child will arrive at the end of autumn, isn't that so?"

"My brother has a good eye. Apparently he can detect the emergence of new life. We've yet to tell anybody, except for Yennego, who knows he'll have a little playmate by the end of the year," I said, avoiding Onneca's gaze.

Her eyes were brimming with sorrow. It sparked in me an old pain I was loath to revisit.

Just then horses entered through the North Gate. This past summer, King Sancho VII, called the Strong because he stood two heads higher than any of his subjects, had appointed a new lieutenant. The man had served him well at Saint-Jean-Pied-de-Port, the starting point for pilgrims following the Way of Santiago. Sancho's lieutenants were military men who came and went, sent to take control of one castle or another. They never settled nor did the soldiers under their command. Sancho's son, Petro Remírez, had recently come of age, and the king was moving his lieutenants around in response to alarming news coming out of Toledo.

Throughout Navarre, there was talk of Sancho's journey south, to the land of the Saracens, where he would seek an alliance with the new caliph, Miramamolín. The king was widely criticized for seeking allies in the land of the infidels; the pope had threatened him with excommunication. Some of the townsfolk in Victoria weren't happy about being forced to pay taxes to a king they did not know, a king who bedded infidel women in southern lands. When the wine flowed in the wayside inns from Tudela to Pamplona, from San Sebastian to Santander, conversations turned to salacious stories of Moorish princesses lying in the Navarrese giant's arms. In our town, many looked favorably on the advances of Alfonso VIII, King of Castile. In Portal Oscuro, the Mendozas and the Isunzas spoke of the Castilian monarch, saying that he had granted them more favors than King Sancho VI, called the Wise, and his son. Under the Castilian kings' charters, minor nobles were treated the same as any other free men within the town's walls.

We had been awaiting the arrival of Martín Chipia, Sancho's new lieutenant, and the detachment of soldiers from Tudela. The lieutenant had shoulder-length hair and a flattened nose, the result of a drunken brawl. His short legs and broad shoulders made him appear top-heavy.

"Here are my new men." He leaped nimbly from his horse. His head was level with my chest. "They will cause no trouble in town. But I bring worrisome tidings from the king's advisers. Alfonso has launched an offensive, and we must be prepared. Tomorrow we will discuss provisions. There will be enough time to bring in the harvest, God willing. The fields I saw along the way looked green. Are your granaries filled?"

"Not yet," replied Alix. "But judging from the summer rains this year, the harvest will be plentiful."

"Then let us pray for sun these next few days so we can reap it all," he said. "King Sancho doesn't trust his Castilian cousin, and my orders are to ensure that Victoria does not surrender."

"Let's hope it won't come to that," Nagorno interjected.

Our nightmare began when darkness fell.

Alix and I had just come home after putting Grandmother Lucía to bed. She had little appetite lately, and every day her voice grew fainter.

We left Yennego capering among the market stalls at Santa

María with the other boys from Villa de Suso. Every Thursday, fish arrived from the northern ports. We had to buy sardines or salted cod to get through Friday, a day of fasting decreed by the Church of Rome.

In the evenings, once the fishmongers had gathered up their baskets, the gravestones in the Santa María Cemetery were strewn with sticky scales and entrails, and the rotten stench of fish pervaded the air.

I went down to look for my son among the few remaining stragglers flitting around the cemetery, but I didn't see him. The curfew had sounded long before, announcing the closure of the town's three gates.

I spied a group of children nearby. "Have you seen Yennego?"

"No, sire," replied the rope maker's son. The lad was tall for his nine years.

"He said he was going to walk around the church three times," said a girl, the eldest child of the farrier who worked for Lyra. "He said it would cure his toothache."

"When did you last see him?" I asked.

"It was still daylight," they replied.

By the time I crossed Rúa de las Tenderías, the town was practically deserted. I ordered one of Martín Chipia's guards to open the South Gate for me and walked around the church, calling my son's name.

Hours later, after the entire town was out looking for Yennego, I finally realized what had happened when the red-wool bracelet with the hedgehog's tooth that Grandmother Lucía had made for him was found, unraveled, on an old tombstone in the Sant Michel Cemetery.

No demon had taken my son.

He'd been abducted by a monster.

34

LOCARD'S PRINCIPLE

UNAI

October 2019

I plunged into the cold water, swimming down one of the pool lanes. I'd become accustomed to swimming a few laps when I visited Arkaute to chat with Doctor Leiva. It relaxed me more than my morning runs: my thoughts flowed better underwater, surrounded by silence.

I had arranged to meet Doctor Leiva at lunchtime. She was running late, so I took advantage of the extra time to get some exercise and to contemplate the theft of Count Don Vela's chronicle. Ramiro Alvar had asked his lawyer to search his private collection. Only the chronicle was missing, and the lawyer had persuaded Ramiro Alvar to report the incident. The police were treating it as trespassing with aggravated burglary.

At the police academy, I had studied Edmond Locard's exchange principle: every crime leaves behind trace evidence. The famous criminologist had speculated that "it is impossible for a criminal to act without leaving traces of their presence." The theft of the diary had left more trace evidence than the culprit imagined. Alvar or Ramiro Alvar could have staged the attack, but at this point I knew it was more likely that the thief had been an outsider—the person had acted on impulse. He had found out what the chronicle was worth and decided to steal it.

Thought number one: The person who had attacked Ramiro Alvar and Estí and the person who had committed the murders were one and the same. By the time the culprit read about the chronicle, they already knew it existed and where it was kept but did not know how valuable it was.

Thought number two: the thief's motive for stealing the copy of the chronicle was money. Ramiro Alvar and Estí had been attacked simply because they were in the way. It hadn't occurred to me that the motive for killing Antón Lasaga, the two sisters, and MatuSalem might also be money. What if that's what it had been all along?

A voice interrupted my reverie. "I've done two laps with you and you haven't even noticed I'm here."

I glanced at the lane to my right in astonishment. Doctor Leiva had joined me in the pool and was studying me with a serene smile.

"Marina!" I gave a start. "I was lost in my thoughts."

We swam to a corner of the pool and propped ourselves up on the edge. It was a most relaxing place for private conversation. I told her about the break-in at the tower and the theft of the chronicle.

"Look at Ramiro Alvar's background," she suggested, after listening patiently to the whirlwind of information. "You need to pinpoint the traumatic experience that caused his personality to split and the lie he told himself to keep going. We all invent things when we can't accept a situation. But patients with dissociative identity disorder take this type of fabrication to an extreme: They invent alters, avatars that symbolize the perpetual reliving of that trauma. They become trapped by what they feel they ought to have done: the bully who took a stand, the impassive victim who ran away. I doubt Ramiro Alvar will tell you about the trauma if you ask him directly. Does he ever speak about his parents?"

"In glowing terms."

"Clichés?"

"Yes."

"Patients with DID occasionally erase periods of their lives and refill them with pleasant but vague memories they never actually experienced."

"They seem to have enjoyed a good reputation among the villagers," I said, "other than the fact that the father had an eccentric penchant for dressing up. Ramiro Alvar attributes it to a hereditary form of the disorder. Although in the literature you recommended, experts seem to reject the idea that DID is inherited."

"As a rule, yes. The infrequency of cases makes even an intergenerational study impractical, let alone a genetic study. But we must keep an open mind. In my view, the condition has more to do with the story the patient tells himself. If Ramiro Alvar was a precocious child, brought up by his family to feel shame and fear about a hereditary illness that kept them isolated from others, then when his traumatic experience occurred, his mind may have latched onto his worst nightmare and he became what he feared the most. It's a self-fulfilling prophecy. If the individual believes a situation is real, it will have real consequences."

"There is one possible explanation for what happened, but I hope it isn't true," I said. "It's possible that Ramiro Alvar woke up and saw that Alvar had slept with my colleague. He then staged a break-in and the theft of the chronicle to divert suspicion. After throwing Estíbaliz off the balcony, he climbed down the stairs, opened the window from inside, and then jumped from the lower height to ensure his own survival. This scenario aligns with Ramiro Alvar's desire to get rid of Alvar, in the same manner as in the novel, and it explains why Estíbaliz no longer activates Alvar—Alvar no longer exists."

Doctor Leiva considered my theory and then nodded. "In my experience, patients with DID often self-harm: they cut themselves, tattoo insults on their bodies, engage in risky behavior. But it's normally the abusive alter who attacks the weaker personality, the ANP—not the other way around."

"Meaning?"

"Make sure the person you think is Ramiro Alvar isn't in fact Alvar pretending to be Ramiro Alvar. Alvar is a survival-driven alter; he'll do whatever it takes to stay alive. He is also theatrical, so if he's impersonating Ramiro Alvar, he'll give himself away eventually. Don't lose sight of your profile. You mentioned that when you confronted Ramiro Alvar with Estíbaliz, she didn't activate his alter."

"That's true, but I don't want to use her again," I said.

"Yet Alvar had already appeared before he met Estíbaliz because the novel predates their meeting. We need to know what triggered his first appearance. Does Ramiro Alvar have other alters?"

"He says there's only Alvar, the priest," I explained. "Apparently, the men in his family start dressing up when they are young, and as they grow older, they develop multiple dissociated identities. He was afraid he might end up like his father, so he wrote the novel as a therapeutic exercise to rid himself of Alvar. He claims it worked—Alvar died when he wrote the novel. He described the experience as cathartic, and he believed Alvar had gone. Then he met Estíbaliz, and Alvar reappeared."

"The abusive personality."

"Yes, and this is what I find puzzling: Why would Ramiro Alvar cast his deceased brother, Alvar, the priest, as the abusive alter? According to the villagers in Ugarte, the two brothers adored each other. Those feelings can't be faked. Young children and adolescents are usually open about their likes and dislikes."

"Is it possible Alvar became abusive later on, perhaps when he became Ramiro Alvar's guardian?" Marina suggested.

"People in the village say Alvar died about a year after becoming ill."

"Ramiro Alvar may have resented having to look after his brother. He was a teenager, and he had just lost both parents. That would be an extremely traumatic time for anyone, and then Alvar died a year later."

"Apparently, although no one in the village remembers a funeral."

"What are you implying?"

"Nothing," I said, "just that there's something not quite right about his death."

"You seem to have plenty to go on. Good luck in Ugarte. I have to go now; my next class starts in thirty minutes."

After Doctor Leiva left, I plunged back into the water and swam for a while longer, contemplating Locard's principle that every criminal leaves some trace of themselves.

What I was about to discover is that the same is true for every act of love.

At that moment, love was forging a path between two people who refused to acknowledge their inauspicious circumstances.

Afterward, I found out how the romance began: the timid Ramiro Alvar persuaded a nurse to deliver a letter for him. Estíbaliz read it with a mixture of surprise and curiosity:

Dear Inspector Ruiz de Gauna,

I'm very sorry things turned out this way due to my condition. Although I remember nothing from the hours or days my alter spent with you, I realize your feelings for each other were sincere. Alvar fell in love with you, and you with him. It doesn't surprise me; Alvar is courageous and strong-willed. I think you were very special to him. He's never brought any woman to the tower before. In fact, the man you spent the night with, in a sense, was a virgin. I'm now convinced he no longer exists, that he died in the fall. I haven't suffered any more blackouts. This has encouraged me to believe I'm cured, that my private nightmare is finally over. I believe I can now lead a normal life. I realize that, for you, this constitutes a loss, because Alvar is no longer with us. I also understand that you must hate me, Ramiro Alvar, and that you see me as—how did you put it?—a "boring nerd." To you I am Alvar's tedious alter, yet I am the real person behind this split personality.

Kind regards,
Ramiro Alvar Nograro,
XXV Lord of Nograro Tower

At the time, though, I knew nothing of the letter. All I knew was that without Estíbaliz, I felt unable to make headway in the investigation. Frustrated, I got into my car and drove to Ugarte. The book club wasn't due to meet, but I wanted to find out more about Ramiro Alvar's family background, especially his brother.

I headed for the village bar.

The place was half empty. A group of young men and women were playing foosball, while a group of senior citizens were busy tallying up their scores after a contested card game. I found Benita dozing in her wheelchair, a blanket draped over her knees.

"You can talk to her. She's only pretending to be asleep," said the young man running the bar. He winked at me.

"Benita, how are you today?" I asked, sitting beside her and warming my hands in front of the stove.

"Ah, the detective!" she said sardonically.

"Inspector, actually. I missed the book club last week. Any news?"

"I'll say! Four more locals signed up: Aurora; Nati, the mayor's wife; and the Ochoas—mother and daughter. Women who've never shown any interest in listening to someone read aloud before . . ."

"I'm glad it's getting more popular," I said. "This seems like a close-knit village, with everything that entails—good and bad."

"Well, you know what they say: 'Small town, big hell,' " she drawled.

"It's curious you should say that. The other day, your son made a comment that I found shocking. He said Ugarte was a town full of bastards. Surely the people here aren't that bad?"

"He didn't mean it in the way you're thinking. Words change over the years; they acquire different meanings, but nuance is important. My son meant it literally. There are the legitimates, children born to lawfully wedded couples. And then there are the illegitimates, children born out of wedlock. We know a lot about them here in Ugarte. We probably have a few whoresons and daughters, too. Of course, there are the naturals, children born to an official mistress who was faithful to her man. I expect we have a few of those, too. Then there are the 'abominations,' children born of incest—an offense against God, don't you think? That shouldn't be allowed to happen. And we mustn't forget those born to concubines."

"Concubines?"

"Women who cohabit with Catholic priests," she explained. "Let's see, who's left? The nuns . . . Did I mention the abominations? Yes, I think I did. And last of all are the cuckoos, children born to an adulterous woman whose husband brings them up as his own. We've had more than one of those."

"Cuckoos, you call them. My grandfather would describe it as a fox bringing up a litter that isn't his."

"It's as old as the hills, isn't it?" she said cheerily.

"Does that cover everyone?"

"I think so. People here don't talk about these things. If they did, we'd find one in every house—and nobody wants that. That's why they tolerate one another, suffer in silence and then send their children away so there's no inbreeding. God forbid."

"What do you mean?"

"You've said quite enough for today, Mother," Fidel broke in. "I'm taking you home."

I was so absorbed in my conversation with Benita that Fausti's shy husband seemed to appear out of nowhere to wheel his mother away.

First thing the next morning, Milán called. It was still dark and I was naked, leaning out of the big window overlooking the square. The wind was already whisking through the streets.

"Kraken, we got a call about an aggravated burglary in Quejana. It's bizarre."

"What do you mean, 'bizarre'?" I said, irritated.

"Somebody broke into the Conjunto Monumental de Quejana. The elderly priest who looks after the place has been injured."

35

QUEJANA

UNAI

October 2019

What the hell? I thought as I listened to Milán.

"Should I come get you?" she asked.

An hour later, with dawn just breaking, we parked outside the abandoned Dominican convent at Quejana, in north Álava.

Other than an ambulance, the cobbled yard was deserted. Leafy trees bordered the yard, their boughs entwined above us, reaching into the red sky.

We walked past the deserted buildings. Unsure where to go, we instinctively made our way toward the fortified palace with its four huge, square towers.

Cautiously entering through a big wooden door, I called out, "Is anybody there?"

A rather tall young man in a paramedic's uniform came out to greet us.

"Follow me. A man has been injured in a fall—we suspect he's fractured his hip. We're taking him to the hospital." He led us to the inner courtyard, which was lined in wet flagstones and boasted pots of well-kept shrubs. Mounds of leaves had been swept into the corners. Clearly, someone was keeping the place more or less alive.

I saw the old priest sitting on a stone bench, surrounded by paramedics. He was wearing striped pajamas and had covered himself as best he could with a black jacket.

"Did you call the ambulance?" I asked him.

"Lázaro Durana, at your service. I'm the parish priest here at Quejana. I live in the old chaplain's house. Late last night, I was awake reading—I only ever sleep for a few hours—and I heard noises. I'm alone here, so I realized it must be somebody up to no good. When I came down, I found that someone had broken into the chapel."

"What did you see?" Milán asked him.

"Not much. The door to the Nuestra Señora del Cabello chapel was ajar, and I saw the beam of a flashlight inside. As I got closer to the chapel, I yelled, 'Who's there?' Nobody answered, but I heard more rustling. I didn't want to confront the thief alone, so I called the police from my cell phone. The thief must have heard me because the light went out, and then I caught a glimpse of a figure running out of the chapel. He pushed me aside, and I fell on my hip. It's terribly painful. And I seem to have lost my glasses. Could someone find them for me, please?"

Milán and I scoured the yard, as though we were processing a crime scene: I divided the area into four, and we examined each section, moving counterclockwise, spiraling from the outside in.

I finally found the glasses in the far left-hand corner, approximately four yards from where the priest said the collision had occurred.

"They're over here," I shouted. "The lenses are intact, but the frame's a bit bent. Did your attacker touch them, do you think?"

"No, he just knocked me over and ran off."

I took several photos of the glasses—a close-up, one shot from medium range, and another from far away. Based on where we found them, the priest was telling the truth: the intruder must have burst through the chapel door and collided with the old man exactly where he had said.

I picked up the glasses and returned them to their owner.

"That's better," he said, "now I can see your faces."

"Do you think you could identify your attacker?" Milán asked.

"No, it was too dark."

"Was there anything specific you remember about him? Did he give off a particular odor, perhaps?"

"Just sweat. I couldn't tell if he was wearing cologne."

"So you believe it was a man?"

"I'm not around many women, but judging from the person's build, I'd say it was a man. Could you check to see if he broke into the convent chapel as well? It's over there," he said, waving his hand toward a gloomy area on the far side of the courtyard. "We keep a rather valuable chalice in the sacristy."

Milán walked over to the small chapel, slipped on some gloves, and tried to open the door.

"It's locked, and it doesn't look like the door's been tampered with. I don't think he came over here."

"Thank heavens for that." The priest sighed. "Would you take a look in the main chapel and see what he was doing in there?"

"Of course, that's what we're here for. Is there anything of particular value we should be looking for?"

"The tomb of Chancellor Pero López de Ayala and his wife, Leonora de Guzmán. On the wall is an altarpiece. It is a reproduction; the original is in the Art Institute of Chicago. I hope he didn't defile the tomb with graffiti. Please check, would you?" the priest insisted. He grimaced and clutched his hip.

The young EMT frowned at us. "We're taking him to Vitoria," he said.

The old priest nodded meekly and pulled a bunch of keys from his threadbare black jacket.

"Would you please lock the main door when you've finished, and bring the keys back to me at the hospital?"

"I'll make sure you get them, Don Lázaro, don't worry," I assured him. "Does anybody else have a key?"

"I usually lock up. The maintenance crew occasionally prunes the trees in the parking lot, and they make sure the outside looks tidy, although we don't get many visitors. In the summer, they hire seasonal workers, usually locals. I suppose there must be a few keys circulating, but that's a matter for the diocese and the Quejana Council."

"We need to take him now," the paramedic insisted.

"Of course," I said. "Don Lázaro, I'll bring the keys to the hospital as soon as I can. In the meantime, I have some homework for you. Will you write down the names of anyone who worked here recently?"

"I'm not sure I'll remember."

"Just do your best. And one more question: Is this the first break-in you've had?"

"I'm glad you asked me that. A while back, I noticed the lid of the chancellor's tomb had been moved. I informed the diocese, the historical heritage department, but they weren't interested because nothing had been damaged or stolen. I wanted to go to Vitoria to report it to the police, but my superior dissuaded me. In the end, I paid to have the lock changed. I did it for peace of mind, out of my own pocket. I live here alone, and I felt exposed. There hasn't been another incident since then. Oh, come to think of it . . . I did have to make copies of the keys for the council."

"When did that happen?"

"I can't really recall. . . . A year, a year and a half ago?"

"I'm sorry to interrupt, but we really need to get this gentleman to the hospital for treatment," the EMT said, helping the old man into a folding wheelchair.

"Of course," said Milán. "Go ahead."

With that, the paramedics whisked away the injured priest.

Milán and I looked at each other. What had the intruder wanted to steal from the chapel?

The courtyard was dank and still. Not the coziest place to live year-round.

I put on gloves before entering the chapel. Milán looked at me impatiently. She thought this was a waste of time. So did I.

Was it a prank? Was the attacker a vandal who had been caught in the act? If the intruder had been a burglar, wouldn't he have broken into the sacristy at the convent chapel, where he might find valuables he could grab and sell fairly quickly?

The fact that the priest surprised the intruder in the chapel with the tomb suggested that whoever it was hadn't done their homework and had simply stumbled through the wrong door.

But it didn't matter. We were here now, and we had to go in.

The chapel was a small oblong space, roughly five hundred square feet, with a few pews, and a wooden latticed choir stall above our heads. The reproduction of the famous altarpiece was on the wall facing us. It depicted men and women in medieval garments, mostly kneeling in prayer. At the center of the painting was an empty throne.

Milán and I weren't looking at that, though. We were staring at the huge recumbent white sculpture.

"Shit, are we dealing with a crazy person? Is this a grave robber?" Milán whispered, shaking her head.

I didn't respond. I wasn't sure just what we were dealing with yet.

The tomb, a huge alabaster slab, was a marriage bed for the chancellor and his wife, where life-size statues of the couple slept together in death. Both the man and the woman at his side had a dog at their feet. A symbol of faithfulness, I supposed.

Fidelitas, Maturana seemed to whisper to me from beyond.

The heavy slab supporting the two stone figures had been moved.

The act would have required superhuman strength. The sun was now rising, and a ray of light seeped through the crack in the door. It illuminated the gloomy chapel, and we witnessed the unthinkable.

I leaned over the open tomb of the López de Ayala family's most illustrious son: author, diplomat, chancellor. A renaissance man well revered even five hundred years after his death.

But there were too many bones in that sacred space, more than those of the husband and wife. I counted six femurs.

Who did the third body belong to, and why had the thief uncovered this secret?

36

EL PORTAL OSCURO

DIAGO VELA

Summer, the Year of Our Lord 1199

"Could he have fallen asleep somewhere outside the town walls? In a barn, perhaps?" suggested someone behind me.

"Maybe he got distracted catching frogs in the River Zapardiel, and by the time he returned, the gates were closed."

Anglesa, Pero Vicia, and Sabat were in a huddle, murmuring.

"If that were the case, he would have returned this morning," I reasoned. "Yesterday, his uncle gave him his first colt. He was eager to ride him again. Keep looking. Search every hedgerow, behind the walls surrounding every garden."

After a night spent calling Yennego's name, I doused my torch in a puddle.

The gates opened at cockcrow, and those who had joined the search now went straight to their workshops or set up the awnings at their stalls.

I went to find Nagorno. He had been searching for Yennego within the town walls, in gardens and workshops, anywhere a mischievous young lad might have hidden.

I heard a commotion and realized something was happening. I looked around and saw an angry-looking crowd beneath the Portal Oscuro.

My brother had seized one of the Isunzas by the neck and had the point of his dagger pressed against the man's throat. A dozen or so others, including the Ortiz de Zárate brothers and the Mendozas, had formed a circle around them.

"Let every family in Villa de Suso and Nova Victoria weep until my nephew is found. If any man here is holding the lad hostage, it's not too late to release him. As long as he's alive, no questions will be asked," he declared. I knew he meant what he said.

I walked up to the group. Several of the men turned around, and some raised their hands to their belts, reaching for their weapons.

"Let him go, Nagorno. This won't help Yennego."

"Yes, it will. If someone is trying to avenge what happened to Ruiz de Maturana, they will pay. I'll enter each of your houses, and you will all die. No one will be able to stop me."

"Drop him at once!" I cried. "That's enough."

Nagorno grudgingly let the man go. With that, the whole group ran off, and within a few seconds the street was empty.

"You're a fool, Brother. That won't bring Yennego back," I rebuked him.

Nagorno was beside himself. I wasn't accustomed to seeing my brother lose control like this.

"And what do you propose, hm?" he replied angrily. "You'll let them spill our blood and do nothing?"

"I came for you. We're leaving for the fortress at Sant Viçente. We'll enlist the lieutenant's best men to help with the search for my son."

We walked through the Angevín district until we came to the South Gate, where we found the lieutenant saddling his horse.

"No sign of him then?" Martín Chipia inquired as we approached.

"No," I replied, staring through the gate.

Alix was still searching outside the town. She had refused to return without Yennego.

"Children get into mischief, they sleep under the stars. . . . He'll be back. He can't have gone far, not with his leg—"

"Yennego hasn't gone anywhere. He's been taken," I cut in. "I found a broken length of yarn—the amulet his great-grandmother gave him. He would have picked it up if it had just fallen off; he would not have wanted to hurt her feelings. No, Chipia, I plan to assemble a search party with some of your best scouts. My son has been taken from the town, and I fear that, by now, he is far from here."

Just then, one of Chipia's men-at-arms came riding through the South Gate. His horse was slick with sweat and on the verge of collapse.

"Lieutenant, several fortresses are under attack!"

"It's started already?" Chipia exclaimed. "I didn't expect it so soon. Tell me, which ones?"

"All the southern garrisons. They're attacking from the west as well: Puebla de Arganzón, Treviño, Salinas de Añana, and Portilla."

"I know the lieutenant who commands Portilla: Martín Ruiz. He's as experienced as he is tenacious. What more can you tell us? Have they repelled the attacks?"

"As best they can. But, sire, that's not all—"

"What is it? Speak."

"Roderico claims he saw a rider on a white horse bearing the flag of Castile, followed by companies of foot soldiers, archers, and crossbowmen, although not many mounted troops. Behind them were cartloads of provisions and a magnificent, covered carriage. It must belong to King Alfonso, and the rider must be his standard-bearer López de Haro."

Chipia gave me a worried look.

"The situation is worse than King Sancho's advisers led me to believe. Alfonso would not have left Toledo simply to conquer a few fortresses. This is a full-blown campaign. He aims to take Victoria; it's the main frontier town. I'm afraid, Vela, I will need you to prepare the town for a possible attack. No other man here has your determination. I shall meet with the mayor and the royal bailiff at the Sant Viçente fortress. Meanwhile, assemble the people who live beyond the town's walls. The townsfolk must find a place for them in their barns and yards: they won't be safe outside in the event of an attack. We've lost the harvest, but tell the farmers to bring as much of their produce with them as they can. Is there anything else?"

Yennego. You've forgotten that everyone should be out looking for my son. I refrained from saying it, to my chagrin.

"Send a man to the Ajarte quarry," I forced myself to say. "Tell him to load the carts with stones and bring them here. We will use them to repel any attempt to storm the walls. He must also bring limestone. I'll explain what it is for later. The forge is freshly stocked with iron from the Bagoeta mines. I'll tell my sister to order her apprentices to make spearheads. We have neither the time nor the materials to make armor, but the tanners can fashion leather breastplates. Send the woodcutters to fetch saplings for lances, arrows, and crossbow bolts—and to collect firewood."

"In summer?" queried Chipia.

"Tell them to collect firewood," I repeated. "The cows, pigs, sheep, goats, and other livestock must be put out to pasture and then brought back inside before curfew. I realize we have much to do, but permit me to take a dozen of your men to make a quick sweep. I want to search Los Montes Altos—"

"I don't think you've understood the gravity of the situation, my dear count," he interrupted. "After we have brought in everything from outside the walls—all the people, animals, everything we need to survive until King Sancho arrives with reinforcements—I shall order the gates to be closed."

"Then we'll go alone, without any men," Nagorno declared.

"No, I need you both here. I am the king's representative. If you leave now, with danger outside the gates, I will have no choice but to consider you traitors to the Crown."

"Give us until the Angelus. We'll be back before then. I promise," I pleaded.

"I know you're a man of your word, but I wouldn't be doing my job if I let you go now." He turned toward the man at the gate. "Close the gate this instant! Then go up to the guard walk and open only for people seeking shelter or bringing their animals inside."

"Wait, let me through!" a voice cried.

Alix was running up the causeway where the vendors sold their fruit. She was drenched in sweat, her hair plastered over her face. Her wimple was nowhere to be seen.

I hurried over to her as she caught her breath.

"Yennego?" I whispered.

"I found no trace of him, Diago. Nothing."

The lieutenant approached.

"I'm aware of your misfortune, my lady, but I urge you to come inside. Alfonso's army is—"

"That's why I returned," she said. "I saw plumes of dust on the Ibida road, only it wasn't dust. . . . Hundreds of soldiers are heading this way. We're trapped."

37

THE OLD LECTURE HALL

UNAI

October 2019

Estíbaliz had called the previous evening. She sounded worried.

"Kraken, I think—"

"It's Unai, Estí. My name is Unai," I corrected her.

"Unai, I want you to come to the hospital. There's something I have to show you. But first, get the keys to my house from Alba, and bring me what's under the heavy sweaters in my bedroom closet."

After I had gone to Estí's house and then visited her in the hospital to hear what she had to say, I called Doctor Leiva and arranged to meet with her the next morning. This time, we wouldn't be in the pool.

Marina was waiting for me in an empty lecture hall at the Arkaute Police Academy. She was dressed as she always was—despite her sixty-odd years, she wore slim-fitting suits and sneakers.

"I haven't been inside one of these rooms in years," I said, glancing around. Not much had changed since my training days. The wooden desks were the same, and the bare walls still offered no distraction. Light streamed in through the windows.

"Teaching is an acquired taste, but you should try it some time. It can be rewarding. I like to have a packed lecture hall. There's a different energy," she said, looking around the room. "Young people hanging on your every word, eager to absorb all your advice."

"I was like that once. Impulsive. Hungry. That was before I worked the streets. It can change you, make you sick of what you do."

"Are you sick of it?"

"That just came out of my mouth, to tell you the truth," I admitted.

Am I sick of it? I thought, puzzled.

"I've brought some documents to show you," I said, changing the subject. "I need your help. You collaborated with handwriting experts on a case that involved forged wills, I remember."

"That's correct."

"And you've given courses on forensic graphology. . . ."

She looked at me sideways, placing her red half-moon glasses on the tip of her nose.

"Come on, show me these documents. What are we looking at?"

I handed her two separate sheets in see-through plastic sleeves and a pair of my latex gloves. They were a size XL—a loose fit on her tiny fingers.

"Letters. From Ramiro and Alvar. Alvar and Ramiro. To Inspector Ruiz de Gauna. She called me from the hospital yesterday. Since his fall, Alvar seems to have disappeared. When she and Ramiro Alvar met face-to-face, it didn't activate Alvar and Ramiro Alvar didn't recognize her. He apologized to her and explained his condition—"

"That's a good sign," she said, interrupting. "A big step toward his recovery."

"I agree," I said. "Then, shortly afterward, Estíbaliz received this letter from Ramiro Alvar, who managed to sweet-talk a nurse into giving it to her."

Marina studied the letter intently. A furrow appeared between her eyebrows, dividing her forehead in two.

"And . . . ?" she prompted once she'd finished reading.

"Estí asked me to stop by her apartment on my way to the hospital to pick up some love letters Alvar gave her. Check out the signature here."

"Alvar de Nograro, the Twenty-Fourth Lord of Nograro Tower," she read.

"Beautiful writing, isn't it? Nothing like Ramiro Alvar's. I'm no expert, and neither is Estíbaliz, but the difference between them is—"

"Startling," Doctor Leiva finished my sentence for me, totally absorbed in her examination of the letters.

She placed the two sheets side by side on the desk. After poring over them, she turned to me.

"This is even better than I expected," she said at last.

"Meaning?"

"Look at Ramiro Alvar's writing. The block script indicates isolation and introversion. But the backward slant, at approximately sixty-five degrees, is the most remarkable feature: It is rare and has negative connotations. It indicates a struggle for self-control, a suppression of the ego that masks fear and inhibitions. This is the writing of a very sensitive person."

"What can you tell me about Alvar?" I asked, pointing to the other letter.

"This man loves himself. He has a strong, mature mind. He likes to surround himself with beautiful things. He's a hedonist. In comparison, Ramiro Alvar is an ascetic. Do you see how his letters contain no loops? In fact, they're almost rigid. But the most interesting thing is that this letter indicates that Alvar suffers from an unresolved conflict over the death of one or both of his parents. See the extended loop at the top of the capital *D*? That denotes orphanhood. By contrast, there's no such loop in Ramiro Alvar's handwriting: his *D* is balanced—"

I had been listening wordlessly. Marina was completely engrossed in her analysis, but at this point I had to interrupt.

"I asked you about this because I'm hoping you can tell me whether Alvar is pretending to be Ramiro Alvar, whether he's still courting Estíbaliz from his hospital bed because he doesn't want to lose her. Could this last letter be from Alvar pretending to be *Ramiro* Alvar?"

"No, these letters are from two different people. You can usually look at the last word of a sentence to spot fraud, or at the last stroke, which in the case of forged signatures, contains a slight tremor. There's no evidence of this occurring in Ramiro Alvar's letter. This handwriting expresses the author's true intention from start to finish. I've seen similar material associated with well-known, well-documented cases of dissociative identity disorder, but this . . ."

"What, Marina?"

"This is more complicated than an individual presenting a dual personality. Unai, I'm going to ask you a strange question: Do you know for a fact that Alvar Nograro is dead?"

"Alvar? He died a long time ago."

"Are you sure? Is there a grave or a niche? Was he buried? Was he cremated?"

"Slow down," I said. "I don't know. But we can't request an exhumation order for a suspect's entire family. According to the residents of Ugarte, Alvar was already ill by the time he returned to Nograro Tower, and he died shortly afterward. Although none of them went to his funeral, as I think I told you."

"Yes, you did. Isn't that strange, given that Ugarte is a small village? Wasn't Alvar a charismatic, handsome young priest?"

"I don't know, maybe that's the reason they didn't attend."

"You need to go back to the apparently normal personality, Ramiro Alvar. He needs to relive the traumatic experience, to pinpoint the trigger that caused his split and created Alvar. Unless this is all a lie, and he, or they, have been deceiving us."

"*They?* As in two separate people?"

"These letters are so different that I don't know what to think. They have nothing in common, nothing. Even the pen pressure is different."

"Ramiro Alvar is recovering from a bad fall," I reminded her. "That might affect the strength in his hand."

"You need to confront him, Unai. You need to get him to tell you everything. This doesn't add up."

She glanced at her watch. Students were beginning to drift into the lecture hall. Marina handed me the two letters and took off the gloves.

"One last thing," she said in a hushed tone. "Your visits to the academy haven't gone unnoticed. You must realize that you're well respected—you're a legend here. The director wanted me to ask you if you'd be willing to give a talk on applied criminal profiling. It would be educational for the students to hear about your experience. What do you think?"

Her proposal took me completely by surprise.

"I don't know what to say. You know how busy I am right now," I said apologetically.

"Just promise me you'll think about it."

At that moment, my phone's ringtone sounded, interrupting us.

I nodded a goodbye to Doctor Leiva and pulled out my phone as I left.

It was Milán, who, it turned out, had had an equally hectic morning.

"Did you go to the Quejana Council?" I asked.

"Yes. It took forever, but I have a list of staff employed around the complex over the past few years—people who worked at the palace, the convent, the museum, the gardens, and the car park. No names tell me anything. I'm e-mailing you a copy."

"Very good. Have you spoken to Doctor Guevara?"

"Yes. She sent the remains to the Forensics Institute for DNA testing. She's discovered something very interesting, Kraken."

"Unai," I corrected her. I wanted those closest to me to treat me like a person, not a goddamned myth.

"Unai," she repeated. "As I was saying, Doctor Guevara unearthed a few surprises in her preliminary examination."

"What are they?"

"As we suspected, the remains belong to three separate skeletons: two females and one male. But, oddly, one of the female skeletons indicates that the person died recently. Doctor Guevara thinks the body may have been kept outside for several months while it decomposed, and then the bones were placed in the tomb. The other sets of remains are much older."

"So, we have the chancellor and his wife, and a contemporary intruder."

"It's too early to speculate. And the analysis will take several weeks."

"Have you told the DSU all this?"

"A separate investigation is being opened; there are no commonalities with the *Lords of Time* case. This was aggravated breaking and entering. If we assume the perpetrator wanted to desecrate the tomb, then the motive isn't clear. We could be dealing with a simple act of vandalism. The diocese and the Quejana Council are going to report the incident to the local police. For the time being, unless something was stolen, the cultural heritage people don't want to get involved. More work for everybody, and Inspector de Gauna is on leave."

"Send the forensics team to Quejana, then," I said, "to see if they can lift fingerprints or find tire tracks. The culprit didn't get there on foot."

"Good idea. If they find anything, I'll check the database and see if it matches previous thefts at historical sites."

"It won't," I told her. "This wasn't a professional job. I'm willing to bet that the culprit has no prior convictions. He didn't go there to steal. Think about it: He went straight to the tomb. When he heard Don Lázaro on the stairs, he stopped what he was doing and knocked the priest over as he fled the scene. I don't think he meant to hurt him; a violent person could have easily finished the old boy off, but our perpetrator simply gave him a shove."

Milán took a while to reply. I imagined her taking notes on one of the Post-its she kept in the pocket of her baggy duffle coat.

"If our criminal isn't a burglar or a vandal, then what is he?" she finally asked.

"Someone who was looking for something in that tomb," I proposed. "Someone who had been there before and moved the lid. Someone who had access to the keys at two separate points: once more than a year ago, and then again recently, after the priest changed the lock. Someone who didn't want this to look like a burglary; if he had, he would've broken down the door. No, he just wanted to open the tomb, steal the bones or whatever he was looking for, and leave—without anybody noticing."

"Or it could be a simple prank that got out of hand," Milán replied hesitantly, "in which case, we may never find the culprit. Either way, we need to prioritize. We have four bodies in the mortuary."

"I know. This is a minor enigma."

"There's more, Kra— Unai," she corrected herself. "You were right to ask about the objects found at the scene of MatuSalem's murder. Forensics analyzed everything lying on the grass: a soda can, an empty bag of sunflower seeds with about fifty shells, an ice-cream wrapper . . . And a number-two pencil with a very sharp point."

"Which has DNA on it," I said eagerly. "There's blood on the tip of the pencil."

You're a damn genius, Matu, I thought. *God bless you.*

"How did you know?"

"MatuSalem spent time in prison. Somebody who's been inside considers a sharpened pencil a weapon," I explained. "And, like all professional hackers, Matu didn't trust the Internet. He carried a pencil with him at all times; when he didn't want something traced, he used the old-fashioned approach. Thanks to him, we have his killer's DNA."

I left the building and wandered aimlessly along the paths I had taken when I was at the academy. I was lost in my own thoughts: finally, there was a piece of physical evidence, a trail we could follow.

I'd been feeling lost for some time now, and not just because I was facing the most disconcerting case of my career. I was starting to lose what it was that made me leap out of bed every morning, ready to go to work. I sensed my life had reached a crossroads, and I didn't want to have to give up any of the paths that lay before me.

Thank you, Maturana, I said silently. *I'm one step closer to avenging your death.*

38

BEYOND THE WALLS

DIAGO VELA

Summer, the Year of Our Lord 1199

I hastened to the ramparts, Chipia at my heels.

"I'll send a rider to Tudela. Alfonso has seized his advantage, knowing that his cousin Sancho the Strong has been in the Muslim lands since spring. But the court will get word to King Sancho and he will send reinforcements."

"I trust we won't need to await the king's reply," I said, frowning. "The message will take a month to reach him, and another will pass before we receive his decision."

"You are right, the situation requires urgency, and custom must be bypassed. The court will obey the king's orders, given to me by his advisers: 'Victoria must under no circumstances be surrendered to my cousin.' They will send troops to help us defend the gateway to the kingdom. We need only hold out until tomorrow. Our first concern is to determine which direction our enemies will take. It will augur well if they arrive from the south," he said, gesturing toward the horizon.

There was nothing to see as yet. All was quiet: green expanses of wheat, the odd oak tree, and a few oxen plowing the land.

"If they approach the South Gate, the sloping terrain and the height of the town wall give us the advantage. If they choose that route, they'll have come to parley, not to attack directly," the lieutenant reasoned. "But no matter their approach, they will soon be here. I'm off to fetch my weapons and armor. I suggest you do the same."

I nodded and rushed to the forge, where Lyra and her men were at work. Every furnace was blazing, and it was devilishly hot inside.

"Here, Brother," she said loudly for everyone to hear. She presented me with my chain-mail snood, helmet, and breastplate. Then she beckoned me over to a secluded corner. "We must leave the town and search for Yennego. Kings can fight over fortresses and frontiers, but we must fight for our lineage."

"Nobody wants that more than Alix and me, Lyra. But Alix came back empty-handed. And neither Nagorno, Gunnarr, nor you have found any sign of him inside the walls. You realize what this means."

I leaned against my sister. I was weary after my lengthy vigil, weary of searching for my son, and weary of thinking about the impending battle. I was able to let down my guard with her, and I felt better for it.

"Just say the word, and I will brave the arrows and the lieutenant's wrath to take Nagorno's horse and search for him," she told me.

"I cannot let you venture alone into territory where almost every town and fortress has been taken by the enemy. It is too dangerous. You'd never make it back alive."

Clanging bells heralded the retreat. One, two, three . . . Some were right above our heads, others farther off. Chipia's men were closing all the gates of Villa de Suso and Nova Victoria.

Lyra went back to her companions and started giving orders. I walked outside, leaving the armor my sister had fashioned for me on the floor. Full carts bearing sacks of fruit, firewood, and suckling pigs were crowding the streets, as were the cutlers and their families who had abandoned their dwellings outside the walls. They bore scythes and sickles and carried small children.

I looked for Alix. She was directing the flow of people entering the town.

"Head for the fort! And the church!" she cried.

Amid the clamor and chaos, I bumped into Onneca as she came out of a courtyard. She seemed agitated and looked surprised to see me.

"What are you doing?" she asked nervously.

"Preparing for the arrival of the enemy troops. Is anybody taking care of Grandmother Lucía?"

"With all this turmoil, I'm afraid she might have been forgotten," Onneca replied.

"I'll bring her to the church with the others," I said, and hurried off to the old woman's house.

"Grandmother, I'm here to take you to the church," I said.

"But I must stay here, in case Yennego returns. I don't want him to take fright if he arrives and finds the house empty," she replied, gazing out the window as she spoke to me.

"You needn't worry. Yennego is much cleverer than you and me. He'll know to look for you at the church," I assured her. "Don't upset him by refusing to take shelter. Come along."

She let me carry her to the church on my back. When we arrived, I put her down on the steps beside the altar. I ran back to the forge to fetch my armor and made my way home.

There I put on a leather breastplate, followed by one of metal. Over that I slipped a long-sleeved cuirass and a tunic emblazoned with the Vela coat of arms: a mountain cat on an azure background with our family motto, *Vela, he who watches*, in sable lettering. I donned the chain-mail snood to cover my head and shoulders and finally put on my helmet, despite the heat on that ill-fated day.

The enemy army arrived from the south, but as they neared the town, they circled around and approached the North Gate. Chipia, Nagorno, and I mounted the ramparts. A soldier bearing a white flag approached the gateway, halting a few yards away.

"King Alfonso the Eighth wishes to parley! Will you honor the truce and lower your weapons?"

"We will!" Chipia replied. At his signal, the archers aiming at the advancing guard lowered their arrows.

"They are four hundred strong," Chipia calculated. "There are fewer than three hundred in the town. But we have nothing to fear, for I see no siege weapons, and without them they cannot enter. We have the advantage, and the king knows it."

Then, let this be over quickly so I may continue to search for my son, I was tempted to say.

We only had to hold out for a day before the army from Navarre would arrive with reinforcements and my family and I could continue our search for Yennego. We could at least find out what had become of him, so that we could find peace.

"These men look rested. Their tunics are clean, not bloodstained," I observed. "They haven't seen battle yet nor lost any comrades-in-arms. They are keen to fight and are at their most dangerous."

"They'll be even more battle ready after forgoing the siege of other towns," Nagorno added.

Several men on horseback approached. A man on a magnificent white stallion came forward, escorted by two riders.

King Alfonso VIII was a fine figure of a man. His shoulders were muscled like an archer's, and he had a regal bearing, evincing a certain disdain and an ease of manner. He had been king for three years now, and he wore it well.

When he removed his helmet, his hooked nose was slightly flattened, possibly the result of a blow sustained in battle. His square face had flowing whiskers, but he was otherwise completely bald.

"I do not seek a bloody conquest," he said, his commanding voice ringing out. "I come here to reclaim what was endorsed in the year of our Lord 1174. These lands are mine by right, and yet when the treaty was signed, I was a mere novice, incapable of holding my own against the expert diplomacy of my uncle, King Sancho the Wise. Now I am a man, and I am here to demand that you surrender the town, open the gates, and let me enter. I will respect your charters and tax exemptions. Unlike the Navarrese, I promise not to seize fortresses and depopulate the estates of the counts and local lords. I will not impose lieutenants from far afield, who are not of your lineages—"

"Before you trouble yourself further, my lord," Chipia cut in, "I must inform you that, on the orders of your cousin, Victoria will not be surrendered to you."

"You must be his lieutenant. And you the town's noblemen." He greeted us with a nod of his head.

"Count Vela and Count de Maestu," I shouted, returning the gesture.

"Count Don Vela, I've heard the sad tale of your son and heir. It's being told in the inns we passed through along the way. It is a shame that the gates are closed; you must be eager to search for the lad outside. Surrender the town, and you may go. I won't try to stop you."

Nagorno made to raise his crossbow, but I restrained him. I, too, could have hit Alfonso with an arrow at that distance and committed regicide. But there was too much at stake. . . .

Instead I replied, "You are a king and are therefore presumed to be noble. I find it hard to believe you would play with the life of a child, even if he is your enemy's heir, to force the surrender of a town."

The king raised his head and looked straight at me.

"Yours is a grave offense, but I forgive you. I, too, am a father, and if anything were to befall my daughter, Blanca . . . I understand your pain."

All I saw was an arrogant man holding my gaze.

"Since we speak as one man of honor to another, do I have your word that this tragedy is not of your making?" I asked.

"If any of my subjects were to resort to such a vile ruse, they would receive the harshest punishment. I regret the loss of your son. Your family's renown extends as far as Castile, and you do not merit such a tragedy. But let us discuss the conditions of your surrender: open the town gates and we will respect the good folk within its walls."

"Alas, it is I who speak on behalf of King Sancho the Seventh," Chipia spoke up once more. "And we will not surrender the town. Indeed, we are awaiting reinforcements that will arrive at any moment. The battle will take place outside the town's walls. There is nothing left to discuss, as your attempt at usurpation is unlawful."

"You speak of laws? Make no mistake, the pope has excommunicated my cousin because of his unlawful pacts with the infidel. He abandoned his territories and his vassals months ago to reside with the Saracens. He now stands alone, for neither Aragon, León, nor Portugal support his claims. What good is paying the yearly tithe to a king none of you know and who shows only contempt toward the nobles of his realm? Why should you give him an ox every March?"

I glanced sideways at the mayor, who shifted his weight uneasily from one foot to the other.

"You have no answer? Then will you open the gates?" Alfonso insisted.

"We shall not. You will camp outside the walls tonight, and tomorrow when our reinforcements arrive, you will lose many men in battle. Is that how a just king treats his soldiers?" retorted Chipia. The parley was at an end.

The king and his escort turned their horses and headed toward the cemetery square, close to the well.

As we descended the tower staircase, Nagorno held me back.

"While the king was parleying, some of the rear guard were chopping down trees."

We looked at each other in alarm.

"This doesn't bode well," I muttered. "Tell Lyra to free up a furnace to heat the powdered limestone from the quarry."

Nagorno stalked off while I made my way to the main square.

The townsfolk from both neighborhoods were gathered there, nobles and craftsmen alike, all of them armed with swords, lances, bows, and hammers.

"Has everybody outside the walls managed to seek refuge in the town?" the mayor asked.

"All but the folk at La Romana Inn. They say they're staying put, that they'll have work and protection with the soldiers," replied the royal bailiff.

"We will defend the gates of Nova Victoria," declared Mendoza. "Deploy your men on our turrets. If they attack from the west, our walls and streets will be the first to fall."

"The lance makers, cutlers, bakers, and grocers will defend the east wall, the North and South Gates, and Portal de la Armería," said Alix, and the townsfolk murmured their approval. "We are higher up and better protected, yes, but the king will want to bring down Villa de Suso and the Sant Viçente fortress right away. If he attacks, he will start with us."

"Very well, I'll place one of my men on each of the twenty-four turrets," Chipia agreed. "They don't have enough men to surround both neighborhoods. But they will send scouts to see if anyone leaves the town. Go to the forge and ask for arrows, and bolts for those with crossbows. Take any weapons they've been able to make. Bring out your pitchforks, knives, and hammers, anything that might help you defend yourselves."

"Is there news from the southern forts?" asked Yñigo, the furrier's son.

"No, you fool. The town gates are shut and we're surrounded by the enemy. Why would I send scouts to bring tidings from the south?"

"Are we to fight them, then?" asked Mendoza. "Shouldn't King Sancho be leading the rescue mission?"

"I've sent a message to Tudela requesting help," Chipia interjected impatiently. "Tomorrow or the day after, reinforcements will arrive from Pamplona. But remain at the ready lest something go awry. If the bell tolls, those who are unable to fight should take refuge in the churches of Sant Michel and Santa María, and in the fortress of Sant Viçente. Meanwhile, return to your homes and wait for help to arrive."

The crowd dispersed slowly, some cursing quietly as they gazed up at the clear blue sky.

I went in search of Alix, who had disappeared. Beneath my helmet, my hair was dripping with sweat.

I found her giving orders to the latest arrivals, and together we slipped inside Grandmother Lucía's courtyard. We hadn't seen each other properly since we'd started the search for Yennego.

"He is lost to us," she said, heartbroken. "We won't find him inside or outside the town amid this chaos."

I embraced her, feeling powerless. She was right. And with King Alfonso at our gates, we could expect no solace, only more danger.

"We won't stop searching for him. If I disappear and you find no trace of me in the coming days, I will have gone through the blockade to look for him. Trust that I will return. I know your instinct will be to follow me, but you must protect our unborn child. For now, you are safer looking for Yennego inside the town. Keep questioning the villagers, and take advantage of the chaos to search the houses of Nova Victoria. Use any pretext you can think of."

"Do you think the soldiers will arrive from Pamplona in time to—?"

But before she could finish her sentence, we heard a massive thud at the North Gate.

A battering ram was pounding at the wooden door, threatening to split it in two.

39

THE OLD BURIAL GROUND

UNAI

October 2019

It's good of you to bring me back to the tower," murmured Ramiro Alvar, who was sitting in the passenger seat of my car. "I could have asked someone from the village."

"I know," I said, parking next to the moat. "But long stints in the hospital can be disorienting. It's good to get away every so often, even if it's just for a few hours. I'll take you back in a bit. How do you feel?"

"To be honest, I have been longing for home, even though they won't be discharging me for several weeks. It's taking me a long time to recover."

To be honest echoed in my head. It was ironic to hear Ramiro Alvar talk about honesty.

"I thought you had come to arrest me. I thought you were going to take me from the hospital to the police station and then to prison. I'm glad you removed the armed guards. I found their presence quite intimidating."

"We can't prove you threw Inspector Ruiz de Gauna over the balcony," I said, my hand automatically gripping the steering wheel tighter.

"You know what I mean," he said.

"I don't. Tell me, I want to understand."

"Even I can't be sure my alter didn't do it." A blond curl fell in front of his eyes as he adjusted his glasses.

"You have a low opinion of your alter."

"If you only knew. . . ."

"That's why I brought you here today. I want to find out all about him. Let's go." I opened the passenger door and lifted him into a folding wheelchair.

"Where are we going?" he asked.

To the Nograro family burial ground.

"You'll find out soon enough."

I headed for the low wall alongside the family chapel. An iron gate barred our way.

"You can push it open," Ramiro Alvar said. "It isn't locked." He sounded tense.

The place had a desolate atmosphere that I found surprising. For a family so proud of its lineage, they hadn't done much to honor their dead. The ivy on the cemetery walls was barely alive, and the cypress trees at the entrance appeared to be shedding their bark.

We stopped in front of a line of headstones, all bearing the name Alvar. This was one of the few cemeteries I'd visited that had no niches. Instead, the graves had been dug into the ground and were all marked by headstones.

I gave Ramiro a sidelong glance. He swallowed hard.

"You know whose grave we're here to visit, don't you?"

"Why are you doing this to me, Unai?" he implored. He made as if to wheel himself to the gate, but I held him back.

"Because I'm committed to solving this case, and I need to see the whole picture. You've only shown me fragments. I'll never understand you if you only show me certain pieces of yourself, and Estíbaliz others. We've reached a dead end. Even you don't even know whether you're guilty. But together we're going to solve this puzzle, Ramiro. Which is your brother's grave?"

Ramiro shuddered. The burial ground was certainly dismal, but this was something more than a sudden chill.

"That one, on the left," he said, signaling toward one of the headstones.

I wheeled him closer, until his chair was opposite the grave.

Alvar Nograro XXIV

Lord of Nograro Castle

1969–1999

Although this headstone was newer than the others, the granite was cracked, as if someone had hit it. It was interesting that Ramiro Alvar hadn't had it fixed or replaced.

"Is the grave empty?" I asked.

"No! For God's sake, how could it be empty?" he protested. "He died and was buried here."

"Were you at his funeral?"

"Of course I was. I arranged everything after he died. I saw to all the formalities," said Ramiro.

"Why such a small funeral? Why were you the only mourner in attendance?"

"Because Alvar was a bad person! He set all the families in Ugarte against one another. They didn't want to meet each other at the graveside."

"Was he mean to you?" I probed.

"During the last year of his life, after our parents died, yes. He was a total idiot."

"But he wasn't always like that, was he?"

"Until I was about thirteen and Alvar was twenty-five, he was my best friend, even though he was a lot older. He was my role model, my mentor. Then he joined the priesthood, and after that he changed."

"What do you think changed him? Your father? Something he saw?"

"No, Unai. It wasn't my father."

"What, then?"

"What if I don't want to remember?" he shouted. This was the first time I'd heard him raise his voice, and my guard went up.

"If you want to get yourself out of this mess, you don't have any other choice."

"You can't force me."

"Listen to me, Ramiro Alvar, because my patience is wearing thin," I said, crouching so I could look him in the eye. "People are dying because of a book you wrote to cure yourself from a condition that you might not even have. You've made decisions that have had horrifying consequences—the worst possible outcomes. My partner, my best friend, nearly died because of you, and she still believes you're innocent. I need you to try here. I need you to confront your past once and for all. What happened to Alvar? What was so serious that it made you create an alter you wanted to kill off?"

Ramiro Alvar's chin quivered. He extended a finger to wipe away the grime on the engraving of his brother's grave.

"It began the way all stories do when you're young, I suppose. It began with love."

40

THE RAMPARTS

DIAGO VELA

SUMMER, THE YEAR OF OUR LORD 1199

They brought more than just battering rams. Hundreds of arrows spiked the roofs of the houses inside the walls. It was terrifying. The sky bristled with sharp points. They dropped onto the cobbles and the graves in the cemetery. At least there, they could no longer take a life.

"Pick them up, we're going to need them!" I called out to a group of children shielding themselves under some wooden planks.

A few of the girls who weren't paralyzed by fear darted out into Rúa de las Pescaderías and grabbed the stray arrows.

Lyra and her apprentices appeared, carrying cauldrons of hot sand.

"Give them cover!" Chipia ordered his soldiers.

I grabbed a shield and joined them, protecting my sister as she and her men scrambled up the stairs to the North Tower.

At the top, I peered over the battlement. Although most of the soldiers were attacking our gate, there weren't many of them. The king and his standard-bearer, López de Haro, must have realized that any men deployed at the other gates would fall victim to Chipia's archers and crossbowmen who could take aim from the safety of their arrow slits.

Below us, eight soldiers wielded the battering ram, a huge tree trunk with a sharpened point at one end. They were ill prepared aside from their metal helmets and breastplates. There was no leather canopy to protect them from above.

Lyra positioned her apprentices above the soldiers' heads and gave the command: "Now!"

The burning-hot sand poured onto the battering ram and the men carrying it. Several of them collapsed, clawing hopelessly at their breastplates as the sand seeped into the gaps in their armor.

The tree trunk lay abandoned, and we were given a few moments' respite.

It did not last, however: Soon the bulk of the rearguard infantry rushed toward the wall. They came in pairs, carrying ladders with a single pole and traverse bars. This time they spread out on both sides of the North Gate.

"Ladders!" I cried from the square. "To the ramparts, everyone, with your stones!"

Anglesa the baker bounded up the steps two at a time, clutching several large stones to her breast. Alix's apprentices were close on her heels as they moved to defend the east side. They threw stones of all shapes and sizes, and our archers gave swift cover, launching arrows at the soldiers attempting to climb the ramparts.

Few made it as far as the merlons. Nagorno ran his sword through the belly of a skinny soldier who managed to scale the west wall, and Gunnarr threw his battle-axes left and right. He was lethal and effective, but his size and his flaxen beard made him an easy target for the enemy archers, and one of their arrows pierced his shoulder.

Alarmed, I ran over to him as he took shelter behind a turret.

"We can tend to our wounds later," he grinned.

"Have you taken henbane?" I asked, surprised to see him so cheerful.

"No need, we're in no real danger yet."

Gunnarr had fought with a band of Norse mercenaries who had

some bad habits. They were trained to use what they called Odin's spume; it was actually an ergot, and it produced a state of euphoria that rendered the mercenaries deadly in battle. I hated to see Gunnarr fight under its influence, for it made him as reckless as it did courageous, and I feared for his life.

Just then we heard several voices cry out, "Retreat! Retreat!"

I glanced around. Everyone appeared paralyzed. Chipia had been about to throw an enormous rock and was now clutching it in both arms. Alix's apprentices exchanged glances, unsure whether to empty their cauldron of burning sand.

I peered over the ramparts. This wasn't a ruse; the few soldiers still able to run were taking shelter in a nearby stand of trees or fleeing farther afield.

A trumpet sounded. The order came from the king himself.

Retreat.

Gunnarr and I heaved a sigh and leaned our heads against the battlement.

The silence was followed by joyful cheers. Some of the townsfolk lost their heads and continued hurling stones.

"Don't be foolish, we might still need them!" Nagorno reprimanded.

"Archers, hold position! No one is to lower their guard!" Chipia ordered. "You, townsfolk, take shelter! Everybody to the cathedral!"

We barged into Santa María, where the oldest residents were reciting the paternoster for the hundredth time.

"We fought off the attackers! The town stood firm!" we all exclaimed.

Mendoza, his face torn by arrows, flung his arms around the weaver women, overjoyed.

Children skipped in circles.

Someone standing close said, "I'll fetch my bagpipe!"

Even Gimeno, the stout curate who had replaced Vidal, refrained from scolding us for dancing in God's house. He sat on the floor, legs splayed on either side of his paunch, and leaned his head against the altar. He closed his eyes and crossed himself.

Soon all the inhabitants, nobles and artisans alike, were reeling to the music from violas, rebecs, and lutes.

I looked for Alix and found her clinging to Grandmother Lucía. The old woman's eyes were creased with joy. She laughed, showing her beautiful, toothless smile.

I went over to sit with them, rested my head on Alix's lap, and closed my eyes, allowing myself to escape for a few moments. I caressed her belly, embracing our unborn child. I thought about our son, Yennego, who wasn't dancing with the other children. She squeezed my hand gently, wordlessly.

Chipia joined us on the altar stairs, interrupting our moment of peace. He reeked of death, and his breath was labored. A trickle of blood ran from his brow down his neck and under his chain mail.

"Miraculously, no one was killed," he declared. "Only arrow wounds. Two are serious: Ortiz de Zárate has four in his leg. It will have to be amputated, before it turns gangrenous. And Milia, the layer-out, was hit in the side and the stomach."

"Send the townsfolk home. If wine begins to flow, they'll be celebrating all night," I warned. I shared their happiness, but I was concerned about what lay in store for us, concerns I knew they did not share.

Chipia stood up and ordered the musicians to stop playing.

"Go home and rest!" he shouted, placing himself at the center of the gathering. "We have resisted them, and tomorrow the troops will arrive from Pamplona. They will repel King Alfonso's army, and we'll be saved."

But Alix, Lyra, Nagorno, Gunnarr, and I did not rest. We continued to search every yard, every garden. I even tapped the walls of the sacristy with a stick lest some monster had the idea of immuring my son.

But we found no trace of Yennego.

Still my family refused to go to their beds, and we spread out once more. Alix and I scoured the alleyways off Rúa de la Astería for the hundredth time.

Dawn had not yet broken, but we saw a glow lighting up the indigo sky. We exchanged a worried glance and ran to the South Gate.

We climbed the steps and peered over the wall.

"Have you ever seen such a thing?" Alix asked, alarmed.

"I'm afraid so. This attack will be like none this town has seen. We must alert Chipia at the Sant Viçente fortress. I'm not sure our town will survive what's coming."

41

THE FORGE

ALVAR

April 1994

Alvar kept looking behind him, even though he knew everyone in the tower was enjoying an afternoon siesta. Ramiro was studying in the library; his father was dozing by the fire in his office. He had double-checked.

He swallowed around the lump in his throat when he thought about his father, Lorenzo Alvar XXIII, Lord of Nograro Tower.

But there was no going back now.

He had done it. He'd gone to Vitoria and signed the papers. Agustín, his best friend since childhood, had recently been ordained. He had agreed to Alvar's request to serve as a witness and would be waiting for them in the chapel at San Viçente Church.

"Gemma," he whispered, as he entered the abandoned forge. "It's me, Alvar. We need to go now, or we'll be late."

But Gemma wasn't there yet. He checked his watch. They had an hour to get to Vitoria. Once it was done, his father would have to accept it.

He checked his watch again.

We won't make it. He was starting to worry. *I told her not to be late, not today.*

Gemma was sometimes a bit impetuous. She had thick wavy hair and strong features, and she was a good student. She dreamed of becoming a marine biologist, although everyone knew it would never happen. She would instead go to university in Vitoria and choose one of the courses available there. But when she and Alvar met in Ugarte on the weekends, she had put all that aside and stopped being so serious. She would arrange dinners with the *cuadrilla*, outings on horseback, hikes and trips to attend festivals in town. That was Gemma, a natural leader. Alvar had always been crazy about her, but she'd never paid attention to him. She was the only one. All the other girls had been desperate to get close to him, but they'd never mattered.

Alvar sat on an old stack of firewood. The forge technically belonged to the Nograro family, but it hadn't been used in decades. He had been thinking about restoring it for years, turning it into a country hotel when he set up his agritourism business.

His father would fight him on it. Lorenzo Alvar disliked change, and the family didn't need the money. But Alvar didn't want to just preserve the family heritage. He planned to reform the estate from the bottom up, although he would have to do it slowly as long as his father was still around. And it was going to take Lorenzo Alvar a long time to get over the marriage, which wouldn't help things.

What did it matter? His father had gotten worse recently. He even wore his embarrassing disguises to dinner, and he insisted on speaking medieval Spanish. His last psychiatrist didn't even believe he *had* multiple personality disorder. He thought he was a transvestite in denial.

Poor Mama, Alvar thought yet again. *She's had to put up with so much.*

He peered out the ancient building's tiny windows. All he could see in the distance were a few houses in Ugarte.

That's how I'll get them to agree: I'll tell them after the fact, when it's a fait accompli.

But Gemma still hadn't arrived, and now he worried that they would be late for their own wedding. He stood up. He was willing to risk it. He would go to her house to pick her up. Gemma's grandmother had always been their silent ally; she wouldn't betray them.

He was halfway to the door when it opened slowly. He heaved a sigh of relief. He didn't often get agitated, but his hands had been shaking all day.

He wasn't expecting her to enter. Not her.

He had worried that his father might find out, that the people in the village might have told him something, and that he would confront them and fly into a rage the way he did when he wore his military uniform. When he dressed in that costume, the whole family knew he would be irascible.

But he wasn't expecting his mother to walk in. Inés approached him cautiously. She was wearing the string of gold bracelets she never took off and had a cardigan tied loosely around her shoulders. It looked as if she had just been to the tanning bed as well. He adored his mother; they were as thick as thieves. She was the only grown-up who took his side.

"Mama, what are you doing here?"

His mother looked serious—too serious.

"I'm sorting out your life, that's what."

Alarm bells rang in Alvar's head, and he instinctively recoiled.

"I don't know what you've heard, but—"

"Sit down, Alvar." She motioned to a sack. She didn't even smile. This was unlike her. She was patient and courteous, and always smiling.

"It's just that I have to go." He looked at his watch again.

If Gemma walked in with his mother there, it would be disastrous. . . . Disastrous.

"The wedding is off," she said, and produced the marriage license Alvar thought he had in his wallet.

His mother tore it into tiny pieces until not one word remained intact.

"I understand that you're angry because I didn't tell you I was getting married. I know how important these things are in our family, and I planned on telling you. Let me explain. . . . Gemma's pregnant. And we want to be together."

"Just like all the others, Alvar," his mother said, clasping her son's hands. She stared down at them.

"No, it's different this time," Alvar said frantically. "And it's not just because she's pregnant. I understand why you're skeptical. You always tell me that I'm fickle, that I've never had to fight for anything in my life, that my future has always been mapped out for me. But don't you see? I want to be with Gemma. I want to take responsibility for the child we're going to have."

They heard a noise outside the forge.

"It's her!" Alvar jumped to his feet, excited.

"Sit down, Alvar. It must be a dog. It certainly isn't Gemma."

Outside, Ramiro was crouched behind the wall, listening. Alvar had been acting strangely, and Ramiro had noticed that his mother was coming and going at odd times as well. She was lying to his father and taking mysterious trips to Vitoria. His home had begun to resemble a den of medieval conspirators, full of intrigue, uncomfortable silences, and nervous smiles. Young Ramiro saw everything from behind his protective glasses. He was convinced that Alvar and Gemma were plotting something, so he had followed his brother. Gemma was eighteen, five years older than Ramiro, and he was madly in love with her. But if she and Alvar were together, he would forget about her. He wouldn't interfere in his brother's life if Gemma meant that much to him.

Ramiro stayed perfectly still, praying to God that his brother and mother wouldn't discover him eavesdropping.

"How do you know she's not outside?" That was Alvar's voice inside the forge. He sounded distraught.

"Because she left Ugarte last night."

It took Alvar a couple of seconds to absorb this; he and Gemma had last spoken on Saturday afternoon. They had had a long conversation to tie up any loose ends.

"Did she go to Vitoria?" he asked, sitting down again, still oblivious to what was coming.

"No, I forbade it."

"You did what?" Alvar echoed, incredulous.

"She won't be coming back to Ugarte or to Vitoria. Not ever."

"I don't believe this. What did you do?"

"I paid her—a lot. To leave here, to never see you again, and to get rid of a child that has no business being born."

No, not my child. It was a terrifying thought.

Alvar realized that, for the first time, he felt like a father. When Gemma had first told him, the child had been no more than an exciting, abstract idea. It was Gemma who really mattered. But now, his child? Gemma was going to get rid of his child? Without even talking to him?

"What are you saying? Why would you say that my child has no business being born? Are you really that much of a snob?"

"Me, a snob? You know nothing, Alvar. You've lived your whole life in Ugarte, and you know nothing."

"What don't I know? Why don't you approve of Gemma or her mother—or anybody in her family for that matter?"

His mother sighed. It was so difficult, so humiliating to have to tell this story to her own son. She didn't want to dredge up memories from twenty years ago. Damn him. Damn Lorenzo Alvar, XXIII Lord of Nograro.

"Because Gemma is your sister," she finally said. She spoke the truth with perfect clarity. It was unambiguous.

"What?"

"Your father got her mother pregnant after he and I were already married. You were six years old. She and her boyfriend had a shotgun wedding. But everyone in Ugarte knew the truth. They could see that the baby wasn't premature. Gemma is your father's daughter. You're half siblings. The idea of you having a child together is madness."

"I fell in love with my own sister?"

"Yes, I'm afraid so."

"I slept with my own sister?"

"Yes."

"And no one in Ugarte told us?"

"Why should they have? You've followed in your father's footsteps and slept with every girl in Ugarte and in the nearby villages. I suppose they didn't think the affair would last more than a few weeks. Why destroy two families a second time by digging up an old scandal?"

"What about Gemma and me? Did anybody consider the fact that this might destroy our lives?"

"That's why I'm doing what I'm doing. Putting an end to this."

Alvar took a while to take in what his mother had said, to believe what he was hearing. Raising his head, he glanced around the forge, the place he had conducted his romantic trysts for years. He felt like he was cavorting onstage while the whole village watched in silence, the whole time knowing how it would end.

I thought that today I would become an adult, a married man, he thought bitterly.

He sighed and acquiesced.

"So you spoke to Gemma. What did you tell her?" he asked. His voice was different, older, deeper. It was the voice he used to seduce, to appear more mature.

"Everything."

"Everything?"

"Yesterday she found out that she was pregnant with her half brother's child. She wept for a long time. I offered her money to go away, to pursue the studies she'd always dreamed about. I offered her a life."

A life without me. And she accepted.

"How much?" he asked.

"Enough."

"How much?"

"I offered her fifty million pesetas to start."

"Are you crazy? Won't Papa find out?"

"Your father has no idea how much money he has; he hasn't known for a long time. Even when he's himself, he doesn't even pretend to care. Our lawyers know what they're doing, and they keep us informed," she said.

She was tired. Tired of playacting, tired of hiding her husband away, making sure nobody found out that the lord of the tower was mentally unbalanced, a lunatic who could be hospitalized. If he were declared insane, they would lose everything.

All that tension. All that control, was it worth it?

I do it to protect them, Inés reminded herself, contemplating the gold rings on her fingers. *To protect Alvar and Ram.*

"You said to start. How much did she accept?"

"She negotiated. In the end, she agreed to leave for eighty million."

"She bargained away the life of our child? She agreed to never see her family again, to never say goodbye to me?"

"Don't hate her for what she did. She was as shocked as you when she found out you were her half brother."

"But she haggled over the money . . ." muttered Alvar. He was no longer talking to his mother; he was talking to himself. He was repeating the words he would tell himself every night until the day he died.

And he wanted to know everything.

"How did you know I was getting married today?"

"Agustín," she replied simply.

¿Et tu, Brute? My best friend. You too.

And then he felt it.

A weight falling at his feet, like a heavy sack.

An almost-physical sensation.

Three masks cracked that day: his mother's, Gemma's, and Agustín's.

His respect for all of them disappeared.

For his mother especially—the woman who gave birth to him, who raised him, who always listened to him, and who had been his ally, someone he could trust.

"Very well then," he said finally, standing. "I won't get married. Not to her, or to anyone. Who knows how many sisters I have scattered across the country. Tomorrow I'm joining the priesthood. And you will not deny me that. It's a family custom. I can do it. Ramiro Alvar will inherit the title. I don't want it. I want nothing to do with you. Goodbye, Mother. Thank you for putting a price on me. Now I know how much I'm worth."

And with that, he left.

Ramiro, now Ramiro Alvar, had to crouch in the wheat field so his brother wouldn't see him when he stormed out of the forge, slamming the door behind him. The wooden door, barely held together with old, rusty nails, couldn't withstand it and burst apart from the impact. No one would be able to fix it.

Ramiro, officially crowned Ramiro Alvar, fell to the ground in shock. His glasses flew off, hitting a stone at the field's edge. A crack like a spider's web formed in one of the lenses.

And he did not see his brother again that day. He was told by their bewildered father that Alvar had decided to enter the seminary in Vitoria. He had felt a calling from God.

That evening they dined in silence. The three of them. His father, devastated, was dressed sloppily, like a servant. Ramiro's mother didn't even notice the crack in his glasses. Dinner was a silent affair, full of vacant stares. The only sound was the clink of silver cutlery on their plates, dishes that belonged to their ancestors. They barely touched the meal, *crestas de gallo*, Alvar's favorite; it felt sacrilegious.

The absence of the impetuous Alvar burst the fragile bubble of daily life in the tower. His mother—who likely already lacked the strength to pretend each day was as perfect as the last, or who perhaps was unable to bear the weight of her guilt—stopped smiling.

Whenever Alvar returned from the seminary, he flipped the household ecosystem upside down. Arrogant, frivolous, and charming with outsiders; cold and distant with his family. He seduced every girl in Ugarte. A worthy successor to his father, Alvar returned frequently to the forge, and never alone. Only now he wore his cassock.

Ramiro Alvar just watched things unfold. He wondered where his older brother, his role model, his best friend had gone, and why he hadn't come back. No one could answer that question.

Just as no one knew why Inés was at the wheel the day his parents' car dove off the Vitoria bypass.

Seeing his father's inert body on the steel gurney, wearing clothing taken from the servants, shook Ramiro Alvar profoundly.

"If your *alter* is dead, then where are you, Papa? Why don't you come find me?" he whispered into a cold ear that could no longer hear anything.

Alvar wasn't listening, either. The two gazed in disbelief at the bodies that had made them orphans. Ramiro Alvar hadn't seen his brother for several years. Alvar had stopped visiting the tower. His mother invented feeble excuses, smoke screens that insulted Ramiro's intelligence.

He finally understood, or at least thought he did, when he saw Alvar enter the morgue. His brother was an old man who walked with a cane. His face was pale and haggard from anemia and chronic pain, and none of his proud vigor remained beneath his cassock. Only bitterness was left. But what he still couldn't figure out was Alvar's new and violent hostility toward him.

"This is what our mother did. And she did it well, don't you think?" said Alvar, finally addressing his brother.

"I don't understand. What did she do?"

"She steered the family's destiny, and we didn't even see it happening. That's what she did."

42

REINFORCEMENTS

DIAGO VELA

Summer, the Year of Our Lord 1199

"Listen, Alix, I have a plan. I need you to talk to all the spinners and weavers." We went out into the square, where I used a stick to sketch a rough picture in the dust.

Alix crouched down, drawing the torch near, and nodded.

"Three yards should suffice. All the townsfolk must quit whatever they're doing and come to the workshop to sew. They mustn't stop until it's finished."

"Do you believe this will stop their monstrous devices?"

"No, but we're desperate."

I made my way to the butcher's house and rapped hard with the door knocker. He came down in a nightshirt that barely covered his hirsute legs.

"Slaughter half a dozen suckling pigs. The fattest you have."

My words woke him from his slumber.

"Should we not save them for later?"

"They'll never be plumper than they are now, and I need every ounce of animal fat you can give me. We have plenty of salt from the Añana flats, so you can cure the remaining meat."

Back at the main square, I found half the village on the ramparts, peering over the wall. I climbed the wooden steps to the tower.

The light from the enemy's torches showed their progress. A large army was approaching.

I found Chipia by the North Gate, giving orders to his archers, who were filling the baskets at their feet with arrows. I ran up to him.

"How many do you think?"

"Three thousand, at least," he said. His sardonic smile had vanished; he was worried. "But none of them are ours, God be damned. I've seen pennants belonging to the orders of Calatrava and Santiago, powerful allies of Alfonso. And they have three robust siege towers in addition to their siege engines. They're bound to attack soon, before our reinforcements arrive. These walls have been well reinforced and will withstand them, at least. By the way, I've been meaning to congratulate you for using hot sand instead of boiling oil."

"Oil is expensive, and our reserves are low. I was reluctant to waste such a precious resource, although it might come to that given what we're facing."

"A novice would have used oil to repel the first attack."

"I'm not thinking about what might happen today, or even in a month's time. I'm preparing for the worst possible scenario. If there's a lengthy siege, we will need oil more than sand. As long as we have walls and cobblestones, they can be ground into sand and heated in the furnaces. But I'll leave you here, I need to speak to my brother and sister."

I hastened to the forge where I found Lyra and Nagorno distributing weapons. Nagorno was about to take several baskets of bolts to the crossbowmen in Nova Victoria.

"Lyra, I need you to make arrows that are sturdier and longer than these. They need to bear weight. We don't have time to make hoops, so send one of your men to the rope makers for rope."

I briefly explained my plan, and they nodded.

"We need good marksmen. Only you and I have the nerve to fire straight," murmured Nagorno.

"I know," I replied. "We'll do it. I'm not even going to share the plan with Chipia in case he tries to stop us. He's still waiting for help that isn't coming, and his false hope will destroy the town if we let it."

I had scarcely finished speaking when the first volley of rocks fell onto the rooftops. The wood splintered from the force of the missiles, and I could hear shouting.

We ran outside.

"They're armed with catapults and trebuchets!" I cried. "Lyra, make those arrows quickly!"

In addition to the huge rocks they were firing from their onagers, balls of burning straw soon began to rain down upon us, setting fire to rooftops.

The streets filled with black smoke and debris from the damaged houses.

"Run for cover!" The cry went up. "To Santa María Cathedral!"

Then the arrows came, only this time no one hurried to collect them. I saw a little girl no more than five summers old, one of Milia the layer-out's children. I ran after her and had almost caught up to her when an arrow shot past me and pierced her back. By the time I threw myself on top of her, she was no longer moving. I carried her limp body to the nearest courtyard and vowed to return after the attack to give her a Christian burial.

But will there be an after? I wondered.

I knew they could obliterate us. They could continue to bombard us with fire, rocks, and arrows until nothing was left, not even the town's foundations. They would repopulate the area, and in two generations, no one would remember the people who had originally built Victoria and had made their lives there.

I ran to the weavers' workshop.

"Did they bring you animal fat?"

"They're still slaughtering the pigs, but they've started bringing us all the fresh lard they already had in store, just as you ordered."

"Then spread the canvas sheets on the floor and smear them with the lard. I'll be back shortly. I doubt we can hold out for long."

I heard several loud thuds. Onagers were launching rocks at the town wall. They weren't precise engines, but a trained solider knew where to aim them to inflict the most damage: opposite a gate tower or to cover an assault.

I looked up at the guard walk and saw that Chipia's archers and crossbowmen were doing a good job of protecting the ramparts. Then I went into every burning building I could see to make sure that nobody was trapped.

After I had gone through several, burning my arm on a beam that caught me unaware, I heard my name being called.

"Count Don Vela, your brother and sister are looking for you! They're waiting for you at the forge, and they ask you to bring the canvas sheets."

Some time later, Nagorno and I climbed the battlement west of the North Gate. We could see one of the three siege towers advancing toward us. It was several stories high, and the oxen had dragged it as far as the first moat. Soldiers were placing bundles of branches lashed with rope across the breach, then putting planks of wood on top to allow the tower to move closer to the wall.

If the soldiers stormed the battlements and entered the town, there was nothing we could do. We would be helpless against so many.

My brother and I each carried a longbow made of yew, the kind used by English archers, and a thick arrow that was fastened by a rope to the corner of an immense canvas.

Nagorno sniffed the air like a wild boar.

"The wind is coming from the south. This promises to be a magnificent spectacle," he murmured gruffly.

We stood several feet apart. The enormous cloth was smeared with lard, making it a deadweight. I drew back my bowstring with my burned arm and took aim.

"Ready. Take aim! Fire!" I cried to my brother, tilting back and holding my breath as I released the bowstring.

The two arrows sped through the air simultaneously, striking the wooden platform at the top of the siege tower. The canvas draped itself around the edifice.

Lyra handed me an arrow with a lit tip. Her men did the same for the four archers who accompanied us.

"Ready! Aim! Fire!" I shouted.

All our burning arrows landed on the cloth and set fire to the pork drippings. Red and blue flames engulfed the siege tower, and the soldiers hidden in the upper platforms leaped to the ground, their clothes alight. The wind appeared to be on our side. Its gusts fanned the blaze until the charred wooden structure eventually collapsed at the base of the wall.

Some of our men let out cries of joy and embraced one another. But Lyra, Nagorno, and I ran down the stairs. A second siege tower was approaching the outskirts where the cutlers lived.

Once again, we climbed to the guard walk. I saw dead bodies on the way, but we were going too fast for me to recognize them: I could make out burned wimples, legs covered in soot, motionless amid the rubble. The weavers were coming up Rúa de la Astería, bearing another huge canvas patchwork on their shoulders. Arrows were flying everywhere, and they were using it as a shield.

The second siege tower didn't collapse completely. The soldiers had been warned, and as soon as we fired the canvas sheet, they began to pull at it from below. We only managed to set fire to the base of the tower.

"That's enough!" Nagorno cried. "We've stopped it for now—

they won't be able to use it to breach the east wall. Let's take the third one!"

"All right, but we haven't destroyed it; they'll just repair it!" I said.

The third siege tower was threatening the walls of Nova Victoria, next to Portal Oscuro. Ortiz de Zárate cleared the rubble blocking our way to the Angevín district.

This time the tower had all but breached the wall. Some soldiers were pushing bound planks onto the crenellations, preparing to cross.

Mendoza and his men fired their crossbows repeatedly, and the planks plummeted to the ground.

"Ready! Take aim! Fire!" I ordered, even though we were only a few yards from our target.

The third canvas wrapped itself around the last tower, and a fresh volley of flaming arrows set the huge siege engine ablaze, swiftly reducing it to cinders.

Old Mendoza carried his family shield—a red stripe on a green background—and gave me a solemn nod. I took it as a gesture of gratitude and responded in kind.

We were ready to set the onagers aflame as well, and then burn the soldiers attacking our walls, but once more we heard the cry.

"Retreat!"

To our astonishment, the cry was repeated all around the town.

"Retreat!" we heard along Camino de la Cruz Blanca.

"Retreat! King's orders!" on Campillo de los Chopos.

The arrows stopped flying and the rocks stopped pounding our walls. Soon the only sounds left were the crackle of the flames consuming the rooftops and the cries of people searching for their mothers, husbands, daughters, grandmothers.

"Sancha! Has anybody seen my Sancha?"

"Paricio, shout if you can hear me!"

"Hold on, Muño!" shouted the butcher's wife. "Somebody help me, he's trapped under the door to the shop!"

There was no rejoicing that day.

Hundreds of blackened ghosts cleared away rubble and screamed at the top of their lungs. Terrified hens squawked, trapped in coops no one expected to salvage.

I threw my bow on the ground and ran down the tower steps.

"Yennego!" I cried.

For hours, my voice rang out through the streets. "Yennego, my son, I'm here!"

43

A SPLIT TOMBSTONE

UNAI

October 2019

Did your alter start appearing after your parents died?"

"No, it was after Alvar's death."

"What happened when your brother returned to the tower, the year you turned eighteen?"

"He made my life a living hell."

"Why? What happened to make him turn against you?"

"Don't you see? His death was my fault."

"How can you blame yourself? He had a fatal illness. There was nothing you could have done to save his life."

Ramiro Alvar clenched his fists, braced his arms against the sides of the wheelchair and rose to his feet. I stiffened, alert to his every movement. I expected him to hit me.

His whole body was shaking with rage: his lips, his chin, his voice.

"Yes, there was. Alvar had a hereditary blood disease called thalassemia. Other men in our family have had it to varying degrees, but Alvar suffered from the most severe form, and the consequences were devastating. He had chronic anemia and was prone to infection. The disease attacked his spleen, heart, liver—even his bones. He developed fractures in his legs, and the pain became unbearable. By the end, he had become addicted to painkillers. Whose wheelchair do you think this is? By the time he returned to the tower, his body was ravaged by the thalassemia. Only a bone marrow transplant could have saved his life. I was his brother, so we were compatible."

"Then why didn't you—?"

"Because no one told me, for God's sake! The relationship between Alvar and my mother deteriorated so much that she hid his diagnosis from me. She could never forgive Alvar for his behavior when he returned to Ugarte. He was the talk of the village, stirring up rivalries among the local girls, causing rifts in families. He humiliated the family—and he laughed in my mother's face. It was his revenge for what had happened with Gemma. So my mother never told my father and me about the thalassemia. At the time, my father's psychiatrist had diagnosed him as schizophrenic and had prescribed antipsychotic drugs. My father was like a zombie. She couldn't bring herself to tell him he was going to outlive his elder son. As for not telling me . . . My mother was good to me, but that's something I can never forgive."

"What about Alvar?"

"He thought I had refused to donate my bone marrow for the transplant. My mother told him that the entire family had disowned him because of his reputation in Ugarte, and he believed her. I still can't believe that he would think me capable of such cruelty. During Alvar's last year, when he came to live at the tower, he was dismissive, rude, verbally abusive. Every day, he reminded me that I could have saved his life. It was impossible to get through to him. He just wouldn't listen. His personality had completely changed, and the constant pain he was in, coupled with his addiction to his pain medication, only made things worse. They say pain can dehumanize a patient to the point where those caring for them need care themselves. I can attest to that. He lived in a kind of parallel reality; he only acknowledged the truth when it suited him. The year I turned eighteen was a living hell."

"And then you were alone."

"Not exactly. They're all still here in my head: Alvar, my father, my uncles and aunts, my grandparents . . . the whole damn family tree. No, I'm not alone in my tower. I have plenty of company. So far, only Alvar has become an alter, but it won't be long before the others start to take shape. Now do you understand why I was desperate to get rid of him?"

I was surprised to see Ramiro Alvar like this. He was never confrontational—and the sudden burst of strength that had him standing on a broken leg was even more astonishing.

"How have you managed to hide your alter?" I asked. "No one seems to know about him—not the villagers, not your lawyer, not your publisher . . . not even Claudia, and she spends a lot of time just downstairs. How can Estíbaliz and I be the only ones who have seen you as Alvar?"

"Because I've been careful. Studying psychology helped me perfect the masquerade. I learned to turn off the lights whenever anyone comes near the tower. But now that I know I haven't banished Alvar forever, I'm terrified that he might return. What if it's just like when I wrote the novel? He went away for an entire year, until your colleague brought him back. She's the only woman he's fallen in love with since Gemma."

This is like a siege, I thought. *Ramiro Alvar is defending his fortress from behind a wall, trying to keep the monster inside.*

"Maybe you don't have to get rid of him," I suggested.

He looked at me blankly.

"Why would I want to keep him?"

"I know he undermines you because he hates how passive you are."

"That's true. I don't want him inside my head. I want to be alone in there, just me. I just want to be myself."

"You're already you," I explained. "And the alter is not your brother. Your brother, or what remains of him, is here in front of you, six feet underground. He's dead, Ramiro. Your alter isn't Alvar; it's you pretending to be him. And that side of your personality, more brilliant, mischievous, captivating—"

"Dynamic."

"Yes, dynamic. That is also a part of you, but because it reminds you so much of your brother, it brings back memories you're determined to suppress. Ever since you were a child, you've heard horror stories about a mental illness passed down through the men in your family—but they're just stories, they can't be proven. So you have a choice: You can accept this role that they've thrust on you, that they've terrified you with for your entire life, or you can walk away. You can tell yourself: 'That isn't my life. It was yours, but I refuse to live like my father and those before him.' You aren't the same as them. You weren't destined to suffer from this disorder."

"But Alvar is still inside my head. I can't get rid of him. He has a life of his own."

"No, Ramiro, that's just a lie you tell yourself. You think you have a split personality caused by a traumatic event that you were unable to assimilate. That final year, when you cared for Alvar, he was abusive, and you were too young to shoulder that burden alone. So you followed your father's example because it was all you knew how to do, even though you knew it was harmful. You're an adult now with a will of your own. Stop hating your alter; he isn't your brother. If your alter could win the heart of a woman like Estíbaliz, he can't be all bad. He's just one part of you looking for an outlet. You need to integrate Alvar, not reject him or try to kill him off him the way you did when you rewrote the chronicle. You need to take the best parts of his personality and make them your own."

"How?"

"If it's too hard to change the way you think about him, then start by adjusting your behavior. Get out of the tower, take part in the sort of activities you think he would like, but understand that, actually, you're the one who wants to do these things. Take up riding again, you love it. Force yourself to go to Ugarte every day, visit the locals who like and respect you. You don't have to be a recluse; you aren't going to seduce every woman you meet. You've been in love with Estíbaliz from the first time you saw her. You, Ramiro, not Alvar. It was your lack of self-confidence that made you take off your glasses, put on a cassock, and style your hair like his when you first saw her in the parking lot. But you were the one who wanted to eat stewed rooster combs, because there's a hedonistic side to your personality, and you like good food, beautiful views, a well-written novel."

"You're right," he said, uneasily. "I'm starting to remember that night with Estíbaliz in the grotto in Florida Park. It was the first time she looked at me with real interest, but I felt as if I weren't good enough for her and I suppressed that memory for weeks. Still, it was there in my head, waiting to reappear . . . as was our first night together in the tower—"

"All right, Ramiro, I get the picture." I cleared my throat, embarrassed.

Keep that memory to yourself, I begged silently.

But Ramiro was trembling as he stood next to me. At some point during our conversation, he had started to cry silently. He took off his fogged-up glasses and wiped them. He sank back into the wheelchair, his gaze fixed on the cracked headstone.

"So, it was never Alvar; it was always me, acting out what I admired and what I hated in him."

I shook my head.

"Not what you hated. The Alvar I met was never distant or rude because it was never truly Alvar, it was your interpretation of him, and you are neither of those things. Take what you think was the best in your brother, and accept that those things have been in you all along."

I thought this observation might split him in half like a bolt of lightning, but in fact the opposite happened: It made him whole again, fusing his broken parts. As Ramiro gazed beyond his brother's grave, the tense grimace he always wore melted away. He smiled openly for the first time, like a child seeing his first dawn. I think he'd realized that life didn't need to be as painful as the one he'd been living.

"You have an amazing brain," I told him, pushing the wheelchair out of the cemetery. "I think you'll find a way to overcome this. Come on. We'll go to the tower now so you can see it with fresh eyes, and then I'll drive you back to the hospital."

44

SANTA MARÍA CHAPEL

DIAGO VELA

Summer, the Year of Our Lord 1199

Alix caressed her belly as she and I gazed in disbelief at the thirty-four shrouds at our feet. We were standing in the market square outside Santa María Cathedral. There was no space left in our cemetery. A few graves had been dug inside Sant Michel Church, and in the tiny cemetery of Sant Viçente, old bones had been pushed aside to make way for the graves' new inhabitants.

"No family has been spared," Alix said, looking into the distance. "Seventeen children orphaned. Each guild will look after its own, but Milia was nursing her newborn and Tello is also dead. I'll pay the fishmonger's wife to feed the baby, and if she still needs milk when our daughter is born, I'll suckle her myself."

I nodded. Alix was convinced we were going to have a baby girl. But even as she prepared for the new baby, she still mourned our son and would slip away to a grave in Sant Michel cemetery, half of which lay in Villa de Suso and half in Nova Victoria. She placed sprigs of lavender and the red wool bracelet on it as a tribute to Yennego, as if she were calling him home. It was her way of saying, *Come back, son, your mother misses you.*

But Yennego was far away from the horrors we were enduring. Part of me was relieved he hadn't had to suffer like the other children who roamed the streets shouting for their parents until someone took pity on them and offered a morsel of bread and a few kind words.

The priest at Santa María said prayers for all our lost souls. Then the townsfolk left to assess the damage to their dwellings and workshops, many of which had been reduced to ashes or rubble.

Alix went to get Grandmother Lucía. Her house had been spared, just as ours had, but the old woman had always been afraid of storms, and she was insisting that the thunder we had heard that morning would return.

While Alix was away, I slipped into the cathedral. I told myself I was searching for peace, but perhaps I was just looking for a place that didn't reek of smoke and blood.

The townsfolk were all gone. Only one lit candle remained, casting dancing shadows onto the wall next to the altar. Then I realized I wasn't alone. I knew that silent presence very well.

Nagorno was down on one knee, and he was weeping. I drew closer, puzzled.

"I've never prayed to him," he said. He didn't turn around. He didn't need to, my brother could always recognize me. "To the man on the cross. I'm still a pagan at heart."

"As am I. Yet when I ask Father Sun and Mother Moon for answers, they are as silent as this Christ figure whom so many worship these days. Were you praying for your life?"

"No. Death means nothing to me. I do not respect it."

"Why this pretense at prayer, then?"

"I'm praying that you will come to my aid," he said. He spoke slowly, weighing each word, and then he rose to his feet to look me in the eye.

"Tell me, Brother," I said. "What is it you want from me? You make me uneasy."

"I want you to bed my wife."

I heard his request in silence. Onneca . . .

"You are not asking me to . . ." My voice was a whisper. "Hush. You are in God's house, and He forbids it in thought and deed. You know not what you are saying—you are weary. Tomorrow we'll meet by the wall, for we have graver matters to discuss than your warped desires."

"She believed herself barren. I told her the truth."

I stared at him, bewildered.

"You told her you're incapable of giving her children?"

He nodded and looked away.

"You've never admitted that to any woman before. You must truly care for her."

"I want you to give her a child," he said.

This was pure folly.

"I am not your stud," I responded angrily, shaking my head. "Find another man to do your work for you."

"He must carry our family's blood."

"What about Gunnarr?" I suggested.

"You know he's celibate."

"Héctor, then."

"Héctor doesn't live in the town."

"You'll find someone willing, I'm sure."

I turned to leave, but Nagorno was too quick for me and blocked my way.

"I want it to be you!" he insisted.

"I'm not your stud. No!" I repeated and hurried to leave the cathedral before we woke the entire town.

"You hate her, don't you?" he said, grasping my arm. "You hate her with the same intensity as you once loved her, isn't that true?"

I took a deep breath to calm myself. I did not want to commit an outrage in that hallowed place.

"Alix is my wife. We are still looking for our missing son, and we are soon to have another child. I won't destroy any more lives, and I refuse to allow you and Onneca to destroy my family."

"I'm not afraid to die during an attack, nor do I fear a siege, but King Alfonso will not give up this town. We must surrender before we are no more. You are familiar with the laws of Castile: should Onneca and I die without issue, Count de Maestu's estate will go into the king's coffers."

"And you want me to place my manhood at the service of your titles."

With that, I went home to sleep with my wife.

45

A BROKEN PENCIL

UNAI

October 2019

Early the next morning, we gathered in the conference room. The lights were switched off as Alba summarized the latest developments in the case. Milán, Peña, and I sat around the table in the gloom, listening.

"We're going to pursue other lines of inquiry," Alba announced. "Until now, we've concentrated on one suspect: Ramiro Alvar Nograro. And the evidence we have against him is circumstantial: the barrel Maturana was drowned in matches those found in the old bodega on his estate, as do the plastic bags. But forensics didn't find fingerprints or footprints—the floor in the bodega had been swept, which could indicate that the suspect was trying to cover their tracks. We also have an unidentified person dressed as a Dominican nun who fled the scene of Antón Lasaga's murder. Inspector López de Ayala chased this person but to no avail. A similar costume that had been on exhibit at Nograro Tower's museum is missing. And there's been a second aggravated burglary at the abandoned Dominican Quejana convent. We know Ramiro Alvar made donations to the Natural Science Museum; however, this appears to be a family tradition: Milán has traced prior donations made by his father, Lorenzo Alvar Nograro. The museum has confirmed that some blister beetles were taken, as well as the snake found in the barrel with Maturana. So far, the novel has not linked Ramiro Alvar to the case, although this evidence has led us to look more deeply into his background and into the village of Ugarte."

"What are you proposing?" asked Peña.

"We're going to approach the case in a different way. The victims were what we would consider low-risk victims in low-risk situations. Looking into their social lives, families, and work backgrounds hasn't provided any clear motive, so we'll have to start assuming the killer picked them at random. We're going to be proactive in drumming up leads."

"What do you mean by 'proactive'?" asked Peña.

"We'll start with the media," Alba said.

Milán looked as puzzled as Peña.

"The media? Won't that just make things worse? It's possible Inspector Ruiz de Gauna is in the hospital because of a press leak."

"I know, and I accept the responsibility. But we're still going to take off their muzzles. In exchange, they've agreed to cooperate."

"How?" Milán asked.

"I've arranged a meeting with local journalists. They'll be here in ten minutes. I spoke to the investigating judge, and she's given her blessing."

We were soon joined by Lutxo, a female reporter who was friends with Alba, and several digital-media journalists.

They looked at us expectantly. Alba welcomed them and I took the floor.

"As DSU Salvatierra has already explained, we need your cooperation. We have developed a multistep plan that hinges on the fact that the killer is following the case. He will read everything you write. So, let's begin with the Nájera sisters."

"What do you want us to publish?"

"These photographs, which their parents have provided," I replied as a series of images flashed across the projector: Oihana aged three playing near Ullíbarri-Gamboa Reservoir, Estefanía at Las Fiestas de la Virgen Blanca, dressed in a *neska* costume. I had also asked for cute snapshots from their most recent birthdays. Their parents had sent one photo of a little girl blowing out twelve candles, and another of a teenager doing the same thing with sixteen candles. The message wasn't exactly subtle: *Because of you, they won't be blowing out any more candles.*

"Why them? Why not the industrialist or the kid in the barrel?" asked Lutxo.

"Because whoever killed these girls felt remorse," I replied. "He put bags over their heads while he was trapping them behind the wall so he couldn't see their faces. He felt bad about what he was doing. We're going to play on that guilt. The industrialist was a random victim. It was a cowardly murder, carried out from a distance by someone who didn't want to see his victim suffer and die. Although we know he didn't want to see the result of his actions, we don't know if he felt guilt or remorse. The same is true of the victim drowned in the barrel."

There was another reason I didn't want to give them any details about MatuSalem. Maturana had spent time in prison for defrauding dozens of people online. He was the protégé of Tasio Ortiz de Zárate, and the two of them had kept in touch—they were in contact the day before he died. I didn't want the public to judge MatuSalem because of his past. I wanted to do what I'd failed to when he was alive: protect him.

"Anything else you want us to run with?" a young journalist asked.

I handed each of them a folder.

"These packets contain some information about the girls' hobbies. Estefanía was studying music and wanted to be a cellist like her mother. This summer, she was going on a trip to Scotland with her *cuadrilla*. Oihana liked to develop computer apps. According to her teachers, she was a gifted child who excelled at robotics and had a bright future. This is what you have to tell the public. The public needs to get a sense of the dreams these girls had that will never come true, the tragedy of two promising young lives cut short. We want to touch a nerve with the killer, so show the parents, grandparents, teachers, and friends grieving at the funeral. Try to use images that show people of different ages so the public sees the scope of the tragedy. All the images you need are in the file. Share your stories, overlap them if possible. We want to manipulate the killer's emotions, show him the pain that has resulted from the loss of these two lives. We want to use the press to reflect his guilt back at him, so that it becomes a daily reminder of his actions. Make it impossible for him to forget."

"Can you collaborate to ensure that an article comes out every day next week?" Alba said. "It's essential to keep up the pressure so we can track the killer's responses."

"And you're sure it will have the desired effect?"

It already has, I thought. *Ask Estíbaliz.*

"We are indeed," replied Alba. "Thank you in advance for your cooperation. If everything goes according to plan, we'll meet again in a few days and move on to phase two."

I'd started driving to Ugarte every Wednesday and Thursday for book club.

From where I was standing on the sidewalk, I could see that the bar was filling up. Several cars were parked outside, and it looked like each week more locals—of all ages—were joining. I walked in and said hello to everyone. I noticed a lot of expectant faces and oblique glances at the newspaper I had tucked under my arm. A week had passed, and the journalists were doing a great job with their coverage.

We were now in phase two of the plan Alba and I had developed over several nights, the reports spread out on our bed. We had vowed never to let the monsters we faced at work invade our sacred space. Unfortunately, we were losing that battle every day.

But our efforts had paid off. The headline that morning provoked an avalanche of retweets.

NEW TWIST IN CASE OF BOY DROWNED IN ZADORRA

> A witness has come forward with a detailed description of the killer. Police sources have announced that an arrest is imminent.

A few days earlier, Peña and Milán had visited Ugarte, taking statements from the villagers and asking for alibis for the three days the crimes had taken place. They had also requested voluntary DNA samples. Not everyone had agreed to provide one.

I sat down between Benita and Fausti. The old lady introduced me to some of the new members: Cándido, who always beat everyone at bowling, and Juani, who worked for the town council. Fausti's husband, Fidel, stood by the door with his arms crossed, as though he wanted a good view of everything that was going on. Even Claudia, the willowy tour guide from the tower, was there. According to Benita, Claudia's sister, Irati, ran the agritourism business at the Forge, where she also had a glassworks. Physically, the sisters couldn't have been more different: one was tall, the other short, one's hair was straight and dark, the other's curly and blond. For some reason, Irati looked familiar. Benita's relentless introductions of the inhabitants of Ugarte had been going on for quite a while, but there were more to come.

"The one in the glasses is the legal eagle, Beltrán," Benita told me.

The young, impeccably dressed man with a waspish face was greeting late arrivals.

"He looks pretty young," I said.

"He is; he only just graduated. Ramiro Alvar lets him take care of some minor affairs."

"Yes, I think he's already mentioned him to me," I whispered with a nod.

"Let's start the reading now, shall we?" Fausti interrupted. The dawdlers took their seats, and a contented Gonzalo brought people drinks.

This week, the reader was an older resident with a husky voice. Half an hour later, our discussion revolved around whether Gunnarr had taken henbane during the siege.

"Isn't the description of its effect a bit exaggerated?" asked Cándido.

"It's fascinating to read an account written in 1192 that refers to drug-induced behaviors we now know to be accurate," I responded. I wanted to remind everyone that I wasn't just there as a reader. I wanted them all to remember I was a police inspector, and I wanted to see their reaction to that revelation. "It appears the character Gunnarr Kolbrunson was formerly a berserker, a mercenary hired by Norse kings. Henbane, the powder Gunnarr is known to ingest before battle, caused hallucinations, followed by amnesia and intense dehydration that occasionally resulted in death," I explained, recalling my time at the police academy. "Gunnarr would have been familiar with the properties of henbane, which made men feel invincible and transformed them into shock troops on the battlefield. I believe this is a reference to the so-called amok syndrome. In my profession, we are trained to deal with the possible repercussions of this type of disorder: an alienated individual kills innocent people in a frenzied attack, and then usually goes on to take their own life. Unfortunately, we've seen a rise in these cases recently."

Everyone was staring at me. The bar was silent. I might have gotten carried away by the subject matter, but I was working a case at a book club, after all. I felt an almost-pleasurable buzz.

"You'd make a good teacher," Benita whispered in my ear, smiling cheerfully.

"Thanks."

Shortly afterward, people got up to stretch their legs. They divided into small groups based on age and interests. Claudia and her sister came over to say hello.

"How are you, Inspector? You're spending more and more time here in Ugarte."

"It's a charming village. I like it a lot."

"Then you should visit Irati's glassworks studio at the Old Forge."

"I'd love to. I can pick up a souvenir," I responded swiftly.

I actually wanted to soak up the atmosphere of the place that had destroyed Ramiro Alvar and sealed the fate of his family.

"In that case, Inspector, follow me. I'm heading back there now," said Irati with a smile.

We set off along a path that ran parallel to the river and wound toward the outskirts of the village, ending at the tower's perimeter a few hundred yards ahead.

Irati was a friendly young woman, easier to talk to than her sister. She told me it was harder to find clients for her agritourism in the winter.

"I have a friend in the hotel business," I said. "I know it can be tough, though I get the impression that being your own boss and not having to work nine to five has its advantages."

"The glassworks saved me. My brand is slowly making a name for itself, through word of mouth."

"I'm glad to hear that. So, this used to be the Nograro family forge."

"The whole place has been renovated," she said, as we entered the stone structure. "We have several rooms, and we're completely free this weekend. Come into the studio and see if there's something that interests you."

The group of locals coming up behind us was taking an opportunity to go for a stroll and purchase a set of blue steins or whatever other glass creation caught their fancy.

I was about to leave with a collection of decorative bottles for Alba when Peña called.

"Kraken—"

"Unai," I interrupted. "Please, call me Unai."

"We just got a report from the lab that upends all our assumptions from the past couple of weeks. Are you sitting down?"

"No, I'm not," I said, as another customer pushed open the door. "Just tell me what it is."

"The DNA on the pencil we found at the scene of MatuSalem's murder matches Ramiro Alvar Nograro's."

I couldn't believe what I was hearing.

"Ramiro?" I echoed. "Are you sure?"

"I'm afraid so. Doctor Guevara says the result is unequivocal."

Numb with shock, I propped myself against the wall of the forge. This news threw everything I had come to believe into question, everything Ramiro had told me about what had happened at the forge. Had he made it up? Was it an act? Was Ramiro our killer, or did he really have dissociative identity disorder, and the murderer was actually his alter, Alvar? Who was I dealing with here: a charlatan, a snake charmer, or a psychopath with an integrated personality and a brilliant compensatory façade?

I forced myself to respond decisively.

"Fortunately, he's still at the hospital. How long before we can obtain an arrest warrant?"

"The judge will take a lot of persuading. This isn't the lead we've been pursuing, and she won't be happy," said Peña, "but hopefully we can get one within a couple of hours."

Customers were still going in and out of the glassworks. Reeling from the news, I hung up and turned around without looking. I bumped into a burly young man with a thick reddish-brown beard.

"Sorry," he said. He had a serious face and seemed distracted. He wasn't even looking at me.

He seemed vaguely familiar, so by force of habit, I followed him with my eyes. It turned out he was just Irati's boyfriend.

"There you are, Sebas," she said affectionately.

How useless. All that information we had accumulated, all those names and faces. I realized the reason I was still in observation mode, registering and cataloging everything in front of me was so I wouldn't to have to think about the truth. Damn it, Ramiro Alvar had murdered MatuSalem—and he'd come close to killing my colleague . . . after sleeping with her.

He was a monster.

How was I going to tell Estíbaliz that Ramiro Alvar had duped us all?

46

PARLEY

DIAGO VELA

Summer, the Year of Our Lord 1199

The next day, Chipia came to tell me that the king had called for a parley and was waiting outside the town gates.

The lieutenant, the mayor, the members of the council, and all the nobles climbed to the battlements. We wore helmets and breastplates. After the recent attack, no one felt safe.

"King Alfonso is here to list the terms of surrender!" exclaimed López de Haro. "Lieutenant Chipia, you have the right to surrender the town without dishonor. You should not fight to the death for a king who will not come to your aid. Admit it, if his troops haven't arrived by now, they are not coming."

"Is that why you've built a rear guard? You know as well as I do that they are on their way," retorted Chipia with a smile.

"My messengers bring news of victories in every town we aimed to reconquer. And almost every fort from here to La Puebla de Argançón has surrendered, with varying degrees of resistance. Give up now, the traders are eager to continue selling their goods in the town. Open your gates so the people can go about their business," declared King Alfonso.

"I believe the forts of Treviño and Portilla are holding out. I know their lieutenants," ventured Chipia.

The king and his standard-bearer stirred uneasily.

Nagorno drew closer to Chipia and the mayor.

"They won't attack again. They don't want to kill the inhabitants, raze the town, and then have to rebuild it. They want Victoria to serve as a crossroads: the only stopping place from Castile, the gateway to Cantabria and Aquitaine."

"Perhaps we ought to surrender while we still have something to negotiate with," suggested Onneca. The Isunzas agreed with her. "If they break through the walls, they'll slaughter us all and repopulate the town. The residents of Nova Victoria are in favor of surrender," she continued.

"And those from Villa de Suso prefer to wait for reinforcements from Pamplona," said the mayor.

"I follow the orders of King Sancho, whose last words were 'Victoria will not surrender,'" insisted the lieutenant. "His forces may have been called to other besieged fortresses or to San Sebastian. They are relying on us to hold out."

"Chipia, I want this to end more than anybody. I want to leave the gates and look for my son," I said. "But why the delay?"

"I'm beginning to think that King Sancho signed a treaty with the Almohads and will come here from the south himself. By my estimation, they will arrive in a month; in the meantime, we must refuse to surrender. If bad weather comes, it will be to our advantage. They can hunt and fish, but their tents won't keep out the rain and snow, and they'll be vulnerable to cold and disease. They don't want a prolonged siege."

"They'll soon bring replacements!" Nagorno snapped. "This is Castile you're talking about. Do you really think their army is only three thousand strong?"

We turned together and looked at the troops deployed below. King Alfonso was growing restless, steering his horse in circles.

"What do you have to say? I don't have all day."

"There'll be no surrender!" cried Chipia.

The king leaned close to his standard-bearer and whispered something in his ear.

Nagorno and I exchanged nervous glances.

We stood motionless, waiting for the king's next command. Chipia gave the signal for the archers to mount the turrets. They drew back their bowstrings ready to fire.

But then, as we looked out despondently, the army fanned out until it had surrounded the entire town. They unloaded canvases from their carts and set about erecting more tents. In another area of the camp, we saw cooking pots and watched men mount trivets. Many of those standing with us who lived in the cutlers' district outside the walls looked on helplessly as the soldiers entered their dwellings, installing themselves in what had been their homes for years.

My brother and I remained on the battlement after the others had descended the stairs. They were crestfallen, muttering about calamities and ill omens.

"You got what you wanted, Brother," he whispered. "An all-out siege. Pray to your gods that the people of Victoria don't end up like the Numantians, cannibalizing each other."

47

THE CHAMELEON

UNAI

October 2019

By the time I arrived at the hospital, I was out of breath. I wanted to be the one to arrest him. I wanted to look him in the eye and see the real Ramiro Alvar. But when I opened the door to his room, I found a neatly made bed and a book lying open on the visitor's chair.

"He got away! I want officers at every exit!" I ordered Peña.

"Let's go to Estíbaliz's room," my colleague whispered nervously.

We hurtled down the hallway and burst into her room.

"Estí!" I cried. "Are you okay?"

"They discharged me. I'm leaving," she said, trying to use her one good arm to pack her sneakers and toiletries. "But I have to come back for physical therapy."

"Did Ramiro Alvar come here?" I asked.

"No, of course not. What's the matter? Didn't you arrest him?" she said, puzzled.

"He's not in his room. I'm afraid he's one step ahead of us," I replied. "Peña, I'm putting you in charge. I'll stay here with Estíbaliz."

Peña nodded, closing the door behind him.

I looked at Estíbaliz. Her eyes were red, and her lips were pressed in a taut line.

"How are you?" I asked, not knowing what else to say.

"I've been sick a few times, but I can't wait to get out of here."

"You're safer away from the hospital," I said. "If Ramiro Alvar hasn't managed to get away, he could be hiding in the building. I'll make sure you have protection."

"I don't want protection! I just want to know what's going on. Is it him? Did he kill MatuSalem? Did he fool us all?" She sank down onto the edge of the bed.

I sat next to her.

"I'm afraid he did."

"And how did he know you were going to arrest him?"

"We still have to figure that out," I said. "Peña said he called to tell you the results of the DNA test and that we were waiting for an arrest warrant. He offered to post two officers on your door and you refused."

"I don't want protection," she insisted.

"Swear to me you didn't do it."

"You think I warned him?"

"Or that you decided to confront him, and he wormed it out of you."

"I didn't refuse protection so I could tip him off. And if you don't believe me, you can check the security camera footage," she replied irritably.

This wasn't getting us anywhere. And besides, this was Estíbaliz, the same woman I had been friends with forever.

"No need. I believe you."

We stared out the window in silence. Both of us needed to get away from that hospital.

"How did he manage to fool us like that?" she asked at last.

"Because I profiled him incorrectly. He was a magician; he made a shiny object vanish and reappear right before our eyes. He seduced us both. You and me."

I stood up. I needed to get moving.

"Finish packing. I'm supposed to give a lecture on profiling at Arkaute in two hours. Why don't you come with me? I could use your support."

Estíbaliz arched an eyebrow.

"Stage fright?"

"Not at all, but if we don't want this case to affect our relationship, we're going to need to work on creating mutual trust again. You've asked me to trust you, and I'm asking you to come with me. It'll be good for both of us."

"It's a deal," she said, giving me the first smile I had seen from her in weeks.

While Estí finished dressing, I returned to Ramiro Alvar's room. Something had caught my attention. He'd made his bed before leaving, which was consistent with his neat, tidy nature, but he had left a copy of *The Lords of Time* open on the chair. I picked it up and looked at the page. He was giving me a message.

That's interesting, Ramiro, I thought. *Most interesting.*

Marina Leiva welcomed us when we arrived at the academy. Estíbaliz and I walked into the packed lecture hall; the lights had been switched off and a blank projector was waiting. Doctor Leiva and Estíbaliz sat in the back row, where Estí's neck brace and bandaged arm generated a lot of interest. Everybody knew who we were anyway. Why bother hiding?

I stood facing the students. My eyes rested on their pens for a moment. They were poised to take notes the instant I opened my mouth. I smiled and decided to put aside the sanitized presentation I'd prepared.

"I'm here today to talk to you about psychopathy and how to detect psychopaths in our midst. As profilers, the first thing we need to learn is to forget our prejudices. The public tends to think we always look for maladjusted monsters, for bogeymen with deformed skulls, as though we were nineteenth-century phrenologists. In fact, the serial killer is more likely to be a skilled professional with an outstanding CV. He's an expert in his field, which happens to be getting away with murder. That's why serial killers aren't easy to catch. They evolve. They become adept at evading arrest, at flying under the radar, because of what we might call their compensatory façade. How often have we heard neighbors or friends, when asked to comment on a recent arrest, say, 'He's a good son' or 'a good brother'? And of course, they are."

A student in the first row raised her hand.

"How can people say that?"

"Because of a cognitive bias known as an attribution error. We are at a disadvantage individually and as a society. It's difficult to believe that we are incapable of detecting evil in a person just because we find them affectionate and charming. Psychopaths use our cognitive dissonance to their own advantage, and they exploit our inability to see manipulation at work when we are deceived by a charismatic individual. It's the same psychopathy whether the person is a murderer or is physically or verbally abusive. I know you've studied the profiles of several psychopaths, so I want you to tell me some of the traits you've detected."

"A parasitic lifestyle," answered a student at the back of the room.

"Good: Their life consists of preying on others. They live in the present—there's no such thing as tomorrow because they have no conception of the future. They usually have brief relationships. Their long-term goals are unrealistic. Other traits?"

"Lack of empathy."

"They learn to imitate emotions and facial expressions," I concurred. "They even claim to master nonverbal language. Psychopaths feel empty inside, but they know they need to fit in so that we can't detect them, for example, when they fail to respond properly to a tragedy, or to a death in the family."

"They're good actors," another voice offered.

"Yes, and they depend on that ability to achieve their goals. Psychopaths don't have friends; they use people and throw them away. They acquire followers, or flunkies, or disciples. They employ their compensatory façade to manipulate their parents, siblings, grandparents, whoever comes under their influence. Only outsiders can detect the way those closest to a psychopath are in thrall to his or her aims, whatever they may be: work contacts, childcare, money, a family support network. Thanks to their cognitive dissonance, their followers refuse to believe the psychopath is anyone other than the construct that friend has conditioned them to believe. And this is why, after a person commits an atrocious series of murders, we often hear that he was a good neighbor, or we see a wife who continues to visit her husband in jail despite the evidence stacked against him, despite his signed confession. This compensatory façade is the psychopath's lifeline, and they work at it constantly."

"What do you mean by a compensatory façade?" the same voice asked.

"It's basically a mask that psychopaths put on every day. They're quite accustomed to wearing it. Underneath, they're incapable of feeling remorse for the pain they inflict. Whenever possible, they convince others to do their work for them, especially their dirty work. They're intrinsically lazy and are often con artists. They're likely to be spendthrifts because they rarely think about tomorrow. They don't know how to save, so they run up debts and borrow money. They are easily bored, fickle. They change jobs frequently because they derive no pleasure from work. They are only interested in instant gratification. Many psychopaths flunk out of university because they can't apply themselves to anything long-term. They have no scruples about how they obtain whatever they want and will happily exploit their parents or partners. Other traits?" I asked.

"They're adrenaline junkies. They may gravitate toward extreme sports or high-risk activities. They lack a sense of danger," someone added.

"Good. What else?"

"They use a kind of hypnosis to get into your head and control you."

"And how do they achieve that?" I asked.

"With a compelling stare. It instantly creates the illusion of empathy. If the psychopath is targeting a romantic partner, it would feel as though the person had just met their soul mate."

"That's the short answer, but it's more complex," I explained. "Psychopaths will get into their victim's head by becoming a chameleon: they mimic their victim. Generally, they follow a four-step approach. First, the ego massage: they praise their victim, especially if the person has low self-esteem. Second, they become their victim's soul mate: *you and I are identical; we were meant to be together*. Third, they gain their victim's trust: *you can rely on me; tell me all your weaknesses*. By the fourth stage, they've become the perfect friend, partner, child, or sibling. They become almost mythical: their reputation is unimpeachable to their disciples, which is useful because they need their followers to carry out the work they don't want to do or to defend them when they reveal their true nature. These followers—family members, coworkers, neighbors, relatives—don't see the psychopath's true personality; they see only the perfect imitation the psychopath has created. Disciples will even cover up the psychopath's crimes because they believe the rationalizations they are told.

"Psychopaths cannot tolerate criticism and will persecute and banish critics from their social milieu. Only a fraction of psychopaths commit crimes, yet on average, a person will meet seven psychopaths in his or her lifetime. One psychopath will victimize approximately fifty-eight people. In this country alone, approximately one million people have a severe psychopathic personality disorder, and four million are functioning psychopaths. They are successful professionals, friendly neighbors . . . Anyone could be a social and domestic predator with a trail of wrecked lives in their wake."

A profound silence followed, and I knew I'd gotten my message across. I was talking to each one of them. And I could see what they were thinking: they were dredging up memories of possible psychopaths they'd met.

"Now for the bad news: psychopaths can't be rehabilitated. They don't respond to therapy. In fact, therapy makes them worse unless their psychopathy is detected at a very early age, when they can be reeducated. Why? Because psychopathy isn't an illness; it's a way of being. Believe it or not, the years psychopaths spend in therapy provide them with an endless supply of emotional resources they can use to manipulate others more effectively, starting with their therapist."

The students all took notes on this point.

"We know about serial killers in the United States, like Ed Kemper, who were in therapy and, according to their psychiatrists, were making progress. Yet, they were committing the most gruesome crimes imaginable. Even within the prison system, psychopaths pose a problem for society because their psychiatric evaluations are based on the responses they provide. A convict who wants to get out of jail will tell his or her therapist whatever they want to hear. We have statements from inmates serving life sentences for serial murders who have said, 'Give me the *DSM*—the *Diagnostic and Statistical Manual of Mental Disorders*. I'll pick a mental disorder at random, and in a couple of sessions, I'll convince any therapist I suffer from those symptoms.'"

I looked toward the back of the lecture hall. Doctor Leiva was beaming at me, and Estíbaliz was listening intently.

"As far as what to do in your own lives," I said in conclusion, "all I can say is that we need to train ourselves to detect psychopaths because they represent a real danger for each and every one of us. Do not try to rehabilitate or change a psychopath; that approach will destroy you. Consequently, my only piece of advice for what to do when you identify a psychopath is to have zero contact. Drop everything and get the hell out of there."

48

LAND OF THE ALMOHADS

DIAGO VELA

Winter, the Year of Our Lord 1200

The months that followed were a living hell. The army cut off our supplies, and the market vendors had nothing to sell. All passage from the outlying towns was stopped, and Héctor Dicastillo's diplomatic attempts to cross the blockade were rebuffed. We received no more messages from outside the wall. Our ignorance as to the fate of the neighboring towns was the worst possible punishment for the lieutenant, whose sardonic smile gradually faded.

Sometimes, at night, King Alfonso's army would sound the clarion for hours on end to wear us down by making us fear an imminent attack. On All Souls' Day, the soldiers galloped around the town walls holding aloft bits of roast game. The aroma of venison in red wine and wild boar with rosemary wafted inside. A number of the townsfolk watched from the guard walk and returned home weeping. Many still recalled the celebrations with anger.

There was a single beacon of light amid all the darkness, though. Alix gave birth to a calm baby girl. We had her baptized quickly, lest a surprise attack take her from us before she received the blessings from Alix's God. Grandmother Lucía became her godmother, and she became the old woman's great-great-great-grandchild.

Gunnarr was named her godfather, and he swore by the Crucified One to protect her. Though he crossed his fingers behind his back as he solemnly recited his vows, I knew he would die to save her.

And just when we believed all was lost, salvation appeared.

A clarion call announced its arrival in the form of a man accompanied by an escort of Castilian soldiers who were wary of the intruder.

The news spread like wildfire and the town's inhabitants congregated on the battlements.

"What is going on?" Chipia shouted from above.

"King Alfonso has allowed me temporary passage to bring tidings. Open the gate before he changes his mind. My journey from Pamplona was arduous. Don't let it have been futile as well," Bishop García said with a smile.

We all heaved a sigh of relief. We had not seen a fresh face since the summer.

The priest had grown thinner and had aged a great deal over the past few months, but he ran to the tower at the Santa María Cathedral and began to ring the bells.

The sound was music to our ears.

Chipia, prudent as ever, positioned his crossbowmen around the North Gate.

Then the rest of us encircled them, armed with the first weapons we could lay our hands upon.

"Open the gate!" commanded the lieutenant. "But just enough to allow a single man and his steed through!"

The rusty hinges on the door made a horrendous din.

The head of Bishop García's horse appeared and Chipia's men hastened to close the gate after him.

The cleric dismounted and Onneca, who had been drawn by the peal of bells along with everyone else, embraced her cousin.

"I never thought I'd see you again!" she cried, heaving a great sigh.

"If this continues much longer, you won't. And I have no wish to hold a funeral Mass for your town, Cousin."

The bishop studied us all with a frown.

"You are a sorry sight. This siege must end immediately," he said.

"If you've come here to persuade us to surrender," Chipia replied, "your journey has been wasted."

"It is not for me to decide such weighty matters. But I fear for your souls, so I am willing to travel to the lands of the Almohads, accompanied by one of the town's nobles, whomsoever you choose. I will speak with good King Sancho and explain to him that the siege must end. I will ask whether he intends to send reinforcements or if he has other orders for us. Does this sound reasonable?"

Separate groups of gentlefolk and vendors formed. Hushed exchanges followed, punctuated by the occasional curse, until finally everyone agreed to the bishop's proposal.

"I'll ride with you, García," I said.

"Out of the question," objected the mayor. "You're the voice of reason in this town. Without you, we would all have perished."

"He's right," Nagorno whispered in my ear. "You and I must remain and stand together."

"Who, then?"

"One resident from Nova Victoria and one from Villa de Suso," interjected Mendoza. "We can only trust our own."

"So be it. Any volunteers?" asked Chipia.

To our astonishment, Onneca stepped forward.

"I will accompany my cousin, riding Olbia. I'm still strong enough to endure the two-month journey."

A murmur spread among the various groups, but no one dared oppose her.

"Anyone from Villa de Suso?" ventured the mayor.

"I'll go," said Alix, who was standing by my side and cradling our sleeping daughter. She handed her to me and I looked at her mutely.

Who was I to stand in her way? This was her town; these were her people.

"Then prepare to leave at once. The road south is a long one," said Chipia.

Of that journey to the lands of the Almohads, I can relay only what was described to me. Part of the story that follows I heard from my wife, Alix de Salcedo. Other details were revealed to me by my sister-in-law, Onneca de Maestu.

The trip was hampered by bad weather, and it took nigh on five weeks for them to reach their destination. Once there, Alix and Onneca waited while Bishop García was given an audience with King Sancho the Strong. They argued at length, but García was a seasoned diplomat and much respected by the monarch. He emerged victorious with the letter of dispensation permitting us to surrender the town.

"What else did our king say?" Alix asked anxiously.

"There will be no reinforcements. The Miramamolín has problems of his own in Tunisia, and he needs the men of the monarchy. He is not keeping our king against his will, nor is he being held prisoner, but he's being showered with gold and jewels, and there are rumors of a beautiful infidel woman. King Sancho is releasing you from your pledge to defend the realm. He vows to retake the town as soon as he returns north, but he cannot know when that will be."

Onneca and Alix looked at each other in frustration, though they dared not question the king's word.

"Is that all? After everything we have endured in defense of his town?" exclaimed Onneca. "Are you sure he won't send an army to save us?"

García looked at her and then, without a word, gave her a consoling embrace.

"We've done the best we can, Cousin," he murmured. "Kings propose and dispose; it has always been so. We must return to Victoria before more of the residents die. If our monarch swears to retake the town, you may trust his word."

The return journey was speedier. Alix was anxious to be reunited with her baby daughter, and Onneca was eager to impart the news to the town and return to her daily life alongside her spouse—riding in the hills on Olbia and Altai, skating on the frozen millpond in the early morning.

When a freak storm arose, though, they were forced to circumvent the road up to the South Gate. Although they were only a few leagues away, it was the dead of night, not a good time to seek an audience with King Alfonso. At Bishop García's direction, they reluctantly took a detour and sought refuge at La Romana Inn.

What happened next is hard for me to recount, but I wish it to be known and not forgotten.

49

JARDÍN DE ETXANOBE

UNAI

October 2019

What does an old man think about before he dies? What thoughts flash through the mind of someone who was born at the turn of the last century? Does he think about the children he has outlived, or the thirty-six thousand dawns he has seen through eyes tired of surveying beauty, destruction, serenity, evil? Perhaps he thinks about his wife, the woman who accompanied him along Villaverde's stony pathways for half a lifetime.

"What do you enjoy doing most in life, señora?" a female oncologist once asked my grandmother after she had opened her up and scraped seven of her internal organs free of the spreading cancer, as though she was filing nails that had grown too long.

"Working outside in the fields," she replied, shrugging. The gesture hurt, but she didn't let her pain show. She was brought up never to complain, even at the gates of death.

"But you're over seventy. You're retired. You don't need to keep working. And you've just undergone invasive surgery. You should take it easy, avoid physical exertion. What do you most enjoy doing for fun?" the oncologist insisted.

"Spending the afternoon in the basement preparing seed potatoes for planting."

This is hard for most people to understand. Preparing seed

potatoes involves sitting for hours in an unheated basement slicing the potatoes with a tiny knife, your hands stiff with cold.

"I enjoy it," my grandmother said resolutely.

The two women fell silent. Because they both knew—operation or not, cancer or not—my grandmother would be in that basement every afternoon.

I know my grandfather would have given the same answer: going down to the basement for the seed potatoes, driving the combine, looking after his granddaughter.

The worst day of my life began with a call to my good friend Iago del Castillo.

"Iago, I'm sorry to keep bothering you, but I need your expertise. Could you come to Vitoria?"

"I'm in Santander today, but I can drive out to you. I'll meet you outside your apartment block in three hours," he replied.

"Do you mind coming to the Álava historical archives instead?"

"Okay. We can meet on the campus," he said.

Several hours later, I was driving along the avenue to the university when my phone vibrated. It was Peña.

"We've checked the security footage from the hospital—Ramiro Alvar had help. He was wheeled out of the building by someone in a white coat."

"Help?" I thought aloud. "Who the hell could Ramiro Alvar have gotten to help him escape?"

"That's what we're looking into. The two figures are only visible from behind, but we have a couple of officers working with hospital staff to see if they can identify the one in the white coat. The fact that Ramiro Alvar has no cell phone complicates matters. On a separate topic, we just got the list of entrepreneurs who attended the meeting at Villa Suso the evening Antón Lasaga was poisoned. You must be familiar with one of the names on the list, because you asked me to check him out recently: Ignacio Ortiz de Zárate. He was representing Slow Food Araba, a nonprofit organization focusing on local food. Incidentally, the day you asked me to find him and take photos of the clothes he was wearing, I couldn't confirm that he was in Vitoria. I didn't see him enter or leave his residence."

"Ignacio was at Villa Suso? That has to be a coincidence. But thanks, and keep looking for Ramiro Alvar. I sent a patrol car to Nograro Tower, but there's no sign of him there. I have to go now," I said quickly, noticing that Iago del Castillo was walking over to me.

We greeted each other warmly and entered the building that contained the archive.

"I'd almost forgotten that tonight is Halloween," he said as we walked the hallways. "I've already seen several people dressed as the Grim Reaper."

"Are you not a fan of Halloween?" I asked. The usually easygoing Iago seemed a little tense.

"I'm not normally superstitious, but our family has suffered quite a few tragedies around this time of year, and I'm reminded of it every time I go outside on the eve of All Souls' Day."

"Well, I got my little girl an *eguzkilore* costume to ward off evil spirits," I told him.

"Good idea, you're a sensible parent," he said, his mood lifting.

I'd spoken to the head librarian, who had agreed to give us access to the Nograro family archives.

"What exactly are we looking at, Unai?" Iago asked as we reached the records room.

"A document from 1306 signed by King Ferdinand the Fourth: 'Privileges and Concessions Granted to the Lords of Nograro.' I need your help explaining it."

The librarian brought us the document I'd requested, and Iago spent a long time poring over it.

"This is a classic example of the rule of primogeniture," he said at last. "*Ius succedendi in bonis, ea lege relictis, ut in familia integra perpetuo conservatur, proximoque duque primogenitor ordine succesivo deferantur.*"

I stared at him blankly. I don't think he even realized he was speaking Latin.

"The right of the eldest son to succeed to the estate of his father, with the proviso that said estate remains in the family in perpetuity and is passed on to the next eldest son in the succession," he translated.

"Okay, now I want you to look at this passage, here," I said. "'May he be neither convict nor prisoner, to ensure the lineage is confined to men of honor.' Is that stipulation still in force?"

"Yes, it would be, unless a subsequent law revoked the privileges granted by the king. It's quite common for provisions like these to be adapted according to later legislation."

"What do you think happened? What made them surrender and what led to Victoria's incorporation into Alfonso's kingdom?" I asked, forcing myself to think about something else.

"We can't look at something like this with a contemporary mindset. The same warring factions in the siege of Victoria, the kings of Castile and Navarre, would later fight side by side at the Battle of las Navas de Tolosa in 1212 against the Miramamolín, who had been Sancho the Strong's ally during the siege of Victoria. The boundaries between the kingdoms of Castile and Navarre were fluid: They were redrawn five times over the course of the twelfth century. The average person didn't feel the same sense of national belonging we do today; they were too busy struggling to survive. They were bound to the social strata they were born into, and their support for one monarch over another depended on the favors granted to their town, not on patriotic sentiment. In addition, kings went to war over territory to preserve status more than anything else. Rulers constantly needed to display their strength because admitting weakness was impossible."

I glanced at my cell phone for the time: hours seemed to pass like minutes for the del Castillo brothers. I called Grandfather. He was going to take Deba to the Jardín de Etxanobe, next to the *Triumph of Vitoria* mural, and let her go on the swings.

I tried his number a couple of times, but he didn't pick up. I assumed he was distracted by something else he was doing.

"Speaking of families, I'd like you to meet my grandfather. He's babysitting my daughter, Deba."

Iago smiled, intrigued.

"He must be a very active gentleman to be able to look after his great-grandchild."

I shrugged. Maybe what I took for granted wasn't obvious to everybody else.

"He's practically immortal. I can't remember him as anything but old, but age hasn't diminished him. He's full of energy. He just started using a cane a few weeks ago, but I don't think he even needs it."

I suspected he'd decided to carry it as a deterrent after the shock Ignacio gave him in Laguardia, but he had played the innocent when I'd asked him about it.

"I'd be delighted to meet him," said Iago.

We headed for the Old Quarter, avoiding people dressed in skeleton and demon costumes. Half an hour later we arrived at the garden, the highest point in the city and one of my favorite spots.

We walked through the iron gate, and all I saw was a sculpture that someone had carved from a sequoia struck by lightning. And it was quiet. No shrieks of joy from Deba as she pranced around in her *eguzkilore* costume, no "Gotcha, little fox!" in my grandfather's comforting voice.

"Unai!" shouted Iago. "Call an ambulance!" I didn't react—I couldn't.

Iago launched himself toward Grandfather, who was sprawled on the ground, motionless.

I was paralyzed, staring at Grandfather and Iago as if they were from another planet.

Iago felt Grandfather's neck for a pulse. His bloodstained beret was lying at my feet, but I couldn't pick it up.

"He's in cardiac arrest! For God's sake, Unai, call an ambulance, he needs CPR right now!"

But I didn't call. Grandfather wasn't moving. Deba wasn't there.

Instead I watched, detached, as a competent man unbuttoned my grandfather's coat, placed his palms on his chest, and began pressing rhythmically.

He straightened Grandfather's head, plugged his nostrils, and gave him the breath of life. Once, then a pause. Twice.

"Unai, get a hold of yourself! Come here!" Iago cried in desperation.

But I was rooted to the spot.

I opened my mouth, but to my horror discovered that my Broca's aphasia had returned. I couldn't utter a single word.

Iago continued performing CPR, but Grandfather didn't stir. Finally Iago sat astride him, using his whole body to press as hard as he could on his heart.

"Unai." He changed his tone, speaking softly, gently, as if to a child. "Unai, take a step toward me, just one step."

I wasn't cognizant of following his instructions. My body just responded to his parental voice. My right foot edged forward.

Iago continued to give Grandfather mouth-to-mouth resuscitation. I was aware of everything that was going on, but it was like watching a movie I didn't want to see but couldn't stop looking at.

"Great, Unai, you're doing great," Iago repeated reassuringly. "Now, take another step toward me. You're almost there."

My left leg obeyed. Another small step. I was just close enough to see that my grandfather's ruddy cheeks looked almost drained of blood. He was pale, lifeless.

"One more step, Unai. One at a time. That's good, keep coming, don't stop," the tranquil voice said. Iago kept breathing air into the limp body in front of him, but every so often, he cast sidelong glances at me to make sure I was listening to him.

At some point I reached them, and my foot touched Grandfather's body. Iago took his phone out of his pocket and called a number.

"There is a centenarian male with a severe head injury at the Jardín de Etxanobe. He's in cardiac arrest and I've been giving him CPR for three minutes. Send an emergency team. Also, you need to start searching for a little girl. She's missing, and we don't know how long she's been gone. The injured man is her great-grandfather, so we're looking at a possible abduction. Call the Portal de Foronda police station. The little girl is Inspector López de Ayala's daughter. I'll keep giving his grandfather CPR."

Three minutes? No. It had been a lifetime. An entire lifetime flashed before me: the swing he made for me and Germán in Solaítas; the day he told me about the family's secret hiding place where the cache of *perretxikales*, or St. George mushrooms, grew; the nights when we lay on our backs near the Tres Cruces crossroads and watched for shooting stars.

Iago dropped his cell phone on the ground beside him, and resumed his task.

I have thought about that day often.

About what could have made me freeze that way.

It was dissonance.

Cognitive dissonance.

My brain couldn't accept losing the two most important people in my life at the same time.

Both of them.

During those endless minutes before help arrived, I couldn't decide who to help first, Grandfather or Deba.

And that dilemma overwhelmed me. It wiped me out.

50

THE STORM

DIAGO VELA

Winter, the Year of Our Lord 1200

The storm forced them to spend a second night at La Romana Inn. Pilgrims following the Camino de Santiago, frightened by news of the lengthy siege, had bypassed Victoria. Without their patronage, the inn was empty, soulless. Not many Castilian soldiers had been calling there lately, either. Their leather purses were empty after months of deadlock, and they could no longer afford a quick release on one of the inn's pallets.

Bishop García had retired to the upper floor, doubtless in need of rest after a long ride. Onneca watched the flames in the hearth as she dried out her robe while Alix helped Astonga bake the rooster-comb pies Bishop García had requested.

A series of thunderclaps sent Onneca to the stables. She knew her mare would be terrified.

"Stay calm, sweet lady," she whispered, stroking the animal's mane. "Stay calm. Tomorrow we shall finally have lunch in the town."

Onneca spent a long while with her mare. She had a great fondness for solitude and avoided lengthy conversations, for they exhausted her. Yet another reason she avoided the chatterbox Alix de Salcedo whenever possible.

While in the stables, she happened to look at her cousin's saddlebags. In their haste to come in from the storm, he had left them behind on the stable floor. She had stooped to pick them up, wiping away a film of muddy straw, when she saw it.

A small wax seal—the royal seal. The seal of King Sancho the Strong. Why did her cousin have a copy of the royal seal? Only old Ferrando the notary was permitted to have one. Possessing copies of that seal was high treason.

Onneca rummaged anxiously in the bottom of the saddlebag and discovered a second seal. An older one, more worn. This one had belonged to the deceased King Sancho the Wise.

She grabbed the two seals and stormed upstairs in search of her cousin. He owed her an explanation. He owed her several explanations.

But before she entered his room, she heard his voice and the voice of a young man. This was puzzling; she imagined that only the landlady and her sisters would be abroad at this hour. She drew closer and listened.

"Here are your powders for tonight. My mother will come up when your fellow travelers are asleep. But I'm here about a different matter." The boy began to whine. "I'm of age now, Father, and I've taken many risks and done you many favors." He sounded upset.

"You misjudge me, Lope. I haven't forgotten the promise I made you when you poisoned de Maestu. But the inn was under suspicion back then, and if I had publicly recognized you as my son, I would have exposed myself unnecessarily. Now years have passed, and the town has forgotten all about de Maestu's death. Have I ever stopped sending money to you and your mother? How else would you have survived the harsh winters, or this ridiculous siege? Don't be ungrateful, son. Here is the document you've long been waiting for," said Bishop García.

You poisoned my father? Onneca thought.

Without stopping to think, she burst into the room, oblivious to the danger she was in.

"Did this boy give my lord father the blister-beetle oil that killed him?" she cried. The bishop looked aghast at the two seals clasped in her hand.

"Calm down, Onneca. I'll answer all your questions; only first you must give me those seals, I beg of you. You'll make me out to be a schemer."

"And what do you use them for exactly? What did you use Sancho the Wise's seal to do? Did you send the letter informing me that Diago Vela was dead? Did you destroy my life to keep him from becoming my spouse?"

García glanced around the room calmly.

Calm.

Calm was always a good thing.

A pallet, a washing bowl, a hearth, a poker, candles. Few objects with which to strike a person.

"Leave us, my boy. Go downstairs to your mother and aunts. Keep Alix de Salcedo occupied. I don't want anybody coming upstairs for a good while," he said slowly.

"What are you going to do, Father?" the young man asked nervously.

"Either you leave the room, or I will renounce the document recognizing you as my son. You decide."

Lope gave the woman a resigned look before closing the door. She was already doomed. But Onneca was not yet afraid for her life; the man before her was still her beloved cousin.

"I was sorry about Bona and Favila, and about your brother. Of all the Maestu family, you have always been most aligned with the interests of the nobles of Nova Victoria."

"And what do you have in common with them?"

"The palace at Pamplona, the lands bequeathed to me for doing my utmost to control King Sancho the Wise and his son. But that's all over now, Onneca. As you know, Alfonso will grant our family many more privileges."

"And for that my entire family had to die? Was there no other way?" cried Onneca. "I would have conspired with you. Why didn't you confide in me? I would have been your staunchest ally. We could have convinced them together."

"With Diago Vela in the middle of things? Do you think it possible to manipulate him, you foolish woman? I convinced Sancho the Wise to send him on a dangerous mission. I was convinced he would never return alive. My mercenaries tracked him on his way home, but they couldn't catch up with him. I've never known a man with so many lives."

When it came, it was quick. He selected the old poker and began to strike her. Onneca defended herself with all the fury the memory of her father sparked in her. When she found herself on the floor she knew she was about to die, so she tried screaming with all her might.

At least they'll know he murdered me. At least my screams will weigh upon their consciences, she thought as the iron blows rained down upon her.

From her vantage point on the ground, she saw the door open to admit a familiar robe. The beating stopped.

"Onneca! García, what savagery is this?"

She knew Alix had leaped onto her cousin, but she saw no more of that struggle. She let her eyelids close and gave way to the darkness.

51

THE CARNICERÍAS DISTRICT

UNAI

October 2019

I regained my voice. Seeing Alba calmly give orders forced me to come out of my shell and begin functioning again.

I picked Iago's cell phone up off the ground and called Germán.

"It's Granddad. Come," I managed to say.

My brother understood. As a lawyer, his job depended on his ability to interpret the nuances of human misery.

"Where?"

"Santiago Hospital."

"What about you?"

"Deba. I'm hanging up."

I'd said enough. I knew Germán would take care of Grandfather so that Alba and I could concentrate on finding Deba.

Alba had already set up an operation and sealed off the Medieval Quarter. She had officers posted at each end of every guild street. She knew this was a race against the clock in more ways than one. The minute Superintendent Medina discovered the missing girl was our daughter, he would force us to stand down.

It made me think of the siege of Victoria. A thousand years ago, the townsfolk had fought to keep the enemy out. Now we were cordoning off the same streets to prevent the monster from escaping.

"Over here!" I heard Milán's voice ring out over the commotion in the park.

Alba and I ran toward the Carnicerías district.

Milán was looking at something on the ground.

"Isn't this Deba's?" she asked as we came sprinting over.

It was the little red wristband with the silver *eguzkilore* charm her aunt Estí had given her.

Clever girl.

I always told her to leave a trail of breadcrumbs if she got lost.

But my daughter hadn't gotten lost. Someone had hit Grandfather with his own cane. Grandfather would never have given his boxwood cane to his attacker willingly. No, he had confronted his assailant and had been knocked down, which left little room for doubt. My daughter hadn't lost her way in the maze of the Old Quarter—someone had taken her.

"Get forensics to process the scene," Alba said curtly.

Iago came down the street toward us.

"This isn't how I'd hoped to meet you, but you must be DSU Díaz de Salvatierra."

"This is Iago del Castillo. He tried to resuscitate Grandfather," I explained to Alba.

Iago gave her a firm handshake and then discreetly pulled me to the side while Alba took command of the scene and continued giving instructions.

"I don't want to get in the way. I just wanted to make sure you have enough help. Do you need someone to stay with your grandfather at the hospital and keep you informed?"

"My brother is on his way there now. And we have plenty of people to help us," I said, though my mind was thinking through a thousand other things. "I can call family, friends from Villaverde, my *cuadrilla*. . . . We're covered, but thanks for the offer."

"If you don't mind, I'll stop by the hospital anyway, in case I can be of any help there. I couldn't go back to Santander not knowing your grandfather's condition. Right now, there's nothing you can do for him. Focus on Deba. Do you hear me? Focus on Deba."

I felt a stab of panic, and Iago must have seen it in my eyes.

"What do you need?" he asked. "One thing at a time. What's most urgent?"

"Circulate a photograph of Deba, check the security cameras in the city center . . ." I reeled off a checklist straight from the police training manual.

I didn't want to stop. For her. For Deba.

"Just one question, Iago, because I can't stop thinking about it right now. Count Don Vela's little boy disappeared. Did . . . did they ever find him? Is his death mentioned in the chronicle or anywhere else in the family archive?"

Iago looked away, closing his eyes like he was suppressing a painful memory.

Then he collected himself. He placed his strong hand on my shoulder. The gesture reminded me of a great sequoia's older branches supporting newer growth.

"No, Unai. I'm sorry. I'm very sorry. Diago Vela's son, Yennego, does not appear again."

52

THE UNDERPASS

UNAI

October 2019

We'd already interviewed the few witnesses who were in the park and on the surrounding streets around the same time as Grandfather and Deba. The fact that many of those who had been at the scene of the crime were dressed up as bloodthirsty killers, half wearing masks, didn't help.

"What leads do we have?" I asked Alba. "Reliable ones. I feel like we're looking for a needle in a haystack."

"Nobody saw a little girl wearing an *eguzkilore* costume. That worries me. We have three eyewitnesses who saw a woman with a stroller near Calle Fray Zacarías Martínez around the time we think Grandfather was attacked, but that's about it."

"We've sealed off the Old Quarter, so either they got away before we sounded the alarm, or they're nearby," I said, trying hard to push aside the memory of the girls trapped behind a wall just yards from where we were standing.

"We're completely in the dark, Unai. We need to go big: I want Deba's photograph posted on the emergency services' Twitter, and her description broadcast on every radio station. We can't forget that Tasio Ortiz de Zárate has made it clear more than once that he wants to see her. He's our main suspect."

"Go for it" was all I said.

Germán had been calling every twenty minutes to give me updates: Grandfather was in a coma and the prognosis wasn't good. He told me we should prepare for the worst.

"But he'd want you to keep looking for Deba, so don't beat yourself up or panic about not being able to say goodbye. I'll call you when . . . if . . . I'll call you if there's any change. Just find her, please."

Soon we were getting calls from all over the city. People claimed to have seen a little blond girl dressed as an *eguzkilore* holding hands with a woman pushing a stroller in Judizmendi, San Martín Park, Calle Zaramaga. We sent squad cars to check out each and every lead.

"Any news?" I asked Milán.

"We're trying to screen the reported sightings. Meanwhile a ticket agent at the train station claims Tasio Ortiz de Zárate bought a ticket to Hendaye. His hair was dyed black, and he was pushing a stroller with a little boy, not a girl, asleep in it," she added.

Alba and I exchanged glances—we didn't need to say a word. I took the first car I could find and headed for the railway station at the far end of Calle Dato.

I didn't have my weapon or a bulletproof vest. Why would I—my Halloween had started with a harmless visit to the archives with Iago del Castillo. The station was packed, although thankfully few people on the platform were wearing costumes.

I got a text from Alba. She had ordered a search and rescue operation and had gotten the station to delay all departures.

But there was no one with a stroller on any of the platforms. I checked the bathrooms, but I saw no sign of Tasio or my daughter anywhere.

Until I ran to the underpass between the platforms.

I saw them at the bottom. It was true, Tasio had dyed his hair black and had grown out his beard. I was amazed the ticket agent had recognized him. A little boy with cropped blond hair was asleep in the stroller, and a blanket draped over his waist hid an *eguzkilore* costume.

It wasn't a boy, though—it was Deba. Was she unconscious? She couldn't be dead. I cast the idea from my mind. He wouldn't be trying to get a train out of the country with her if she were dead.

"Tasio, step away from my daughter and let's talk," I said, holding up my hands so he could see I wasn't armed.

"She isn't your daughter. When I spoke to her in the park in Laguardia, I gave her a lollipop. It was the perfect DNA sample. You chased me, but you didn't even realize I had it."

"You're a good actor. I thought you were Ignacio. I even talked about police work to test you, but you convinced me. You're damn good at impersonating him," I spluttered.

"I just told you that she's not your daughter; she's my niece. I got the test results. They confirm that I'm her uncle. She's my flesh and blood."

"I know. I've always known."

"I just told you that she's not your daughter and you're not even batting an eye? My twin and I are the only family she has."

"I knew she didn't have my DNA from the moment she was born. But you're wrong: she does have a family. She has my surname, and I've brought her up. And the family she has loves and protects her, they don't abduct her, drug her, and cut off all her hair. You're guilty of aggravated kidnapping of a minor. As her second-degree relative, you're facing between two and four years in prison, as well as a restraining order. I doubt you'd be able to apply to be her legal guardian when you get out, because what you just did carries a four- to ten-year disqualification. The prosecution will certainly try for the maximum penalty because you tried to take her out of the country."

I was still twenty feet from Tasio and the stroller, hands in the air. I was afraid to get any closer in case he threatened to hurt Deba. But behind him, at the other end of the tunnel, Alba was advancing soundlessly, gun at the ready.

I kept talking.

"Or you can hand her over now and plead remorse. We can get you a reduced sentence. I'm sure you don't want to spend any more time in prison than you have to after what happened the last time. I shudder to think what they'll do when they find out you abducted a two-year-old girl."

"That won't happen," Tasio replied tersely. "Because you're unarmed and you won't come near the girl. You're going to let me go, unless—"

"Unless nothing," Alba hissed in his ear. She kept her cool but pressed the gun barrel against his neck and immobilized him with her free arm. "This is the closest you'll ever get to Deba. I'm arresting you for kidnapping a minor and for attempted homicide. Santiago López de Ayala is in the ICU. You'd better pray he has a few more years to bring up his great-granddaughter."

The ambulance doors closed. Alba and I sat on either side of Deba, each of us holding a limp hand. Tasio had cut off her blond curls; she looked like a naughty little boy and seemed strange, alien. The sedative Tasio had administered hadn't worn off yet; our daughter was fast asleep.

"How much did you hear?" I asked Alba.

"How could you know she wasn't your daughter on the day she was born? Did you get a DNA test without telling me?"

"I'd never do that. They took a blood sample from Deba after she was born, standard procedure. You're type A, but she's type B. I remembered that your husband's autopsy listed his blood type as B. You never asked me for my blood type. I'm type A. So I lied when I said I was type B as well. You chose to bring her up without knowing which one of us was the father, and I respected that."

"Who else knows?"

"Grandfather, who, as you know, is wilier than a fox. I couldn't hide it from him. But when I held her in my arms, Deba and I decided right away that we are father and daughter. So that's what we are. We transcend blood. I'm not sure you'll ever understand that bond, the same way I'll never understand the bond you have with her after carrying her for nine months."

"Did my mother know?"

"No, Nieves never knew. And that's fine. Deba was her granddaughter, and she died thinking I was Deba's biological father. Our families have come together, and we've all been there for Deba. Don't throw that away because of a few strands of protein. It's just DNA, Alba. I refuse to let something physical define the people I love and share my life with."

"Aren't you afraid she might inherit her father's psychopathy?"

"So far she hasn't presented any of his traits. Deba's empathic. She is not manipulative, and she expresses her emotions spontaneously. She's not faking them. But if she ever did show signs of following in his footsteps, then she was born into the right family, don't you think? A strong mother who was a deputy superintendent, a father who's a profiler. We're perfectly placed to detect early warning signs and to try to instill the right values in her. I'm sure Doctor Leiva would help us. They have special programs for reeducating psychopathic children."

"I *was* deputy superintendent?" she asked, stroking Deba's cheek.

"I know you're going to quit. You deserve your castle with your sea of vineyards, and Deba deserves to be safe. She can't possibly live in Vitoria now that the whole city has seen her photograph. You both have to go back to Laguardia."

"That will split your life in two. You don't need to raise her as your own if you don't want to."

"What the hell are you saying?" I yelled. I was mad, and I squeezed Deba's hand harder than I should have. "No matter what happens, the three of us are joined together. It's right here in a strand of red wool."

But the truth was that the red wristband, and even the *eguzkilores*, had failed to protect the people I loved most.

There was a zombie-hunter costume back at my apartment, but I wouldn't be wearing it for Halloween. I'd only bought it because I felt obliged to double-down on what I had said to my daughter about carrying twenty zombies around on my back.

In fact, the number of those who had died because of me was getting alarmingly close to that amount.

Dissemble, *deceive*, *double-down*—the verbs that ruled my life.

Even someone as blind as I was had to realize he couldn't go on like that.

53

THE FAITHFUL MUNIO

DIAGO VELA

WINTER, THE YEAR OF OUR LORD 1200

Onneca woke up in the middle of the night. She was cold. It had stopped raining, but she was chilled to the bone, a feeling exacerbated by the fact that her battered body was bruised and trembling.

"What happened to García?" she asked Alix.

"You need no longer concern yourself with him," Alix replied, as if the matter were closed.

"Where are we?"

"In the old mill by the river. It wasn't safe for us to stay at the inn, and we can't ask King Alfonso for permission to reenter the town. He will want to know why Bishop García isn't with us."

"What about the message from King Sancho? We need it to persuade the townsfolk to surrender."

Alix coughed. She felt unwell, but she hid it from her sister-in-law.

"So what do we do now?" insisted Onneca.

"I'm going to venture as far as the wall. You stay in the shadows," Alix directed her.

With that, Alix slipped out into the chilly night. Thankfully, Mother Moon, as her husband called it, was resplendent in a sky now free of storm clouds.

She drew within earshot of the town walls and whistled several times.

Nothing happened.

The night crawled on, but Alix didn't desert her post.

At last her angel arrived, his enormous wings blocking out the sky for an instant.

"Munio!" she whispered, overjoyed.

Her faithful snowy owl, who was old and needed her help catching mice in recent years, had responded to the call of the woman he loved.

"Munio, take this to Diago and bring him to me," she commanded, tearing off a strip of cloth from her sodden robe and tying it to the owl's talon.

Then she went to fetch Onneca. She helped her up to the wall as best she could, terrified that they might bump into a patrolling enemy soldier.

Just before sunrise, Gunnarr descended the wall on a rope secured by Nagorno and the author of this chronicle, two noblemen keen to be reunited with their wives at last.

54

THE APPLE GRAVE

UNAI

November 2019

We had been reunited with one López de Ayala, but we were losing another.

Germán managed to sneak the apples into the hospital. Grandfather was still in the ICU, and there was no sign of improvement. Some people from the funeral insurance company approached us, and I told them where to go in no uncertain terms. But the nurses advised us to make arrangements. This would be our patriarch's last autumn.

Late on a Friday evening, when everything was calm and the hospital noises were muted, I set to work on my last mission as his grandson.

It took me a while to rub the quartered apples from his garden all over his knobbly skin. We reminisced, or rather I did, about the houses we used to build out of bales of straw after the August harvest in Las Llecas. Or about the time I woke him at four in the morning, coming home from the fiestas in Bernedo, and we ended up putting sprinklers out in the fields because of the drought that year.

I found his silence almost unbearable. Eventually I was finished, and I got in the car and drove to Villaverde.

We had whisked Deba away from the hospital and the city of Vitoria: she'd been through enough that day. I'd never seen her as upset as she was when she saw herself in the mirror with cropped hair. I hated Tasio for that.

Tasio Ortiz de Zárate had spent the night in jail and would remain in custody. I doubted he'd be free anytime soon. I tried not to waste my thoughts on him; Deba and Grandfather had filled my mind since last night. As soon as we had arrived at Grandfather's house in Villaverde, my daughter found one of his berets and refused to take it off even though it was much too big for her. Exhausted, she had fallen asleep next to her mother still wearing it. I made another red wristband for her, my way of telling Fate that I took care of my own.

All Souls' Day marked the first of November, the month when my family was responsible for ringing the bell for Mass and for the Angelus. It was village tradition on that day to ring the bell every three hours in remembrance of the dead, so Germán and I made our way to the bell tower with our big iron key before the sun rose.

We opened the church door and mounted the spiral stone staircase. The bell tower itself was just a few old wooden planks. It wasn't very safe. In the distance we could see the looming black expanse of the sierra, while, near the foot of the church, a feeble yellow streetlight barely illuminated the nearby rooftops.

Other than that, the night was dark.

Germán and I began to ring the bell in silence, the way Grandfather had taught us. The deafening sound of the clapper next to our heads stopped my thoughts. It gave me a few moments of peace, the only peace I can remember from those dark days.

Not thinking.

"Do you remember the way he taught us how to draw the sun years ago?" Germán asked, motioning with his hand as we released the bell rope.

I'd forgotten. I looked where he was pointing and could make out the crude outline of a tiny sun on the north wall of the tower.

"Look, boys, I'm going to show you something in case I'm no longer here one day," I remember Grandfather telling us. We had been at the top of the tower on a mild August morning. Outside a combine was harvesting the ripe corn beneath a cloudless sky.

"No longer here!" I had exclaimed. "I don't like it when you talk like that."

Germán and Grandfather had looked at me tenderly until I calmed down.

"I think Granddad is trying to pass on a family secret, like when he took us to San Tirso and showed us where vervain grows," said Germán. He had always been the more levelheaded brother.

"It's family tradition to pass on this secret when a member of the family takes his or her turn ringing the bells," Grandfather said, scratching his head. "Don't tell the neighbors about it. There's a little drawing here in the stone, beside the bell. I think it's a miniature sun. Granddad Santiago told my father about it; it's the last thing he remembered Santiago telling him before he left. It must have meant a lot to him."

"The Santiago who left when your father was ten?"

"The very same. I don't know why, but I think he wanted us to know that he drew this sun, or this flower. I was a little boy when my father brought me here, and I didn't pay attention. I can't remember whether he called it Grandma's Sun, or Grandma's Flower. But he said it protected Villaverde. And that protecting Villaverde was something our family had always done."

Ever since then, whenever it was our turn to ring the bell, Germán and I would take a knife to the tower with us and retrace the lines of Grandfather's little drawing if it looked as though dust and time were causing it to fade.

I checked the time on my phone. It was late, so I changed the subject.

"Do you know Beltrán Pérez de Apodaca? He's a young law graduate."

"Yes, I've bumped into him in court a few times. Why do you ask?"

"Tell me about him."

"He's ambitious, smart—a young shark. He lacks the wiliness that comes with experience, but I'm sure he'll learn. We're on good terms."

"You're on good terms with everyone. Would you employ him in your practice?"

He thought for a moment.

"No."

"Why not? He seems to have a bright future."

"I'm sure he does," said Germán. "But I only take on men and women with integrity and principles. That's always been my rule. Over the years, you learn to judge people's character pretty well, if you catch my drift."

"I understand perfectly, Germán. You've been helpful. Now let's head down, I have a couple of things left to do today."

"Is Beltrán a suspect?"

"He gave us a DNA sample when we canvassed Ugarte. It wasn't a match. He certainly didn't kill MatuSalem. No, I'm just trying to pull together a better picture of our main suspect," I explained.

"You're going to continue working on the *Lords of Time* case, aren't you?"

"Somebody has to do it."

"And you're the only one who can?"

I started to explain. "I know it's taking a heavy toll on our family—"

"If you put yourself at the center of a hurricane, it'll end up destroying everything and everyone around you," he interrupted. "Out of everything you could have done with your life, why did you choose to work in homicide, Unai?"

"Somebody has to protect people," I said, repeating something I had told myself many times. "Maybe it's in my blood. Grandfather was the mayor of Villaverde for years when nobody else wanted the job; he felt it was his duty. And that's the way he brought us up. You're no different. You're doing the same job as I am, but you do it from behind a desk. Domestic abuse, unjust terminations . . . You accept cases in order to help others. You and I are the same."

"I don't carry a gun or wear a bulletproof vest, that's the difference. If only my brother were a lawyer."

It was pointless trying to explain. . . .

"There's something I've been wanting to ask you for a long time," I said, soldiering on. "I don't like to nose around in your personal life, but everybody knows you haven't been dating for the last two years. Have you put your life on hold in the hope that I'll quit my job?"

He didn't respond.

"Is that why?" I insisted. "Are you afraid your girlfriends might end up dead?"

"I didn't say that. I'd never blame you for what happened, but—"

"But that's what you think," I concluded.

My brother had become celibate because of me. He adored Deba, he'd always loved children, and I know he longed to have kids of his own. But was he waiting for me to quit my job?

We climbed down from the bell tower in silence, disinclined to speak to each other. I stopped by Grandfather's house to pick up the basket with the quartered apples. I was unable to find any old newspapers, so I wrapped them in some pieces of paper Deba had been drawing on the day before. She and Alba were still asleep. I tiptoed into the bedroom, planted a kiss on both their foreheads, and went downstairs.

I entered the garden. The apples were back in the basket, wrapped in Deba's paper and tied with string, the way Grandfather did before burying them. I grabbed a hoe and set to work beneath our enormous pear tree. The glow from a streetlight shone golden on my back, projecting my shadow onto the grave I was digging.

Grandfather would sometimes mention the Roman coins his father had discovered while plowing. As a child, I had heard countless other stories as well: field hands unearthing treasure troves, small pouches of toughened leather buried two thousand years ago, which were sometimes handed over to the authorities but, more often than not, kept. The local museums were full of these treasures: coins, shards of pottery, and other archaeological artifacts.

When we were boys, Germán and I had spent months searching for sacks of gold. We dug holes everywhere, and we'd even saved up for a metal detector. Then we grew up and forgot about buried treasure. What lay buried didn't glisten. It was lifeless. We had learned the difference the hard way.

I shook off my dark thoughts.

Kneeling, I began to bury the apple pieces in the earth. I wanted them to decay. Quickly.

And then I noticed what my daughter had drawn on the sheets of paper I'd wrapped the apples in. I brushed off the loose earth and shone my phone light on them, intrigued.

Chimeras and monsters. My brain recalled seeing them somewhere recently.

But where? I struggled to remember.

I investigated, recorded, and classified so much information from crime scenes, suspects, and witnesses that sometimes I had trouble retrieving the data from the part of my brain where everything was stored.

Sometimes these myriad facts were as useless as this one seemed to be.

"What are you doing?" I heard Estíbaliz's voice behind me.

I jumped, startled, and had to prop myself up with the hoe.

"More to the point, what are *you* doing in Villaverde at this time of night?" I retorted once I had recovered.

"I wanted to visit my niece, but I just went upstairs and everyone's fast asleep. Germán told me you were down in the garden. I know I've been taken off the case, but I'm here to bring you the list of Quejana Council employees. Milán meant to give it to you yesterday, but with everything going on . . ."

"Let me see."

I sat on the low wall and scanned the list of names. None rang a bell, except . . . Claudia. Claudia Mújica.

"The tour guide?" I said out loud.

"I hadn't noticed. Is that her last name?"

"It's written on the plaque at the reception desk in Nograro Tower. Of course, she has keys to the tower, so she could have gotten in and stolen the copy of the diary. She's very tall and skinny. Could she be the person who attacked you?"

"I couldn't see anything in the dark, and it all happened so quickly, but the person I tried to fight off was extremely strong and heavily built."

"She also had access to the Dominican nun's habit," I mused, "but the person I chased was definitely a lot shorter. On the other hand, according to this list, she was hired as a museum guide by the Dominican convent a couple of years ago. So she could still have the keys to the Quejana complex. But she doesn't fit the priest's description of his assailant, either. Still, we'll need to contact her to answer some questions. First thing tomorrow morning, we'll ask her to provide alibis for the days the crimes were committed."

But Estíbaliz was already on her feet.

"What are you waiting for?" she asked when she realized I wasn't moving. "Let's call Peña and get him to go to Ugarte right now to check her alibis. Who cares what time it is? This is urgent."

"May I remind you that we already have a suspect on the run, and that the person who helped him get away wasn't a woman," I said.

"Milán told me you've been unable to identify the accomplice, that none of the hospital staff recognized him from behind. What if Claudia is involved? You're obsessed with the idea of a homicidal alter who murders real people to prevent his fictional character from being killed off, so you can't see that it doesn't add up."

"What doesn't add up, in your opinion?" I asked.

"The victims. Like all profilers, you're focusing on the killer and his MO, and you're forgetting about the victims."

"Isn't it your job to remind me of them?"

"Yes, and that's exactly what I'm doing. But you only seem to listen to me when my life is hanging by a thread. The first victim, Antón Lasaga, fit your theory of similar MOs because of his profession and the location of his death. He could be a stand-in for Count de Maestu, Onneca's father. MatuSalem, your collaborator, was a Maturana, and he died the same way as the Maturana in the novel. But the Nájera sisters who were trapped in a wall like Onneca's sisters have nothing to do with Ramiro Alvar's alter, or with what happens to Bishop García."

"Bishop García?"

"I noticed that he shares several traits with Alvar. I think the bishop's character is modeled off Alvar. García's a young priest who's attractive and wealthy. He wears only a cassock, even in midwinter; he loves to ride; he adores offal dishes . . ."

"I have to admit, I didn't make the connection," I said.

"That's probably because you've spent more time with Ramiro Alvar than with Alvar. What I'm trying to make you see is that whoever is imitating the murders in the novel knows nothing about Ramiro Alvar's dissociative identity disorder, or his reasons for writing his own version of the chronicle."

"Ramiro Alvar has escaped, Estí. What if Alvar is back? What if he never went away, and he drew you in again at the hospital? What if he threw you over the balcony and then staged the chronicle's theft?"

Estíbaliz drew her knees up to her chest and hugged them.

"You have no idea what kind of person Ramiro Alvar is. None whatsoever. We talked for hours at the hospital. We took things slowly this time. Even though I was no longer on the case, I didn't forget my training. Ramiro is a good human being, and nobody can fake that."

"Okay, convince me," I said.

"He donated his bone marrow."

"To Alvar? That's not what he told me."

"No, not to Alvar," she said. "To Alvar's son."

"Alvar has a son?" I asked.

"Yes, the kid who runs the bar."

"Gonzalo Martínez?"

"Yes, that's him. About eighteen months ago, after his mother disappeared, he came to Ugarte. When he discovered that Gemma's parents were dead, Gonzalo went to Nograro Tower. He had never finished school, but Ramiro Alvar gave him money so that he could take over the bar."

"Why did Ramiro Alvar donate his bone marrow to Gonzalo?"

"About a year ago, Gonzalo was diagnosed with the deadliest form of thalassemia. As his sole living relative, Ramiro didn't hesitate to help him. He's telling the truth; I saw the scar on his back the night that . . . that night."

"Gonzalo is Ramiro Alvar's nephew?" I echoed in a whisper.

"Neither of them wanted anyone to know. Ugarte's a small place. He told me the Nograro family paid for Gonzalo's mother to have an abortion. That's not a story you want to brag about in a bar."

"Sure," I replied, pensively.

"What's wrong? You're as white as a sheet. Do you think Gonzalo has something to do with the murders?"

"No, he gave a voluntary DNA sample. That rules him out," I explained. "No, it's something else."

That damn village with its secrets and its lies. Ramiro Alvar hadn't told me that his brother had a son who now lived in town.

How many more lies, Ramiro Alvar? What else haven't you told me?

"Oh God . . ." I realized aloud. "The chimera."

I pulled my daughter's crumpled drawing from my pocket.

"What is it?"

I gaped at the piece of paper, dumbfounded, as though it were an aleph that held the key to the entire universe.

"Fuck, Estí. What is it we always say? When you rule out the impossible, all that remains is—"

"The improbable," she concluded.

"What is statistically improbable but possible. It's been documented."

"What's been documented?"

"The chimera, Estíbaliz. The chimera."

"You need to draw me a diagram, because I don't understand what you're saying."

I stood up, elated.

Neurologists say that when you solve a puzzle, your brain rewards you with a shot of dopamine. It's addictive. It makes you feel good.

I was definitely addicted to that *eureka* sensation.

Thank you, Grandfather. I sent up the prayer as I walked past his buried apples.

"Where are you going?" Estíbaliz called after me.

"I have to talk to Doctor Guevara!" I shouted, running up the garden's stone steps.

She'll understand everything.

55

THE CIRCLE

UNAI

November 2019

I spent all of the next day in my office. My conversation with Doctor Guevara had cleared up several questions. Now all I had to do was close the circle. Spread out on my desk were the photographs from MatuSalem's funeral. I was looking for family likenesses, and at last my search bore fruit.

I called Milán.

"I need you to access the Álava Emergency Services database for me."

"What are we looking for?"

"I'll know it when I see it. How long will it take?"

"Consider it done."

Shortly after, I got another call. It was Iago del Castillo.

"Good morning, Unai. How's your grandfather doing?"

"He's still in the ICU. Th doctors say it's a matter of days. He's almost one hundred, so they can't understand how he's still alive. All of the medics think he should already be dead. They expect his heart to fail slowly and then just stop."

"That heart has been beating for almost a century. You're doing the right thing letting it end its journey in its own time," he said gently. "On a happier note, I'm so glad Deba is back with you. No parent should have to suffer the loss of a child."

"Thanks, Iago. I was actually going to call you this morning. I have another question, since you're the only one besides the author who knows the differences between the factual events narrated by Diago Vela and the liberties taken in the novel."

"Ask away."

"Does Bishop García die in your ancestor's version?"

"No, he doesn't die. The chronicle is true to life—it coincides with Jiménez de Rada's account in *De Rebus Hispaniae*, although he was writing in the first half of the thirteenth century. That's why Don Vela's chronicle has so much historical value. It's a firsthand account from one of the protagonists."

"So this is one point where *The Lords of Time* diverges from the original?"

"Yes. Bishop García rode back to Victoria with a nobleman from the besieged town to inform the residents that King Sancho the Strong had given them permission to surrender. This next part doesn't appear in the chronicle, but other documents from that period place Bishop García in Pamplona after the siege, specifically in 1202, where he leases land to Don Fortunio, the archpriest of Salinas."

This fact worried me—a lot.

Estíbaliz said Bishop García represented Alvar. Ramiro Alvar gave García Alvar's personality, his obsessions, his quirks. If the bishop died in the novel, who did Alvar think killed him? Who did he want to eliminate? Should I worry about the possible nemeses of an alter who hadn't appeared since the theft? I didn't know Ramiro Alvar's whereabouts or what his next move might be, and that made me uneasy. Would he just be happy to have escaped and leave it at that?

When Iago cleared his throat politely, I realized I'd been lost in my own thoughts.

"I also have a question about the charter that grants privileges to the Lords of Nograro," I continued. "Does it mention the inheritance rights of illegitimate sons?"

"There is no need. Contemporary inheritance laws make no distinction between legitimate and illegitimate children. However, three years ago, in a Supreme Court ruling, illegitimate children were barred from inheriting noble titles and privileges. In this particular instance, holding the title of Lord Nograro is a prerequisite for inheriting the family estate because of the law of primogeniture. But in the document signed by Ferdinand the Sixth, there is the following proviso: 'In the absence of an elder legitimate son who fulfills the conditions, the eldest illegitimate son will be next in line to inherit the estate.' I don't know if that helps."

"I'll say it does. I'm going to let you go now, I have a lot to do."

"Good luck. I'll call later to see how your grandfather is doing."

"Thanks for all your support," I said, and hung up.

The person who walked through the door was the last person I expected to see. Estíbaliz was still on sick leave, even though she had a lot more mobility in her arm, and, of course, she was no longer working the *Lords of Time* case. But this was Estíbaliz. To her, rules were meant to be bent.

She perched on my desk, knocking several photos to the floor without noticing.

"I think I know where Ramiro is," she announced, a mixture of triumph and exhilaration in her voice.

"So do I, but we're going to need help to catch him."

After a lengthy discussion, we came up with a plan.

Soon afterward, I called the bar in Ugarte run by Ramiro Alvar's nephew.

"Hi, Gonzalo, Inspector López de Ayala here."

"How are you, Inspector? Are you coming to book club this evening?"

"Actually, that's not why I'm calling. This is about something much more serious."

"I'm listening," he said, swallowing hard.

"You may be aware that Ramiro Alvar de Nograro is on the run. I think he'll try to contact you. We can't offer you police protection because it would jeopardize our operation if he found out. I can, however, give you some advice about how to protect yourself, and I'll give you my direct number as well. I'm also going to give you instructions about what to do if he calls. We're worried you could be his next victim."

56

A SEA OF BOTTLES

UNAI

November 2019

That same night, young Gonzalo received an urgent call on the bar's telephone.

"Uncle," he whispered uneasily, "the police are looking for you."

"I know. Can you help me get out of here?"

"Of course, I'll help you. I don't have much money, but we'll figure out an escape plan. You know I'd never leave you in a bind. I haven't forgotten what you did for me. You saved my life."

Ramiro Alvar heaved a sigh on the other end of the line.

"Thank you."

Shortly afterward, Gonzalo called me.

"Inspector, Ramiro Alvar has been in touch. But there's something else I need to tell you."

The moment had finally arrived.

"Is he within earshot?" I asked.

"No, I'm at the bar. But I'm going to the place he's been hiding out for the last few days right now. He's nervous," said Gonzalo.

"Did you tell anyone else about this? I need to know how much backup to bring."

"I wasn't sure what to do, so I called Beltrán Pérez de Apodaca. I trust him, and he's a lawyer. I don't know if I did the right thing."

I thought for a moment.

"I have no problem with that. Ramiro Alvar trusts him, too, and I'll rest easier knowing there are two of you. I'm going to tell you what to do when you meet him. I'll be leading the operation, and we'll surround the building, so you won't be in any danger. I'll see you there in just under an hour."

By the time we arrived, daylight was fading. A unit of officers fanned out around the glassworks. Milán, Peña, and I were armed and wearing bulletproof vests.

I called Gonzalo. He had last been in touch twenty minutes earlier, and I was getting worried.

"Is everything okay?" I asked when he picked up.

"I'm in the agritourism, in the downstairs hallway. Ramiro Alvar is hiding in the room at the very back of the glassworks. He's still really agitated. Beltrán and I are doing our best to calm him down."

"How did he get there?" I asked.

"He called Irati's boyfriend, Sebas, from the hospital," he whispered. "Sebas drives an ambulance. Ramiro Alvar told him he'd been discharged and asked if he'd take him home. Then Ramiro persuaded Sebas that it'd be easier for him to stay at the forge while he's still in a wheelchair. Irati and Sebas didn't know he'd escaped, or that they were harboring a wanted man, until I told them just now."

"Typical Ramiro Alvar. He manipulates everyone," I said calmly. "Make sure he stays where he is, and don't let him convince you to help him escape. He'll make something up, tell you whatever you want to hear. We're coming in."

Irati was waiting at the entrance to the forge. I motioned for her not to make any noise, and I holstered my gun. Our uniforms must have looked daunting, because she seemed anxious, her elfin face locked in a grimace.

She led us through the workshop. Ten of my officers spread out among shelves crammed with blue glass bottles and round jugs that puffed out like blowfish.

When we reached the back of the workshop, I took a deep breath and rapped on the door. Milán and Peña stood on either side and just behind me, weapons drawn. I didn't want anybody inside the room to see them; one wrong move, one knowing look, and the whole plan could go wrong. The volatile emotions in that room could explode at any moment, breaking the sea of bottles that surrounded us.

"Come in," the young lawyer's voice rang out.

Irati and I went in. Ramiro Alvar was sitting in his brother's wheelchair. He swallowed hard when he saw me. Next to him was a comfortable camp bed, which he'd probably been sleeping on for the past few nights. I recognized Sebas, not just as Irati's boyfriend, but as the gigantic young ambulance driver who had attended to the elderly priest at Quejana.

Gonzalo was the first to speak.

"I'm sorry, Uncle, but it's over," he said simply.

I pulled out my gun and took aim. Ramiro Alvar didn't even bother raising his hands. He stared forlornly at Gonzalo.

"You're turning me in? I gave you money to buy the bar, I donated my bone marrow to save your life, and this is how you repay me? How you repay our family?" His voice oozed disappointment.

"But you didn't let me join you in the tower, in the family seat! You banished me to the village, like a second-rank Nograro, one more bastard."

We looked at Gonzalo in astonishment. It was hard to believe that such an easygoing, polite young man carried so much anger, but his fists were clenched, his voice quaking.

"I did it to protect you! I didn't want to expose you to all the evil in this family—you have no idea how bad it is," Ramiro said, raising his voice as well.

"Protect me? From what?"

"From my alter, and from the mental illness that has plagued all our male ancestors. You reactivated Alvar, the very worst of Alvar, your father's dissociated personality. I didn't know how he'd react to you. I was afraid he might hate you for being born and make your life hell as he did mine. That's why I stayed away from Ugarte and from you. I didn't want to become the womanizing priest who tore families apart the way Nograro men have always done."

"What on Earth are you talking about?" asked a bewildered Gonzalo.

"Many men in your family have suffered from dissociative identity disorder," I said, cutting in. "You probably know it as multiple personality disorder. Your uncle believed that your return triggered his illness, and he took on your father's personality. He helped you in every way he could, protecting you from himself and from the demons in your own family at the same time."

And then I gave the order.

"You can come in."

Peña, Milán, and several officers burst into the room, pointing their weapons at everyone except Ramiro Alvar. I'd been very precise with my instructions.

"Gonzalo Martínez, you're under arrest for the murder of Samuel Maturana. Beltrán Pérez de Apodaca, you're under arrest for the murder of Antón Lasaga. Irati Mújica and Sebastián Argote, you're under arrest for the murders of Estefanía and Oihana Nájera."

57

BENEATH THE WALL

DIAGO VELA

WINTER, THE YEAR OF OUR LORD 1200

The two women slept until late morning. When Nagorno saw how badly hurt his wife was, he cursed all the pagan gods as well as the Christian one.

Alix didn't feel any better. She took our baby girl in her arms, and the three of us lay together beside the warm hearth. I stayed awake that night praying that my worst fears would not take shape the next day.

Outside, the tired, starving townspeople hammered on our door, impatient to hear the news the two women had brought back. Everybody wondered at the absence of the worthy Bishop García, who was transformed into a martyr within hours. He was considered a saint, our selfless protector.

By the time Alix awoke, I knew what was wrong with her. She had blood in her urine, and when I opened her mouth, I saw the blisters in her throat.

"What happened, my love?" I asked.

"García," she whispered in my ear. "I attacked him because he was beating Onneca. He tried to kill her at La Romana Inn. He put the powders in my mouth. I tried not to swallow, and I made myself vomit, so that I wouldn't end up with my guts burned like Count de Maestu."

Alix coughed and winced. I could only imagine the agony she felt each time she spoke.

"Lope, the innkeeper's son, poisoned Count de Maestu," she explained. "The bishop offered to recognize Lope as his son if he would do it. And the seal . . . Onneca told me everything. It was García who faked the letter announcing your death, using a copy of King Sancho's royal seal. Don't surrender the town. Onneca and I didn't meet with the king; the bishop spoke with him alone. He brought a document releasing the residents and the king's lieutenant from their promise not to stand down. The bishop said we have King Sancho's permission to surrender, but I'm not certain that is the truth. The bishop also had a copy of our present king's seal."

I bit my lip in frustration. In saving Onneca, Alix had condemned herself to death. Her mouth and throat were blistered from the powders. All I could do was give her belladonna to alleviate the pain of her final moments. In less than an hour, she would be dead.

"Rest now, Alix. I'm going to fetch Grandmother Lucía. She is upset and keeps asking after you."

I left her cradling our baby daughter and hurried to Grandmother's house.

That's how Alix died, embracing her grandmother and her baby, who clung to life despite the famine.

I asked Lyra to disperse the townsfolk camped outside our door. I did not want anyone to see me when I came out bearing Alix's shroud. I fastened my red bracelet around her wrist: the time had come for her to join Yennego.

I walked through La Astería district. Everyone closed their wooden shutters when I went by, as a mark of respect. Gunnarr helped me push aside the lid of the tomb beneath the wall next to Sant Michel Church, where Alix used to go every morning to pray for our son's return. Dried seeds from the lavender she brought with her were still strewn over the stone, despite the snow and storms of that accursed winter.

I gathered as many as I could and sprinkled them over my wife before we sealed the tomb again. My grief was so intense that I refused to pray to any god.

I entered my brother's house in that lamentable state. Onneca's wounds were healing, and she seemed greatly improved.

"How is Alix?"

"I've just come from burying her. Bishop García forced her to swallow Spanish fly. It poisoned her just as it did your father. What do you have to tell me, sister-in-law?" I asked.

"My cousin Bishop García was responsible for the murders of my father, my sisters, and my brother. I will take up the matter with him when we meet in the hereafter. But now we have to inform Lieutenant Chipia that the king has given his consent for us to surrender the town. He will not be sending any reinforcements, dear brother-in-law. The document is at La Romana Inn, you must request King Alfonso's permission to fetch it, or he must send his own men to the inn."

"The royal document, Onneca?" I shouted, losing my patience at the deception all around me. "Weren't you going to tell me about the counterfeit seals your cousin possessed, the ones he used to prove I was dead?"

"The ones that separated us, Diago, say it," she retorted, holding my eyes with her golden gaze.

"I kept that from my lips out of respect for my brother," I replied. "What's done is done. But I cannot trust a royal dispensation delivered by a man possessing counterfeit seals. What will happen if we surrender the town without the king's permission? We will fall into Castilian hands and the Navarrese will be our enemies. When King Sancho returns from the south, he will reconquer the town and we will suffer and die."

"Diago," interrupted Nagorno. "Look at what has happened in recent months with a cold eye. King Sancho has had more than a year to dispatch a messenger to Pamplona, commanding them to send reinforcements. And yet he has not. Look around you now. The townsfolk of Nova Victoria and your beloved Villa de Suso are starving to death. You are a learned and wise man, like King Solomon. Remember the story of the two women who both claimed to be the mother of a child. Solomon awarded the child to the woman who would rather give up her son than see him cut in two. He knew she was his true mother. What kind of lord are you, Brother? Will you let your children be slaughtered, or do you prefer to see them live under a different ruler?"

"You have always wanted to surrender the town to the Castilians because they will favor your people."

"You know what happens in a prolonged siege: a few days from now, people will start to dig up the dead, and after that, they'll eat the sick. Do you think any of us will be alive by spring? And even if there are survivors, will they ever forgive themselves for what they are about to do?"

58

THE GLASSWORKS

UNAI

November 2019

"We've got you," I told them.

All four were too shocked to react.

The day before, Ramiro Alvar had called Estíbaliz, explaining that he hadn't fled the hospital. Sebas had shown up at the hospital and urged him to escape, saying that the police were about to arrest him. Ramiro Alvar played along, but not before leaving me a message: *The Lords of Time* opened to the beginning of "The Old Forge" chapter.

"You four conspired to have Ramiro Alvar arrested in order to avoid suspicion, because none of you has an alibi for all three murders. That's why you all agreed to give voluntary DNA samples. Irati, you have an alibi for the murder of Samuel Maturana, and another very clever one for the murder at Villa Suso, even though you were there disguised as a nun. Since you were already selling your glassware at a stall on the Plaza de Matxete as part of the medieval market, it was easy to slip into the nun's habit and run past me. You wanted to divert our attention from what had happened a few hours earlier: a meeting of entrepreneurs where Beltrán laced Lasaga's canapé with cantharides. You must have known your name would come up sooner or later, or that someone would place you at that meeting. Was Antón Lasaga a random victim or did you target him?"

"No comment," Beltrán replied.

I was expecting that. He was the strongest link in the chain.

"Sebas, you and Irati don't have an alibi for the hours around Estefanía and Oihana Nájera's disappearances. Irati knew Estefanía, and you and Samuel Maturana's girlfriend are in the same *cuadrilla*. We have photos of you consoling her at his funeral. You, Gonzalo, murdered Samuel Maturana, and you don't have an alibi for that day. So, when the newspapers mentioned that a witness had come forward with a description of the killer, you were quick to provide us with a DNA sample. You wanted to make sure we'd rule you out in case you fit the description."

"I didn't kill the kid in the Zadorra," Gonzalo replied calmly. "You and I both know the DNA you found doesn't match mine."

His composure and self-assurance seemed incongruous with the display of pent-up anger we had seen a few minutes earlier.

"No," I replied, "and you know that the DNA in that blood sample belongs to your uncle, Ramiro Alvar."

"Exactly."

"The DNA places Ramiro Alvar at the scene, and you were counting on that. The evidence is misleading, however—the blood was yours even though it contained your uncle's DNA. That's why you gave us a saliva sample. You're a chimera. After receiving the bone-marrow transplant, you developed a condition known as post-transplant hematopoietic chimerism. You never told your uncle about the condition."

"What?" asked a bewildered Ramiro Alvar.

"Gonzalo's blood contains two different types of DNA," I explained. "His and yours. To monitor his condition, his doctors have been testing his DNA sequence polymorphisms, or variations, regularly since the transplant. Gonzalo gave us a saliva sample, because he knew it wouldn't match the blood DNA found on Maturana's pencil. He also knew that the blood DNA on the pencil would match his uncle Ramiro Alvar, making him the obvious suspect. You felt untouchable up until right now, Gonzalo, that's why you flaunted that chimera T-shirt all over the village, right under my nose. Handcuff him."

Milán placed herself squarely in front of Gonzalo, her face like thunder. Gonzalo stared at her defiantly but held out his wrists.

"Why would you do this?" Ramiro Alvar cried. "Irati, I helped you set up a business. Beltrán, I gave you legal work, valuable experience that would look good on your résumé."

"You still haven't figured it out, have you?" I said. "They grew up thinking you were their uncle. Ugarte was full of rumors about Alvar's children. Beltrán, I'll bet you became a lawyer and went to work for Ramiro Alvar to gain access to documents about the family inheritance. Irati and Sebas, your situation is more tragic. When you started dating, your mothers were afraid you might be half siblings, and they turned their backs on you, didn't they?"

My chat with Benita at our last book club meeting had been extremely informative.

"Irati, Sebas, and Beltrán had grown up suspecting they were Alvar Nograro's bastards. Their mothers, Cecilia the pharmacist and Aurora the grocer, have hated your family for years. Both got pregnant after a brief encounter with Alvar during one of his weekends away from the seminary, back when he made Ugarte his private hunting ground. Both women had shotgun weddings and endured ongoing suspicions about who fathered their children. Irati and Sebas both felt different and excluded, and this common experience brought them together. When they started dating, their families were horrified and did everything in their power to end the relationship. It was a tragedy.

"The three of you hate Ramiro Alvar and what he represents as the legitimate son. But your main motive was money. Gonzalo, you were eager to steal the chronicle when you found out how much it was worth. You weren't sure the DNA evidence you'd left was enough to send Ramiro Alvar to prison, and the chronicle was your insurance plan."

Gonzalo looked at me, and then said, very calmly, as though he were speaking to a child, "You call it murder, but I call it theft with collateral damage. The victims were a diversion so I could steal the diary. That book is worth millions of euros—it's a family fortune. We could split it four ways: If I suffered a relapse I'd be able to pay for treatment at the best hospital. Beltrán could open his own practice and hire the best lawyers without having to waste years building a reputation. Irati and Sebas could finally leave this village and never have to work again. We've been victims of the Nograro family since the day we were born: Don't we deserve what Ramiro Nograro refuses to share?"

"No, Gonzalo," I said. "You're just telling yourself that to justify your actions. You manipulated Beltrán, Irati, and Sebas, you got them to do your dirty work for you. You only got personally involved because Maturana discovered that the e-mail Malatrama received about *The Lords of Time* was sent from Nograro Tower. The e-mail could only have come from Claudia's computer. Claudia, Irati's sister. Maturana's girlfriend told Irati that Kraken had asked her boyfriend to look into the source of the e-mail, and later on she told her what Maturana discovered. That's when you understood that your plan was about to go off the rails. Maturana realized there was more than one killer, so before he drowned, he scratched a message for me on his arm: *Kraken, more than one*."

We handcuffed the other three, and they were led away to spend their first night in the cells at Portal de Foronda.

When I got back to my apartment at midnight, I put a black cross in my balcony window.

"I kept my promise, Matu. The monster is back in his box."

59

IN THE RAIN

RAMIRO ALVAR

April 2017

Ramiro Alvar had gone for a walk in the rain. He didn't mind getting mud on his boots; he loved the way the countryside smelled after a storm. He walked along the path leading to Ugarte, veering off into the poplar grove where he strolled contentedly for a while. He contemplated going into the village to talk to the locals, but the wind was picking up, and he decided the most sensible thing to do would be to go home, light a fire, and lose himself in a good book.

But as he passed the church, he noticed something off: the gate to the family cemetery was ajar. He always kept it shut.

Ramiro Alvar entered hesitantly. His glasses were foggy, but he could just make out a figure standing next to one of the graves.

"Hello, may I help you?"

The young man gave a start and wheeled around when he heard Ramiro Alvar's voice. His eyes were puffy from crying.

"I'm sorry. I shouldn't be here, should I?" he replied.

"No, this is private property. . . . Do I know you from somewhere?"

The lad's face looked familiar; there was something about his square jaw, his dark, wavy hair. He looked soaked through and bedraggled, but he was well dressed and seemed polite.

"My name is Gonzalo Martínez. My mother is Gemma Martínez, she's from Ugarte. I recently found out that my father was Alvar Nograro, the man buried in this grave. I don't know anything about him or his family, yet here I am looking at his grave. At least, I assume it's his. He was born in 1969."

"Yes, and he died in 1999," Ramiro Alvar confirmed.

Gemma's son. So she didn't have an abortion. She took the money and kept the baby, her half brother's son.

"How did he die?"

"He suffered from a hereditary blood disorder called thalassemia." It struck Ramiro that he had never told anyone what had killed his brother. He didn't know why he was telling a total stranger now. At eighteen, he hadn't had the strength to tell the villagers.

"Did you know him?" Gonzalo asked. Ramiro looked more closely at the young man. He had a cleft palate that made him look feline, and perhaps explained why he seemed a little timid and aloof.

"I'm his brother."

Gonzalo stared at him for a long time.

"I'm sorry, I've never met anybody on my father's side of the family before."

"What about your mother?" asked Ramiro Alvar. He wasn't usually so direct, but the boy had stirred up long-buried memories.

"She's been gone for a while. I think she left with her new boyfriend. I guess after the money ran out, they saw me as a burden. The police haven't been able to locate her anywhere in the country; they suspect she doesn't want to be found. Just before she left, I asked her to tell me something about my family, and finally she told me about the Martínez family in Ugarte, and about Alvar de Nograro. I asked around the village and they said my grandparents are dead, too. So I'm alone. There's nobody left. I just came to ask about my father. I'm sorry I trespassed on your property—I'm leaving."

"Don't worry. Where are you staying tonight?"

"There's an agritourism place nearby called the Old Forge. The girl who runs it says she has a vacancy. I'll leave town tomorrow," he said, turning to go.

"Wait!" cried Ramiro Alvar. "Where . . . where did Gemma go when she left Ugarte, when she was pregnant with you?"

"I was born in a small village in Asturias, but we moved around a lot when I was a kid." Gonzalo was being deliberately vague, and he noticed that Ramiro Alvar was taking the bait. "Listen, I wouldn't blame you for thinking I'd just come here to claim my father's inheritance, but I promise you, I don't want money. If you want me to take a DNA test, I would, because I believe my mother. She wouldn't have lied to me and then run away. I'm twenty-three, and I've grown up with no family, no roots. Now that my mother's gone, I'm all on my own. I just wanted to know a little more about where I'm from, but I can see this place doesn't have much to offer, and it means nothing to me."

With that, he walked off in the rain. The girl at the agritourism place, whatever her name was, was waiting for him. They'd slept together the night before, and Gonzalo knew he'd be able to get a free room for a few days.

Ramiro Alvar watched his back get smaller as he walked along the muddy path to Ugarte. He looked like his mother.

The next day Ramiro Alvar woke up shivering. Somebody had left the windows in his bedroom wide open and rain had soaked the bedspread. He had fallen asleep on top of the covers. He looked down and, to his horror, realized that he was wearing Alvar's cassock. Where did he get it? Hadn't he thrown all Alvar's clothes away after the funeral? He felt for his glasses on the bedside table, but he couldn't find them.

Alvar had hidden them. Alvar had gotten inside his head and was starting to play games with him.

60

THE INTERVIEW ROOM

UNAI

November 2019

Beltrán and Gonzalo had both refused to comment, but Irati and Sebas were ready to talk. I went to my office early and closed the door. I was working out a strategy, but I still had to clarify a few points and I didn't want to miss anything.

I called Peña.

"Take Irati Mújica to one of the small interview rooms. I'll be down to question her in a couple of hours."

She would have plenty of time to think, to get nervous. I was counting on her growing impatient during the long wait.

Finally, around midmorning, I entered the interview room carrying several report files, a notebook, and a pen. It was a rather clumsy way of getting into character, but I wanted information. The setting and props were supposed to make her think that I assumed she was going to answer all my questions.

"How did you sleep?" I began, taking a seat at the table. I positioned myself at a slight angle from her; I didn't want her to see our conversation as a confrontation.

"Oh, I was very comfortable," she replied sarcastically.

"Good," I said, nodding. "I heard you wanted to talk to me. You're doing the right thing cooperating; we have plenty of evidence. Now tell me, how did all this start?"

"I'm not sure what you mean by 'all.' Sebas, Beltrán, and I have always been friends. Apparently you already know about the rumors we had to put up with in Ugarte, about Alvar de Nograro and our mothers, and you know that Beltrán asked Ramiro Alvar for work to gain access to his private papers. Well, Beltrán's dreams about claiming his share of the inheritance were intoxicating, and we all wanted in. We used to spend hours talking about what we'd do if we took Ramiro Alvar to court and a judge ruled in our favor. It was like dreaming about winning the lottery and becoming millionaires. I think, eventually, we started to count on that money. It was no longer a fantasy born out of resentment; it became our lives."

"Did Beltrán encourage you to take the next step?" I probed.

"Beltrán went to the tower a lot. He managed to get a sample of Ramiro Alvar's saliva, and we sent it to a lab along with our own samples for a DNA comparison."

"And there was no match."

"No. None of us is related to Ramiro Alvar. We aren't Nograros. It was partly a relief, because it meant Sebas and I weren't half siblings. But I confess, we felt deflated. We weren't going to be millionaires after all, and we couldn't even tell the whole village that we weren't bastards without admitting that we'd obtained Ramiro Alvar's DNA without his consent. Sebas and I told our parents so they'd stop talking about what they called our 'incestuous relationship.' But our mothers still aren't speaking, and I doubt they ever will. Their feud has gone on too long."

"So you were disappointed about the money."

"It was like the day after the Christmas lottery. You spend Christmas Eve dreaming about what you're going to do when you win the prize money, and then you find out you didn't win and you have to accept that you're never going to be a millionaire. Yes, we were disappointed. It felt as though we'd been doused with a bucket of cold water."

"And then Gonzalo Martínez showed up in Ugarte in"—I leafed through my notes—"2017. He made friends with the three of you, and he told you he was Alvar Nograro and Gemma Martínez's son."

"We didn't believe him. We told him that we'd been through the same thing because of rumors, that spreading gossip about the Nograros was a tradition in the village, and that he shouldn't believe anything he heard. But then Gonzalo was diagnosed with thalassemia, and Ramiro Alvar offered to help him. The preliminary tests showed that they were a match. So it seemed as if Gonzalo really was a Nograro. They kept in touch, and occasionally Gonzalo would visit him at the tower. Months later, after Gonzalo had recovered completely, he showed us the manuscript he'd seen in Ramiro Alvar's study. Gonzalo had scanned it and replaced it without Ramiro Alvar's knowledge. We had no idea it was based on a priceless antique text. But Beltrán knew the Malatrama publisher, because he'd handled copyright questions when the council published a catalog for the temporary exhibition at the tower. In fact, around that time Ramiro Alvar started to give him other minor legal matters to handle."

I sighed. All of this had taken place in the analog world, while we were focusing all our efforts online. No one had hacked into Ramiro Alvar's computer.

"And thanks to Beltrán Pérez de Apodaca's legal inquiries, you knew that inheriting the Nograro fortune was conditional: 'May he be neither convict nor prisoner, to ensure the lineage is confined to men of honor,'" I quoted.

"Beltrán assured us that if we managed to frame Ramiro for a crime, he would be stripped of the Nograro fortune and his title would pass to the next male in line. That would be Gonzalo, who had legal proof that Alvar was his father. Beltrán also told us that the heir was no longer legally obliged to bear the name Alvar. In any case, Gonzalo could easily go to the registry office and change his name."

"But he would have legally inherited the title and fortune after Ramiro Alvar's death anyway."

"When? In forty years maybe, when Ramiro Alvar died and it was too late for us. Why would we run the risk of Ramiro Alvar having children of his own?" she exclaimed. "No, Gonzalo wasn't about to wait around, and, anyway, he hated Ramiro Alvar for not letting him live at the tower. He loathed running a bar; he thought it was beneath him. Gonzalo was a dropout who never did a day's work in his life—he and his mother lived off Nograro family money. But he knew that if he killed Ramiro Alvar in order to claim his inheritance, he'd be the prime suspect. Besides, Gonzalo wanted to see Ramiro in prison, stripped of everything. Disinheriting his uncle became Gonzalo's obsession."

"Even after Ramiro Alvar gave him the money to buy the bar and donated his bone marrow to save Gonzalo's life?"

"Ramiro Alvar only did that to atone for the way his family behaved," she said, with a wave of her hand. "He felt guilty. Don't defend him."

"He also gave you the forge and paid for the remodel, so you could set up the glassworks and the agritourism. Are you even the slightest bit grateful to him for all that?"

"Honestly, I saw it as compensation for emotional distress. I believed he knew about the rumors, and he gave me the forge to make up for what the Nograro family did to me. And I still see it that way."

I put an *X* in my notebook and stayed silent. We had reached the next stage: self-justification. This was the most unpleasant part of my job. I hated listening to the despicable excuses every felon created when faced with admitting their guilt. Every rapist, murderer, fraudster, thief, and abuser walked into that room under a kind of moral anesthesia, something I found increasingly hard to tolerate.

"Let's move on to the two sisters," I said, forcing myself to continue. "You're going to have to explain how you abducted Estefanía and Oihana Nájera."

"Who said anything about abduction? We didn't abduct them. Fani told me her parents were going out to dinner and that she had to stay in and look after Oihana. I arranged to meet her in the empty apartment on Calle Cuchi."

"That explains why she had no registered calls and why there's no CCTV footage of you outside her building," I said.

"Exactly, words die on the wind and leave no trace. I went back to basics, something I learned from all my hours in the studio. There's no technology there, and it's less messy."

"And how did you get into the apartment on Calle Cuchi?"

"The building was being renovated, and the door had been left open. Me and my *cuadrilla* discovered it one night. We had been out partying, and we took a break and sat on the stoop. Most of the apartments weren't finished, but it looked like the work had stopped. We started to meet up there to smoke and drink. Fani came with us a few times."

"So you didn't abduct them."

Nobody had dragged the two sisters over the rooftops.

"No, I just called out to her, and she snuck into the apartment through the back."

"The back?"

"The interior courtyard. She always came in that way. It was August, the neighbors weren't awake at that time of night, and it was dark. I knew she'd leave her bedroom window open to get back into her house. When she and her sister got to the apartment, Sebas dealt with Fani and I subdued Oihana. We put them in the bags we'd brought from Ugarte, and Sebas finished bricking up the wall. We cut Oihana's arm and collected some blood so we could plant it in their house and draw attention away from the apartment. We were worried about how close the two houses were, afraid the police might find them alive. Then we climbed through the window into Fani's apartment, smeared the blood on the floor, climbed out again, and closed the sliding window from the outside. We wiped our fingerprints off the glass. That was our first task and it went well.

"We each picked the crime we were best suited to carry out. We figured if there was more than one perpetrator, it would confuse the police. They'd focus their attention on the author of the novel, and that was our plan: to frame Ramiro Alvar. There were lots of crimes to choose from in *Lords of Time*. Sebas and I opted to re-create the immurement of the two sisters. He's the kind of person who does what he's told, and he doesn't ask too many questions. Beltrán chose the poisoning. Lacing a canapé with Spanish fly was simple. He didn't care which entrepreneur died; he hated them all."

"And you carried out the murders in the same order as they appear in the novel."

"Yes. We ruled out the complicated ones. In fact, we would have stopped after Lasaga, but then MatuSalem confided in his girlfriend. She told me, and I told Gonzalo. I said he had to stop Matu before he could speak to you. But he didn't want to get his hands dirty."

Like every good psychopath, Irati, I felt like saying to her. *He manipulated all of you. He preyed on your frustrations, made you believe he shared them, and got you to do his dirty work.*

"Matu was a clever kid," she continued. "Sebas was furious and wanted to put Matu in the barrel himself, but it was too risky because Matu knew us, so in the end, Gonzalo did it."

"You didn't count on the fact that an ex-con uses a sharpened pencil as a weapon. Matu left me Gonzalo's DNA."

"Actually, Gonzalo left you that clue. It's true, Matu tried to stab him with his pencil, but he didn't hit his target. Gonzalo left his own blood, knowing it would prove Ramiro Alvar's guilt."

"And what about Claudia? You stole the keys to the tower from your sister so Gonzalo could take the chronicle, and before that you stole Magdalena Nograro's habit. And you also stole the keys to the Quejana complex. But why? Why did you break into Quejana then, and why again a few weeks ago?"

But Irati folded her arms, stared at the wall, and refused to reply.

"You're going to have to explain it to me, because I still can't figure out why someone broke into Quejana a year and a half ago—"

I fell silent then. I kept quiet because I had just remembered: *A year and a half ago, when Gonzalo arrived in Ugarte.*

And then it struck me.

Eighteen months.

61

ALTAI

DIAGO VELA

Winter, the Year of Our Lord 1200

Seventeen days had passed since Alix and Onneca's ill-fated return. The town had never been more divided, and if the Nova Victoria residents had been strong enough they would have attacked those in Villa de Suso. They wanted to surrender unconditionally, while Villa de Suso would have rather died waiting for King Sancho's army to save them.

Chipia had stopped scanning the horizon from the battlements and had even given his men leave to play a board game, alquerque, when months earlier he would have punished them for the infraction with several nights in the cells.

There were no more animals in our yards: no pigs, no hens, not even rabbits. Walking through the cobbled streets felt like walking through a graveyard. The squawks, clucks, and whinnies had given way to a heavy silence.

Only my daughter and Grandmother Lucía compensated for the loss of Alix. My insides churned with grief at her passing, and at the thought that, after all she'd been through on that arduous journey, she wouldn't see the end of the siege. And still the siege showed no sign of ending.

I took my daughter with me to visit Grandmother Lucía. Lately she was barely more than skin and bones, despite the fact that all the townspeople, from Sancha de Galarreta to Lorenço the shepherd, secretly brought her some of their rations.

As I entered the yard, I whistled to alert her to my presence. I couldn't even bring her a leather belt to chew on—something we all did for the scant nourishment it provided—because there were no teeth left in her mouth. Instead, I brought strips of the vellum I was using to write this chronicle. I intended to boil the vellum and make a fortifying broth.

But as soon as I entered her chamber, I knew.

She was gone.

Grandmother Lucía's presence no longer filled the room, all that remained inside those bleak walls was cold air.

I found her sitting on the floor, arms draped around an open chest.

She had left us a gift: cured pork, cheese, chestnuts . . . All the food we'd brought her over these last few months, which she knew we wouldn't take back. She had saved it all for us: her children, her grandchildren, her great-grandchildren, and her great-great-grandchildren.

I sat beside her, my sleeping daughter in my arms, and permitted myself to weep.

I wept for her, for Alix, for Yennego, for all the people I'd left behind.

I was failing in my duty as a father. I was choosing to let the world cut my child in half rather than entrust her to strangers.

But Gunnarr's cry roused me from my stupor.

I could hear his voice booming from the street below. He sounded especially agitated.

"What is it, Cousin?" I asked, leaning out the window. I was still clutching my daughter.

"It's Nagorno, you must come immediately! He's threatening to set fire to the town. He's out of his mind," Gunnarr exclaimed.

"Nagorno, out of his mind?" I repeated incredulously.

I hurried downstairs and followed Gunnarr to the stable yard at my brother's house.

I found Nagorno lying on the last of the remaining straw. Our sister, Lyra, was holding him down as best she could, the tip of her dagger pressed to his neck.

"What's going on? What is this nonsense?" I demanded, taking in the pitiful scene.

"Some people broke into the stables last night. They've eaten Altai," Lyra explained. "He and Olbia were the only animals left in the town. They must have known Nagorno would exact a bloody revenge, but maybe they decided they'd rather gorge themselves and then wait for our brother to finish them quickly than wait out this siege. You talk some sense into him; he won't listen to me."

"Let go of him," I told her.

"I will not."

"Let go of him, Sister. I'll deal with this," I repeated.

Lyra frowned at me but gave in.

Nagorno leaped to his feet. His eyes normally resembled a dark tunnel, but they seemed even more dead than usual.

"Grandmother Lucía is dead. We're going to surrender the town. This no longer makes any sense," I announced simply, placing a hand on his shoulder. "Come, Brother, I want you to be in charge of organizing her funeral. Talk to the people of Nova Victoria. Lyra, summon everyone from Villa de Suso. Ring the death knell and we'll gather at Sant Viçente Cemetery the way we always have, ever since this hill was called Gasteiz."

And what neither hunger nor the town walls could unite, Grandmother Lucía brought together. There were no candles lighting the streets, and Milia the layer-out did not display bread offerings, for there was no Milia and there was no bread. Nor were there any hired mourners left to grieve for her.

But what need had we of hired mourners when grief was inside each of us? We thought Grandmother Lucía was immortal. She had always been part of Villa de Suso, there in her little house watching life go by as she plaited her red bracelets for us.

The hundred or so survivors formed a circle around her shroud. Nagorno brought out her chest with all the food she'd saved for us. We sat on the tombstones and shared it: Mendozas with rope makers, Isunzas with fruit sellers, the finest feast we could remember in ages.

"Are we all agreed, then?" I asked after we'd finished every last morsel.

They nodded in unison.

"Every one of you?" I insisted.

"Every one of us," they cried.

62

THE CHANCELLOR'S TOMB

UNAI

November 2019

As I sprinted to my office, I bumped into Alba in the hallway. I looked to the left and to the right and couldn't see anyone. I was euphoric.

"Come here," I said, pulling her in and giving her a quick kiss.

"What's that for?" she asked, grinning.

"I need to check a couple of things, then I'll tell you," I said.

I closed my office door behind me. I was elated—it was the same feeling that had kept me hooked on my job for so many years. I picked up my cell phone and dialed the forensic pathologist's number.

"Doctor Guevara, I think I know who the remains from Quejana belong to. I want you to see if they match the following DNA sample."

I explained my theory to her, and she wrote it down.

"I have some important news for you, too. I think you should be sitting down," she said. "It came as a complete surprise, and I asked the lab to run the tests again just to be sure."

"What's this all about? You're making me nervous," I said, sitting down and preparing for bad news.

"It's about the other two bodies found in Chancellor Ayala's tomb. As you know, we routinely check all our DNA results against the DNA of those working on the case in order to rule out false positives from cross-contamination. It turns out the man and the woman in the tomb are your ancestors, although they aren't related to each other. We've been in touch with the diocese and it's safe to assume that the remains are those of Chancellor Don Pero López de Ayala and his wife, Leonor de Guzmán. They were placed in that tomb in 1407 at the chancellor's behest."

"And yet that part of the family supposedly died out centuries ago. None of the present-day López Ayalas are descended from them," I struggled to respond.

"Well, we've just proved that this branch of your family tree survived."

I had a thousand-and-one questions to ask her, but I didn't know where to start. Just then Alba flung the door open so fiercely, it ricocheted against the wall.

"Unai, it's your grandfather. . . . We have to go to the hospital."

I saw her face and leaped out of my chair. I forgot to grab my coat, and I even forgot to take off my badge. She got behind the wheel—I was in no state to drive.

Germán had called to give us the news. He was watching Deba when the hospital told him.

The hospital elevator was the slowest, most exasperating I'd ever been in. I sprinted down the corridor and burst into his room.

"What's new, my boy? You look frightened," Grandfather said with a smile.

"How on Earth . . . ?" I shot Germán a quizzical look. I felt a knot in my throat and found I couldn't finish my sentence. For a moment I was afraid my Broca's aphasia had come back.

"The nurses told me he just opened his eyes and asked them if they were crows come to pick over his bones," Germán replied.

Grandfather just kept smiling, as if he didn't know what all the fuss was about. He playfully placed his beret on Deba's head.

Alba squeezed my hand tightly. I knew she wished her mother could share this miracle with us.

But she couldn't. Nieves was dead, and there was nothing I could do to bring her back.

I looked down at my cell phone. My screensaver was the photograph we had taken at the book launch in Villa Suso. We were all smiling: Grandfather, Nieves, Alba, Deba, and me.

Dazed, I sat on the sofa, the same place I'd spent hours watching Grandfather and praying for the impossible.

And I made a decision—or perhaps the decision had already been made and was simply waiting to be put into words.

"I brought all four of you a present," I said, rising to my feet. "Here, this is no longer mine. You've earned it."

I placed my badge next to Grandfather on the bed.

He picked it up happily and hung it around his neck.

"It's about time, son," he said with a shrug.

Alba looked at me, and for the first time, I felt as though we were on the same path. I'd taken a different route to get there, but she'd had the wisdom to wait for me.

Germán's chin began to quiver as he launched himself at me. I stooped to return his embrace.

"Thank you, thank you, thank you . . ." he whispered between sobs.

Then everybody, including Deba, gathered around me and enfolded me in their arms.

"Why are we crying, Mama?" my daughter asked after a while.

"Because your father's chosen us," Germán whispered to her.

63

KRAKEN

UNAI

November 2019

And so, little by little, life returned to normal, with Grandfather back among us. One morning, I went into the barber's shop where I had been getting my hair cut since I was a teenager. There was something I needed to get rid of.

"Short. Very short. The way I used to wear it," I told the owner.

"You don't mind your scar showing?"

"No, not anymore."

It was time to embrace my scars.

And as the clumps of hair fell to the floor, I let go of Kraken, of the impossible burden I had shouldered. I let go of my self-destructive sense of duty that had caused so much loss. I was a serial killer, too, in my own way. The lie I told myself—*I am the only person who can keep the city safe*—had killed or endangered the lives of so many people I loved that I deserved a life sentence. Without parole.

I left the barber's feeling new, strange.

And that hopeful feeling was nice.

I was walking through the Carnicerías district, heading toward la Torre de Doña Otxanda, when I thought I spotted a familiar bald head.

"Lutxo?" I called.

He wheeled around and looked surprised to see me.

"What are you doing here at this time of day? Aren't you working?" he asked, puzzled.

"I want to organize a dinner with the *cuadrilla* on Friday. You'll come, won't you?"

"You haven't answered my question. Why aren't you at work?" he insisted.

"I can't wait to see all of you. We haven't met up in forever. It's going to be a celebratory dinner. What do you say?"

"I say there's nobody like you when it comes to being evasive. Will you please tell me why you're not at your office?"

"I've been telling you from the beginning, Lutxo. On Friday I want to have dinner with the *cuadrilla* to celebrate leaving my job with the Criminal Investigation Unit. Feel free to write about it, if you want. In fact, you'd be doing me a huge favor. 'Kraken Retires.' You can say it's for personal or professional reasons, whichever you want."

"And what are you going to do now?"

"I'm joining the coach's bench: I'm going to train profilers. I won't be working on any fresh cases. There's another headline for you."

It took Lutxo a minute to digest the news. Then he stroked his goatee and smiled.

"Well . . . I'm glad to hear it. Really glad. Honestly. We can pick up our Sunday hikes in the mountains again without the constant tension between us."

"Yes, I'd really like us to be friends again, too."

We said goodbye, looking each other in the eye for the first time in a long while. But I hadn't told him the whole truth. I still had one last task to carry out: Quejana.

I always made sure to present the examining judge with detailed reports, and this case would be no different. After all, it was the last case of my career. There were still a few loose ends to tie up in *The*

Lords of Time investigation, and I needed to make sure everything was perfect.

Judge Olano once said my work was "impeccable and implacable."

I glanced at my red wristband as I gripped the wheel.

No loose ends, I told myself as I headed toward the north part of the province.

A few miles from the seat of the Ayala family, my phone rang. I was taken aback when I saw the name on the screen: Ignacio Ortiz de Zárate. I pulled onto a side road that led to a small chapel bordered by green hedges.

"Yes?" I said.

"Hello, Inspector."

"What do you want, Ignacio?"

"First, don't hang up on me, and give me a chance to explain."

"I'm not going to hang up on you, Ignacio. You aren't Tasio."

"That's what I want to talk to you about. That's why I'm calling, obviously. I can only speak for myself when I say how deeply sorry I am about what happened to your daughter and your grandfather. I heard he came out of the coma and is no longer in critical condition."

"That's correct."

"Then I'll be brief. This is as uncomfortable for me as it is for you. I'm moving to the States. For good. My twin brother is in prison for abducting a minor, and I already went through that hell twenty years ago. I'm selling the house in Laguardia as well as the apartment on Calle Dato. I have no intention of ever coming back. Our lawyer, Garrido-Stoker, explained what Tasio learned about your daughter's DNA. I have no intention of bothering you or interfering in your daughter's life. If she ever learns the truth about her father and wants to know more about his side of the family, I'd be more than happy to step in as her uncle. But if she doesn't, and I hope for her sake that's the case, then she'll never hear from me. I don't have much more to say. I'm sorry your family had the misfortune to cross paths with mine."

And with that, he ended the call.

More collateral damage, I thought.

The actions of narcissists are like stones tossed into a pond. They create ripples that become waves and end up devastating the lives of those around them.

Soon afterward, I parked beneath some bare trees, their boughs entwined with those of their neighbors, creating thick knots. I prayed that the priest would be in the old chaplain's house.

"Don Lázaro!" I yelled, rapping on the door with the knocker.

"Who's there?" a hoarse voice called from across the courtyard.

I asked him to let me into Chancellor Ayala's chapel. Once he left, I slipped on my gloves, possibly for the last time. I entered the crypt and faced the tomb of the couple whose DNA said they were my ancestors.

I was still coming to terms with the implications, but once I was there, in that solitary place, I had the overwhelming sensation that their story was part of mine, and everything around me felt familiar. Those stone slabs that had held a branch of my family through the centuries, the copy of the immense red-and-gold altarpiece, even the silence—it all somehow belonged, in part, to me.

I approached the alabaster tomb. The forensics team had examined every inch of its interior and found nothing other than the three sets of remains.

The tests I had asked Doctor Guevara to carry out had confirmed that the other woman's corpse belonged to Gonzalo's mother, Gemma Martínez.

Gonzalo hadn't confessed to his mother's murder. Irati told us that, in exchange for a reduced sentence. Alvar's son killed Gemma after she spent all the money Inés Nograro had given her. She and Gonzalo returned from Asturias with the intention of demanding more from the family.

But Gonzalo was fed up with his mother's financial management. He hated constantly having to ask her for money, justifying his expenses, lying. They had a fight. It ended with Gonzalo digging a hole in the rain with his bare hands in a eucalyptus grove in Cantabria.

It was the same day he arrived in Ugarte. He took a room at the Old Forge, where Irati filled him in on the villagers and the Nograro family. The next morning, he went straight to the Nograro family cemetery, where he met his next victim: Ramiro Alvar.

Over time, having gained Irati's trust, he persuaded her to get the key to the Quejana complex, where her sister, Claudia, worked. It was a secluded place that attracted few visitors, and there's nowhere better than a tomb for hiding a body . . . and something else.

I went to the altarpiece and tried to pull it away from the wall. It wouldn't budge. Patiently, I ran my fingers around the edge until I found it. One corner, which depicted the chancellor kneeling, was loose. I felt gently behind the canvas.

And there it was: the copy of Count Don Vela's chronicle.

A book with a stitched leather cover and parchment pages.

I slipped it out of its hiding place. I had to admire Gonzalo's logic.

What better place to hide a copy than behind another copy?

64

RAMIRO

UNAI

NOVEMBER 2019

I looked out at my students. The entire class had been listening to my lecture intently for more than an hour. I had decided to use my most recent case to demonstrate the practical reality of criminal profiling. And I had resolved to include all my mistakes and false leads.

"At first I believed we were dealing with a serial killer. Then I thought the murderer suffered from dissociative identity disorder. It took a long time before I finally realized there was more than one killer. By focusing exclusively on the medieval lead, I lost valuable time. I failed to see that each crime bore the mark of its perpetrator: cowardice in the case of the Spanish fly poisoning, which was done at a distance; shame in the case of the immured sisters; and cruelty, inherent in *poena cullei*.

"But the key to this case is the instigator, Gonzalo Martínez. He persuaded his followers to see the murders as 'collateral damage,' as he called it. The aim was to steal Ramiro Alvar's family fortune, worth hundreds of millions of euros. But this was no simple bank robbery with guns and bags of money. The strategy was to strip Ramiro Alvar of his fortune with the law in one hand and his own novel in the other. If he was successfully framed for the murders, then legally he could not hold his title and wealth. And his own method of healing, his version of the chronicle, was the very weapon that implicated him in the murders."

I scanned the back row for Doctor Leiva. She'd promised to attend my first lecture to put her stamp of approval on this new phrase of my career, but the class was over and she hadn't made an appearance.

The students filed out of the lecture hall, and I was left to put away the audiovisual material. Then I saw her, and she wasn't alone.

Estíbaliz was with her, and she was pushing Ramiro Alvar in a wheelchair.

"We're too late, I'm sorry," Marina apologized the instant she walked in.

"It's my fault," Ramiro Alvar said. "We waylaid her."

"Now I'm curious," I said. "What brings the three of you here?"

"Ramiro has agreed to undergo therapy with Doctor Leiva," Estíbaliz said solemnly.

"To put it bluntly, Estíbaliz told me I had to if we were to continue seeing each other," he corrected her.

"Yes, but I'm making no promises," she went on. "You have to choose whether you want to follow the path to recovery or not. And once you've decided who and what you are, I'll decide whether I want to be with you."

"In fact, Ramiro will be my last clinical case before I retire," said Marina. "Although I'm also going to give up teaching, I'm confident I can help Ramiro. I doubt many of my colleagues would be able to make an objective diagnosis."

"I'm really happy to hear that," I said. "Could I talk to you alone, Ramiro Alvar? I have a couple of questions I want to ask you."

"Call me Ramiro, Unai. From now on it's plain Ramiro. The name feels less onerous. Ramiro Alvar is for official documents only."

"All right then, Ramiro," I said with a smile.

Doctor Leiva and Estíbaliz said goodbye and left us alone in the empty lecture hall.

"What can I do for you?"

"I need to tie up one last loose end to completely understand this case. I'd like you to confirm a theory of mine—you're not obligated, but if you do I give you my word that it will remain between us. I believe your alter identified with Bishop García because he was your ancestor. You didn't explicitly say in your novel, but Bishop García's illegitimate son, Lope, was the founder of your lineage. During a visit to the historical archives, I came across documents that named the first Lord of Nograro, Alvar López de Nograro, son of Lope Garceiz. The same Lope Garceiz who was the bastard son of the woman who ran La Romana Inn, am I right? You murdered Bishop García in your novel to change the ending and symbolically kill off your alter. That's why you feared the bishop might kill his enemies. It made sense to you that he would kill Count de Maestu's counterpart in the real world, so you were afraid Alvar would kill Estíbaliz. But you couldn't believe Alvar would murder the two sisters, because in the novel they weren't Bishop García's enemies."

Ramiro pushed up his glasses, his nervous tic, and lowered his gaze.

"It's true," he finally said. "According to the documents, he's the first of our lineage. Our family is descended from a brothel-owner who sold her own sisters, albeit to avoid starvation, and the murderer of Count de Maestu. But it's always been a closely guarded secret. That was the other reason I was so horrified when the novel came out. In reality, Lope was Bishop García's illegitimate son, and when his father died, he inherited everything. The Nograro family always hid their origin story, but Lope inherited what was considered a fortune at the time. He sold the Pamplona palace to King Sancho the Strong and moved to the Valdegovía region to escape his notoriety in Victoria. That has always been the Nograro family's biggest secret."

"I'm beginning to understand the way secrets and lies accumulate in old families. I also have something to tell you about another of your family's secrets. We've recovered the missing copy of Count Don Vela's chronicle. Gonzalo hid it behind the altarpiece in the crypt of Chancellor Ayala at Quejana."

"I don't want it!" Ramiro snorted. "I don't want to go anywhere near that thing. It's a reminder of everything I'm trying to forget."

"One last thing. This is delicate, and confidential, so I won't mention any names. The descendants of a branch of Count Don Vela's family possess the original diary along with the documents to prove it. I think an appropriate gesture might be to return their property."

"Then there's an end to it."

Shortly afterward, I called Iago del Castillo

"I think I have something that belongs to you here in Vitoria."

65

ONE TOWN

DIAGO VELA

WINTER, THE YEAR OF OUR LORD 1200

We all ascended the steps to the ramparts above the North Gate. One of Chipia's men sounded the trumpet, and presently López de Haro rode up.

"What is it you want?" he asked. He looked gaunt, though nothing compared to the emaciated figures lined up along our wall.

"Tell King Alfonso we're ready to parley," I declared.

Chipia and the mayor were on either side of me. Next to them were Nagorno, Onneca, Lyra, Gunnarr, the Isunzas, the Mendozas, the rope makers, the butcher, two little girls, and an old man.

Alfonso appeared on his white stallion. He looked at me expectantly and motioned for me to begin.

"Speak up, Vela," he said.

"We hereby surrender the town of Victoria to you. All of it, both Villa de Suso and Nova Victoria. Your cousin Sancho the Strong has released us from our duty to defend it and will not be sending any troops, so it's safe for you to dismantle your defensive line. This ordeal is over for all of us."

I noticed the tension fall from his men's shoulders at once. The soldiers to the rear, whom the king couldn't see, embraced each other in relief. There was a muted joyful outpouring from the besieging troops.

"I accept your surrender," the king proclaimed solemnly. "Open this gate once and for all."

"There are conditions," I said.

López de Haro laughed. "You're in no position to demand conditions."

"There are conditions," I said, standing firm.

"Let him speak," the king interjected.

"There are to be no reprisals."

"Continue."

"Any person wishing to leave Victoria to make a new life elsewhere in the kingdom is to be free to do so without fear of persecution. We do not want to find bodies hanging from the trees in Los Montes Altos."

"That will not happen, you have the word of your king. I appreciate the dignity with which you have defended what is yours, and your bravery will not be forgotten."

"There is to be no pillaging," I continued, "not that much of value remains. The townswomen must be respected, and no one will be put to the sword when we allow your men inside these walls. We want to know we can sleep safely in our beds without locking our doors, for we are used to keeping our yards open in this town, and that must continue if you want to keep your new subjects happy."

"Once again, you may rest assured. Your new king is no butcher."

"You speak of meat—bring in some of that delicious-smelling wild boar, rabbit, venison—whatever is cooking out there, and do it quickly."

"Standard-bearer, give the order. My new subjects deserve a feast."

López de Haro nodded and obeyed his king.

"And do not stop favoring the market of Santa María, rather, lift the gate taxes," I added. "This is a town of merchants and artisans. Without them there will be no market, and without a market there will be no tribute paid to the king. Do not lose sight of your ultimate goals."

"Do you seek to give a king orders?"

"I am counseling a wise man, as I did your beloved uncle Sancho the Sixth."

"The art of listening. Yes, he was a good teacher. But I've heard enough. Let me pass, I am eager to greet my new subjects."

I gave the order to Yñigo, the only son of Nuño, the furrier.

The North Gate creaked on its hinges and opened for our new king. A cart filled with bread and roasted meats arrived with him. The food never got to grace a table, for the ravenous townsfolk emptied the cart there in the deserted marketplace.

Several days passed before the town started to come to life again.

A few of the local artisans packed their tools and set off for Pamplona to open new workshops.

Lyra prepared to travel to the Bagoeta quarry to replenish her forge.

"We surrendered Victoria, but now it is one town not two," she said, trying to console me before she left.

"But at what price, sister?" I murmured as I watched her cart leave. "Never again will I blindly defend any land, town, or fortress. Only people. Nothing can compensate for the loss of a beloved."

Gunnarr and I set off to visit Héctor in the village of Castillo. We knew he must be worried for us, and that he would want to meet his new niece.

Gunnarr left for the port of Santander that same night. His crew was waiting for him to ferry pilgrims to Santiago, and I knew he missed the sea, the freedom of being unconstrained by walls. He had a giant's soul that was too large for any town; he only felt whole in big spaces.

I was strolling near the fortress of Sant Viçente with my daughter in my arms when I met Martín Chipia mounted on a horse borrowed from the Castilians.

"I have received a message from the king's counsellors. Sancho is sending me to Mendigorría. He believes that my work here is done. We leave tomorrow."

"Won't you wait for your men to regain their strength?" I ventured.

"We are Navarrese soldiers, and the streets have been taken by Castilians. It's best we don't cross their path. After all, beneath every breastplate is the beating heart of a man. And we've all lost brothers-in-arms to the enemy. We leave tomorrow. Count Vela, it has been my privilege to fight alongside you."

"I wish you Godspeed, lieutenant. We'll remember you with fondness here. I doubt we'll ever meet again, but I hope that death continues to elude you," I said, bidding him farewell.

Life continued, inside and outside the town. We each followed our own destiny.

I took my daughter to visit the tomb where her mother and brother lay. I began to tell her the story of our family, which, for the moment, ends here, in February, the year of our Lord 1200, in the town of Victoria.

66

THE LORDS OF TIME

UNAI

DECEMBER 2019

The month started with a gentle but abundant snowfall. We awoke to a silent, white city, as if somehow the snow had washed away all our bad memories. I leaned out of the balcony and let the cold air slip into my apartment.

I could see Iago and Héctor del Castillo crossing the Plaza de la Virgen Blanca. I'd called to tell them about the DNA that proved I was a direct descendant of Chancellor Ayala. I wanted to know what they thought of it, or if they could find any historical document to back it up. I knew that the news had come as something of a shock to them, and I was eager to talk through it.

Héctor embraced me enthusiastically at the entrance to my apartment. Iago was carrying a briefcase. I ushered them inside.

We sat around the coffee table in the living room, and I gave them the salvaged copy of Diago Vela's chronicle.

"Here it is. The current Lord of Nograro is going to begin the necessary paperwork to donate it to you legally. But it's finally yours again."

Iago brushed the leather spine with his finger, forgetting to put on his glove in his eagerness to examine the book.

"It's been so long . . ." he whispered.

"Our family has had to wait many years for this moment," said Héctor. "We can't thank you enough for all that you've done, Unai.

Iago has something for you, too—a letter. We'd like to show you what's in it."

Iago pulled out a plastic sleeve with an old parchment inside. It looked like he had brought it back with him after a trip through time.

"The day Deba was abducted, you asked me about Yennego. I didn't want to trouble you during this hard time, but I've brought something for you to see today."

"What is it?"

"A letter from Onneca de Maestu addressed to Diago Vela just before she died in 1202, not long after the siege ended. She had the white plague, what we now call tuberculosis. She sent him this, knowing she was dying."

Iago handed me the document. I waited for him to read it aloud. He recited it from memory:

> "My beloved Diago,
>
> "Yennego fell into the moat. I found him drowned, but I feared you would not believe me, after I behaved so deplorably upon learning that Alix de Salcedo was with child a second time. His remains rest in my father's tomb. You will find two bodies there. This tragedy was followed closely by the siege. I never even found the courage to tell my husband, Nagorno, who adored the boy. I was not a good aunt to him; I was never affectionate. I saw in Yennego the son who was denied to me, the son you and I should rightly have had. And yet, all that matters to me now is your soul, for mine is already departing my body. I have no wish to leave with this burden. You must grieve for him at my father's graveside.

"This letter is a part of the Vela family's private correspondence and has remained in the family's possession over the centuries. It postdates Count Don Vela's chronicle, which explains why he makes no reference to it. And why we never learn what becomes of Yennego in the novel *The Lords of Time*."

"So, Yennego died in an accident," I murmured. "If only Onneca had revealed what she knew, she could have spared a great deal of suffering."

Iago nodded silently as he carefully put the parchment away.

"There's something else we want to share with you," he said. "Let's go out for a stroll around the Old Quarter. I haven't walked these streets after a snowfall in ages."

I looked at my phone for the time.

"All right. But Grandfather has taken Deba to play at the Jardín de Etxanobe, and I have to pick them up soon."

"We'd love to say hello to him. It's good to know that old heart of his is still going strong," said Iago.

The three of us headed toward the Plaza de Matxete.

"You told us the DNA tests prove that you're related to Chancellor Pero López de Ayala. There are a couple of important details about your ancestor's legacy that we feel you ought to know," said Héctor. "The Nograros were one of the rival families during the feud between the Ayalas and the Callejas. But it's a shame there's nothing on these streets to show what the Ayalas did for Vitoria. Look, can you see that building over there?"

They had brought me to the top of the San Bartolomé steps.

"That was the South Gate, where people and goods arriving from Castile entered the town. You see that rough section of wall?" Héctor pointed to the entrance of Villa Suso palace. "Those stones are over a thousand years old. They are part of the first wall erected by Diago Vela's ancestor, the first Count Don Vela. The Vela family always served as the town's protectors. Back in the seventh century, they erected the Old Forge, beneath what is now the Old Cathedral. They lived in a long house called the chieftain's dwelling. They also built the well, the cemetery, and the carved headstones that archaeologists have recently uncovered."

Then the brothers asked me to turn around and look at one of the buildings, currently home to the city council's social services department.

"That's where the Ayala family built their palace in Vitoria, next to the earliest Gasteiz chapel, now the Chapel of Nuestra Señora de los Dolores inside Sant Viçente Church. That's where the city's charter was granted. They held meetings and carried out trials here, on hallowed ground. And if you look farther down, at the Arquillos del Juicio, you can see that the tradition was preserved, passed down to us in the form of a name."

"You're saying that we're standing on hallowed ground?"

"This is the site of the first cemetery in the village of Gasteiz," Héctor said, nodding. "The old Sant Viçente fortress had its own cemetery."

"We want to tell you that the Velas and Chancellor Ayala belonged to the same branch of the family," Iago said. "Back in the fourteenth century, Chancellor Ayala's father, Fernán Pérez de Ayala, recorded his family genealogy in a book called *El árbol de la Casa de Ayala*. He stated: 'My ancestor Don Vela made the town walls in Victoria, Álava.' Contemporary historians never gave this much credence, as it was common for noble families to seek legendary status for their lineage at the time. Count Don Vela was already a legend, so it made sense that Ayala would claim kinship. Yet one detail didn't match up: the date when the wall was built. Historians had always believed that Sancho the Sixth, Sancho the Wise, built the wall when he granted Victoria's charter in 1181. It made perfect sense: he bestowed privileges on the townsfolk and then built the wall to defend them against the King of Castile."

"But that's not true?"

"Carbon dating has recently proved that these walls are at least a hundred years older than we had previously thought. They date from around 1080, during the reign of Alfonso the First, the Battler. But if that was the case, who was behind their construction? Archaeologists began to look at Fernán Pérez de Ayala's book again. How did he know the walls were built a hundred years earlier? Maybe he was telling the truth after all."

"But that doesn't prove that the Ayalas were descendants of the Velas," I said.

"No, and this is where we need you to promise confidentiality," Iago said.

"You have my word. You know that."

"In Lope García de Salazar's *Bienandanzas e fortunas*, which he wrote at the end of the fifteenth century, he says, and I quote: 'The said Count Don Vela, Lord of Ayala, who lived in the Basques and Latin speakers, died and is buried in the Cathedral of Santa María de Respaldiça.' "

"Why is that confidential?"

"It isn't. There is documentation of Count Don Vela's funeral, which confirms that the body buried at Santa María de Respaldiça was indeed his. As there were properties at stake, and Héctor and I want to keep the family estate intact, we were obliged to prove that our ancestor, Don Vela, was a direct descendant of the Ayala family branch in Quejana. So a few years ago we obtained permission from the bishop to take some DNA samples from the chancellor's bones. The results confirmed that the two men were related and came from the same branch of the family, which enabled us to recover our family inheritance, retrieving lands and lost legacies. It was all done privately, and the newspapers never found out about it. We'd like it to stay that way."

I gaped at them, as if I were seeing them for the first time.

"Then you also belong to a lost branch of the chancellor's family," I managed to say. "I just assumed that side of my family had died out and that the surname López de Ayala came from somewhere else. That's why I'm finding it hard to assimilate the result of that DNA test."

"Yes, that's the common assumption, and we hope it stays that way. We don't want to attract people's attention. And yes, our DNA matches the chancellor's."

"So that means we're family?" I said, a slight catch in my voice.

"Apparently so," Iago said with a smile. "Come on. Don't you have to pick up your daughter and grandfather?"

We walked down Fray Zacarías Martínez, formerly Calle de las Tenderías, and found the two of them in the middle of a snowball fight.

Deba was wearing a little red beret Grandfather had given her to cover her cropped hair. He said it helped him see her more easily. He had stubbornly kept on bringing her to the park where Tasio had assaulted him before kidnapping her. Grandfather had instilled his philosophy in me and in Germán, and now he did so with Deba: we wouldn't let bad things get the best of us and turn our setbacks into trauma.

"Santiago, how are you?" Iago asked, walking straight over to Grandfather.

"Haven't I seen you somewhere before?" Grandfather asked, wiping the snow off his beret.

"This is Iago del Castillo, Grandfather," I said, introducing them. "He found you after the fox took Deba. He gave you CPR and called the ambulance. It's thanks to him that you're still alive. And this is his brother, Héctor del Castillo. And it turns out we're family."

Grandfather extended his enormous hand to both of them.

"What's this about us being family?" he asked, bemused.

"Remember when I told you about the tests they ran on the DNA samples taken from Chancellor Ayala's remains at Quejana?

Well, Iago and Héctor ran the same tests and they're related to him, too. We all come from the same branch of the family."

"I knew it," said Grandfather, scrutinizing Iago. "You have blue eyes just like my grandfather Santiago, who left Villaverde when my father was ten."

"It was a different time, I imagine. I'm so glad your father thrived, and that you lived to see your grandchildren and your great-granddaughter grow up."

"As am I. And that we're family," Grandfather replied. "You know you always have a home in Villaverde."

"Unai, there's something we'd like to show all three of you. It's an old family tradition," said Iago.

"Of course. Where are you taking us now?"

"To the Old Cathedral's bell tower."

"What?"

"As researchers, we're allowed to access it. And we've worked with the director of the Santa María Cathedral Foundation in the past," Héctor added with a mischievous grin, dangling a bunch of keys in front of us. "Santiago, are you all right to walk up to the tower?"

"With the little one on my shoulders if I have to," Grandfather replied valiantly.

Soon afterward, the five of us stood behind the guardrail on the Santa María bell tower contemplating the snow-covered rooftops of the white city.

"Magnificent, isn't it?" murmured Iago.

Even Deba was speechless for a moment. Grandfather broke the silence.

"Look, lad, Grandma's Sun!" he declared, pointing at some scored lines on one of the stones next to the bell. "Somebody drew one here, too."

"That's what we wanted you to show you. Grandma's Sun, or

Grandma's Flower, is really an *eguzkilore*, a sunflower," Iago explained. "Our family has always drawn the symbol to protect the places we've lived. Grandmother Lucía drew this one. She is Alix de Salcedo's great-grandmother in Count Don Vela's chronicle, and the matriarch of our branch of the Vela and then the Ayala family. The *eguzkilore* has been passed down through the generations as a reminder."

And it came to me.

"Do you think I could have inherited this sense of duty? Does protecting the old town run in my veins?" I asked.

"I don't know, maybe it has more to do with the way your grandfather brought you up. But maybe he inherited it and passed it on to you. Didn't you say your daughter wanted to open a hospital? Oddly enough, the chancellor's daughter-in-law founded what later became Santiago hospital."

"Did you hear that, Deba? You're the last of the López Ayalas. And if you have children, you must bring them here to show them the drawing of the *eguzkilore*. That way we'll all be safe."

"I like the hospital better," Deba replied with her delightful self-assurance. "I wanna save lots of lives."

"Let's go downstairs. We have one more family secret to share with you," Iago said.

I suppressed a shiver as we crossed the threshold of Villa Suso.

"Where are we going?"

"This way," Iago indicated.

He guided us over to the glass lid that covered the remains of the immured lady of Villa Suso.

"This is the resting place of Alix de Salcedo. Diago Vela buried her here," Iago whispered.

He knelt and placed his hand on the glass that separated them, as though speaking to her.

We all respected his silence, even Deba, who seemed to understand the gravity of the situation. She gripped my hand solemnly.

"Then this lass is our grandmother," Grandfather observed pithily.

"That's right, Granddad. She's Alix de Salcedo; she and Diago had a child."

"A daughter named Quejana," said Iago.

"And we're the descendants of those descendants," I explained to Deba, filled with emotion.

Then I bowed before her, too, and said my prayer for the last time:

"This is where my hunt ends, Mother. And this is where my life begins, daughter."

Acknowledgments

This novel forms the crossroads of my two literary universes: the White City Trilogy and the Ancient Family Saga.

As a writer, it has been one of my greatest pleasures to write about the common origin of both families and to reveal that Iago del Castillo; Diago Vela, Lür; and Héctor Dicastillo, Nagorno, Gunnarr, and Lyra are the direct ancestors of Unai Lopez de Ayala. After three decades of creating fiction and living with these characters, they are very dear to my heart and to my readers.

I am very thankful to the entire team at Planeta for their professionalism and good work throughout the editing and publication process of the novels in the White City Trilogy.

Thanks to Antonia Kerrigan, for her effective defense of my editorial interests.

To my readers, thank you for your patience in understanding that writing a five-hundred-page novel is an arduous task that requires several years of intense creative and intellectual work and research. I will always appreciate your common sense and generosity in waiting for my next work.

And finally, thank you to my children and to my husband for making our days the best place to live.

Selected Bibliography

This novel is the result of intensive research, which was very important to me. The following lists are the bulk of a collection of sources I have used to depict, in the most vivid way possible, a fascinating time period.

For the history of the city of Vitoria and medieval Álava:

Andrés, Salvador. *Historia de una ciudad: Vitoria. Vol. I. El núcleo medieval*. Vitoria, Spain: Bankoa, 1977.

Azkárate Garai-Olaun, Agustín and José Luis Solaun Bustinza. *Arqueología e Historia de una ciudad. Los orígenes de Vitoria-Gasteiz (I)*. Bilbao: Universidad del País Vasco, 2013.

———. *Arqueología e Historia de una ciudad. Los orígenes de Vitoria-Gasteiz (II)*. Bilbao: Universidad del País Vasco, 2014.

Bazán, Iñaki. *De Túbal a Aitor. Historia de Vasconia*. Madrid: La Esfera de los Libros, 2002.

Díaz de Durana, José Ramón. *Álava en la Baja Edad Media: Crisis, recuperación y transformaciones socioeconómicas (c.1250–1525)*. Vitoria-Gasteiz: Diputación Foral de Álava, 1986.

———. *Vitoria a fines de la Edad Media*. Vitoria-Gasteiz: Diputación Foral de Álava, 1984.

Elizari Huarte, Juan Francisco. *Sancho VI el Sabio: Reyes de Navarra*. Navarra: Editorial Mintzoa, 2003.

García Fernández, Ernesto. *Bilbao, Vitoria y San Sebastiá. Espacios para mercaderes, clérigos y gobernantes en el Medievo y la Modernidad*. Bilbao: Universidad del País Vasco, 2005.

———. *Gobernar la ciudad en la Edad Media. Oligarquías y élites urbanas en el País Vasco*. Navarra: Diputación Foral de Álava, 2004.

González Mínguez, César and María del Carmen de la Hoz Díaz de Alda. *La infraestructura viaria bajomedieval en Álava*. Bilbao: Universidad del País Vasco, 1992.

González de Viñaspre, Roberto and Ricardo Garay Osma. *Viaje a Íbita. Estudios históricos del Condado de Treviño*. Self-published. Ayuntamiento del Condado de Treviño, 2012.

Imízcoz, Josemari and Paloma Manzanos. *Historia de Vitoria*. San Sebastián: Editorial Txertoa, 1997.

Inclán Gil, Eduardo. *Breve Historia de Álava y sus instituciones*. Bilbao: Fundación Popular de Estudios Vascos, 2012.

Lasagabaster, Juan Ignacio. *La catedral de Santa María de Vitoria: Primer Congreso europeo sobre restauración de catedrales góticas*. Vitoria-Gasteiz: Diputación Foral de Álava, 2011.

Llanos Ortiz de Lándaluce, Armando. *Álava en sus manos*. Vitoria-Gasteiz: Caja Provincial de Álava, 1983.

Martínez Torres, Luis Miguel. *La ruta de la piedra: Camino medieval desde las canteras antiguas de Ajarte hasta la Catedral Vieja de Santa María en Vitoria-Gasteiz*. Leioa: Universidad del País Vasco, 2010.

Rivera, Antonio. *Historia de Álava*. San Sebastián: Editorial Nerea, 2003.

I have always tried to make the historical part of my novels reflect the daily life of the characters who inhabit them. I am obsessed with documenting their occupations, dress, gastronomy, and rituals.

In this case, the books on my bedside table have been:

Ayuso Sánchez, Cristina. "El mundo laboral femenino en el País Vasco Medieval." *Sancho el Sabio: Revista de cultura e investigación Vasca* 30, (2009): 115–35.

Hennessy, Kathryn. *Moda: Historia y estilos*. London: DK, 2013.

Iziz, Rosa and Ana Iziz. *Historia de las mujeres en Euskal Herria. Prehistoria, romanización, y Reino de Navarra.* Tafalla: Txalaparta, 2017.

Leventon, Melissa. *Vestidos del mundo desde la antigüedad hasta el siglo XIX. Tendencias y estilos para todas las clases sociales*. Barcelona: Blume, 2009.

Manzanos, Paloma and Francisca Vives Casas. *Las mujeres en Vitoria-Gasteiz a lo largo de los siglos*. N.p.: Ayuntamiento de Vitoria-Gasteiz, 2001.

Ventureira San Miguel, Aitor and Imanol Bueno Bernaola. *Araba. Mitos, creencias y tradiciones*. 2014.

Despite the scarcity of primary sources from the period, both the archaic expressions and all the medieval names in the novel—Diago, Lope Garceiz, Dicastillo, Paricio, Yñigo, Alix, Onneca, Bona, Pero, etc.—appear in the original:

Jimeno Jurío, José María. *Colección documental de Sancho VII el Fuerte (1194–1234). Archivo General de Navarra*. Pamplona: Pamiela, 2008.

An important part of the plot takes place in la Torre de Nograro, located in Valdegovía. Even though it is in ruins, I took the architecture of the fortified building as inspiration and used it as a model for the Tower of Varona, though its family history has no connection to the novel.

Arechaga, Susana and Francisca Vives Casa. *Arquitectura fortificada en Álava*. N.p.: Ayuntamiento de Vitoria-Gasteiz, 2009.

Martínez Álava, Carlos J. *La torre-palacio de los Varona: Historia y patrimonio*. Vitoria, Spain: Diputación Foral de Álava, 2009.

Vélez Chaurri, José Javier. *Las tierras de Valdegovía. Geografía, historia y arte*. Vitoria, Spain: Diputación Foral de Álava, 2003.

I have drawn on the following volumes for the common origins of the Vela and Ayala lineage:

de Mendía, Santiago. *El condado de Ayala*. Avila: Diputación Foral de Álava, 1994.

Diputación Foral de Álava. *Guía de exposición Canciller Ayala. Conmemoración del VI Centenario de la muerte del Canciller Ayala*. Vitoria-Gasteiz: Diputación Foral de Álava, 2007. Exhibition Catalog.

García Fernández, Ernesto. *La tierra de Ayala. Actas de las Jornadas de Estudios Históricos en conmemoración del 600 aniversario de la construcción de la Torre de Quejana*. Vitoria-Gasteiz: Diputación Foral de Álava, 2001.

Pérez de Ayala, Fernán. *Libro del linaje de los señores de Ayala, desde el primero que se llamó D. Vela hasta mi D. Fernán Pérez.*

Verástegui Cobián, Federico and Félix López López de Ullibarri. *El linaje del Canciller Ayala. Aiala Kantzilerraren leinua*. Vitoria-Gasteiz: Diputación Foral de Álava, 2007.

I am grateful to Ismael García-Gómez for his willingness to clarify some points regarding his monumental work *Vitoria-Gasteiz y su hinterland. Evolución de un sistema urbano entre los siglos XI y XV*, from *Colección Patrimonio, Territorio y Paisaje* published by Universidad del

País Vasco. I have made some changes to fit the plot. All adaptations and variations are my own.

Regarding the siege in Victoria, we only have the chronicle *De rebus Hispaniae*, by the archbishop Jiménez de Rada, a registry of the Cathedral of Pamplona, and various administrative documents from the Chancellery of King Alfonso VIII de Castilla, from which we know he participated in the siege. For the technical aspects of re-creating the siege, I have been guided by:

Akal. *Armas. Historia visual de armas y armaduras*. Madrid: Akal, 2017.

Davidson Cragoe, Carol. *Cómo leer edificios*. Barcelona: Blume, 2017.

de Montoto y de Simón, Jaime. *Las guerras medievales y el renacimiento de los ejércitos*. Madrid: Libsa, 2017.

Dougherty, Martin J. *Armas y técnicas bélicas de los caballeros medievales. 1000–1500*. Alcobendas: Libsa, 2010.

Glancey, Jonathan. *Cómo leer ciudades. Una guía de arquitectura urbana*. Madrid: Blume, 2017.

Hislop, Malcom. *Cómo leer castillos. Una guía sobre el apasionante mundo de las fortificaciones*. Madrid: Blume, 2015.

I have endeavored to keep some street names based on fourteenth-century sources. To re-create the layout of the old streets of Victoria, I studied the following volume:

Knörr Borràs, Henrike and Elena Martínez de Madina Salazar. *Onomasticon Vasconiae: Tomo 27. Toponimia de Vitoria I. Ciudad/Gasteizko Toponimia I. Hiria*. Bilbao: Euskaltzaindia, 2009.

I decided to set a part of the novel's plot in an imaginary town in Ugarte for obvious reasons. I chose the unpopulated region of Ugarte in Ayala, which appears in a document from 1040, because it participated in the area's tithes. The following volume contains research on the hundreds of medieval towns in Álava that subsequently disappeared:

López de Guereñu Galarraga, Gerardo. *Onomasticon Vasconiae: Tomo 5. Toponimia alavesa seguido de mortuorios o despoblados pueblos alaveses*. Bilbao: Euskaltzaindia, 1989.

In order to understand the dynamics of a complex and poorly documented disorder such as DID, dissociative identity disorder, I studied the following psychiatric manuals:

American Psychiatric Association. *DMS-5. Manual de diagnóstico y estadístico de los trastornos mentales.* American Psychiatric Association. Buenos Aires: Editorial Medical Panamericana, 2016.

González, Anabel. *Trastorno de identidad disociativo o personalidad múltiple*. Madrid: Síntesis, 2015.

Because the protagonist in the trilogy is an expert in criminal profiling, these academic books have accompanied me throughout the years. I have also included the courses I have taken:

Bartol, Curt R. *Comportamiento criminal*. Mexico City: Pearson Educacion de México, 2017.

Jiménez Serrano, Jorge. *Manual práctico del perfil criminológico*. Valladolid: Lex Nova, 2012.

———. *Psicología e investigación criminal. Psicología criminalista*. Valladolid: Lex Nova, 2015.

Soria Verde, Miguel Ángel and Dolores Sáiz Roca. *Psicología criminal*. Madrid: Prentice Hall, 2012.

Xandró, Mauricio. *Grafología Superior. Estudio morfológico de la escritura y método de interpretación psicológica*. Barcelona: Herder, 1991.

Ytam, Augusto Vels. *Tratado de grafología: El conocimiento del carácter por la escritura*. Barcelona: Vives, 1945.

COURSES

- *Curso Avanzado de Policía Judicial* (Advanced Course on Judicial Police)
- *Curso de Inspección Técnica Ocular* (Course on Ocular Technical Inspection)
- *Curso de Investigación Policial en el Proceso Penal* (Course on Police Investigation in the Criminal Process)
- *Curso de Medicina Forense aplicada a la Investigación Policial* (Course on Forensic Medicine Applied to Police Investigation)
- *Curso de Perfilación Criminal* (Course on Criminal Profiling)

The #1 Internationally Bestselling

WHITE CITY TRILOGY

Inspector Unai López de Ayala, also known as Kraken, investigates gruesome murders in his beloved Vitoria. Set against the backdrop of Spain's beautiful and historic Basque region, this trilogy interweaves mythology, ancient legends, and archaeology with heart-pounding suspense.

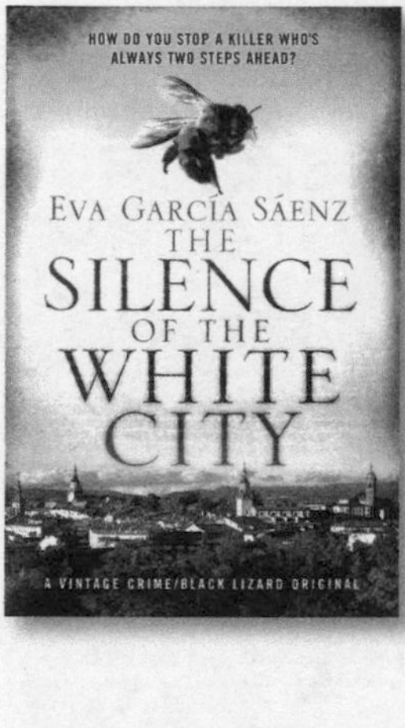

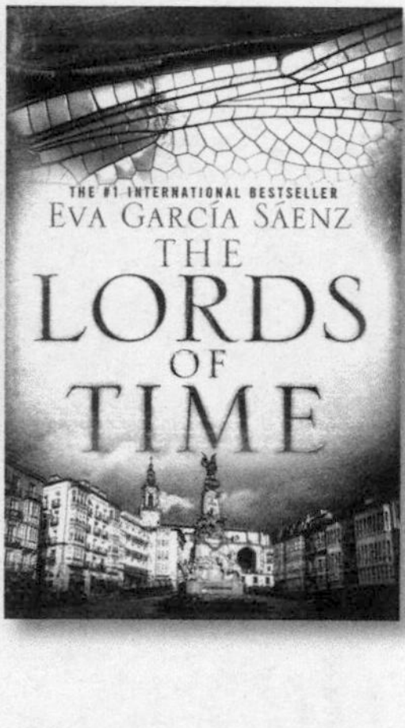

Available wherever books are sold

Vintage Crime/Black Lizard **www.blacklizardcrime.com**